I0784400

NEEDED IN THE NIGHT

A COZY SCI-FI ROMANCE

THE FORTUSIAN MATES
BOOK 2

LISA EDMONDS

ISBN 978-1-963525-19-9

Edited by Grey Moth Editing

Cover Art By Lindsey Staton (@honeyy.fae)

Cover Typography by Megan Van Dyke

Isla and Mikas Portrait by @FlavulousArt

Chapter Headers and Chapter Art by Carly at @CarlysBookishBeasts

Published in the United States

By Storybook House, LLC

ALSO BY LISA EDMONDS

The Fortusian Mates Series

Sheltered in the Storm

Needed in the Night

The Alice Worth Series

Heart of Malice

Heart of Fire

Heart of Ice

Heart of Stone

Heart of Shadows

Heart of Vengeance

Heart of Lies

Heart of the Pack

Heart of the Damned

Alice Worth Short Stories and Novellas

From the Ashes

Just For One Night

Blood Money

Ghosting 101

Perfectly Magical

Alice Worth and the Elite Death Machine

The Alice Worth World Novels

Mortal Heart

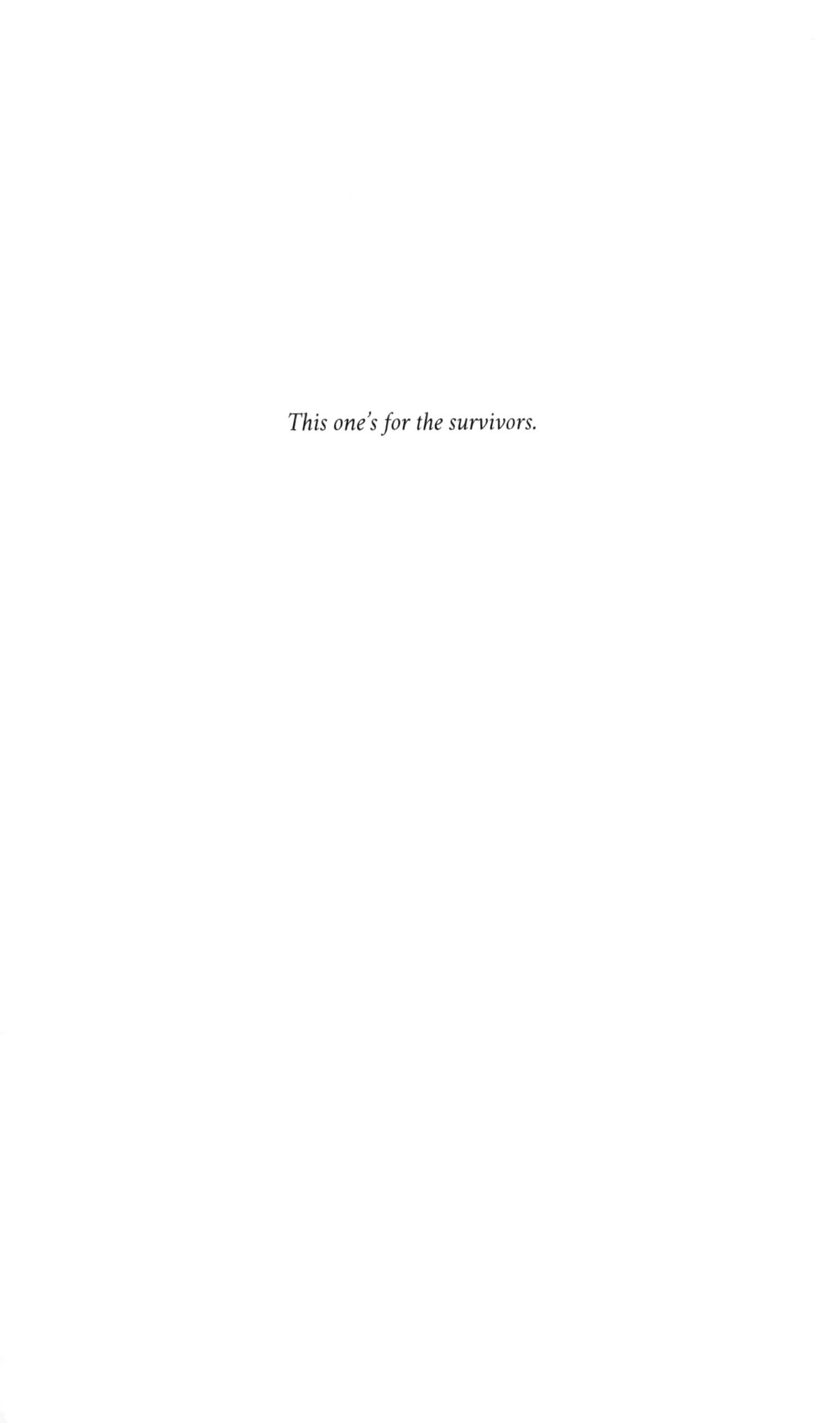

This one's for the survivors.

CONTENT NOTES

This book, as with all other titles in this series, contains scenes that depict violence, death, physical intimacy, and some topics that may be disturbing to some readers. Please always read safely.

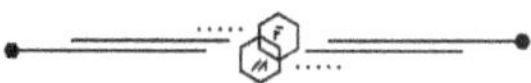

A complete list of content notes can be found on my website at LisaEdmonds.com/contentnotes.

CHAPTER 1

ISLA

"I CANNOT DO THIS," MY COMPANION SAID, HER VOICE SO WISPY I had to strain to hear her. "I can *not*."

"Yes, you can," I countered, also in an undertone.

Our footsteps echoed off the marble floors and walls as we made our way along the palace hallway toward the back stairs. The air reeked of wealth and privilege: the heavy fabric of fine tapestries, bouquets of flowers replaced daily to fill the halls with cloying perfume, purified air so no offending plebeian odors from outside the palace walls reached our noses. My skin crawled with the vulgarity of it all.

"Keep your head high and smile," I reminded the woman at my side. "We're going to get some food from the kitchen and then we're going to your theater to rehearse, the same as we've done every morning for the past two weeks. Nothing's different about today, at least as far as anyone besides us is concerned."

In reality, today would be life-changing. Today—in the next ten minutes or so, in fact—we would either walk out of this palace and board a cargo transport bound for a distant planet, or face execution. Given the Erotovo's brutality, there really was no third option.

"Ninety-nine percent of success is looking confident," I added. "Even when you're not."

Or especially *when you're not*, I thought, but didn't say. Because the woman at my side was hanging on by a thread already.

Beautiful Novee, a long-limbed Tivoran zero-G dancer whose lithe body could take shapes and transform in midair in ways my humble human body could only dream of, took a deep breath. She plastered a performer's smile on her face, but her cerulean skin had a sheen of perspiration that sparkled in the mid-morning sunlight streaming through the tall windows lining the hall.

Novee wasn't the only one of us projecting calm she didn't have. My stomach had been roiling from the moment I woke up this morning. Adrenaline? The Ngaran moth soup from last night's banquet? Or were my instincts trying to tell me something?

Whatever the reason for my fluttery insides, it didn't matter. Wheels were in motion, the ship delivering supplies to the palace was on the landing pad, its crew were ready for us, and there was no turning back.

Novee deserved freedom. I'd looked myself in the eye in the mirror yesterday and sworn last night was her final one in this gilded hellhole.

As long as palace guards didn't suddenly block our path, or my shadowbat didn't tell me to run for it, or Novee didn't lose her courage, we were all right. We just had to make it to the end of this hallway, down the stairs, through the kitchens, and out to the cargo carrier. That was four things. We could do four things, one step at a time.

I took deep breaths to slow my heart rate, checked my data-pad, frowned as if concerned about the day's schedule, and resisted the urge to put a comforting hand on Novee's arm or back.

Forcing myself to appear uncaring was tough but necessary. The Web had inserted me into the palace household as Novee's chaperone and personal assistant after my handler had arranged for her previous one to suddenly find more lucrative employment elsewhere. I wasn't Novee's confidant or friend, at least as far as the Erotovo or his staff were concerned. Novee was the Erotovo's possession, and possessions didn't get to have friends. They didn't get comforting touches. I knew that better than most.

I flexed my fingers and kept walking toward the beautifully etched floor-to-ceiling mirror near the stairway.

My own tastes were simple, so I hardly recognized myself in a floor-length green gown with the enormous and very impractical puffed sleeves popular in the Erotovo's court. I'd also styled my shoulder-length dark brown hair according to his preferences, in a halo of curls pinned back from my face with clips. I hated this version of myself for how well I blended in with the Erotovo's entourage.

As necessary as it was to wear these clothes and style myself to suit a cruel despot, I drew the line at jeweled dermal piercings in my face and upper chest. Those were popular in the court and among Ngaran aristocracy and their servants, but to me it was a sign of ownership and I couldn't bear it, even as part of a disguise.

While my skirts rustled and my shoes made sharp staccato sounds as I walked, Novee moved silently. The very tall and willowy Tivoran woman with long, almost translucent hair wore a skintight, silver-blue bodysuit and slippers designed for practicing her artistry in the zero-gravity theater the Erotovo had built for her.

As much as he clearly enjoyed filling his palace with elegant people wearing the latest and most ostentatious fashions, the

Erotovo required Novee to wear dancer's clothing at all times. It permitted him to always see her not as a person, not as Novee, but as *his dancer*—and as a bonus, she could hide nothing in the suit, especially weapons.

Today she'd be leaving the palace with nothing but the clothes on her back. I wondered if she'd destroy this suit the moment she had something else to wear. I would, if I were in her slippers.

In fact, I *had* done so, once upon a time, when it was me being secretly escorted out of my pretty prison by a mysterious operative who'd appeared in my life suddenly, and vanished just as quickly once I'd made it to safety. I'd never known her real name, just as Novee would never know mine. To her and the palace staff, I was Halena Onsulus, a hardworking recent arrival from Havel Prime with a long set of references and haughty demeanor that had led the Erotovo's chief of staff to hire me almost instantly in the wake of my predecessor's abrupt departure.

Two palace guards emerged from the east stairwell just before we reached it. Novee's breath hitched.

"Madame," the taller one said to me, inclining his head. "It is a good morning."

They didn't acknowledge my companion at all. That was the safest choice. The Erotovo was a jealous owner.

"Masters," I said coolly, dipping in a tiny curtsy without missing a step.

From my first hour in the palace, I had established myself as not one for chatting with other staff. Feigning extreme aloofness meant my days were lonely, but the fewer interactions I had with others, the easier it was to play my role without arousing suspicion.

Today we definitely didn't have time for delays. Timing was crucial. Our extraction had to go like clockwork, or it wouldn't go at all.

As the guards continued down the hall, the shorter one muttered, "Frigid bitch."

My fingernails dug into my palms, but I kept walking. It wasn't the first time I'd heard some variation on that particular insult. Apparently my predecessor had been very friendly with the guards. I didn't judge her for it, but I wasn't interested in clandestine threesomes with the Erotovo's armored palace defenders. I was here on a mission and I didn't mix business with pleasure, even to relieve stress. Too many ways that could go wrong. Too many lives at stake.

Not to mention, men who signed up to serve a despot didn't exactly moisten my panties.

Our walk down the winding staircase from the palace's third floor to its first underground level took less than two minutes. Every step, every breath, seemed to simultaneously take an eternity and not long enough, as if I both desperately wanted to reach the kitchen but dreaded it.

No signs of trouble. No indications that our journey to the kitchen had attracted unusual notice. No frantic warning from my shadowbat. Everything remained quiet, except the chatter of voices drifting up from the kitchens, where the staff was hard at work unpacking the provisions brought by the cargo carrier, clearing up from breakfast, and preparing the midday meal.

Still, the little hairs on the back of my neck prickled more intensely with each step and my uneasiness grew. Desperation led me to reach out for some kind of reassurance.

Brae, I thought. My mental voice sounded strained even to me. *Give me news.*

Tell me my instincts are wrong, I willed him, while giving Novee the tiniest of reassuring looks so maybe she'd stop shaking.

His reply came just as we reached the bottom of the stairs and the wide hall that led to the main kitchen.

All seems well. Brae's voice in my head was quiet. My shadowbat companion probably sensed my tension and was doing his best to ease my fears from a distance. *The Erotovo hasn't emerged from his council chamber. All guards appear to be on routine patrols. No unusual activity.*

I let out a breath. *Thank you.*

I wished Brae was with us, but his job right now was to slip through the palace, keeping watch and reporting any concerns or potential dangers. I feared for his safety as much as ours, though he was all but invisible.

Novee and I had made it down the third floor hall and the stairs. That was two of the four tasks before us. Only two more to go.

No guards in the hall that led to the main kitchen. There seldom were, but I breathed just a little easier seeing an empty, echoing corridor before us. No Vorcian marble or Fylorian tapestries or fine sculpture down here, either. The Erotovo didn't care about impressing anyone who lived or worked in the bowels of the palace. The kitchens contained the finest foods and the most high-quality prep equipment built by monk-gastronomists on Bacora to ensure his banquets were second to none, but this hall and the staff quarters on this level were mean at best.

Our steps sounded much different on cold, damp stone than on marble. I liked the sound far better, though, and not just because it meant we were getting close to the doors. Marble reminded me of my own former prisons. Every footstep on its gleaming surface catapulted me back to nightmares I'd give anything to banish.

The main kitchen bustled with activity. Chefs, cooks, assistants, assorted household staff, and the uniformed crew of the cargo carrier rushed in all directions, carrying crates, platters, dishes, ingredients, and utensils.

Novee's chest was heaving now. She reached out as if trying to grab my arm before she dropped her shaking hand back to her side. At least we'd made it to the kitchen before she started hyperventilating. If I couldn't calm her down, the odds of a successful clandestine exit would dwindle even further.

A trilling voice cut through the clamor. "Ach…Halena, Novee, my loves." Vila, one of the cooks, hurried to meet us in the doorway. The little four-armed Manorian clapped both pairs of hands, sending puffs of sweet-smelling flour into the air. "I am late getting your basket ready. I am sorry, I am sorry. You will come with me to the pantry to choose what you like?"

I let out a breath. If the basket of high-calorie, carbohydrate-laden food Novee needed to sustain herself during a strenuous practice session had been waiting for us, something had gone wrong and we needed to abort the plan. An invitation to the pantry meant everything was going according to schedule. The lack of a warning from Brae supported that assumption.

If only my stomach and those little hairs on the back of my neck would get the message.

The carrier's crew hurried in and out through the wide doors that led to the landing pad, bringing in fully laden anti-grav sleds, unloading them, and returning to the ship with the empty sled for another load.

The clock in my head was now ticking so loudly that I almost expected it to be audible to everyone in the kitchen, if not the palace itself.

If timing had been crucial before, now it was everything.

I used the mild pandemonium as an excuse to put my hand reassuringly on Novee's lower back and guide her as we followed Vila across the kitchen and into one of four main pantries.

Provisions filled shelves and cold storage units floor to ceiling on three walls inside the pantry. A cargo carrier crew member wearing a full-face breathing apparatus and coverall was busy unloading when we entered.

"Is full," Vila said to another crew member, a diminutive

Ymarian who approached the door with a full sled. She pointed to the storeroom next door. "Unload there."

"Yes, madame," the Ymarian said, all three of their eyes downcast as they guided their sled away.

Vila was no taller and weighed less than the Ymarian, but she had an aura of authority that demanded respect. I worried about her safety once we were gone, but I had to trust the plan we'd put in place with her help. I had to have faith.

The carrier crew member with a covered face put a crate down near the door. I heard a very quiet *beep*.

The hidden holo projector activated. To hide us from prying eyes, it created the illusion in the doorway that Vila, Novee, and I went about the pantry collecting items for the basket.

"Now," the crew member said, her voice tinny and rough through the respirator.

We had three minutes. Three and a half at most.

Hidden by the holo projector, and with Vila and the female crew member on watch, I opened a crate at the back of the pantry with a visibly damaged bottom corner.

I pulled out a coverall and handed it to Novee. "Put it on over your suit," I said. "As fast as you can. Leave the front open."

As she quickly stepped into the uniform, which had additional padding and body armor to protect her and disguise her slim figure, I was already halfway out of my gown. Unlike Novee's suit, this ridiculous dress could not be hidden under any coverall. It would go into the crate along with my shoes and other discarded items.

Under the gown, I wore a bodysuit similar to Novee's. I kicked off my high-heeled shoes, stepped into my bulky coverall, pulled it up and over my shoulders, and sealed the seam in the front.

At the bottom of the crate, under the rest of our disguises, I found a medical kit.

Nausea rose. I swallowed hard, steeled myself, and opened it. Gloves, plasma scalpel, transdermal analgesic and tranquilizer patches, extraction instruments, suture kit. And a collection tube.

"Gods above," Novee whispered at the sight of the kit's contents. She sat—nearly fell—onto a nearby crate, her face ashen.

If we had more time, I would have held her close and stroked her hair and said reassuring things until she felt brave or at least less afraid. But we had no time to spare. I could be brave for her if I had to be. Someone had done the same for me only three years ago. I'd been just as desperate to escape as Novee, and just as frightened.

"You won't feel any pain," I said. "Keep your eyes on my face or close them. Just don't look at what I'm doing. I only need thirty seconds. But it is now or never, Novee. Freedom is right outside on the landing pad."

"A lot of people have risked their lives for you," the crew member in the respirator said, her voice harsh. Her name badge read *ERGIN*. "If you cannot be brave for your own sake, be brave for ours."

I glared over my shoulder. Novee inhaled sharply and straightened her spine. "You are unkind," she told the woman. Then she startled me by meeting my gaze and adding, "Do it, then, and let us be gone."

I didn't appreciate Ergin's tone, but it had snapped Novee out of her paralysis. Sometimes kindness only got you so far.

With the scalpel, I cut a hole in the fabric of Novee's practice suit so I could access her bare skin just below her ribcage. The tracking device had been implanted where it wouldn't affect her muscles or ability to bend in the sinuous, almost boneless way necessary for her style of dance.

I slipped an analgesic patch under her suit near the hole I'd made and pressed it to her skin. The drug was strong and its effects would be swift—an absolute necessity for an operation of this kind.

"Put this against your stomach," I said, handing her a towel. "Press it tight and hold."

Trembling, she did as I asked.

For her sake and mine, I didn't hesitate. No time to think or second-guess, or remember when it was me who had to sit still while a virtual stranger cut into my flesh.

I checked to make sure Novee was staring at something above my head and not at her abdomen, and then I cut.

With the scalpel's plasma edge, I incised a three-centimeter opening into Novee's smooth cerulean flesh. She didn't so much as gasp. No pain, as I'd promised, and such a fine edge—only nanometers thick—did not even tug at her skin, but blood gushed from the wound. My right side ached in memory.

I dropped the bloody scalpel into the kit and picked up the extraction instrument.

"How many times have you done this?" Novee whispered, her gaze on the ceiling as her green blood soaked the towel.

Not enough times, was what I wanted to say. Not enough to save as many as I wanted to save. Only enough to be a drop in a vast and endless ocean.

"Many," I said instead.

I slipped the long tip of the extraction tool into the wound. Its sensors found the tracker immediately. The fine teeth at its tip gripped the device, which was no larger than my thumbnail.

Holding my breath, I attached the collection tube to the back of the extractor and activated it. Novee's blood filled the tube. Any contact with air would activate the tracking device, alerting the Erotovo that it had been removed—and more critically, cause it to either release deadly poison or ignite an explosive. Trackers served as jailers and merciless executioners.

Clink. The tracker landed in the tube and was sealed inside by the extractor. I exhaled.

Ergin took the extractor from me and hid it on a shelf. I sealed the wound with a suture patch, took the towel from Novee, wiped up the blood smears on her skin, and glanced at my wristcomm. Time was almost up.

I tossed the towel into the crate. "Seal your coverall," I told Novee, offering my hands to help her stand. "And put on the respirator."

She still trembled from fear, adrenaline, and maybe a little blood loss and shock, but she stood more quickly and with more fire in her eyes than I'd expected. Maybe making it through arguably the worst and most dangerous part of this process had given her some confidence.

In any case, the moment that tracker landed in the tube, we'd officially passed the point of no return.

Quickly and silently, Novee and I finished putting on our cargo crew uniforms, complete with gloves, boots, respirators, and extra padding that changed our body shapes and disguised plates of body armor that covered our chests and backs.

The tracker we left on the shelf so anyone watching its location would see Novee was still in the pantry. Everything else went into the crate, which Ergin sealed and left on her sled. The glowing red symbol on the crate indicated it had been rejected as damaged goods.

While I'd focused on removing Novee's tracker, two empty antigrav sleds had been left outside the doors of the pantry, ready for us to pilot to the carrier.

In my mind, I reached out to my shadowbat. *Brae, we're ready to go.*

Understood. Brae's tension crackled through our telepathic link. He knew as well as I did how deadly dangerous the next few minutes would be. *I will meet you at the kitchen door.*

A surprised sound and a burbly snore made me spin around just in time to see Ergin lower Vila's limp body to the floor. She'd knocked her out with a transdermal injection.

Novee took an angry step forward. "I wanted to say thank you and goodbye."

"She knows you're grateful," Ergin said shortly.

Novee bared her teeth and hissed. It was the first time since I'd met her that I'd seen the soft-spoken woman so angry.

I'd met Web operatives like Ergin before. It wasn't uncommon for an agent to adopt a cold and even unkind manner as a way of keeping emotional distance from those we rescued. I didn't like it, and that wasn't my way. I couldn't make myself be harsh toward people who'd already suffered so much, even if it meant my heart might ache less. Still, I couldn't pass judgment on those who chose that path. We all had to find ways to cope with our own nightmares *and* the pain of those we tried to help.

Some Web agents were in it for the money—especially the highly trained operatives who specialized in the most dangerous missions. But most of us were survivors turned agents, inspired to join the organization that had rescued us and given us our freedom.

As Novee struggled to rein in her anger, the holo projector continued to show a scene of Vila rummaging through the shelves and putting items in the basket as the real woman who'd helped us snored, curled up against a cold storage unit. Thanks to the drug, once she woke she'd have no memory of what she'd done for us and be looked at not as a conspirator but as a victim of our scheme—or at least that was the plan.

"Get ready to step out of the pantry and grab your sled," Ergin told us. "Do not speak. Keep your eyes down and walk quickly. You will go ahead of me to the ramp. As soon as we have boarded, the carrier will depart."

"Understood," I said.

Novee nodded, her long, triple-jointed fingers clenching and unclenching in what was probably a combination of anger and fear. I couldn't see her expression underneath the respirator mask.

I took a deep breath and let it out, banishing my unease and doing my best to replace it with the role I was about to play: busy, hard-working crew member ready to be done with this unloading job and get on to the next one.

"Confidence," I reminded Novee, touching her gloved hand with mine. "We are leaving this planet right now, for good."

"Thank you," she said. "Thank you both."

"You are welcome," I replied. Ergin grunted.

As the doorway hologram continued to show Vila, Novee, and I browsing the shelves of food, Ergin grabbed the manual control handle of her sled and jerked her chin at the doorway. "Go. I am right behind you."

CHAPTER 2

ISLA

Side by side, Novee and I stepped through the hologram into the bustling kitchen.

Only two other crew members were still unloading the last of their cargo. We would all be heading to the carrier together, the last of the crew to board before its departure. It didn't escape my notice that in bulky coveralls and respirators that hid every square inch of our bodies, all five of us were almost identical in height and size, making us all but indistinguishable from one another.

If Ergin had planned this phase of Novee's extraction, she had done well. I owed her a drink, at least. Assuming we ended up docking somewhere with a decent bar and she'd accept my offer.

A familiar warm tingle caressed the back of my neck just as I settled my gloved hands on my sled's control handle. Brae. *Finally.*

I expected him to land on my upper back and ride my shoulders out of the palace as a shadow. Instead, I sensed him above us, traveling along the ceiling as our little group made our way toward the wide exterior doorway. He must feel uneasy enough to want a higher vantage point.

For the first time in weeks, through the open doorway, I saw the sun-drenched morning outside the palace walls without thick blast-proof glass separating me from its beauty. I inhaled deeply to fill my lungs with fresh air that wasn't purified or perfumed. Heavenly. Nothing in recent memory had smelled better, even Vila's fresh-baked, fruit-filled cakes, the only thing about the palace I would miss.

Ngara was a lovely planet ruled by aristocrats like the Erotovo who hoarded their wealth and cared less about the common people than the art and treasures that filled their palaces. I doubted I'd return, even if it were safe to do so.

Thirty meters beyond the kitchen door's threshold were the landing pad and cargo carrier, its massive hold doors open and ramps extended like waiting arms.

A familiar and comforting weight settled onto my upper back as Brae sank his claws into the padded shoulders of my coverall for a better hold. In shadow form he was nothing but a wisp of darkness, and on the coverall he was all but invisible, even up close or in bright sunlight.

Four bored palace guards stood outside the doorway. I smothered a spike of dread and anxiety with sheer will. To her credit, Novee didn't react as they scrutinized us and our sleds.

"What happened to this crate?" a guard asked, indicating Ergin's sled.

"Isssss damage," Ergin replied, her voice suddenly thick with a feigned accent to disguise her own natural way of speaking. She waved her hands as if in warning. "Rot. Isssss smell very bad."

With a grimace and sound of disgust, the guard motioned us to continue. I didn't feel any relief, though. We still had a long walk ahead of us.

With the other two crew members in front, Novee and me in the middle, and Ergin behind us, we made our way across thirty meters of sun-warmed walkway. The only sounds were the hissing of our respirators and the hums of the antigrav sleds.

My ears strained, listening for any alarms or noises behind us. I'd never been so acutely aware of my back—to the point I itched between my shoulder blades, and not because of the rough material of my coverall or the plate of body armor.

No weapons fire and no shouting, but the silence did nothing to ease my nerves. Why hadn't the guards started closing the kitchen doors?

Even with Brae keeping watch behind and around us and the ship now only fifteen meters away, that fluttery, gut-churning feeling came back with a vengeance.

No, something was wrong. Something was very, *very* wrong. Every cell in my body activated, flooding me with adrenaline. My chest heaved, and my breaths rattled in the respirator.

Brae, go! I thought.

The gentle weight on my shoulders vanished as he took to the air with a flap of shadowy wings.

Twin blasts of plasma shot from the shadows under the carrier's enormous landing struts, striking the two crew members in front of us.

As they went down, holes smoking in their chests, something punched me in the back and sent me sprawling face down on the rough surface of the palace's cargo port.

At first I didn't feel pain—just numbness. Through my respirator, I caught the acrid smell of burned fabric, hair, and flesh, and the odor of superheated body armor. Had I been shot in the back?

Then the agony arrived and took my breath away. My cry of pain had no air to give it sound. I choked on it instead. The filthy sons of bogworms had shot me with a plasma rifle. If I hadn't been wearing the body armor, I would be dead.

Darkness threatened to sweep me away. As much as I wanted to escape the agony of my wound, I feared falling into an abyss I might never escape.

Desperately, I clawed at the ground, my fingers in their thick gloves scrabbling as though I could stay awake and alive and not be dragged into unconsciousness or death if I were able to hold onto something.

Fragments of memory tumbled through my mind, each blurring into the next in a cascade of painful moments. My own captivity. The tearful faces of those I'd rescued. The haunting visions of all those still living in torment we hadn't yet freed.

I shut my eyes, but that didn't stop the torrent of nightmares. I let out a broken kind of sound. All the gods above and below, don't let those memories be the last things I see…

More bolts of plasma fire seared the air over my head. Through a fog of pain, I struggled to drag myself out of the past and make sense of anything going on around me.

A battle had broken out between the crew of the carrier and the palace guards. How did they know? Where had we erred in our planning? What had given us away?

Get up! Brae shouted in my mind. *Get up and get Novee to the ship!*

Oh, gods…I hurt so badly. There was no way I could stand up. But there was also no way I was going to just lie here and wait to die either.

So I got my hands under me, and then pushed myself up to my knees. I shook my head to clear it.

The air was thick with billowing smoke that hid both the palace and the carrier. I hadn't heard an explosion. Ergin must have detonated something to conceal us from weapons fire.

Novee lay next to me, groaning and wheezing. The back of her coverall was burned away, exposing the scorched and broken layers of body armor hidden inside it and her bloody skin. The armor had mostly absorbed that first shot, but offered no protection now. I was certainly in no better shape.

Ergin had taken a hit to her right shoulder, but she was on her feet, firing a plasma gun back through the smoke toward the palace and keeping the guards at bay.

"Go," she rasped at me. "Take her and go. I will follow."

The smoke cleared just enough to reveal the shape of the carrier and two bodies crumpled on the landing pad below the open cargo bay door: a pair of palace guards, their chests smoking. They must have fired on us from behind the landing struts before Ergin or one of the other crew members took them out. Three crew members stood in the cargo bay door, firing over our heads back in the direction of the palace.

The agony radiating through my back and chest made it difficult to think, so I grabbed one thought and held onto it: *Get Novee on her feet and get on that ship.*

My arms and legs shaking with pain and shock, I crawled to Novee.

"Get up." I made it a command, though my voice was little more than a croak. "Come on. We've got to go."

"Leave me," she whispered. "I am not strong or brave like you, Halena."

"Bullshit." I gripped her thin arm and hauled her up with me as I rose. She could barely stand. "You're plenty strong and brave," I snapped. "You dance thirty meters in the air without fear. If you can do that, you can walk thirty steps and get on a gods-damned ship. I'll drag you if I have to."

She let out a ragged sob.

Plasma fire sizzled above our heads. Ducking, Novee and I half-ran, half-stumbled toward the ship's one remaining ramp. The other had already been retracted in preparation for takeoff.

"Ergin," I shouted, my voice muffled by my respirator. Damn thing was pointless now, so I pulled it off and tossed it over the side of the landing pad. "Come on!"

A volley of shots cut through the smoke from the direction of the palace. A searing bolt of plasma sliced through the upper right arm of my coverall, leaving a streak of fire across my bicep.

My cry of pain startled Novee. She tripped and almost fell. Cursing, I dragged her forward. Only a handful of steps to go.

A winged shadow with a pair of shining eyes swooped down in front of us.

"The Erotovo and his guards are behind you," Brae said, his voice raspy, maybe from inhaling the smoke. "Run."

Novee tried to backpedal from my shadowbat, but I tightened my grip on her arm and kept her moving toward the ship.

"*DANCER!*" The Erotovo's enraged bellow rolled across the palace cargo port. Novee cringed as if he were beside us with a hand raised to strike her.

Another volley of plasma fire cut across the landing pad. These shots hit the surface in front of us, obviously intended to get us to stop rather than cut us down.

"Your name is not *Dancer*," I hissed when Novee seemed frozen. "Come on. Forget him."

I pushed her ahead of me and glanced over my shoulder. The smoke had cleared enough for me to see the centaurian Erotovo and a dozen of his personal guards pursuing us, running on all four stocky legs. The guards held rifles.

"Stop, thief!" the Erotovo commanded, his face flushed. His eyes blazed with fury as they locked on my face. "Halena Onsulus, I will hunt you down across the galaxy for this crime!"

Realization dawned: he actually thought I was *stealing* Novee rather than rescuing her. Truly, the Erotovo couldn't think in any way other than as an abuser.

With a curse, Ergin stopped and turned to face the Erotovo and his entourage. She planted her feet, braced herself, and began firing, sending the Erotovo and his men scrambling for cover. "Go!" she shouted over her shoulder at us.

The finality in her voice turned my stomach to lead. Oh, no. No, no, *no*. I couldn't let Ergin sacrifice herself for us. There had to be another way—there *had* to be.

I got Novee to the ship's ramp and shoved her as hard as I could toward the crew members coming down to meet us. "Take her," I shouted as Novee stumbled into one's arms. "And throw me a weapon."

The rest of the crew continued firing back at the Erotovo and his guards. But instead of giving me a plasma rifle, the two Ymarians who'd met us grabbed Novee and me and dragged us up the ramp.

The engines powered up, sending a blast of energy and displaced air across the landing pad. The sound of the engines drowned out all other noise, including the weapons fire behind us.

My rage and panic gave me strength despite the agony of my wounds. I fought to free myself. "No! Let me go back for Ergin!"

"She is gone," one of the Ymarians grated, tightening their grip on my arm. They were far stronger than they looked. "There is nothing to go back for."

I twisted around to look behind me.

Ergin, or what was left of her, lay in a heap on the landing pad. Anger and grief sliced through my insides like a scythe. The cry that came out of my mouth was so guttural that it didn't sound human.

"It was fast," the other Ymarian crew member said, their voice strangely distant as if they were speaking to me down a long tunnel. "She did not suffer."

A last volley of plasma fire drove us back from the open door as the ramp retracted. Brae darted into the cargo bay unnoticed by the crew and slipped into the shadows on the ceiling.

With a roar of thrusters, the carrier lifted off the platform. I lost sight of the Erotovo, his guards, and Ergin's body.

Every ounce of adrenaline and determination that had kept me on my feet and allowed me to all but carry Novee to the ship evaporated. As Novee let out a cry of alarm, my vision grayed and my knees gave out. No one caught me before I hit the deck.

Merciful darkness swept me away.

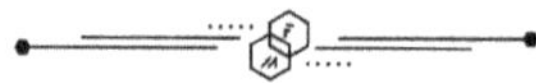

I WOKE TO FULL-BODY ACHES AND THE SOUND OF SOBS.

Once my vision cleared, I found myself on a bunk in a tiny crew cabin smaller than my closet in the palace on Ngara. Novee had curled up with me, her face buried against my unburned arm as she cried. I didn't have the strength to find something comforting to say.

At some point while I'd been unconscious, our half-burned coveralls had been cut off and our boots removed, leaving us in bare feet and what remained of our bodysuits. I was shivering. The ship was colder than I expected, or maybe I was in shock. Or both. At least they'd given us a blanket to share.

Someone had put analgesic patches on us so our pain was muted. Whatever drug was in the patch was strong. My stomach churned, my brain felt cottony, and my thoughts echoed inside my skull.

Brae? I asked, blinking up at the ceiling as it faded in and out of focus.

I frighten Novee, my shadowbat replied, his voice quiet—or maybe that was a result of my brain fog. *So I'm keeping watch on the ship and its crew to make sure you're safe. Rest.*

I wanted him beside me for comfort and reassurance, but it did help to know he was monitoring what the crew was doing since I was in no shape to do so myself. *Thank you,* I told him.

Through the bunk and the bulkhead next to us, the steady thrumming of engines told me we had left Ngaran space and were now traveling at hyperspeed.

I had no idea what our destination might be, when or if someone might come to treat our injuries, and whether the way we were all but ignored meant the crew hated or resented us because Ergin had died.

What I *did* know was that I ached from my soul outward. The gutting memory of Ergin's ruined body lying crumpled and still replayed in my mind in an endless loop. Every mission, whether it ended well or badly or somewhere in between, contributed fuel for my never-ending nightmares.

Unbidden, the Erotovo's rage and roar echoed in my head: *I will hunt you down across the galaxy for this crime!*

I took a deep, shaky breath that hurt my ribs and back. Where would I go now with him hunting me, hells-bent on retribution?

My false identity as Halena offered some assurance, but nothing was certain. Not only did the Erotovo's vast wealth and connections put me in danger, but they infinitely complicated future missions because if he or his agents found me, he'd blow my cover and possibly endanger the Web's operations. My handler might opt not to use me as an agent anymore, or at least until the furor over Novee's rescue died down and the Erotovo lost interest in me—however long that took. Whether my churning insides were the result of those fears, my wounds, or both, I couldn't tell.

By the time a grim crew member came with a medical kit, Novee had cried herself out and fallen asleep, my painkillers had mostly worn off, and the air in our little cabin had become thick with the odors of burned hair and flesh.

Two hours later, the medic departed, leaving us bandaged, mostly healed, and acutely nauseated from intensive muscle, tissue, and dermal repair procedures. We would have some scars on our backs, but not as severe or extensive as I'd feared. We'd also gotten new analgesic patches, so at least we weren't in pain anymore—at least, not physically.

Just as my nausea began to lessen, I received confirmation from my Web handler via long-range transmission that I had been deactivated as an agent indefinitely. I was too numb and sick to my stomach to feel much at the news except hollowness and the sensation of being adrift.

The brief message stated that when this ship arrived on Fyloria, I would be given assistance with altering my appearance. I would also receive a new identity, one-way transport to a world of my choosing, and a small stipend to tide me over until I found work. I was not to reach out to my handler under any circumstances.

At least I wouldn't be cut off completely. Once I chose my destination, I'd get the name of a local agent who'd be my contact there. They would help me if I found myself in danger.

And just like that, not only had I lost my job but my identity and sense of purpose too. The enormity of it all hadn't sunk in yet. It probably wouldn't until after I got my new identity and boarded a transport for some world a long way from Ngara.

Everything about who I was now was tied into my work for the Web. Who was I without my mission? I didn't know.

When Novee asked to share my bunk for the night rather than move to another cabin, it didn't occur to me to refuse. I needed comfort too.

As the crew went about their business outside our closed door under Brae's watchful eyes, Novee and I lay in near darkness, watching stars and planets streak by at hyperspeed outside the window. Our heads lay next to each other and her cool hand rested on mine.

The crew had given us spare uniforms to wear, food, water, and a bottle of Probytian moonshine, which was now open and two-thirds empty. We'd lost the cork somewhere in the bedding.

"I am sorry," Novee said, her gaze on the window that slanted over us above the bunk. Starlight reflected on the blue tears rolling down her face. "You have lost everything because of me."

"Nothing that happened today was caused by you. It was the Erotovo's doing," I stated, my voice quiet but firm. "And I haven't lost everything. This is only temporary. I'll be an agent again as soon as it's safe."

"If that is what you want, I hope it comes to pass." Her long fingers curled around mine. "Your work is never really *safe*, though, is it?"

"No." I couldn't pretend otherwise. "But it's worth it."

"Damn the Erotovo." She trembled. "If he finds you…"

"He won't. It's a big galaxy." I'd keep telling myself that until I believed it. "He'll lose interest after a while. People like him always find a new obsession. This is like a furlough, or a vacation." I took a breath that was shakier than I wanted it to be. "Maybe it's for the best. This was my fifth mission in a row. I'm tired."

"Then you are due for a rest." She squeezed my fingers. "Halena, how do I live knowing Ergin died so I could be free?"

This wasn't the first time someone had asked me such a question. My own extraction had gone smoothly, so I couldn't claim I knew how Novee felt. Time and experience had granted me insight, though, and I'd come to understand what survivors needed was honesty—and never to offer empty platitudes. As such, I had a better answer now than I'd had in my early days as an agent.

"Every day you live as a free woman, you honor her," I said. "Every happy moment you experience, every milestone you reach, even every perfectly ordinary day you have in whatever life you choose to live after this—they're all a blessing on her memory." I swallowed hard around the lump in my throat and said the hard part. "You won't get to the point that you accept and believe that for a while, and you'll have hard days. *Dark* days. Sleepless nights. But there will be happiness, Novee. I promise."

"I think you were once in my place." When I didn't deny it, she asked, "Are you happy?"

"Not at the moment," I admitted. "My heart hurts. But overall—yes, I am happy. Because I'm free. And now so are you. Give yourself time to adjust and be kind to yourself. You've been through a lot."

She nestled her head closer to mine. "I will try."

Her natural scent was sweet. I hoped my own wasn't too off-putting. The ship only had sonic cleansers and neither of us had any scented toiletries. At least we no longer smelled of smoke and our own burned skin.

"After tomorrow, I will never see you again?" she asked.

We both already knew the answer, but she'd phrased it as a question, so I replied, "No. It wouldn't be safe for either of us, especially you."

"All right." Her voice wobbled. "Where will you go? What will you do?"

For better or worse, I'd made those decisions after a talk with Brae and three big gulps from our bottle of moonshine.

I couldn't tell Novee exactly what my plans were since that would undermine the security of my hiding place, but I could answer in broad terms so she knew I had something good to look forward to—something more than months or years of hiding from the Erotovo.

"I'm going someplace beautiful," I said. "It's a planet I've always wanted to visit. And I think I might try to be a singer there."

"A singer?" She'd started to reach over me for the bottle of moonshine, but paused to look down at my face. Her eyes lit up with real interest and excitement for the first time since we'd met. "Oh, Halena, do you sing?"

Despite my heavy heart, I smiled, at least for a moment. "I do."

"I did not know." She took a drink from the bottle and offered it to me. When I shook my head, she returned it to the table and settled back in beside me. "Will you please sing for me?"

I thought of how beautifully Novee danced and grimaced. "I haven't warmed up, and my throat is scratchy—"

Her cool fingertips caressed my arm in a very pleasant way. "Please."

I relented. "What would you like to hear?"

"Anything you like."

I sifted through the list of songs I knew and settled on a simple tune from Havel Prime that was wistful but not sad, and not particularly vocally demanding.

Thanks to my injuries and smoke inhalation, my voice was rough and shaky, my vocal range was limited, and my lungs were unable to get the full breath I needed for long notes, but I sang for her anyway. Novee stroked my arm and listened.

My voice had once been the reason for my captivity and had belonged to my owners. Now my voice was my own. When I sang, it was my way of being free. And if Novee danced in her new life, I hoped it would be for herself, on her terms. It was the very least she deserved.

When I finished the song, Novee kissed my bare shoulder very lightly. "Thank you," she said, and pulled the covers over us. "Gods grant, your beautiful voice is what I will remember of this day and the rest will fade from memory," she murmured, and tucked herself against my arm.

I leaned my head against hers, closed my eyes, and listened to her breathe and the engines hum until sleep claimed me.

CHAPTER 3

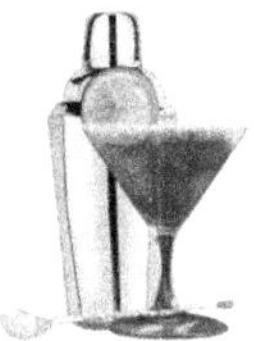

MIKAS

At precisely 1400 hours, I switched the bar's setting from *Auto* to *Staffed*, activated all the lights that illuminated the rows of bottles, casks, and other assorted beverages behind me, took off my shirt, and tossed a bar towel over one shoulder, careful not to snag it on any of my spines.

Out of habit, I checked my reflection in the mirrored wall behind the shelves and smoothed my thick, black hair. Like my back and shoulder spines, my hair tended to bristle when I was angry or irritated—or tired.

I scanned the room, noting the patrons and what they were drinking. After three straight days working double shifts, I was fatigued and in even less of a mood to deal with bullshit than usual. Thankfully, none of the current customers had a history of causing problems. Maybe today would be smooth sailing.

My earpiece beeped. "Turn on the hologram," the bar's owner, Nubo Wex, snapped in my ear. "If you want wages, that holo had better be on."

He could have activated the holo from his office, but my

employer took particular satisfaction in making me do it myself.

Without comment, I activated the hologram of myself outside the bar's front doors that beckoned passersby to come inside for live bar service.

Even in a resort city like Onat'ras, an old-fashioned bartender was a novelty. To keep costs down and reduce the number of employees on payroll, most bars preferred patrons to order at their tables or via kiosks. Drinks were picked up from serving stations or delivered by service 'bots. During off-peak hours, when I was not working, Zaa'ga operated the same way.

But with several interplanetary luxury cruisers currently in orbit, the city had filled with wealthy tourists. Nubo wanted their money. Offering a live bartender ensured he would get a generous share of it. He would force me to work day and night if labor laws did not prevent it.

I wanted tourists' money too, if I were to be honest, which was why I had taken off my shirt and donned form-fitting pants. The more blue-green scaly skin I showed and the more I flashed my fangs and bristled my spines, the more I earned in tips.

Many visitors to Fortusia wanted to marvel at our genetically engineered bodies, which combined humanoid DNA with genetic material from nonhumans, animals, and even plant life from across the galaxy. My creators had used DNA of the reptilian Pallasian bosor, as well as several mammalian species from J'Nora.

Showing skin did not bother me; I had never suffered from self-consciousness or modesty about my body. And any such feelings I had ever experienced disappeared during my years of military service, where privacy was virtually nonexistent.

I did not, however, enjoy seeing myself in larger-than-life holographic form—especially since Nubo had manipulated my image to exaggerate the size of my muscles and groin. If nothing else, it amounted to deceptive business practices. I also found it insulting, as if my natural attributes and my efforts to maintain my physique were somehow insufficient.

As always, Nubo had met my objections with a derisive snort and a dismissive wave. I made good money here, so I had let the matter go. At least I did not have to see the hologram unless I stepped outside, which typically only occurred when I had to remove a troublesome patron from the premises.

Despite the crowded streets, in the middle of the afternoon only a dozen customers sat at tables with drinks. All were locals. Clear skies, sunshine, and the lure of endless entertainments on the main boulevard meant tourists were occupied elsewhere. Zaa'ga would get busier later in the day. This was the calm before the storm.

Bartending was good, easy work for a weary former soldier with a head full of bad memories, a bum leg, few other marketable skills, and no interest in fighting anymore.

As I refilled a pipe of Engareni wine for one of the regulars —an amphibious Prylothian who sat in a small pool next to the bar—my earpiece beeped again.

"Workers will be coming later today to update the stage area," Nubo said, as usual without bothering with any pleasantries. "They told me the disruption should be minimal."

The small, dark stage had seldom been used in the nearly two years I had worked at Zaa'ga. Whenever the bar offered entertainment, it typically took the form of holos or vidscreen, which were the norm in clubs of this size.

"Thank you for informing me," I said, returning to the bar as the Prylothian gurgled contentedly on the pipe of wine. "How do you plan to use the stage?"

Nubo huffed as if my questions annoyed him. "I have posted a job notice seeking a singer."

"A live singer, rather than holos?" My eyebrows raised. "That will be novel."

"Some of the bars on the boulevard have added them. If a live bartender brings in customers, so will a singer." Another huff. "And it will be less costly than replacing the holo system and vidscreens with new models."

I might have guessed. Nubo's primary concern always boiled down to profit.

"So we may expect performers to come in for auditions, beginning today," Nubo continued. "With any luck, we will find someone with at least *some* talent willing to work for reasonable compensation."

Inwardly, I snorted. Nubo's definition of *reasonable compensation* was markedly different than most employers and the wage guidelines set by the province.

"And speaking of pay," Nubo said, "if someone comes in looking like they expect the same wages as clubs pay on the boulevard or aboard the cruisers, tell them the position has been filled. If they look desperate for a job, I will speak to them myself."

Gods, my employer was scum. It was at moments like this I felt most compelled to march directly to his office and strangle him with my bare hands. I would be doing myself and all the good citizens of Onat'ras a favor.

"Understood," I said instead.

My earpiece went blessedly silent. I resisted the urge to take it out and drop it into the Prylothian's wading pool, but only just.

The thought of having a singer in the bar had been interesting, even appealing, for only as long as it had taken Nubo to reveal his plan to exploit whoever he might hire.

Maybe I could warn vulnerable applicants away somehow. A difficult prospect, given Nubo kept constant watch on the bar from his office and listened via devices around the bar. He likely eavesdropped via my earpiece too, though he had told me it only activated when we spoke to each other. I did not believe that at all. When it came to Nubo, it was most prudent to assume everything he said was a lie.

It was rather an open secret in Onat'ras that Zaa'ga was a way for Nubo to show legitimate income while the bulk of his fortune came from far less legal sources. He was just well-connected enough, and paid the right people, to operate in plain sight.

Other than citing how much money I made here, I would have been hard-pressed to explain why I stayed at Zaa'ga knowing the kind of person I worked for. Maybe I could have found bartending work elsewhere—if not in Onat'ras, in another resort city. But after so many years as a soldier, rarely knowing from one day to the next where I might lay my head, my desire to wander had all but vanished.

I busied myself behind the bar pouring drinks, mixing cocktails, and chatting with the regulars. At least I could count on their friendliness and generosity regardless of how many tourists wandered in and how freely they parted with their Alliance credits.

I had my back to the bar and my focus on uncorking a cask of Tocanian ale when an unmistakably human female voice came from behind me.

"Excuse me," she said in Alliance Standard. "Who do I speak to about the audition?"

I glanced up from the cask and into the mirrored wall behind the shelves. The speaker was indeed a human female, with long blonde hair that shimmered in as many colors as a nebula and violet eyes that met mine in our reflection. Unlike the wealthy tourists who packed the streets of Onat'ras in their expensive and fashionable clothes, she wore a very plain long-sleeved jumpsuit, boots, and cross-body bag.

Human women often found my height, reptilian skin, and spines startling or even frightening, but her expression showed only polite inquisitiveness.

I had no time to wonder why that might be because in the next moment, her scent reached me—sweet, delicate, and light, like a single petal of a flower.

My world tilted ninety degrees.

My senses filled with peace, joy, and the comfort of home. Every thought and sensation that was not of *her* disappeared, swept away by a tidal wave of need, desire, and want. My body came alive and filled with warmth as if I felt the bliss and heat of sunshine for the first time.

In the mirror, her beautiful violet eyes held me in thrall.

Oh, all the gods above and below...I had to grab the counter with one hand to steady myself.

"Are you all right?" she asked, her eyes wide with concern. Her voice was the only sound I heard, as if the bar and everything in it had been muted somehow.

I tried to answer, but a dozen images flooded my mind: sleeping beside this woman...walking hand-in-hand with this woman...cooking and eating meals with this woman...this woman above me, her thighs astride my hips and her head thrown back in ecstasy. I heard her call my name in her release as clearly as I had heard anything else today. Blood rushed to my cocks and my head swam.

My mate. My true mate is here.

All Fortusians studied the science of our physiology in school. We understood our own genetics and biology almost as well as those who created us. Our ability to detect the proximity of a true mate—someone with whom we would not only be biologically compatible, but with whom we would resonate in every way—was one of the best and best-known aspects of our engineering. But after thirty-four years, thoughts of finding a true mate had receded until I seldom if ever considered the possibility I might experience such wonders.

Certainly no description of what this moment would feel

like had prepared me for its arrival, or come close to doing it justice.

My chest heaving and my hearts thundering in my ears, I fought to regain my equilibrium. The last few moments felt like an eternity, as if I had already lived a lifetime with my mate in the handful of heartbeats between the moment I caught her scent and now.

Carefully, I relinquished my grip on the counter and cask of ale and turned.

"Are you all right?" she repeated, her expression now wary.

Her gaze swept over me in a quick, evaluating way that reminded me of a soldier's trained assessment, though my instincts told me she had not been a soldier. Interesting.

"I…am fine," I said, my voice rough.

I was *not* fine, though—I was floating. Untethered. A onetime soldier, more than two meters tall and nearly one hundred and twenty kilos, now as light as a cloud.

"Well." The corners of her lips turned up. "You must not see many humans around here, judging by your reaction."

I must look like I had been struck by lightning. Gods, what must she think of me?

"Mikas." Nubo's sharp voice cut through my euphoria like a scythe.

He was not speaking in my earpiece, however—my employer was lumbering our way from the direction of the hallway that led to his office.

Like most Forbian males, he was enormous, as tall and wide as a Gandarian mule-ox and just as graceless, with spiky white hair, a wide-set pair of bulbous eyes, and thick arms and legs. Today he wore a long caftan over trousers and had left his wide, thickly padded feet bare, as was customary for his species.

Nubo ignored me completely, his calculating gaze fixed on the human woman standing across the bar from me. My stomach dropped, and anger and protectiveness made a low rumble grow in my chest.

"I apologize for my bartender," he said, his wide, blue face splitting into a grin. "Mikas pours very fine drinks, but sometimes he forgets his manners. I am Nubo Wex, proud owner of this establishment. You have come to audition?"

Lost in awe and wonder, I had nearly forgotten what had brought my mate to the bar. Oh, gods. My mate must be nowhere near a dangerous criminal like Nubo Wex.

"Yes, I have." She gave him a tiny bow of greeting. "If the position is still available."

"It is," Nubo said, his grin widening. "What is your name, dear?"

My spines bristled, but if being called *dear* annoyed her, she did not show it. "Isla," she said.

Isla. My true mate's name was Isla. Two more beautiful syllables could not exist in the universe.

"Isla…?" Nubo prompted.

"Isla Mair." She glanced at the dark stage. "Your notice said you're looking for someone who can start immediately, but it doesn't look like you're really set up for a live performer."

Warmth and desire rolled through me at the fearless way she met Nubo's sharp gaze without blinking or backing down, even when he drew himself up and frowned at the implication of her words.

Keeping a wary eye on my employer, I busied myself making a Bacorian fullwell, the most complex cocktail I knew, as if an order for one had just shown up on my screen behind the bar. I did not want Nubo to feel my scrutiny and invite Isla to his office for privacy.

"The stage will be ready by tonight, or tomorrow at the latest," Nubo said, and now he was all charm once again. "But we are getting ahead of ourselves. Are you prepared to audition for me now?"

"Of course." Isla took a small device from her pocket. "This will provide music for me to sing, unless you prefer I sing without it?"

"I think I would like to hear you sing in my office," Nubo said, and I vibrated with unease and anger I fought to hide. "There is no need for you to audition on the stage."

I nearly crushed the bottle of Bacorian brandy I held before I steadied myself and poured a measured amount into the glass. No way in hells would I stand by and watch her follow Nubo into his office, which was soundproof and could be locked.

"Respectfully, I disagree," Isla said, with a smile that made my hearts stutter because it was so coolly polite and confident. "I would like to hear how music and voice sounds in your establishment. Not all environments are acoustically suited for live singers."

In other words, she was auditioning the bar as much as Nubo was auditioning her. If it did not meet her standards, she was not likely to want the job. And judging by the tension in Nubo's body and his long silence, I was not the only one who had come to that conclusion.

Everything about the way Isla faced Nubo indicated she had no interest in going to his office for a private audition, in whatever form that might take—or any interest in him as anything more than a potential employer *if* she liked the terms of employment. She was not the desperate, easily manipulated singer he had said he preferred. And I could not have been more pleased by that fact. Surely he would send her away.

Though it meant I would lose my apartment and must seek new employment, likely in some other city, I would leave my own job without hesitation just to ensure their paths did not cross. My future was with Isla, if she would have me—wherever and however that would be.

Nubo's response sliced through my half-formed plans, then straight through my flesh and into the bone.

"Then by all means, go to the stage," he said with a sweeping gesture. He raised his voice. "If our patrons are willing to listen to lovely Isla sing for us?"

A chorus of approval erupted from the regulars—except the Prylothian, who gurgled obliviously on his wine.

As Isla made her way toward the stage, Nubo turned to me, his eyes gleaming and expression nearly gluttonous. "You heard me, Mikas. Turn everything on for our Isla."

Our Isla.

Rage filled me and the sickness in my stomach grew. Isla's fierceness had the opposite effect on Nubo than I expected. Rather than send her away, he was all the more determined to keep her. He clearly considered her defiance a challenge.

Damn it. Damn it to *all the hells*.

Nubo's gaze dropped to my clenched fists. His expression dark with suspicion and anger, he stepped to the bar and lowered his voice. "Unless you relish the thought of being on the street tonight with fewer appendages than you have now, you will keep your eyes and hands to yourself. As long as she does not sound like a screeching Hardanian war-pig, she will be my singer, and she will be under my protection from this moment on."

No, she was under *my* protection. She was my hearts, and my world.

Isla, meanwhile, had climbed the steps to the stage and stood on the platform, her hands on her hips as she studied the bar's interior like a queen surveying her lands. And she watched us out of the corner of her eye in a way that made me wonder what she had been before she sought employment as a singer.

I caught a flutter of nearly invisible wings and a glint of light in a pair of eyes in the shadows along the far side of the bar, traveling along the wall near the ceiling. I could not see any details of its form, as if it was nothing more than shadow itself.

My spines bristled. A Pallasian shadowbat. A rare sight on

any planet but their homeworld. I had certainly never seen one in Zaa'ga. But to whom did it belong?

The creature settled into a dark nook in the ceiling right above Isla. Her gaze flicked up, and a fleeting smile crossed her face before she returned her attention to the stage and the audience around it.

My unease turned to amazement and curiosity. Isla had a shadowbat companion? How many more secrets and wonders did my mate contain?

Nubo, meanwhile, was quite oblivious to my turmoil and not done making threats.

"You lay *one finger* on her," he hissed, drawing my attention away from Isla and her mysterious shadow and back to him. "Or say something to her I do not like, you are a dead man, and she will join you in the incinerator one minute later. Am I clear?"

Rage and fear for Isla turned me cold. A thousand scenarios flashed through my mind, from removing Nubo's head from his body to fcigning indifference about Isla and everything in between. Indifference he would not believe because I had already given myself away—at least that I found her appealing, not that I had recognized her as my true mate. So that was not an option.

Kill him? No, I could not. Nubo had many connections in the city. He was wealthy and powerful. Even if Isla wanted to flee with me, we would not get far.

And more importantly, my body, hearts, and soul had recognized her as my true mate, but Isla knew nothing about me but my first name and that seeing her had left me speechless. She would have no reason to trust me, much less run from a crime lord or his cronies with me. The very thought was ludicrous.

To protect Isla, I had only one choice: convince Nubo I had no feelings for her beyond simple initial physical attraction and bide my time.

I forced my shoulders to slump as though he had cowed me. "You are clear," I said, and activated the controls for the stage.

The lights came on, and suddenly Isla was surrounded by bright colors, like a flower in a garden. The sensor detected someone on the stage and bathed her in a spotlight that made her hair glow. Even her plain jumpsuit shimmered. My knees turned watery. I leaned against the bar to steady myself.

Evidently believing he had put me back in my place, Nubo slapped the bar top with his webbed hand. "Good." He put his back to me to face the stage. "Whenever you are ready," he called.

Isla raised her hand to acknowledge him, then used the device in her hand to play music. I recognized the melody: a Fylorian ballad about a woman longing for her lover who was away at war.

Before her mouth opened, I had the ridiculous thought that if Isla *did* sound terrible, she might yet escape Nubo's attentions. Even as that vain hope crossed my mind, I knew her voice would be as beautiful as she was, and not just to my ears.

"My love, I am waiting here at home for you," Isla sang. Her voice was truly lovely—pure and sweet, and a little husky on the low notes. I found myself caught between utter despair and joy like I had never known.

Gods, she was perfect.

I could not curse that Isla had come into Zaa'ga today in response to Nubo's notice, but I cursed everything about Nubo, from his spiny hairs to his flat feet. Most of all I cursed his power to follow through on every one of his threats.

I stirred the very complex and very expensive cocktail I had just spent the past several minutes painstakingly making, poured it into a cup, and downed it in a single gulp without tasting it. It could have been seawater for all I cared. The burn of the liquor did, however, cut through my despair and enable me to think more clearly.

Isla and I would be colleagues. We could get to know each other as friends. I yearned to know everything about her and to share myself with her. And someday, if and when I earned her trust and we found a way to escape Nubo's reach, I would tell her the truth.

Hopefully that day would come soon. Until then, I would ache for her with every breath and every beat of my hearts.

CHAPTER 4

MIKAS

THREE MONTHS LATER

FIVE NIGHTS A WEEK, ZAA'GA WAS PACKED WITH TOURISTS AND locals who came to hear Isla sing.

Nubo's gamble on choosing a live singer over replacing the bar's holos had paid off handsomely. And even on a planet populated by genetically engineered people who usually attracted the most attention from offworld visitors, a *human* singer drew crowds. Thirsty crowds. Despite assistance from the bar's drink kiosks and service 'bots, I could barely keep up with orders some nights. My tips had never been more generous and my savings had swelled.

And yet my hearts felt as hollow as the great caverns north of the city and as abyssal as the deepest ocean because my love and devotion remained unspoken.

Tonight, Isla took the stage at 2100 hours in a dark red gown that clung to her curves while still covering her arms and back.

The dress's high front slit bared one leg almost to her hip whenever she moved, and its deep-V neckline enticed me with visions of resting my head on the tantalizing softness of her breasts.

Her gaze swept over the bar's patrons, then met mine. Her smile was wonderfully warm, and she gave me a tiny wave. I let my lips turn up at the corners—the closest to returning her smile I could do without risking Nubo's ire.

When her attention returned to the crowd, I smoothed my features and grabbed three tankards to fill for a trio of Hardanian brothers who had already consumed a remarkable amount of ale but seemed only mildly inebriated. Regardless of their level of drunkenness, I did not like the way they murmured to each other with their gazes fixed on Isla. They were far from the only patrons watching her closely, but my spines prickled in warning. These males could be trouble.

When the opening notes of Isla's first song poured from the sound system, the bar fell quiet. She smiled and bowed to acknowledge her audience. My chest ached. Gods above, how could she grow more beautiful by the day?

"My love, hold me close and never let go..." Isla sang in Tivoran. The words were so low-pitched they were nearly a purr, but her amplified voice filled the room completely.

My earpiece and one of the screens behind the bar provided a translation since I did not know Tivoran well. From my mate, those words would have sounded lovely to me in any language.

As if she were some kind of celestial being, Isla's gown shimmered and her nebula-colored hair virtually glowed in soft light while the rest of the stage remained dark.

Nubo had wanted to use a bright spotlight and colorful holo screens as a backdrop like most bars on the boulevard, but Isla had insisted on a simple, muted overhead light and that we dim the lights throughout the bar during her set. The first night she sang onstage for patrons, even Nubo had to admit she had been entirely right about the staging. She was so elegant, and her voice so velvety, that bright lights would have been a sin.

Before she had signed her contract, she also won disputes over her right to select her attire and hairstyle, all her own songs, and the length of her sets. I had never seen our oafish boss lose so many arguments in a row as those he lost to Isla's confident and seemingly guileless smile.

Every night, Nubo watched and listened from his office, ensuring I kept my distance from my lovely coworker…a feat that became more difficult by the hour.

When Isla was nearby, it took all my willpower to go through the motions of tending bar when all I wanted with the entirety of my hearts and soul was to go to my knees before her. For now, the best I could do was be her friend and colleague while I secretly let her sweet voice and even sweeter scent soak into my soul as I poured drinks and kept my workspace tidy.

The Tivoran love song led smoothly into a more upbeat tune from Fyloria about the end of winter and arrival of spring, and then Isla bowed and thanked the patrons in Fortusian for their attendance and enthusiasm. Human vocal cords found Fortusian difficult, especially our vowels, but her sincere attempt at speaking the local dialect rather than simply using Alliance Standard added to her charm—and encouraged listeners to show their appreciation in the form of credits and coins into her tip jar. Patrons could also leave gratuities via the screens on their tables, but Nubo, like most business owners, took a cut of those transactions, so the more thoughtful listeners tipped with currency.

Locals and most offworld visitors knew a performer's primary source of income was tips. Strictly speaking, both Isla and I received little money from Nubo. Our main compensation was our apartments on the fourth level above this one. The arrangement was common in tourist-oriented cities like Onat'ras, where living quarters were in such high demand.

Once her set was underway, drink orders arrived without pause, forcing me to focus on meeting those demands while I listened to her sing. While Isla performed, a significant percentage of customers chose to order their drinks directly from me rather than kiosks. A live singer apparently whetted their appetite for live bar service. I did not mind, as it inevitably led to more tips.

Nubo had briefly suggested hiring another bartender, but I had assured him I did not need one and he had dropped the idea almost immediately. I did not want to split my tips, and he likely did not want to pay for another employee's living quarters. As long as I could keep customers happy, we were both content to leave things be. Nubo's profit margin grew and my savings swelled.

Someday, I hoped to use those savings to begin a new life with Isla, if she would accept my love. If we could get away from Nubo and Onat'ras. If whatever had brought Isla and her mysterious shadowbat to Fortusia did not interfere.

If, if, *if*. A word I had grown to hate.

But even my flash of bitterness faded when Isla's voice soared in a beautiful soprano aria from a Valodian opera. It was one of the pieces Nubo had tried to tell her not to sing, arguing no one who visited a bar wanted to hear fine opera. Isla had simply smiled and included it in her performance the following night, and Nubo never mentioned it again.

A rough voice cut through my thoughts. "Commandant Mikas Auren. I'll be damned."

I glanced up from the cocktail I was mixing and stilled.

Kona Landus—formerly Lieutenant Kona Landus of the Cludian Corps—slid onto a barstool across from me. Despite being designed for species larger and heavier than even Fortusians, the chair creaked.

The very tall and red-skinned Atolani female grinned, displaying sharp teeth. The gold rings on her horns and metal beads strung through her waist-length black hair glinted. She wore a leather vest and pants that emphasized her muscular build—and revealed a dozen scars, half of which she did not have the last time I had seen her. The one on the side of her neck would have severed her spine or taken off her head if it had gone much deeper.

"So this is where you've been hiding." Her grin vanished as quickly as it had appeared, and her black eyes with their bright blue pupils narrowed almost into slits. "*Commandant.*"

A tidal wave of memories tried to surface—all of them bad. I squashed them back and filled a glass with ale. "I am not hiding, and I no longer hold that rank." I slid the ale across to the customer who had ordered it, dried my hands on a towel, and reached for an empty glass to start a new order. "Bar chairs are for customers."

She flashed her teeth. One of her long incisors was chipped. "I came in to have a drink."

I very much did not want to serve Kona anything, but as long as she did not violate any of the house rules, I had no justification for telling her to leave. "What do you want?"

She barely glanced at the drink I was making. "I'll have one of those."

I could not claim to be any kind of expert on what beverages Kona preferred, but a honey wine aperitif did not seem likely to please an Atolani's palate. Then again, the odds she had come into this bar by accident were infinitesimal, and that she simply wanted a drink nonexistent. What the hells could she want with me years after we had parted ways?

I gestured at the payment screen to her right. With another flash of teeth, she scanned her wristcomm to authorize a charge.

Without a word, I finished making both drinks, handed the first to a Biltrobian at the far end of the bar, slid the second across to Kona, and immediately charged her account and closed the transaction without waiting for her to add a gratuity. I did not want to encourage her to linger.

"So, the mighty commandant." She rested her fingertips on her cup, clearly disinterested in consuming the drink she had paid for. "Serving drinks and toting barrels of ale."

My fingers itched to grab her by her collar and drag her outside, where we could settle whatever grudge had brought her here tonight.

"Kona." I gritted my teeth. "I have nothing to say to you, and I am very busy earning an honest living. You should try it."

"Oh, so smug." Slowly, deliberately, she scraped her talons on the glass, leaving scratches down its side. My chest rumbled at her casual disregard for the bar's property. "You forget I watched you on the battlefield, Commandant," she added. "On Ryoxv and Ymar III. I know who you are."

She clearly wanted to needle me, so I chose to ignore her use of my former military rank.

"You do not know who I am," I countered, my focus on the process of mixing two Bacorian fullwells ordered by a pair of well-dressed traders at the far end of the bar. They looked the type to tip well for well-made drinks and prompt service. "Nor did you know who I *was*. I played the role of a soldier, but it was a role I was conscripted into. Even then you saw only what you wanted to see."

Kona scoffed. "Do you sleep well at night telling yourself these lies? Or do you doubt them as much as I do?"

"I sleep very well," I lied, pouring a carefully measured draught of bitterflower extract into each of the cocktails. "You have your drink. Others want theirs. I have no interest in dredging up the past, and no obligation to let you sit here and be insulting." I hooked my thumb at the placard on the wall behind me that stated my right to refuse service to customers who violated the house rules for hospitality. "Either take your drink and go somewhere else or drink in silence."

With a chuckle, she picked up her glass and turned on her chair to face the stage, where Isla had just begun another song—this one, a popular local tune about sailing on a vast pink ocean searching for a mythical island. Some patrons were singing along, which Isla clearly enjoyed, and even directed them when to sing louder and then more softly.

"Beautiful singer," Kona mused, sipping her drink. Her lip curled in distaste. "Not your type at all, of course. Too fragile. But I see why you were staring at her earlier."

Out of sight behind the counter, my fingers tightened on the flask of onyx-colored syrup that was the final ingredient in the fullwells, leaving a dent in its side.

I had not seen Kona in the bar watching me earlier, but she might have found a place to sit or stand out of my line of sight. Or she might not have seen anything at all, and simply trying to get under my skin in a different way.

Best to ignore her. She would not give up, if our previous interactions were any indication, but I did not have to give her the satisfaction of reacting.

Carefully, I poured three drops of syrup into each glass, watched it spread into a thin, even layer across the top of the liquid, and corked the flask before setting it back on the shelf. I delivered the drinks to the traders, accepted my gratuity—which was more than the cost of the drinks—and slipped the credits into my collection box behind the bar.

With my back to the stage, my spines prickled. A familiar warmth spread over my shoulders. Isla was watching me.

It was a curse and a blessing that I was always aware when my mate's gaze fell on me. That warmth reminded me she was nearby. It soothed my hearts and quieted my beastly rage, and promised tomorrows full of joys and contentment. The pleasure far outweighed the ache.

But when I turned around, Isla's attention had moved to

Kona, who was now leaning with one elbow on the bar and staring back, her expression hard and dark eyes flinty.

Atolani were a fierce warrior race. Many found them intimidating even when not on the receiving end of a glare. Isla showed no sign of fear or being intimidated, though. After a beat, she redirected her attention to a boisterous group of young Engareni females sitting near the stage who squawked their appreciation for her singing.

"Hrm…maybe not so fragile," Kona said over her shoulder. She drained the last of her aperitif, grimaced, and slid the glass down the bar in my direction, forcing me to lunge to catch it before it flew off and broke on the floor. With a smirk, she stood. "Still, not someone who'd think much of you, I suspect."

"Why did you come here?" I dropped the damaged glass into the refuse chute. "What is it you want? You chose your path after our service in the Corps and I chose mine. I never wronged you."

"You don't think so?" Her hands clenched into fists. "I vouched for you with my squad. I stuck my neck out for you to make sure you had work once they put your leg back together. And what did you do? You *left*. You slunk back here to pour drinks and listen to a little human screech for credits."

My anger at her disparaging comments about Isla far exceeded my feelings about her accusations against me, but I did not want to engage with Kona about Isla.

"I never asked you to do anything on my behalf," I said, my voice cold. "I would never have joined up with a mercenary squad, not even if the alternative was starvation. The fact you thought I would proves you did not know me and never will."

"Yes, how dare I think the male who'd shared my bunk readily enough when he wanted comfort and pleasure between battles would come with me to a better life." Her caustic laugh made my spines bristle. I had to force them to lie flat again. "I knew you were a beast, Mikas, but I didn't know you were such a hypocrite—or self-righteous bastard."

To be a mercenary raider was no better life—it was a life of cruelty, robbery, and often cold-blooded murder. I could not fool myself into believing everything we had done as soldiers had been honorable or just, but there was little similarity between our service in the Corps and what she had done as a mercenary. My stomach churned even contemplating what horrors she might have participated in during the past two years.

Damn Kona to all the hells for coming here, for dredging up memories I had tried so hard to bury. For reminding me of decisions I had regretted almost from the moment I made them, and for speaking vicious words that stung not because they were not true, but because they were.

For giving voice to my own fears that someone as wondrous as Isla Mair could never think me worthy of more than friendship.

"I have work to do," I said again. "If you have said your piece, the door is that way."

"I'm happy to use it." She gave me a careless facsimile of the Corps salute, her mouth twisted in a vicious grin. "May you have the life you deserve."

"You as well," I said.

After one last lingering glare at Isla, Kona disappeared into the crowd in the direction of the main doors that opened onto the street. I gripped the counter behind the bar so hard that it creaked and my knuckles turned pale.

Why had Kona come to Fortusia? To seek me out? If so, why? And why did her fury and hate burn so fiercely this many years later? We had made no claims on each other, and my refusal to become a mercenary should not have been enough to earn such venomous wrath.

Four drink orders awaited my attention on the screen in

front of me—one blinking red because it had been in the queue for a while. I raised my hand by way of apology and acknowledgement to the customer who had placed the order and hurried to make the drink. Staying busy would allow me to push Kona's words and my memories aside.

As I worked, Isla's sweet voice and the familiar rhythms of tending bar eased my anger and disquiet and allowed my spines to relax. I also kept one eye on my wristcomm, noting the time and counting down to the end of Isla's set, when she would come to the bar for her usual brandy and a chat.

Only an hour to go before I could drink in her scent and find my peace once again.

CHAPTER 5

ISLA

Damn near two hours of singing, and for all the audience's appreciation of my music selections, my tip jar remained only a third full. Tonight's crowd hadn't been quite as generous as I would like.

So I ended my set not with a rollicking Fortusian folk song like I'd planned, but with "Warm Waters," a melancholy ballad. The song had been written for a contralto voice, not a soprano, which was one reason I rarely sang it.

As I warbled my longing for the seas of home, nearly twice as much Alliance credit chips and local currency dropped into the jar as I'd earned all evening. Even the extremely intoxicated Prylothian lounging in the shallow pool on the right side of the bar waddled to the stage and spat some coins from his cheek pouch into the jar.

Behind the bar, Mikas finished pouring a drink, caught my eye, and raised an eyebrow. For the stoic Fortusian bartender, that little movement was the equivalent of a belly laugh.

Well, let him laugh. He owed me a hundred credits. He'd

wagered I'd never get the Prylothian to tip, no matter what I did, wore, or sang. For two standard years the Prylothian had been coming to this bar and never tipped Mikas once—not even when Mikas told him it was his job to clean the shallow pool where the very ungenerous amphibian sat to drink.

I could really use that hundred credits, but I'd probably tell Mikas to keep it. He deserved it after cleaning that pool for years. The bar's owner didn't pay him any extra for doing it. My own conscience was my worst enemy sometimes.

My worst enemy on this planet, that was.

"*Warm waters of home,*" I sang in Fortusian. My eyes brimmed with tears that were mostly but not all an act. I'd never had a home, not really, and that ache made that line especially hard to sing. "*I am so cold now, and I want to be there instead of here...all alone...*"

I held the last note of the song long past the final notes of the prerecorded instrumental accompaniment, the playback of which I controlled with a device in my hand. For maximum effect, I let my voice crack at the end before I closed my eyes and bowed my head.

Silence.

I rarely ended a set with a song like this because patrons didn't come to a bar to leave sadder than when they arrived. But as the applause and shouts of approval began, and more patrons came to the stage to show their appreciation in the form of tips, I decided I'd made the right move by choosing such an emotional song.

"Thank you," I told my audience in the local dialect of Fortusian, though the language was hard for me. The patrons appreciated the effort, if nothing else.

I bowed and made my way down from the stage, holding the long skirt of my gown with one hand so I didn't trip.

With my set done, I would have preferred to retreat to my little apartment, change clothes, and rest or read until Brae returned from gorging himself on insects during his nighttime feeding flight. Unfortunately, my contract stipulated I had to remain in the bar for at least an hour to interact with patrons. Thankfully, I could do so off my feet and with a drink in hand.

I weaved through the crowd to the bar, sidestepping a few wandering hands, claws, and tentacles on the way, and sat on a tall human-sized chair with a sigh.

As usual, Mikas slid a glass of Bacorian brandy across the bar top, along with a bowl of sweet jampa berries that perfectly complimented the smoky bite of the brandy.

"Lovely rendition of 'Warm Waters,' Isla," he rumbled. "The tears and trembling in your voice were particularly effective."

"It's an emotional song. So much longing." I took a sip of my brandy and sighed again, this time with contentment. "Thank you. I needed this."

He glanced over my shoulder at my tip jar, which seemed to be still collecting patrons' appreciation, judging by the *clinks* behind me. "Longing. Yes. You channeled your longing for credits well."

From someone else, I might have taken offense at that statement, but not from Mikas.

I hadn't told him much about my past, but he knew I'd arrived on Fortusia with only a handful of credits in my pocket. To him, it made sense that I'd chosen a song that elicited more tips. After all, he bartended shirtless nearly every night, and I'd seen his shirts disappear more than once when a group of admiring tourists came in. I didn't judge him for it. We were both working people in a resort city, just trying to get by.

I sipped my brandy, summoned a ghost of a smile, and picked out some jampa berries from the bowl. "We all long for something. I think that's why that song always resonates so well. Everyone thinks of who or what they yearn for most when they hear it."

I expected Mikas to scoff at the idea of yearning for

anything. I'd never met anyone *less* likely to yearn. He seemed made of stone, or nearly so.

Instead, when I looked up—up, up, *up,* since the man was so damn tall—he was watching me, his head tilted and vertically slit yellow eyes thoughtful rather than disdainful.

"Maybe they think if they drop a few credits in your jar, they might get their wish," he said, his tone neutral.

"Well, whatever their reason, it works for me." I toasted him with my glass. "And as long as it continues to work, I don't plan to tell them any differently."

"Your secret is safe with me," he promised. I laughed, and he smiled.

We passed several minutes in comfortable silence as Mikas mixed drinks and I sipped my brandy. Over the past few months, the rhythms of the bar and the methodical way he made each order had become as steady and soothing as a heartbeat or the gentle rocking of a hammock. I relaxed, crossed my legs, and watched Mikas work.

Just as I was about to ask him about the angry Atolani female who'd stared at me earlier, three raucous, green-skinned Raxians climbed onto chairs at the other end of the bar.

"Excuse me for a moment," Mikas said and left to deal with the newcomers.

They were already inebriated and thus even more obnoxious than the average Raxian. But when he snarled, they quieted, paid, and sullenly accepted their drinks. Mikas wouldn't get much of a tip after that growl, but he'd probably trade those few credits for less trouble. He might get extra tips from other patrons, especially the regulars. Nobody liked a rowdy Raxian.

Our place of employment was located on a side street just off a popular entertainment boulevard. *Zaa'ga* translated to Alliance Standard roughly as "Friends and Drinks," and its prime location made it popular with both offworld visitors who wanted to escape the noise and crowds and locals who appreciated a quieter and more intimate atmosphere.

Zaa'ga offered three main draws: an enormous variety of beverages from across the galaxy, a gorgeous bartender who doubled as security whenever the situation demanded it, and the novelty of a human singer. Out front, our larger-than-life holographic images beckoned those passing to come in and drink.

The only reason I allowed my image to be used was that I looked very different than before I arrived on Fortusia. My hair's color and length had changed drastically, from shoulder-length and brown to long and multicolored. My eyes were now violet—a popular color among humans living on Fyloria, where my appearance had been altered. I'd even gone so far as to undergo vocal modification to help ensure the most advanced scanners could not connect my current appearance or voice with how I looked before.

None of the Erotovo's agents had been spotted on Fortusia. My local contact had reported Novee's former owner had focused his search for Halena Onsulus on Havel Prime, Halena's alleged homeworld, and nearby worlds. That didn't mean I was safe, but with each week that passed, my back itched a little less.

As for my safety inside the bar, Mikas's mere presence tended to dissuade even the most inebriated patrons from causing trouble. With spines on his broad shoulders and upper back, a shock of thick black hair that ruffled when he was angry, shimmering blue-green scaly flesh, and fangs courtesy of his reptilian DNA, Mikas exuded "Behave yourself" at all times. And when he growled…well, trouble tended to run the other way.

In more ways than one, he was a good friend to have on a planet where I knew almost no one—and in a bar where some tourists chose to interpret my stage persona and attire as flirtation.

A heavy hand landed on the back of my chair, making me jump. The scent of smoke and leather swirled around me.

An enormous Hardanian male with metal-studded black and green skin, wearing animal pelts and armor from shoulders to thighs, grinned down at me, his sharp teeth on full display. His fingers grazed my upper back, not at all accidentally.

How dare he touch me. A wave of hot fury washed through me, followed by icy hate and the strong desire to punch him hard enough to knock that grin off his face.

"Beautiful song, lonely human," he said, his voice as rough as his hands. "You are lovely and your voice is pleasant."

"Thank you." I narrowed my eyes and leaned away from more unwanted touching.

Either he didn't notice my scowl and body language or he ignored them. "If you long for touches in warm waters," he said, nodding over his shoulder, "my brothers and I will gladly provide them."

Behind him, at a large table befitting their size, two other Hardanians raised their heavy tankards to me in a toast. I didn't recognize the sigil on their armor, but it signified they were scions of a noble family.

Hardanian males' biological imperative was to seek females to share among small groups, usually comprised of brothers or male cousins. I had nothing against the practice, but these potential suitors didn't interest me, even if all they wanted was a few pleasurable hours. My instincts told me these were not males to be trusted. I never ignored my instincts.

"I'm not lonely." I sipped my brandy, striving for polite disinterest. Hopefully he'd take the hint. "Those were just lyrics to a song. Please go back to your drinks."

His grin didn't waver. "We see no rings, no collar, no tattoos." He leaned closer and inhaled, his broad nostrils flaring as he treated me to a close-up view of the metal studs along his jaw before I moved away. "You do not bear the scent of a mate.

We are honorable, handsome males who find you appealing. Why do you pretend you do not want us?"

At the other end of the bar, Mikas was opening a bottle of expensive Bacorian mead for a pair of wealthy-looking traders. He wasn't looking in our direction, but the tension in his shoulders indicated he was listening.

"Who's pretending?" I put my drink down. "You just sniffed me—which was rude, by the way. Do I *smell* like I'm interested?"

The Hardanian's smile vanished. His orange eyes lit up, glowing like coals. *"Hr garagh,"* he spat, and stepped forward until my left breast pressed against his abdomen. This time, I didn't move back. Nobody was going to push me around—not at my own workplace.

His brothers rose, growling, their drinks forgotten. The bar fell silent—except for the Prylothian, who squatted in his pool gurgling into a pipe of Engareni wine, happily oblivious to the drama playing out nearby.

At my side, where the Hardanian couldn't see it, I flexed my right wrist. A dagger slipped silently into my hand from its sheath on my forearm. All my gowns, regardless of their designs, had long sleeves and thigh-high slits for a reason, and it had nothing to do with tips.

"Step back," I said, very clearly.

He bared his teeth in a snarl. "What will you do if I stay where I am, little human?"

At a glance, I noted the Hardanian's armor had six weak points. Those hides—trophies of hunts on other planets— provided no protection from my blade. He was big. I was faster. My dagger was sharp. With a touch in the right place on the hilt, its blade would drip untraceable poison. I had three other weapons on my person at this moment that could dispatch him just as quickly as my blade. No one touched me without my permission. Not anymore.

But I was posing as an ordinary human singer, and ordinary

humans didn't fight Hardanians and win. They certainly didn't kill an angry Hardanian male in a single blow. If I killed him, I'd reveal secrets about myself I needed to keep hidden.

Then I'd have to flee this city—possibly this world. And I didn't want to. I hadn't left my job as a Web operative behind by choice, and I'd come to Fortusia to hide from the Erotovo, but I liked my life here, humble as it was. By all the gods above and below, I was tired of running from one mission to the next. I wanted a *home*.

His flesh demanded to feel my blade, though, especially the hand that had touched my back as if he had the right to do so. My hand tightened on the hilt of my dagger.

"Human," the Hardanian said, his voice low and dangerous. "I said, what will you do?"

"She will need to do nothing," Mikas said from the Hardanian's side, his spines bristling.

In a heartbeat, my friend wrapped his massive arm around the Hardanian's neck, dragged him away from me, and squeezed until the man's eyes bulged. Mikas had him in a hold that nearly paralyzed his body. I feigned a frightened gasp and covered my mouth with my hand.

Now even the Prylothian set his wine pipe aside to watch Mikas, his cluster of bulbous eyes quivering nervously.

Over his shoulder, Mikas told the snarling brothers, "You move, your brother dies. And then you join him in Novomord, where your shame marks you for eternity."

The brothers exchanged a glance.

Like me, Mikas had recognized the symbol etched on their sigil. They were adherents of Novod, a sect of warriors who believed those who died at the hand of fewer numbers died in shame. Three warriors falling at the hand of one opponent? The disgrace would be eternal.

Apparently the Hardanians thought Mikas was perfectly capable of making good on his threat, because none of them moved—two by choice, and one because he could probably no longer feel his extremities. His eyes had glazed over. He'd be unconscious soon. I had to fight to keep pretending to be scared and not let on how pleased I was to see the bastard's knees start to buckle.

This wasn't the first time I'd witnessed Mikas shed his gruff but laid-back bartender persona in favor of the hard former soldier I glimpsed in his eyes in unguarded moments, especially when he interacted with our vile crime lord boss. As impressive as he was in his role of part-time bouncer, I'd long suspected there was a third, more true Mikas in there somewhere—not the bartender, not the soldier, but the man he really was underneath the roles he played. Maybe it took someone who'd spent a lifetime playing a series of roles herself to recognize those secret depths.

"You will all leave now," Mikas added, his tone now conversational. "And not return."

He didn't need to sound threatening with his bicep crushing the Hardanian's airway or in the wake of his reminder to all three brothers that an abrupt exit from this plane of existence to an afterlife spent in darkness and shame wasn't how they wanted to end their visit to Fortusia.

"Are we agreed?" he prompted, with a little extra squeeze that elicited an audible *pop* from something in his captive's neck.

"We are agreed," one of the other brothers said, with a deferential bow of his head.

Damn it to all the hells, this was not how I'd planned for my night to go.

All I'd wanted to do was have my usual brandy and friendly chat with Mikas and watch the patrons drink and socialize. I was an observer both by nature and profession. So was Mikas. Even when he appeared focused on pouring a drink or mixing a complex cocktail, he was alert and watchful —more so than strictly necessary, especially in a bar where trouble was rare. Hypervigilance was common among former soldiers.

The Fortusian word *amat'ganor*, or *watcher of people*, applied both to Mikas and myself. Unsurprising, then, that we'd both ended up working in a bar, where the people-watching was often quite excellent.

At the moment, *we* were the people being observed, and not in the way I preferred. This was the wrong kind of attention.

"Go on, then," Mikas said, jerking his head in the direction of the main doors. "I will follow you out to ensure no harm befalls you on the journey."

Wordlessly, the brothers drained their tankards, slammed them on the table, and shouldered their way through the crowd. I turned in my chair to watch them leave.

Before he followed, Mikas glanced at me, clearly concerned for my well-being. I gave him a shaky smile to keep up the charade that the Hardanian had scared me. The only thing hurt was my pride, since I hadn't dealt with him myself.

Mikas's gaze dropped momentarily to my hidden right hand, then returned to my face. His expression remained as unreadable as ever, but the shape of his eyes had changed. Shit—had he seen my blade?

Then he wheeled around and half-carried, half-dragged the Hardanian toward the door. The crowd parted for him, and not just because his spines had flared. Mikas had the respect of everyone in here, especially the locals.

In his wake, the quiet became a murmur, and then the crowd's volume resumed its previous levels. Laughter, shouts, squawks, and conversation in a dozen languages filled the space. The Prylothian belched, mumbled an apology, and resumed gurgling his wine.

I slid my dagger back into its sheath and let out a breath.

The sooner I started to act as if nothing had happened, the sooner everyone would forget the incident. I smoothed my dress, sipped my drink, and chased it down with a couple of ripe, juicy jampa berries.

I expected Mikas to return as soon as he'd had time to make sure the Hardanians left, and I planned to ask about the Atolani female when he got back. Instead, I looked up from my drink to see that Nubo had emerged from his office to confront Mikas about something. Whatever they were discussing, it wasn't a pleasant conversation. Mikas's tense shoulders and frown radiated anger and frustration.

Nubo pointed to the hallway that led to his office, apparently asking—or telling—Mikas to go that way. Mikas gestured at the bar. Nubo's reply was terse. Maybe he was reminding Mikas the bar could be switched to auto mode.

Without a word, Mikas stepped behind the bar, switched it from *Staffed* to *Auto*, and stalked to Nubo's office as several patrons expressed their displeasure at the change.

Why the sudden meeting? Was Mikas in trouble because of how he'd handled the Hardanians who'd harassed me? Uneasiness churned in my stomach.

And with that, I called an abrupt end to my shift. If Nubo had a problem with that, he could yell at me later.

I finished my drink and the last of the jampas, slid off my chair, and returned to the stage. I dumped the contents of my tip jar into my bag, wished the regulars a pleasant evening, then threaded my way through the crowd in the direction of the back hallway.

CHAPTER 6

MIKAS

"Stay away from the singer," Nubo grated, his enormous blue fist striking the top of his desk hard enough for me to feel the vibration through the floor and my boots. "I have told you this before. I will not tell you again."

In my imagination, I crumpled this pompous thug into a lump of broken bones and flesh and tossed him into the closest refuse chute. It was not the first time I had fantasized about doing so.

"The Hardanian touched her. Twice," I said instead, without inflection in my voice. "After she had told him to go away. Did you not expressly state that no one may lay a hand on her?"

"This is not about the Hardanian." Nubo sat in his throne-like chair, his webbed fingers gripping the armrests. "Despite my warnings, you still want Isla Mair for yourself. I see it in your eyes when you look at her."

"I only want to do my job and keep her safe from unruly patrons." I folded my hands behind my back so I was less tempted to wrap them around Nubo's throat. "Isla is pretty by human standards, but I am Fortusian. I am not interested in delicate human women. She is my friend and my colleague only. I simply had to make an example of the Hardanian so everyone in the bar knows you do not permit such behavior."

Nubo studied me. "Go on."

"Zaa'ga is known for the quality of its service, drinks, and environment," I continued, since flattery always worked better on Nubo than simple denial. "If customers want to act badly, they can go elsewhere. I am thinking only of your reputation and of your singer's safety. If Isla does not feel safe here, she may not stay. Human women are notoriously weak and fearful."

Isla was nothing of the sort, of course, but my life *and* hers depended on keeping Nubo convinced I thought of her only as a vulnerable friend and coworker who needed saving from drunken patrons. I would say or do whatever was necessary to protect her.

Nubo tapped his fingers on his chair. "This is true," he mused. "Security is an important matter for her. On the day she applied for the position, she asked for your candid opinion on whether she would be safe working here and living in an apartment in this building."

"Yes, she did, sir." The honorific tasted bitter on my tongue. "That is why I acted so swiftly tonight."

"Very well." Nubo sat back in his chair. "If I see further evidence of any feelings for Isla, you will not only be out of a job—you will be running for an off-world transport with my wingwolves on your heels. Am I clear?"

Kill him, my instincts urged. My belly roiled as if it were full of angry insects. *Kill him. He means her harm.*

Nubo wanted Isla for his own, but according to my sources, her murky past had forced him to bide his time. He could not make a move on her until he knew who she was—who she *really* was.

A man in his position had to be cautious. She might have come here under false pretenses. She might have been sent by an enemy. He wanted to confirm her story that she was an orphaned human with no family and no connections, simply looking for work. And if that was the case, he would take her away, make her his captive, force her to be his. He had done it before with others.

To my trained eyes, lovely Isla was clearly *not* who she pretended to be. Her watchfulness, the way she evaluated everyone who came into the bar like a soldier sizing up an adversary, how she never panicked when someone like the Hardanian confronted her, her faithful shadowbat companion… it all added up to an unavoidable conclusion: Isla was far from weak or fearful.

That fact offered me very little solace. If Nubo came to the same realization, he would kill her. Well, he would *have* her killed. Men like Nubo Wex did not live so freely or for so long by getting their own hands dirty.

By all the gods, this scum would never lay a hand on Isla. Not as long as I had breath in my body. But I could not allow him to so much as glimpse the truth of what I kept hidden in my hearts.

"You are most clear," I said, with another deferential nod. "And understood."

"Good." Nubo switched on his wall vidscreen, which showed a dozen live views of the bar's interior. "The bar can run on auto for the remainder of the night," he added, his thick lips twisting into a smirk. "I think you need to take some time to think about your situation."

In other words, as punishment for his suspicions about my feelings for Isla, no more wages or tips tonight.

Five more hours of work, surrounded by increasingly inebriated tourists wandering in from the boulevard, would have meant hundreds of credits in tips I would have put toward my future escape with my mate.

"Good night, then," I said, an edge of anger in my tone. I did not try to suppress it. Nubo would expect a reaction after cutting my work hours short. His smug smile reignited my desire to crush him with my bare hands. At least if he was smug about punishing me, he was less suspicious.

He would also be self-satisfied about making me angry. I did not anger easily—at least, not outwardly. On the outside, I was as hard and immovable as Vorcian marble.

Inside, I was volcanic. I was a raging thunderstorm. In my soul, I roared like a beast in the night.

I turned on my heel and left Nubo's office with his chuckle following me out. Rage made my hands shake and ears ring.

But the moment I stepped into the hallway and the office door closed and locked behind me, everything changed.

Isla's scent was everywhere, swirling around me, filling my lungs until her sweet smell turned my soul peaceful once more. My beastly hearts quieted, and my fury and hate dissipated like a puff of smoke in a strong wind.

My nose told me Isla had come this way only minutes ago on her way to the lift and stairway that accessed the residential levels above the bar. A scent this strong meant she had paused outside the door.

She could not have overheard our conversation—no sounds from inside the office reached the hallway. And yet she had lingered before going on. Why?

She had seen Nubo order me to come to his office. I had sensed her gaze on me as clearly as I felt the ache in my right leg from standing for so long behind the bar. Had she wondered about the confrontation? Been concerned about its cause? Had she worried about my welfare? The thought warmed my hearts.

Gods, I hated Nubo, but I hated myself more because I had

not found a way to close the distance between myself and my lovely mate.

For nearly three months I had been Isla's friend, as much as I could with Nubo watching our every move. For three months, she had sat across the bar from me, conversing or lost in thought, and I could not touch her or even speak with too much friendliness without endangering us both.

Danger to myself, I welcomed. But danger to the one whose every breath filled me with joy and reason for being, for whom I yearned with every beat of my hearts, I could not bear.

Tonight, I could have torn the Hardanian limb from limb for touching her without her permission. He was lucky to have staggered away down the street supported by his brothers, muttering curses and coughing. *Doubly* lucky, considering the dagger Isla had concealed as the Hardanian loomed over her. That dagger stayed on her right forearm at all times, in a sheath, ready to drop into her hand in the blink of an eye. She took great pains to keep it hidden, but I had noticed its outline.

No, Isla was not at all who she appeared to be. She was infinitely, wonderfully more.

I shook myself out of my reverie and considered what I might do with my time off.

I could stay in my apartment upstairs, alone with my thoughts. I could go out, try to distract myself with liquors or entertainment, which in the resort city of Onat'ras were available all hours of the day and night. But even as I considered that option, I knew it would do no good. My mind would be filled with dreams and visions of Isla wherever I went. At least if I were here, close by, it eased the churning in my gut.

Decision made, I headed down the hall away from the bar and toward the stairs, following the faint traces of Isla's passage. Her scent had an angry note, a kind of sharpness that made my spines bristle and nose twitch. She was supposed to stay in the bar and chat with patrons for at least another half hour, but she had left not long after Nubo called me into the meeting. Something had caused her to ignore her contractual obligations. Illness? Overwhelming emotions?

Thankfully, I did not smell sickness or tears. I could not bear the thought of her weeping. Perhaps she was angry about the Hardanians' rudeness and decided she did not want to remain in the bar in the aftermath of their inexcusable behavior.

Under the watchful eyes of Nubo's extensive surveillance system, I stalked to the stairs, scanned my palm to gain access to the residential floors, climbed to the fourth level, and continued down the stark white corridor, past Isla's apartment to my own near the end of the hall. These apartments were small, but the area was well-kept and relatively safe. I had been if not happy, at least comfortable here, pouring drinks and killing time, until Isla arrived.

Now I spent my days veering wildly from aching need when she was not near to longing mixed with contentment when she was.

I paused outside my apartment door, my hand halfway to the scanner.

We all long for something, Isla had said tonight, her lips turned up in a faint smile that looked sad and maybe a little bitter.

Gods, if she only knew.

I pressed my palm to the scanner, waited for the door to slide open, and started to go inside.

"Mikas?"

For a moment, I thought I had imagined her voice. But when I turned, Isla stood in the corridor outside her apartment, and she was smiling at me. My breath hitched.

She was so lovely—like a nebula, or a sun. She had changed from her gown into a short dress with long sleeves and left her rainbow-colored hair loose down her back. An empty cross-body shopping bag hinted at her plans.

Mindful of the eyes and ears of Nubo's surveillance system, I drew myself up, folded my hands behind my back, and gave her a nod. "Isla." Her name felt like music on my tongue. I cleared my throat and forced myself to sound merely polite when I added, "I did not have a chance to confirm that you are unharmed."

"Thanks to you, I'm fine." Her smile turned rueful, and she fidgeted. "Thank you for intervening. I didn't know *what* to do when he didn't back off. Hardanians are scary."

Anyone watching or listening to her now would think the incident had shaken her deeply. But I had looked into her eyes in the moment, and if she had been truly scared of the Hardanian or his companions, I would eat my boots and wash them down with rotgut Raxian liquor.

She was, among other things, a consummate actress. I would wager her life depended on her ability to fool those around her.

"They are," I said, very seriously. "Especially to human women. Thankfully, our employer has strict rules about patron behavior and no tolerance for anyone who assaults an employee."

Her eyes narrowed ever so slightly when I referenced our employer, but she managed a shaky smile for the benefit of the surveillance. "Yes, I'm very thankful to Nubo for providing a safe work environment for us. And speaking of safety…" She gestured at her shopping bag. "Can I beg a favor? I need to go shopping at the market, and I feel vulnerable right now after my narrow escape. If you could come with me, I would be really grateful. It won't take long. Maybe you need to buy a few things too?"

I would have felt less precarious walking across a minefield. In fact, I saw little appreciable difference between that and Isla's request.

"Please," she said, and now her lower lip trembled. She wiped her eyes with the back of her hand. "I really need a friend. Or even a kind colleague."

I did not see or smell actual tears, but my resolve crumbled to dust at the mere thought of my mate weeping.

Gods above, I was utterly lost.

Acting as a kind colleague and bodyguard during a shopping trip with Isla was not precisely the opposite of what Nubo had ordered me to do, but damned close. Isla had asked me to go with her, though, and if he overheard the conversation, surely I could not be faulted for giving in. She had *pleaded* with me. If I refused, been unkind, that might be more suspicious than agreeing.

And more importantly, why did Isla want me to go with her to the market? If it was not because she was truly shaken, what might her motive be? I did not know, but I must find out.

"I do need a few items." I glanced down at my bare chest. "Give me a few minutes to change."

My attire—or lack thereof—was perfect for tending bar, and probably would not raise any eyebrows at the local market, but I did not want to attract attention I would be forced to rebuff. My hearts, body, and soul belonged to Isla alone.

"Oh, thank you so much, Mikas." Her smile returned. "You're so kind. Take your time. I'll wait in my apartment."

I gave her a brusque nod. "All right."

Once she returned to relative safety, I entered my own living quarters. With the door shut and locked against prying eyes and ears, I leaned against the wall and took a deep breath.

Safely away from the bar, perhaps I could...*hint* at how I felt. See if she might find my attentions agreeable. The prospect made my hearts race.

Right behind my rush of anticipation came trepidation. She thought of me as a friend. I *was* her friend. If she did not want more than that, I risked losing our friendship.

For months, I had stood on this precipice, teetering on its edge, buffeted on every side by desires, dangers, and unease.

Beyond lay the joy of life with my true mate, or a plunge into nothingness.

I took a deep breath, exhaled, and snarled at myself.

I had served as a soldier. Fought on battlefields on distant worlds and risked my life—and nearly died—for causes far less precious to me than Isla. If I could do that, I could do this. I could take this step.

First, though, I had to change my pants and put on a shirt.

CHAPTER 7

Our trip to the market was the first time Mikas and I had socialized outside working hours.

I didn't really need a bodyguard for this outing. This sector of the city was relatively safe and very busy. Floating globes provided soft light, drawing nighttime insects and ensuring no dark corners where danger could lurk. But I had some questions for Mikas—questions that required us to leave our building, where Nubo's surveillance meant everything we said or did was seen or overheard. And I wanted to get to know him better, maybe even find out who he really was when he wasn't being a bartender or bouncer.

Who *was* Mikas Auren? Even after three months and a hundred conversations, I couldn't really say I knew, and that bothered me. A lot.

Despite his height and the length of his legs, Mikas kept his pace even with mine so I didn't have to scurry to keep up. In fact, whenever I paused to marvel at something, he stopped too. And I marveled at *everything*.

Most cities on Fortusia, including this one, embraced eco-architecture, blending artificial construction with trees, grasses, gardens, and even rivers and waterfalls. Onat'ras had as many beautiful natural spaces as buildings, streets, and walkways. While large cities I'd visited on other planets were urbanized to the point of being nearly devoid of any wildlife or plants, here animals roamed the parks and soared overhead. The air smelled fresh rather than full of urban odors that burned my eyes or made me sneeze. If I had to live in hiding, Fortusia was at least a wondrous place to be.

At night, countless species of insects sang, buzzed, and glowed, dancing in the breeze among pedestrians and vehicles. Brae ate so well here that he'd gotten plump. We'd had too many dangerous and lean years for me not to enjoy the *thump* he made when he landed on furniture in my apartment, or the way his butt wiggled when he got ready to fly.

Tonight, my walk with Mikas from our building took us past one of my favorite locations: a waterfall that cascaded from a nearby tower and plunged twenty meters into a small lake.

With Mikas trailing behind, I left the busy walkway and crossed the damp, fragrant grass to the low stone border along the lake's edge. The wind shifted, bringing with it the scents of flowers and foliage and the cool mist from the waterfall. I closed my eyes, tilted my head back to feel the moisture on my face, and inhaled the sweet, familiar smell of Fortusia's pink-tinged fresh water. Heavenly.

In moments like this, I could almost forget why I'd come here in the first place and what I'd had to give up after my mission on Ngara blew up in my face.

The first month after I'd left my job as a Web operative, and even after I arrived on Fortusia, I'd struggled mightily to adjust to not being an operative anymore. Guilt and restlessness and nightmares about Ergin's terrible death led to miserable days and sleepless nights.

But with each passing day—with every singing shift I worked and every evening I spent talking with Mikas over brandy and berries—my unhappiness, regret, and guilt faded to a dull ache that eventually gave way to a new yearning.

Now more than anything I wanted a home. Peace and quiet. Stability, safety, and happiness. To sing five nights a week, wear lovely dresses, earn good money, and watch Brae get fat on insects. All the things life as a Web operative would never allow. When I pictured Brae and I with our own home, I could convince myself I'd done enough for the Web and making a new life was possible.

The waterfall's sweet vapor cooled my face and the wind smelled of flowers. All my memories of cages and plasma rifle wounds seemed light-years and a lifetime away. I licked my lips to taste the cool mist.

Mikas made an odd sound. Had he just taken a shaky breath?

I opened my eyes and found him beside me at the wall, hands at his sides, facing the walkway behind us. Watchful, stoic, and as far as I could tell not at all interested in the lake or waterfall or any other wonder of the cityscape.

Yes, this was his homeworld, so maybe nothing about Onat'ras seemed remarkable to him. Or maybe he was taking his job of bodyguard far more seriously than I'd intended. If I'd known he would treat our walk as a deadly serious mission, I might have come up with another excuse to get him to come with me to the market.

I should try to draw him into conversation. I hadn't intended for this outing to be a chore for him.

"Isn't it beautiful?" I pointed out a massive tree with purple foliage growing in a grassy park across the lake. "What kind is it? Do you know?"

He glanced over his shoulder. "It is called oth'canto," he said very matter-of-factly. His tone softened when he added, "They live to be thousands of years old. They are the longest-lived organisms on this world."

His voice was so deep and soothing. I wished I could get him to talk more, and more often.

I spotted a familiar grim-faced human woman on the walkway, pretending to study the city's colorful skyline over our heads. I clenched my fists in irritation. Damn it. As usual, Nubo had sent someone to follow us—or to follow *me*, anyway. I doubted he'd have any reason to keep an eye on Mikas.

This was an ongoing argument, one I had yet to win. Whenever I asked Nubo not to have someone follow me whenever I left the building where I lived and worked, he reminded me I'd expressed concern about my safety when I first applied for my singing job. He claimed he was concerned for my welfare, but we both knew this wasn't really about my safety, or not entirely about my safety. He was controlling and possessive. He wanted to know where I was, and what I was doing, and who I was with. I hated being watched.

Once I had enough money saved up, I *could* relocate, but I dreaded uprooting myself yet again and searching for another job. I'd auditioned for nearly a dozen gigs before Nubo hired me, and I made good money at Zaa'ga. That plus my friendship with Mikas were the primary reasons I gritted my teeth and put up with Nubo's surveillance.

I'd given my watchers nicknames so I could tell Brae who followed me each time. This was Scar, so-called because of the jagged mark that ran along her entire jawline on the right side of her face.

I wanted to ask Mikas about the Atolani female, or even just ask what was on his mind that had made him grumpier than usual tonight. But if Scar had eavesdropping tech, we might be overheard. So instead I admired the oth'canto tree and then we resumed our walk.

Mikas had swapped his work attire for very nondescript—

and even unflattering—gray pants and a plain black shirt with openings designed to accommodate his spines. Even so, his height, physique, and looks attracted admiring looks from a variety of species, sexes, and genders as we made our way from our building four streets over to my favorite market. He must have noticed all the attention, but he ignored it. But why? In my experience, men this good-looking, who clearly spent time and energy eating well, staying healthy, and maintaining their body, enjoyed being noticed.

Then again, Mikas wasn't typical in a lot of ways.

"What is on your shopping list tonight?" he asked as the market's enormous sign came into sight.

"Food, for one thing," I said, waving in the direction of the market. "I'm bored with what I have in my apartment. I want to find something unusual that's still within my ability to cook. I'd also like to buy some perfume at that little shop on the far end of the market—the one with purple lights and little trees out front."

Mikas's brow furrowed. "Perfume?"

Maybe I didn't seem like the type to like perfume. "I rarely wear perfume," I admitted. "But I've always dreamed of having real Engareni perfume."

He opened his mouth to say something, then seemed to catch himself. "I am intrigued," he said instead. "So, do you enjoy cooking?"

"I do, now that I have an apartment with a kitchen." I smiled. "I don't just live on brandy and jampa berries, you know."

"I suspected as much." He gave me a fleeting smile before returning his attention to our surroundings.

As long as I'd known him, Mikas had been about as chatty as a Bacorian monk. During our first conversation, in fact, he'd spoken only three words. And though he was always polite and thoughtful, he rarely smiled and never laughed.

On my first night working at the bar, he'd asked me about

myself and listened attentively to my cover story of being an orphan without family who'd drifted around the galaxy until I ended up on Fortusia. And every evening since, he'd hung on my every word, regardless of the topic I chose for our chats after I finished my sets.

Mikas had volunteered some information about his past too when I asked. He'd served as a conscripted soldier and received an honorable discharge after a serious injury in battle. Why exactly he'd chosen bartending for a civilian career, I didn't know. And why he would work for a thug like Nubo Wex, of all people, was an even greater mystery. I certainly couldn't ask him about it at the bar with our boss listening in.

My gut told me Mikas wasn't as grim and humorless as he seemed. The omnipresent shadows in his eyes and a heaviness about him made it clear something weighed on him. I had yet to find a way to get him to tell me why he was so despondent. I'd give a lot to see my friend happy.

"What about you?" I asked, still hoping to draw him into a conversation despite Scar's presence. "What are you looking for at the market? Or are you not going to buy anything?"

Mikas showed me a shopping bag he'd brought folded up in his pocket. "Like you, I am here for food. And I welcome the change of scenery."

"Oh, yes—me too. I like peace and quiet, but I spend too much time in our building, just going back and forth between the bar and my apartment." I smiled up at him again. "Thank you again for coming with me. I know it's an imposition. You probably had something else planned tonight."

"It is not an imposition," he said, but without returning my smile. "And I had no other plans."

That wasn't quite true. According to the schedule, he was supposed to work tonight until 0300 hours. He had yet to mention that or explain why he wasn't behind the bar. My guess was Nubo had been angry about something Mikas had done and given him the rest of the night off as punishment. But if Mikas didn't want to talk about it, I wouldn't push the issue.

And speaking of Nubo…

I feigned a stumble. "Ouch," I yelped, and fell against Mikas's side as if I'd turned my ankle or tripped.

Reflexively, he caught me and set me back on my feet, his massive hands wrapped around my forearms with surprising gentleness even though I'd startled him. The strength and heat of his grip was instantly reassuring.

"Are you all right?" He scanned the ground, plainly wondering what had caused me to lose my footing.

"I'm fine," I said, with an embarrassed laugh and a glance around, as if to confirm my mishap hadn't been noticed. "I'm just clumsy."

His grip tightened ever so slightly, and then he let me go. "An uneven walkway," he said, his gaze searching my face. "We must watch our step."

"Definitely." Wincing, I steadied myself on his arm and rubbed my lower leg. "Mind if I take your arm for a minute? I twisted my ankle."

"Of course," he said automatically, but the crease remained between his thick eyebrows.

Could he tell I'd faked that stumble so I could hang onto his arm and talk more quietly to make listening in more difficult for Scar? I suspected so—just as he'd probably seen me palm that dagger in the bar.

He studied me for a beat, his vertically slit yellow eyes scanning my face as if trying to read something there that might reveal my motives for this trip to the market, and maybe hoping for something more, like the truth about why I'd come to Fortusia. I'd had the sense for a while that he didn't buy my cover story—at least, not all of it.

He'd been a soldier. He probably recognized training when he saw it, and was better than most at seeing through my helpless human female act. He had to be wondering why a singer who liked pretty dresses not only carried weapons but knew how to use them.

I opened my mouth to bring up the dagger...then thought better of it. I couldn't be sure we wouldn't be overheard even if I whispered and we were in a crowd.

My heart ached when I opted to stay silent. But why? What was it about Mikas that compelled me to trust him when I'd rarely trusted another soul?

We made our way slowly through the market's arched gateway and onto the promenade. Even this late at night, it was busy.

"Sorry about this," I said, hanging onto Mikas's forearm. "I'm sure my ankle will stop hurting soon."

"I am sure it will," he said, and that time his tone sounded almost...amused. But when I looked up, his expression was as inscrutable as always.

Since his size encouraged others to move aside, I let him guide me through the crowded market. Tourists and locals alike shopped here for everything from food and drink to pets, medical supplies, employment opportunities, clothing, and more, including fortune tellers and recruiters for private militaries. Even after a dozen visits to the market, it remained a sensory overload of competing voices, odors, sights, and loud noises.

A merchant selling imitation Fylorian tapestries argued loudly with a customer over price as we passed their shop. In the next stall, a Bacorian monk-gastronomist was cooking vegetables on an open-air grill and chanting blessings on the food. My stomach growled. Hopefully Mikas couldn't hear that over the din.

In addition to the lure of the market's many shops, street performers had set up throughout the main promenade and the web of walkways that led to smaller courtyards with fountains and gardens. The performers sang, danced, performed acrobatics, and in one case even demonstrated precision tricks with blades, enticing shoppers to drop credits or coins in their collection bins.

One female singer in particular drew my attention. I didn't recognize her species, but she was tiny and almost birdlike, perched on a tall chair near the perfume shop, singing in a high, clear voice that made me misty-eyed with its crystalline beauty. The crowd around her appeared enthralled—so much so that several listeners held credit sticks or coins in their hands but seemed rooted in place instead of coming forward to drop their tips in the little box in front of the singer's chair.

Mikas startled me when he covered my hand on his arm with his own. I couldn't recall a single time he'd touched my hand before this.

He bent so his mouth was near my ear. "Isla, do you weep?" he murmured, his voice rough.

I blinked away my tears. "Her voice is perfect," I whispered. "Gods, I've never heard anything like it."

"She is one of the Sirrah," he said very softly. "They are prized for their voices."

I went cold. *"Prized?"*

Mikas nodded, his expression solemn.

Prized meant *wanted, target for kidnapping, desirable for ownership. Prized* meant misery and suffering. I hated that word with every fiber of my being.

I bit my lip and turned my head away, hoping to hide my reaction, but it was too late. More tears spilled over—this time, in anger. The Sirrah's singing had made me uncharacteristically vulnerable, and then Mikas had unwittingly made the situation worse.

He rubbed my fingers. "This one is free, though," he said, his tone gentle. "You see, she wears no collar or cuff."

No, she didn't have any signs of being someone's property,

but nausea surged at the thought of this beautiful little singer in a cage. I clenched my jaw. A little sound escaped that sounded perilously close to a whimper. Mikas's expression darkened.

Hoping to distract myself, I reached into my bag and took out a handful of local coins. To my surprise, my companion scooped them from my hand, combined them with some of his own from his pocket—a *lot* of his own, in fact—and left my side just long enough to drop them into the singer's box. Without missing a note, the birdlike woman dipped her head in thanks.

Mikas's gift broke the dam. A flood of others came forward, jostling their way through the crowd in their enthusiasm to contribute. Hands clasped, the Sirrah sang an almost effervescent aria in gratitude.

With surprising gentleness, Mikas put my hand back on his forearm and guided me away from the crowd, across the promenade, and into the perfume shop.

CHAPTER 8

ISLA

The shop's doors were wide open to welcome customers. The Sirrah's voice followed us inside and blended with the soft music playing in the showroom.

To my relief, we were the only shoppers, so we had some privacy while I tried to rein in my runaway emotions. I didn't mind so much if Mikas saw my anger and tears, but I didn't want Scar to wonder why seeing and hearing the Sirrah had upset me so much.

Mikas bent his head again, squeezed my hand between his arm and the hard muscles of his torso, and murmured, "You forgot to limp, Isla."

Oh, damn it to all the hells—I'd been so captivated by the singer, and then so angry and upset, that I *did* forget. Only four months after starting my involuntary leave of absence from the Web, I was already getting rusty on basic ruses.

His gaze searched my face. "I did not mean to upset you. I am sorry."

"I'm fine," I said, and forced a smile.

He didn't believe me; that much was clear from the furrow between his dark brows. When he started to speak, I raised my free hand.

"She's right outside," I murmured, with my back to the shop's doors like his so our lips couldn't be read and even eavesdropping tech would struggle to catch our voices. "Our shadow. You saw her, didn't you?"

"Yes." His expression hardened. "I was not sure you had noted her presence until you feigned that stumble so we could speak quietly."

I liked very much that he'd seen what I'd seen and understood why I'd wanted to hang onto his arm. And even after only knowing him a few months, I felt so comfortable and safe around him—even more so now away from the bar, despite Scar's presence.

That wonderful sense of safety was one of the reasons I'd brought him with me to the perfume shop...which like me was more than what it seemed.

With a real smile this time, I gestured widely at our surroundings. "Have you ever been in an authentic Engareni perfume shop?"

"I have not." He scanned the seemingly endless shelves of bottles, jars, and flowering plants gathered from a hundred planets. "It is certainly wondrous, although the scents are quite strong for those of us with keen senses."

I winced. "Oh, I'm sorry. I didn't think about that."

He smiled slightly. "There is no need to apologize."

We turned at the sound of footsteps. A beaming, feathered Engareni woman emerged from the back, her hands outstretched.

"Hello, hello!" she crowed, her voice tinged with a squawk. "So lovely to have such beautiful customers come into my shop."

"Thank you." I inclined my head in a traditional Engareni greeting. "I'm Isla Mair."

"I am Madame Ycari," she said, returning my nod. "Purveyor of the finest perfumes on all of Fortusia." Feathers ruffling, she craned her neck to look up at Mikas. "My, you are a big one. A beastly beauty of a male."

Mikas blinked twice. This was certainly the first time since I'd met him that I'd seen him at a loss. I bit my lip to stifle a chuckle.

"I am Mikas Auren," he rumbled, with a nod.

"Mikas and Isla. Yes, yes." Ycari trilled. "What a lovely couple you are."

Mikas's expression remained neutral, but his spines bristled. Did her assumption that we were a couple upset him? But why would it?

"Oh, we're not a couple," I said quickly. "Mikas is my good friend. And we work together."

"Hmm." Ycari made a strange clicking sound with her tongue and teeth and eyed us, as if unconvinced. "Not a couple, not a couple. Hmm."

"Thank you for coming out to meet us," I said to distract both of them. "I'm here to sample some scents. I've heard good things about the Centenian gregarus."

She clapped her hands. "Oh, very good, very good. Yes, that is a personal favorite." She looked up at Mikas again and chuckled. "Big, beastly man, I will have to put you two in our largest sampling room."

Ycari turned and half-flew, half-walked back in the direction of the rear of the shop. "Come, come," she called over her feathered shoulder. "Come, come."

I affected a limp once more and leaned heavily on Mikas's arm as we followed.

"What is happening?" he asked in an undertone.

"Madame Ycari is a master perfumer," I explained. "You don't simply buy a pre-blended perfume from her. She gathers the ingredients and creates the perfume to match each customer's body chemistry. You leave with a bottle of scent that is unique to you alone, and smells precisely how you want to smell."

"Yes," he said patiently, still keeping his voice low. "I understand how the establishment works. But what is *happening?*"

Ah. I'd wondered if—or when—he'd catch on.

"Bear with me a little longer," I said with a smile, and limped a little extra for Scar's benefit.

When we reached the back hallway, Ycari shooed us into the third suite on the left. This sampling room contained several very plush sofas, a counter with chairs on both sides, and very little else. The air and furniture were completely sterile and odor-free.

"I will join you soon," Ycari said, dipping her head to me and sliding a glance at Mikas for some reason. "Perhaps...one hour?"

"Perfect," I said with a smile.

Ycari squawked and closed the door to the hallway, leaving us alone.

I let go of Mikas's arm, took a deep breath, and exhaled slowly to release my tension. No place could be called *safe*, but this room was the closest to it I had found on this planet, or any other I'd been on recently.

"Isla."

I looked up. Mikas was studying me, his brow furrowed in concern rather than anger. "You believe we can speak freely in this room?" he asked.

"Yes." I settled on the enormous sofa, took off my cross-body bag, and set it on the cushion beside me. All the furnishings were clearly designed for Fortusian customers, making me feel like a child using adult-sized furniture. "How could you tell? My body language?"

"That, and your scent." He hesitated, then sat in a chair to my right, his back very straight—and not because he worried his spines might poke the chair cushion. He still seemed very uneasy. "Forgive me for noticing it."

"There's nothing to forgive." I smiled, hoping to get him to relax a little. "I understand your senses are keener and more finely tuned than mine. It doesn't bother me. I do try not to dwell on the fact that as a human living among Fortusians, I have a fraction of your abilities. If I did, I'd develop quite an inferiority complex."

"Nothing about you is inferior," he said automatically. "Your voice, least of all."

My face warmed at the very unexpected compliment. Hopefully he didn't think I'd been fishing for one.

"Well, thank you," I said. "So, you're probably wondering why I think we're relatively safe in this room."

"I am." He leaned forward, his forearms on his thighs and gaze searching my face. "And why we are here. It is not to sample perfumes—or not *just* to sample perfumes."

How much should I divulge? The question had gnawed at me for at least the past month or so. My instincts told me Mikas was a good man and I could trust him at least to some extent. What those limits were, I wasn't quite sure yet, so I couldn't risk anyone else's safety by revealing too much.

Maybe I could confide in him a little and give him a chance to earn more trust by inviting him to confide in me in return. My stomach churned, but I took a deep breath and took the plunge.

"If you can tell when I feel protected, or at least less on edge, then you know I'm often worried about my safety," I said. "Without getting into any details, I'm in hiding. I came to Fortusia for a fresh start. Which you probably already guessed."

"I did guess that." Mikas's tone was gentler now than I'd ever heard him be, but his brow remained furrowed. "And this shop and its owner?"

"A designated safe harbor, vouched for by people I trust completely." I managed a small smile. "That's as much as I can tell you other than this room is swept for listening devices almost hourly and nothing we say in here can be heard beyond these walls. It takes about an hour to select a perfume blend, so that's about how much time we'll have before our watcher becomes suspicious about what we're doing. You have no reason to trust me, I suppose, but it's the truth."

"I believe you." His frown faded. "But why did you trust me enough to reveal this?"

"Instincts," I admitted. "Gut feeling. You've always been so kind to me, but more than that, I just feel…safe with you. And that's not a feeling I get very often."

Mikas smiled then—a real smile, the first I'd seen on his lips in all the time I'd known him. "I will accept that as the highest praise."

His golden eyes with their vertically slit pupils really were remarkable—and very piercing when his gaze locked on mine.

"Since you have been honest with me, I will be honest as well," he said. "I saw your dagger tonight when the Hardanian touched you. I have known you wear it at all times and you can use it to great effect because you fear some threat. And I spotted your shadowbat companion the day you auditioned at Zaa'ga. I have said nothing of these secrets to anyone and never will."

Up until now, I'd feared anyone, even Mikas, would notice either my forearm sheath or Brae's presence. But to my surprise a weight lifted off my shoulders knowing those secrets were safe with him.

Much to my chagrin, tears welled up at the feeling of being safe. I blinked them away, but not before Mikas slid to the edge of his seat.

"Please do not weep," he said earnestly, his voice suddenly rough. "I swear on my life you do not need to fear I will betray you."

"No, it's not that." I took a shaky breath. "I've held these secrets in for a while. I guess talking about them and thinking about what a good friend you are just hit me all at once."

Something flashed in his eyes—some emotion I couldn't quite identify. And then it was gone, replaced with kindness. "I am glad to be your friend, Isla. And very honored to be trusted with this information."

"How about returning the favor?" I asked.

He tilted his head. "How do you mean?"

"Something's been bothering you." I curled up against the arm of the sofa to bring myself closer to him. "The other reason I wanted to bring you here is so you could tell me what's made you so grim lately. I'm sure you don't want to say anything in the bar, but I'm here to listen. I can keep secrets too."

Mikas bowed his head, obviously struggling with himself over what to say and how to say it. I might have been hurt by his reluctance if I didn't know how painful secrets could be. He'd been a conscripted soldier, so he probably had nightmares in his past I couldn't dream of.

"Does it have anything to do with the Atolani female who was at the bar tonight?" I prompted gently. "Did you know her from before?"

"Yes." He raised his head, his expression dark with memories. "I knew her from my time in the Cludian Corps. I had not seen her or even thought of her since. She bears a grudge at how we parted ways…and because I refused to join a mercenary squad with her after our service ended."

Well, that explanation fit with my assessment of the Atolani. My instincts had warned me loud and clear at the sight of her that she was untrustworthy and dangerous. Everything about her oozed menace.

Reading between the lines, they had once been a couple, or at least had an intimate relationship. At the thought of Mikas being close to the Atolani female, I felt a little stab of something. Not jealousy, which would have made no sense—more like protectiveness and a lot of indignation at the ridiculous thought that kind, honest Mikas would sign up to be a mercenary.

"She wanted you to be a raider?" I demanded. "*You?*"

"Yes." To my surprise, the corners of his mouth turned up. "You do not see me as a likely candidate for that life?"

"No!" The very thought turned my stomach. "Not at all. Mercenaries are nothing more than thieves and cold-blooded killers. How could she have even thought you'd want that?"

"I do not know," Mikas said. He seemed pleased by my reaction. Maybe he liked that I had a better sense of who he was than the Atolani female did. "Once my injuries healed, I returned here to my homeworld," he added. "To a peaceful life and an honest profession. I may not be wealthy, but I am content."

"How did you end up working for Nubo?" I asked. "You're such a good man. And he's…not."

Once again, he smiled. Three smiles in less than an hour. A record.

"Why did *you* accept his job offer?" Mikas countered. "You surely knew what kind of man he is."

It was my turn to smile. "A fair point. I needed the job. I'd had a lot of auditions before that one, and no one in Onat'ras was interested in a human singer. I'd given up, honestly…and then I saw the job notice and told myself I'd try one more time."

His smile faded. If I didn't know better, I might have thought his skin paled a little.

"So you almost did not come to Zaa'ga to audition?" he asked.

"I almost didn't," I admitted. "I argued with myself. But Brae said I should try or I'd always wonder if this job was the one that was meant to be." At his quizzical expression, I added, "Brae is my shadowbat."

"Ah." He laced his fingers between his knees, his expression grave. "I owe a great debt to Brae, then."

It was so wonderful to finally know for sure how much Mikas valued our friendship.

"I owe him too." I smiled. "I would have missed out on a good-paying job, a safe place to live, and a good friend."

I started to added something about Brae, then stopped. Wait. Mikas had said he hadn't thought about the Atolani female until she appeared in the bar tonight, so that wasn't what had been bothering him lately.

"So, what—" I started to say.

"Isla—" Mikas began at the same time, then fell silent.

"Go on," I said, smiling to encourage him. "I'm listening. We've still got plenty of time before we'll need to leave the shop."

He took a deep breath and started to speak.

His wristcomm beeped twice. He glanced at the screen and snarled. I jumped a little at the sound.

I'd never heard him snarl like that—not even when patrons caused trouble. In the bar, his growls had more of a warning note. This snarl was truly ferocious.

I touched his hand. "What's wrong?"

For a moment, he didn't answer. His enormous hands clenched into fists, and then he flexed his fingers. "Nubo says there is a problem with the drink kiosks," he grated. "He requests that I return to work my shift."

He very clearly didn't believe it. Neither did I. The coincidence was too great. I'd bet my best boots if there really was a problem, Nubo had engineered it as an excuse to bring an end to our outing.

Gods, could I have nothing? Not even an hour of privacy and heart-to-heart conversation with my friend without our boss interfering?

If Mikas refused, it would arouse Nubo's suspicions even more, though there was nothing more to our time together than two good friends looking for mutual comfort about our present and our pasts. As much as we resented and hated Nubo, we didn't need to make an enemy of him. Judging by Mikas's expression, his thoughts mirrored mine.

He sent a terse reply and turned off his wristcomm screen.

"I'm sorry," I said, reaching out to touch his arm again in an attempt to comfort him.

Mikas started to move away, possibly out of habit, but then seemed to remember we were in private and covered my hand with his much larger one.

"It will not always be like this," he said, his voice quiet. "We will not always have to answer to him."

"You have some plan to get us out of here?" I asked.

Only after the words came out did I notice he'd said *we*, and I'd said *us*. When had we become an *us*? And why did the thought warm my insides like a cup of hot tea?

Another flash of emotion in his eyes I couldn't read. His hand squeezed mine, very gently. "Goals and dreams, but no plans," he said. "Not yet."

What did he mean by that? He wanted to figure out a way to get us both away from Nubo? How long had he been thinking about this?

If we had more time to talk, I would have asked him all those questions. I would have asked again what was bothering him and where he might want to go if he left Onat'ras. I might have confided how much I wanted to find a place where Brae and I could make a home and feel secure and comfortable and I wished he could find the same.

Instead, I picked up my shopping bag and quietly followed him out.

CHAPTER 9

ISLA

"I think we should leave Onat'ras," Brae said. It wasn't the first time he'd said so—only the first time tonight.

My shadowbat had returned from his nightly feeding just after I got back from the market. Safely inside my apartment, which he accessed through a window I left partially open for fresh air, he shifted out of his shadow form.

In his solid form, his furry body was bright blue with dark blue wings, purple ears, and a purple tail with a fluffy tuft of gray fur with colorful tips on its end. His little horns and fangs were more decorative than functional, since he preferred insects over larger prey, but his fangs produced a paralytic venom and his claws were razor sharp.

A year ago, on Valodia, he'd asked me to put two small hoop earrings in his ear after seeing similar piercings on a frilled bat belonging to a local gamekeeper. I didn't dare tell him I thought they made him look more adorable than threatening.

He settled into a nest made of my clothing at the foot of my bed. When he needed more of my scent, or had nightmares, he slept on my pillow, curled up against the back of my head. I grumbled about it, especially when his claws or fangs got caught in my long hair, but we both knew I didn't mind. We comforted each other.

"Nubo has you followed everywhere." Brae rubbed his pot belly with his wings. "As if it's not bad enough to live under surveillance in this building. You don't need to live like this. *We* don't need to live like this."

"I know." I sat cross-legged on my bed in my pajamas with a glass of wine in my hand. It was my second glass. "I hate it—you know I do. I don't want to be watched like I'm somebody's possession. It reminds me of…" I swallowed hard. "Before."

"And yet," he said with a sigh, "we're still here."

Brae groomed his belly fur while I sipped my wine. Despite working in a bar and frequently enjoying a glass of brandy after I finished my set, I didn't drink much off the clock. Everything about the night's events had driven me to open a bottle of Tocanian wine. It was sweeter than I usually liked, but full-bodied and velvety enough to enjoy.

"I love singing at Zaa'ga," I said, my shoulders sagging. "I love making enough money to feel secure for the first time in my life. Nubo aside, I feel safe in this building. I'm lucky to have this job and an apartment when it's so difficult to get them in this city. I love Fortusia. It's the first truly beautiful place I've ever lived, and the first place that ever felt like it could be our home. Ycari is watching over me. And it's not like there's any place in the galaxy that's completely safe."

"All that is true." Brae curled his tufted tail around his body. "But you and I both know Nubo wants you as more than his singer. Sooner or later he'll act on that."

"Ycari says he's got people digging into my identity." My stomach, already uneasy, began churning, so I set my wine glass on my bedside table. "He wants to know who I am before he does anything. You know how people like him operate. He's greedy and possessive and a thug, but he's not dumb or reckless. If he was, he wouldn't be where he is. He'd be dead."

"So you're living on borrowed time and you know it." He nailed me with a glowing, angry stare. "Isla, there are other cities, other bars. Other places you can sing. Nubo might think you belong to him and that you owe him for giving you a job, but you don't. You aren't obligated to stay here."

My temper, already shorter than normal, flared. "I know I'm not," I snapped. Not because he deserved my ire, but because he was right and I didn't want him to be. "I'm tired of running. Just *once* I don't want to be the one running. I don't want to be the victim anymore."

Those words all but hung in the air in the long silence that followed. My chest rose and fell with ragged breaths.

"I'm sorry," Brae said quietly. "I should have understood that without you needing to say it."

He went back to grooming his belly as I curled up with my back to the headboard, my arms around my knees.

Should I tell him the thought of leaving Mikas behind made my stomach hurt? I wasn't sure I could explain why in a way even I could understand.

"Mikas thinks we should go, though," I said, my voice quiet. "Both of us. All three of us."

His wings fluttered. "You told him about me?"

I pictured the earnestness in Mikas's expression when he'd sworn my secrets were safe with him and smiled. "He already knew."

I told him what Mikas had confided in the privacy of Ycari's sampling room, what else we'd talked about, and how much I'd enjoyed our trip to the market despite its abrupt end and Mikas's dark mood on the walk back. Brae licked his belly and listened quietly.

"So Mikas thinks he can get you both away from Nubo?" Brae asked when I finished.

"He said he wanted to." I gazed absently out my window at the grassy rooftop of the building next to ours. "No definite plans, but goals and dreams. His words."

"Goals and dreams, you say," he mused. "He dreams of escaping Nubo with you?"

"Not like that," I said with a chuckle. "As a friend. He's so kind beneath that grumpy exterior. He worries about me."

He made a snuffly chuffing sound—the shadowbat equivalent of a snort. "That makes two of us."

Talking about Mikas made my chest hurt, but for an entirely different reason than talking about leaving Onat'ras. It was more of a heartache.

"He's so unhappy," I said, "but he doesn't want to say why. Tonight he was more grim than I've ever seen him and it wasn't just because of that Atolani female who showed up at the bar. He seems miserable."

"I think your friend needs someone to talk to, if he could bring himself to open up," Brae observed. "The man's sealed up tighter than an airlock."

I sighed. "I tried at the perfume shop, but before we could say much, Nubo demanded he come back and that was the end of that. Even if we hadn't been interrupted, though, I'm not sure how far I would have gotten. He doesn't trust anyone."

"Sounds familiar."

I bit my lip. "I think I could trust him, though."

Brae paused mid-lick and eyed me. "Enough to tell him how we ended up here?"

"Maybe." I rubbed my knee. "Not the details I'm bound to keep secret, of course, but the story in general terms, and the identity of the Erotovo who might be hunting for me. I know to you it probably seems like a bad idea, but I really do feel like Mikas is trustworthy. He's already been keeping some of my secrets without me knowing."

"You have good instincts, for a human." He licked his belly

for a bit, then added, "I feel the same about him, for what it's worth. I didn't say so because I wanted you to come to your own conclusions. I haven't spent as much time around him as you have, obviously, but he seems honorable."

Honorable was high praise coming from Brae.

As much as I didn't want to feel like a victim anymore, when I thought about leaving Onat'ras with Mikas, the knot in my stomach eased. The galaxy seemed full of possibilities rather than simply loneliness and the misery of yet another relocation.

When had he become so important to me? It had happened so gradually that I hadn't noticed until he'd squeezed my hand tonight and it felt like all my fears washed away as if by magic. Thinking about that moment eased the tension in my shoulders that never seemed to go away, even while I was singing.

Happiness and the warmth of not being lonely were new feelings. Brae had been my one and only true, trusted friend until now, and we'd only been together two years. I'd had intimate moments with people like Novee, and now I counted Ycari among my trusted friends, but my feelings about Mikas were different. His friendship warmed my soul.

I worried Brae might feel jealous or resentful of Mikas's new place in my heart, but my shadowbat closed his eyes and settled deeper into his nest with a rumbly purr I seldom got to hear because it meant he was content—and he was rarely content unless I was.

"How soon can you go back to the perfume shop with Mikas without it seeming too suspicious?" Brae murmured sleepily.

"Ycari is going to send me a message when my perfume is ready," I said.

He opened one eye. "I thought you didn't actually sample any scents?"

"I didn't. As we were leaving, she said she knew what would be perfect for me and we'd have to come back for it in a few days."

"Hmm." He closed his eye again and folded his wings over his belly.

First Ycari had *hmm*'d at me when I said Mikas and I weren't a couple, and now another *hmm* that implied Brae was very uncharacteristically keeping an opinion to himself.

I scowled. "What do you mean, *hmm?*"

He let out an exaggerated snore.

With a sigh, I used my wristcomm to shut my bedroom window and turn them all opaque. I hated to block my view of the city, but dawn was only a few hours away and the suns' light would pour straight into my room. I had to at least *try* to get some sleep.

Under the covers, I curled up on my side and tucked my arm under my pillow. My apartment wasn't cold and my bed had radiant warmth—a common amenity on Fortusia—but I still felt chilly.

Very unsurprisingly, a few minutes later, the bedding rustled as Brae made his way on foot from his nest at my feet to my pillow. He settled in with his back against the crown of my head, moving carefully so he didn't pull my hair.

"If Nubo tries to touch me," I murmured, "I won't hesitate to do whatever I need to do to protect myself. Nobody will touch me without my permission ever again."

His reply was equally quiet. "I know."

Much later, around 0500 hours, as Brae snored but sleep still eluded me, I thought of Mikas. Hopefully long before now he'd finished his shift and returned to his apartment for some much-needed rest. I pictured him in bed, comfortable and asleep, and willed him pleasant dreams.

That vision vanished, replaced by the memory of the hollowness in his eyes I'd glimpsed during the walk back from the market and the almost lifeless way he'd wished me good night at my door. My own eyes filled with tears.

How could I get him to tell me what was bothering him?

The only thing I could think of was to get him back to Ycari's shop and find a way to prevent Nubo from interfering a second time. There, in private, I could trust him with my own big secret, and maybe he would open his heart and do the same.

Again, I pictured Mikas in bed, but this time he was curled up next to me instead of alone. Not like a lover, but close enough that I could feel his warmth and he could feel mine. What a lovely thought that was.

Brae snorted in his sleep, wiggled closer, and resumed snoring. What did shadowbats dream of? I wondered. Tasty insects and warm breezes? Comfortable nests?

I counted shadowbats until sleep finally came.

CHAPTER 10

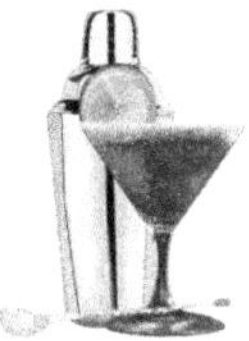

MIKAS

An hour before dawn, I sat on the edge of my bed in the dark, my forearms resting on my thighs and head bent.

Madame Ycari's refuge had allowed Isla and I to speak freely and touch one another for the first time and it had been truly wonderful. My hearts, my soul, my entire body had experienced peace and contentment like I had never known. The thought this was only a taste of what my life might be like with my mate had nearly left me speechless.

I had been mere moments from broaching the topic of our friendship with Isla, fully intending to test the waters to see if she might want more, when Nubo's message cut our time short. The yearning in my hearts went unspoken, and now I ached. Gods, how I ached.

Every word Isla had said during our walk back from the market had hurt my hearts like tiny stabs. Her scent, her smile, even the sound of her footsteps and the rustle of her dress seared me like a sandstorm on unprotected skin. By the time we returned to our building, my guts churned, my spines prickled, and my knuckles itched to pound Nubo to paste.

Isla's mood had soured noticeably too as I escorted her upstairs to our floor. I supposed that was my fault for exuding frustration and anger during our walk. Guilt joined longing and loneliness as weight on my shoulders.

I had ensured she got safely inside her apartment, changed back into work clothes, and returned to the packed bar, where I worked at a frantic pace two hours longer than my scheduled shift, until 0500 hours when Zaa'ga closed. By the time I returned to my apartment, my legs were nearly leaden with exhaustion.

And yet sleep eluded me and I could find no peace.

My peace was alone in her apartment just three doors down the hall—so close, but just out of reach. The same as since the day we had met.

With heavy hearts and heavier steps, I rose and walked to the window.

From here, if I stood in the right spot, I could just see the towering pink waterfall Isla clearly loved. It was such a ubiquitous part of the skyline that I hardly noticed it until she confided it was her favorite element of the city's eco-architecture, which she found wondrous. Now it held a very special place in my hearts. When I gazed upon it, I envisioned Isla doing the same, and that forged another connection between us.

Isla's wide-eyed wonder during our walk to the market had made me look at Onat'ras more clearly and truly see it as both beautiful and an architectural marvel. Even our trees and water captivated her. Replaying every moment of our walk to the market again and again had kept me calm and sustained me during my unexpected extra-long shift.

In a long-ago conversation, she had told me she enjoyed swimming, especially in Fortusia's fragrant natural lakes. It was an offhand comment, but I had filed that information away. Everything she revealed about herself was a treasure.

Someday, I would swim with her. Someday, I would wrap her in my arms in warm waters and feel her body against mine. Someday, I would kiss her, and she would hold me tightly and kiss me back.

Someday my hearts would be at peace, but not today.

In the meantime, I had another source of comfort. I left my clothes in an uncharacteristically careless pile on the floor and lay on the basking stone I had installed between the bed and my window. Sensors activated the radiant warmth within the stone and the infrared heat from the fixture in the ceiling above, bathing me in the heat my reptilian nature craved.

I closed my eyes and tried to relax despite the vicious ache in my right leg. My extra-long shift and our trip to the market had made the pain much worse than usual.

To distract myself, I thought about my walk with Isla to the market—especially our stop at the pink waterfall. After the feeling of Isla's hands in mine in Madame Ycari's back room, those minutes at the water's edge were my favorite memory of our too-brief outing.

Most clearly of all I recalled Isla standing beside me near the lake, her eyes closed and her face turned up to feel the waterfall's mist. Her damp skin had shimmered under the soft lights and her lips had curved up in a rapturous smile I would see in my dreams.

Gods, what I would not do to be the cause or recipient of such a smile.

I had longed to kiss her in that moment—so much so that my need had felt as strong and irresistible as the pull of gravity itself. Despite the presence of Nubo's spy and the knowledge doing so would put us both in terrible danger, I had come perilously close to thinking *fuck it* and kissing Isla with all my pent-up need, and then kneeling at her feet to show her and all the world she was everything to me. Resisting the urge had taken every last shred of willpower I had.

I took a deep, shaky breath and licked my lips to imagine what Isla's might taste like. She would be sweet, surely, but with that edge of spice and heat that so uniquely *her*. Her lips would be softer than even her skin, but her kiss would be fierce, even if it were tender.

Thinking about tasting her was a mistake. My cocks responded immediately, beading with lubrication along their lengths, hard and ready to please my mate. My nipples tightened too, aching to feel the heat of her lips and the sweet pain of her bite. My body did not care about Nubo's threats or that Isla remained oblivious to my dilemma. Gods, I craved her.

The more I fought to think of anything else, the more longing drove me to the edge of despair and desperation. With a resigned groan, I gripped my cocks in my hand and stroked.

Isla. Her full lips, her violet eyes, her nebula-colored hair. Her voice and sweet scent that calmed my rage and soothed my hurts. Her fearlessness that made my blood rush.

The way she had palmed a dagger and stared at the Hardanian as if deciding whether to let him live. *Yes, my fierce mate.*

I groaned again, bracing my heels. My hips lifted from the hot basking stone to thrust into my hand, which was now Isla's sweet body.

I could fight beside her. I could feed her berries and every delicacy her heart desired from my own hands. I could make love to her. I could live every moment of my remaining days in bliss as long as I was at her side.

Blazing heat rolled through my body. With a growl, I let my beastly hearts feast on carnal fantasies.

With my tongue, my fingers, my cocks, I would draw cries from her, hear my name fall from her lips. Make her thighs squeeze my head or hips. Pin her hands above her head into the bed or against the wall and bring her to release until she could take no more.

My movements became a frenzy.

The way Isla had let her head fall back tonight to feel the waterfall's mist on her face…but instead it was my own release falling on her lips, her cheeks. Streaming into her mouth and over her tongue—

Growling and then roaring, my hips bucking and balls clenching, I came in great spurts, first from my upper cock, and then the lower. Oh, gods…

My vision grayed and my hearing faded. I knew nothing but my thundering hearts and the sensation of every muscle going rigid, then warm and relaxed.

Lost in a haze of pleasure, I envisioned beautiful Isla beneath me, her eyes closed as she gasped for air, adrift in her own release as I filled her doubly with mine.

My chest heaved with ragged breaths edged with growls. *My mate. My mate. My mate.* The words became a kind of song, or prayer.

I would give anything to have her in my arms now, to see my cum streaming down her thighs, to hear her panting and whimpering against my chest. What sweeter sound could there be? What more enjoyable sensation than her fluttering around my cocks, knowing it was I who had brought her so much pleasure? I could not imagine anything better.

With my desire sated, my hearts filled with quiet contentment. My limbs relaxed, now heavy with tiredness, and at last I felt as if I would be able to sleep.

My fantasy morphed again: this time, to Isla tucked safely against my side, drowsy and satisfied, her head on my chest and her hand in mine. Yes, that was a good vision too—as gratifying as the images of bringing her to release again and again, but in a different way.

This was not the first time I had resorted to easing my

yearning the only way I could, but it was the first time I had done so with hands that had held Isla's hours earlier. Thanks to our closeness after her feigned stumble, my skin and clothing still carried traces of her scent.

My thoughts went to our stolen moments in the sampling room. *You have some plan to get us out of here?* Isla had asked, her eyes wide and hopeful.

I might have thought she meant herself and Brae if not for the way her hand had squeezed my arm. Somehow, despite the necessary distance caused by Nubo's surveillance, to Isla we had become an *us*.

I was alone tonight, but I had more reason to hope than ever before. I had given her my word that we would not always be under Nubo's thumb. Now I must make a plan to free us. Everything good in my life depended on that.

Thanks to my extended work hours tonight and the generosity of late-night bar patrons, I had made a significant deposit into my savings at the end of my shift. So Nubo's plot to separate Isla from me had instead helped fund our future.

With my heartache eased and need sated, I drifted in the warmth of my basking stone and dreams of Isla.

CHAPTER 11

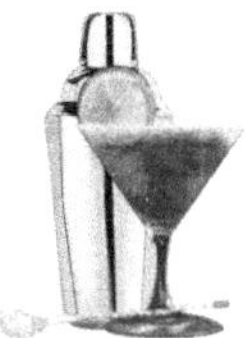

MIKAS

I EXPECTED NUBO TO CONFRONT ME ABOUT THE MARKET TRIP, demanding answers about the time Isla and I had spent out of sight of the spy he had sent to watch us, but he did not. In fact, I saw very little of him for the next two days. He emerged only to meet with a few new vendors and bark orders at me about inconsequential things like how I had rearranged the shelves behind the bar to feature recent additions to our beverage offerings.

Rather than relieve my worry, my uneasiness and need to protect Isla grew by the hour. Day and night, my spines prickled and my skin itched as if a thousand Muravii fang beetle larva were crawling over me. Nothing lessened my tension—no drink, no music, not even my basking stone. I had to choke down food. No matter what I tried to eat, it tasted like dust.

Only when I was behind the bar and Isla was onstage or sitting on her chair across from me were my hours tolerable. I spoke to her kindly and served her jampas and brandy as always, but I felt certain she saw my hands tremble sometimes.

She kept up the ruse too that nothing had changed between us and smiled when we spoke, but worry lurked in her violet gaze.

At night, alone in my apartment with Isla out of my sight, my chest felt tight and I struggled to breathe.

The mere thought of losing Isla filled me with rage and threatened to unleash something dreadful and monstrous within myself I had glimpsed only a handful of times in my life, on the battlefield and in my darkest dreams.

I did not want Isla to see that part of me. I could withstand anything else from her, even disappointment or anger, though my stomach churned at the prospect. But if she ever looked on me with fear, I did not think my hearts could take it.

Other than Nubo's conspicuous and very sudden preference for staying in his office, I had not seen or heard anything that led me to think danger was imminent, but every fiber of my being rang out like bells.

I did not know what had triggered my most primal instincts, but something had. Perhaps Nubo had finally satisfied himself about Isla's background, or some other danger lurked just out of sight. Regardless of the reason, I must get us away *now*, somehow.

Isla did not yet know the depths of my love and devotion, but she did want us to get away from Nubo. She had said so, or she had very nearly said so. Now instead of merely dream, I could plan.

The safest choice would be to leave Fortusia. To do that, we would have to get from Zaa'ga to one of the city's spaceports and aboard an off-planet cruiser, which would be very difficult given Nubo's surveillance. For extra security, we would also need new identities.

Using a secure transmission via my wristcomm, I contacted an old friend from my Corps days to begin that process. The price of two completely new identities so well-crafted they would pass scrutiny was exorbitant, but the value outweighed the cost—at least, to me. I considered it an investment.

Isla loved Fortusia, as did I. My hearts ached at the prospect of leaving, even if Isla were with me. But there were many beautiful worlds in Alliance space and more beyond its borders. Surely we could find another planet that would fill our hearts with as much joy as this one. It was only a matter of choosing a destination.

On the third day since the market trip, about a half hour before I planned to leave my apartment for my shift, something tapped on my window. I jumped to my feet from my sofa, where I had been trying unsuccessfully to focus on reading about Engareni perfumes, and snarled, my spines flaring.

A shadowy winged form perched on the tiny ledge. Sunlight glinted on a pair of large eyes—the only part of the creature that was more than a silhouette.

I strode to the window. "Brae?" The window was soundproof, but he should be able to read my lips.

The shadowbat balanced on one clawed foot and raised the other to give me a little wave. Why was he at my window? Had something happened to Isla? My never-ending uneasiness turned to dread.

I used my wristcomm to open the window. Once Brae slipped inside, I closed it again.

Still in his shadow form, he flew through my entire apartment—living area, kitchen, bedroom, and bathroom, as if checking to make sure I was alone—and then landed on the back of my sofa. He turned solid then, and from black and gray to bright blue and purple.

"Is Isla all right?" I demanded, without bothering with a greeting.

He studied me. "She's fine," he replied finally, and I started to breathe again.

I had never spoken to a shadowbat before. His voice was

scratchy and sibilant, but clear enough that I could understand him easily.

"But she won't be if we don't get out of here soon," he added, and my gut wrenched. "If she's your mate, you need to do what's right for her."

I stood frozen, my hearts pounding in my ears. How did he know? How long had he known? And most importantly…

"Does she know?" I rasped.

"No." He stretched his wings and wiggled more deeply into the sofa's plush backrest, as if making a kind of temporary nest for himself. "She finds it difficult to see what's in her own heart because of everything she's been through. I won't say any more about that because Isla's secrets are hers to tell when she's ready. It's not that she doesn't want your love or devotion. She does, very much. And she deserves it. She cares about you deeply."

"As a friend." I did not intend for my voice to sound so hollow, but it did.

Again, Brae eyed me, as if debating what to say.

"That is what she tells herself," he said. "But when she speaks of you, I see her change. She worries about you constantly, and she says your name in her sleep. If you tell her I told you that, you will regret it very much."

I found myself short of breath again, but for an entirely different reason.

His eyes glowed. "I love Isla. So if you hurt her in any way, or let her come to harm, I swear on all the gods above and below I will make sure you suffer for it."

"You do not need to worry," I said, without rancor because he spoke out of devotion to Isla. "I love her with all my hearts and soul."

I had never spoken those words aloud. Giving voice to my most profound secret made my skin tingle and hearts race.

"Then you'd better tell her so and get her away from here."

Brae's stare was intense. "You've sensed it too, haven't you? Something in the air. Something closing in."

"Yes." My chest rumbled. "What do you know about it?"

"Nothing more than you do," he said, which was a disappointment. "I've been keeping watch and listening in whenever and wherever I can, and I'll continue to do so, but—"

"I will protect her," I stated.

He made a chuffing sound. "Isla needs someone to stand beside her, not in front of her. If you're smart, you'll remember that."

I frowned. "Why would she not wish to be protected?"

"I didn't say she doesn't want to be protected," he countered. "I said she wants someone to fight *beside* her, and someone to fight beside. If she's your true mate, isn't that what you want too?"

Stunned, I stared at Brae. A Pallasian shadowbat understood the physiology of true mates that well?

I thought of the confrontation between Isla and the Hardanian. The way she faced him had thrilled and satisfied—and yes, aroused—me as much or more than anything else about my mate. Truly, in my hearts and soul I did not want to stand in front of her and fight her battles for her. I wanted to do as Brae described.

"Yes, that is what I want," I said quietly. "It would be my greatest honor and privilege to fight at her side."

"Then do it." He rose and stretched his wings. "I don't keep any secrets from Isla. You can tell her we spoke today when the time is right. Soon, she'll ask you to go with her back to Madame Ycari's shop to pick up her perfume. Start planning now what you're going to say to her when you get there, and what you're going to do to get us the hells away from here."

I had been planning my future with Isla from the moment we had met.

"I will," I said.

"Good." He glanced at the window. "If you wouldn't mind…?"

I activated the window. Brae took to the air, faded to a shadow, and flew out of my apartment, disappearing from sight before I could reach the window.

My shift was due to start in minutes. But rather than close the window immediately and leave, I let the breeze and sunshine caress my skin and the familiar scents of Onat'ras fill my nose and lungs.

Yes, Fortusia was my homeworld, but Isla was my home. If she accepted me as her mate, I would be her home as well, though human physiology was not the same as mine. I would provide her with deep contentment and security and love. It was not a pink waterfall or a towering oth'canto tree, but it would be good.

Finally, the time forced me to finish getting ready for work and leave my apartment. Mindful of Nubo's surveillance and the looming threat neither Brae nor I could identify yet, I forced myself to keep my expression neutral and not reveal either the effervescent feeling in my hearts or that I was keeping a much closer watch on my surroundings than usual.

Passing Isla's door without pausing required focus too. I pictured her on the other side of the wall, reading or listening to music, or resting, or maybe practicing ahead of her shift later tonight.

Finish her perfume, I willed Madame Ycari. *Summon us to your shop so I can open my hearts.*

When Isla had first mentioned buying perfume, I had almost let slip that I wished she would not change her scent because it was everything to me. Even then I knew it was a selfish thought and I was ashamed of it. But now I would have bathed her in any perfume she wanted and loved it, especially if it meant a return to the privacy of Ycari's sampling room.

Envisioning being alone with Isla once again lightened my

hearts *and* my steps despite the prickling of my spines and never-ending uneasiness in my gut. I scarcely noticed my long walk down from the fourth residential floor to ground level and the hallway that led to Zaa'ga.

I came around the last corner to the short corridor that went past Nubo's office and ended in the door that led to the bar, eager to start my shift and earn more tips that would go toward my future with Isla.

A tall, leather-clad figure leaned against the wall opposite Nubo's office, flipping a dagger in her hand. I paused mid-step. What the hells was she doing in the private area behind the bar?

"Afternoon, Commandant." As I approached, Kona caught the handle of her knife one last time and slid it into the sheath on her thigh. "Right on time for work. Nice and punctual. Our boss will be glad to see it."

Our boss.

A dozen emotions hit me at once—chief among them, fury that made my spines bristle, skin heat, and claws emerge.

Damn Kona to all the hells. Did Nubo recruit her after seeing her in the bar? Had she sought employment as part of her grudge against me? Or some combination of the two?

With effort, I squashed my rage and continued toward the bar without stopping or replying.

"Good news, Commandant." She chuckled as I passed. "It'll be my job to make sure the singer stays safe whenever she leaves the premises." She grinned so widely that the scar on her neck rippled.

Gods, I could have finished the job someone had started and ripped her head off her shoulders. And then done the same with Nubo's.

Was Kona the danger Brae and I had sensed, or was her assignment only part of some bigger threat? Had Nubo told her to confront me today and imply Isla was now in imminent danger from a cold-blooded mercenary and killer appointed to haunt my mate's every step?

"Aren't you going to congratulate me on my new job?" Kona taunted, her voice following me. "Come on, Commandant. We're colleagues now. Just a couple of former soldiers trying to make an *honest living*—"

I moved so fast, I had no memory of turning around or closing the distance between us. Between one heartsbeat and the next, I went from walking toward the bar's closed door to pinning Kona against the wall with my forearm across her windpipe.

With a hiss, she drew her dagger. I caught her wrist and slammed it against the wall. A bone snapped, and her knife clattered on the floor.

Her other hand gripped my arm and tried to pull it off her throat. When that did not work, she sank her talons into my forearm. Blood streamed from the wounds, but I barely felt the pain.

Fear flashed in her eyes. She hid it quickly and dug her talons in deeper, but I had seen it, and she knew I had. Her fury seemed to double because I had frightened her.

I could not kill her. I could not demand she leave Isla alone. I could not tip my hand that I loved Isla, or that I planned to escape with her—tonight, if possible. Only the fact my happiness and therefore my life depended on these things stilled my hand.

"Stay away from me, Kona," I said, my voice cold despite the rage that filled me and made even my eyes feel hot. "If you have chosen to work for Nubo, so be it. You do your job and I will do mine. Do not speak to me, or sit at my bar, or come near my door. I will not warn you again. Do you understand?"

"I live on your floor now," she wheezed, her eyes blazing. "I will have to pass your—"

"You heard what I said." I twisted her broken wrist just enough to make her squirm. "Do you understand?"

The more rational part of my brain wondered why Nubo had not emerged from his office to intervene. Surely he was watching. The fact he chose not to interfere told me he probably hoped for a confrontation. Maybe he wondered what would be said in the heat of the moment and who would prevail.

"You're a dead man," Kona hissed. She spat in my face. "Your singer too."

Her gaze flicked to Nubo's door. She was goading me, trying to force me to fight, to get me to reveal what was in my hearts. Had he ordered her to say and do these things?

"We both answer to Nubo," I said, because he was listening. "So you will not do anything to me or the singer unless he tells you so, will you? No more than you would have killed someone without orders from your squad leader or your *commandant*."

Kona's mouth compressed into a thin line. Her chipped incisor drew a bead of blood from her lip. She had chosen to work for Nubo to get further under my skin, but to do so she had traded one ruthless boss and subservient life for another. She would have gutted me here and now if she could have for reminding her of that fact.

I released her throat and wrist and stepped back.

She thought about attacking; I saw it in the way tension rolled through her body and her fingers twitched, no doubt yearning to pull another blade with her good hand. I also saw the moment she glanced at Nubo's closed office door and decided against it.

I checked my wristcomm. One minute to the start of my shift. If I hurried, I would get behind the bar just on time and use the small medkit I kept there to treat my talon wounds.

I left Kona where she stood, breathing hard and glaring at my back until I stepped through the automatic door and into

Zaa'ga to start what I hoped would be my final shift behind its bar.

CHAPTER 12

ISLA

Something was going on, and I wished to hells someone would tell me what it was.

Since our trip to the market, Mikas had been ten times pricklier and more grim than ever before, Nubo hadn't criticized either my music selections or my changes to the stage lights, and even Brae had taken to keeping watch around the building all night and even throughout the day, sleeping in small increments instead of with me in my bed. He denied he'd seen or heard anything that made him think we might be in danger, and I believed him, but his behavior only added to my unease.

Most infuriating of all, I had a new watcher who followed me everywhere: the menacing Atolani female who'd shown up at the bar to harass Mikas and now apparently had ended up on Nubo's payroll. I didn't know her name yet, so I called her Slug because she'd actually thought Mikas would want to be a mercenary raider.

The worst part of the past few days was that I hadn't had one single moment of privacy with Mikas, and not one touch. We couldn't risk it. Somehow I'd gone from being fine to longing for him to squeeze my hand.

So when just before my shift on the third day since the market trip I received a message from Madame Ycari summoning me back to the shop to pick up my perfume, I nearly danced with happiness. Thankfully, Brae wasn't in the apartment to see it, or I might not have ever heard the end of it.

I let myself smile and be joyful, knowing once I left to walk downstairs for my shift I had to pretend I wasn't beside myself with excitement about going to the shop with Mikas.

Maybe someday soon I wouldn't have to hide my feelings anymore. What a lovely dream that was.

I wore a new dress tonight, one I'd been eyeing for a special occasion. The teal fabric had microscopic prisms woven into the threads that would catch the stage lights and glimmer as if I were a galaxy of stars. I owned a few dresses, but most I rented from a local shop that loaned clothing and costumes to performers who worked in Onat'ras and whose tastes and wardrobe needs exceeded their budget, like me.

Unfortunately, this teal gown was rented and I'd have to return it, but for tonight, I could pretend it was mine. And Mikas would love it. He might even smile.

I finished styling my hair and stepped into my shoes with barely enough time to get downstairs and have a few minutes to compose myself and warm up before I'd have to be onstage.

The screen above my door showed the corridor outside—a common feature in apartment buildings on Fortusia, even in relatively safe areas. A familiar shadow passed back and forth in view of the camera: Brae, waiting to go with me to the bar. He'd been doing that since Slug started following me around.

With Brae keeping watch as a shadow along the ceiling, I took the lift from the fourth level to the ground floor. No sign of Slug, but that didn't mean she wasn't nearby. My good mood soured and my stomach churned.

The impassive watchers I'd had before like Scar were bad enough, but Slug's overtly menacing presence was too much. And worse, Nubo could have ordered her to be less threatening, but clearly he hadn't. He *wanted* me to feel afraid.

The realization brought with it a wash of clarity that felt like chains breaking.

I *did* love singing at Zaa'ga, but because I loved singing and spending time with Mikas, not because of the bar itself. I didn't like or need this job remotely enough to put up with this misery anymore.

By the time I stepped out of the lift, my hands trembled with rage. *No more*, I thought, my jaw set as I made my way down the long hallway toward the bar. *No more being watched. No more waiting for Nubo to pounce. Just...no more.*

I stopped midway between the lift and the bar and leaned against the wall, pretending to adjust something in my shoe.

Isla? In shadow form, Brae tucked himself into the ceiling line above my head. *Are you all right?*

Yes. My mental voice was quiet. *I'm ready to go.*

Good. His relief was palpable even through our telepathic bond. *When? Now?*

As soon as Mikas is ready. I'm not going without him. The vehemence of those words startled even me. *I'll talk to Ycari tonight after my shift,* I added. *I need to make some plans. Keep an eye out for any trouble in the meantime.*

You know I will.

With my decision made, my steps lightened as I made my way down the hall. I'd expected to feel sad or angry or bitter, but instead my insides fluttered with anticipation.

I didn't have a dressing room adjacent to Zaa'ga, much less a practice room, so usually I prepared for my shift in my apartment. On days when I came down without much time before showtime, I resorted to a quick warm-up in one of the large storage rooms behind the bar area. The acoustics weren't good, but the bar noise and the thick walls ensured I couldn't be overheard even if I sang at the top of my lungs.

Let me know if you see Slug, I told Brae.

He fluttered his wings in acknowledgement and slipped away along the ceiling toward the bar before I closed the door for privacy.

I'd finished my scales and was midway through rehearsing my most vocally demanding song of the evening, a Fortusian folk song that was always a popular choice, when the storage room's door slid open and Nubo appeared, his bulk filling the wide doorway.

I cut myself off mid-word and silenced the music playing on my wristcomm.

"Hello, Isla," Nubo said, smiling widely. He lumbered into the storage room, which suddenly felt much too small. "I did not mean to interrupt. Please, go on."

"I'm done practicing, actually." I forced a smile as if I didn't hate him with the fire of a thousand suns. I didn't want to tip him off that I planned to leave as soon as Mikas and I were able. "I'm due to be on stage very soon, so I need to have a few minutes of quiet to clear my head."

"I am sure the boss will forgive you for being late today." Nubo's grin didn't waver. "I have it on good authority he is very accommodating…and generous, to a fault."

An icy chill swept through me. *Brae,* I thought, while I held onto my smile with such determination that I feared my face would crack. *I need you to come back to the storage room.*

"Someone as talented and lovely as yourself could take advantage of such generosity," Nubo continued, leaning against a heavy-duty shelving unit filled with casks of ale.

He was doing his best to appear casual and friendly and nonthreatening, but his eyes remained as cold and calculating as ever. He'd deliberately cornered me in the storage room because he wanted to scare me. He wanted me to know no place would be safe if I didn't do what he wanted.

The sensation of my forearm sheath and the dagger it held had never felt as reassuring as it did now.

A winged shadow appeared near the ceiling just inside the doorway. I kept my gaze on Nubo's face and hid my relief.

"You could have every luxury," Nubo said. "A penthouse residence. Chef-prepared meals. A wardrobe filled with the loveliest clothes in Onat'ras. There is no need for you to hire cheap gowns when with a word you could have the best."

I'd expected some version of this speech from the moment I met Nubo. And I'd been prepared for almost anything, from seemingly sweet persuasion to threats and even a physical attack. And the latter two might still be coming my way.

But what I hadn't braced myself for was Nubo Wex to corner me in the storage room, smile in my face, and refer to the most beautiful dress I'd ever seen or worn as a "cheap gown." And it hurt way, *way* more than it should because on purpose or not he'd gotten me right in what might have been one of my few soft spots.

I had no idea what my expression looked like, but his smile evaporated like a drop of water under the Solani desert sun.

"Thank you for the offer," I said, forcing a tone that was polite at best. "I don't want to keep everyone waiting tonight, though."

"Give my proposal due consideration," His smile was cold now, to match his flat stare. "I have a lot to offer someone like you."

"I know you do," I said, as if I didn't know what he meant by *someone like you*. This time my smile was sweeter, and I made my tone conciliatory. "Can I have some time, and some space, to consider it?"

"You have had months to think," he said flatly. "I am not stupid, Isla Mair."

Time for a different approach—one I'd used before with people like Nubo. I'd known what kind of man he was from the moment we'd met. Reading people had been essential for my survival before I came to Fortusia, and that hadn't changed.

"Of course you aren't stupid." I let my smile grow and become almost smug, as if it was me who'd cornered *him* and not the other way around. "But neither am I. Maybe I want to negotiate my terms?"

His eyes widened. I'd startled him by flipping the power dynamics. He'd landed a punch with that offhand comment about my dress, but we were going to play things *my* way now.

"You've got something I want, and I've got something *you* want." I smoothed my hands over my hips. "We both know the game. But it would be a lot more fun if we played it a little differently than what you're used to, don't you think?"

"I do not think so," he said, but a beat too late for it to be true. I'd hooked him, all right.

"Oh, I think you'll really like how I play," I purred, emphasizing the word *play* for maximum innuendo.

Nubo eyed me and huffed in an almost oxen-like way.

I glanced at my wristcomm and strode toward the door as if I planned to plow right through him. "Showtime, Nubo. I'll come see you tomorrow. Be ready to talk terms."

A second before I ran into him, he moved aside. I trailed my fingertips over his massive leg on my way past. He huffed again and licked his lips. I had to resist the urge to wipe my hand on my dress.

Chin high and without looking back, I strode down the hall to the door to the bar, feeling Nubo's stare on my back the entire way. I kept my expression blank, but my stomach roiled and my hands trembled with adrenaline.

Are you all right? Brae asked, his shadow following directly above me. *Gods above, Isla, you really outdid yourself making him think you might* actually—

I didn't have much choice. I took a deep breath and exhaled to slow my racing heart. *I'm okay, but we're officially out of time to plan a getaway. We're going to have to wing it. I hope Mikas will go too.*

I think he will, Brae said, his tone dry.

No time to ask why he thought so, or why he sounded so wry. I plastered on a brilliant smile, scanned my palm to open the door, and strode into Zaa'ga with Brae following close behind so the door didn't close between us. He'd be stuck to me like a Barmian barnacle for the rest of the night.

I scanned the bar as if taking in the size of my audience, then looked for Mikas, who was busy behind the bar pouring a couple of drinks. He glanced up, gave me a nod, and put the drinks on a tray for a service 'bot to deliver to a table. At least he appeared less grim tonight.

I wanted to stop and say hello before I went onstage, but it would have been ill-advised even if Slug wasn't leaning against the wall with a tankard of ale. Nubo must have asked her to wait in the bar rather than follow me downstairs from my apartment because he planned to accost me in the storage room.

I made sure to thank the regulars for their patronage on my way to the stage. One notable absence was the amphibious Prylothian who usually occupied the small pool near the stage. Tonight a serpentine Altasian had coiled up in the water, his head, shoulders, and vestigial wings resting on stone as he sipped an unfamiliar bubbly beverage through a long tube that ran into a small cask next to the pool.

Given how impatient I was to go to the market with Mikas after our shifts, I expected my set to drag on interminably, but instead it flew by. I didn't avoid looking in Mikas's direction since that would be as suspicious as watching him too much, but each time I looked that direction, he was busy fulfilling orders.

My heart ached as I watched Mikas drop a hefty handful of credit chips into his collection box. He made good money here. Would he come to regret leaving with me, especially if he struggled to find a job that paid equally well wherever we ended up? That was a concern I could bring up at Madame Ycari's shop later, I supposed. I tried not to let it worry me for now. I had plenty of other things to worry about in the meantime.

Earlier in the week, when I'd chosen the songs for tonight's set, I hadn't planned on this being my final performance on this stage—but maybe I'd subconsciously made my selections on the chance or hope it would be. Every song was one of my favorites and the patrons certainly seemed to appreciate the music. My tip jar filled more rapidly than usual.

I did make one alteration to my set list, though, near the end. Right before my final song, which was the folk tune the audience habitually joined in on, I sang "Warm Waters" because it meant something different to me tonight than ever before—especially its poignant first line: *"When I remember all the places I have left behind, it is your touch I ache for the most."*

Unlike earlier in the week, I hadn't chosen to sing "Water Waters" as a ploy for more tips, but the magic worked again tonight. Before I even sang the final note, patrons were coming forward to drop credits and coins into my jar, which was now my escape fund. And during the final song, the generosity continued, nearly bringing me to tears as I bowed and thanked everyone for listening.

I wouldn't miss Zaa'ga, or Nubo, or the strain of living under surveillance the past three months, but I *would* miss singing and being onstage very, very much. My heart ached thinking about the prospect I might not find another singing job for a long time, if ever.

But I couldn't stay. I wouldn't. I deserved better than this.

The Isla who'd arrived on Fortusia with a single case of donated clothing and a few hundred credits to her name hadn't thought she deserved anything good at all. So however tonight turned out, believing I deserved a good life was a victory worth celebrating.

CHAPTER 13

ISLA

When I slid onto my chair at the bar, Mikas set a bowl of jampas and a glass of brandy in front of me. The last time for this tradition? Another pang.

"Excellent music choices again tonight," he said. "Your Fortusian pronunciation has improved significantly from your early days here."

"I would hope so." For the benefit of our eavesdropping boss, I added, "I don't have any plans to go anywhere, so I've been practicing my vowels. Before too long, I want to trick people into thinking I've been speaking Fortusian all my life."

I worried Mikas might not understand why I'd said that, but when he smiled, I knew I needn't have been concerned.

"I am glad to hear it, Isla. Zaa'ga would not be the same without you." He glanced at the bowl of berries. "Would you like anything else?"

I didn't have much appetite, but the berries looked particularly ripe and sweet tonight, so I tried a handful. They tasted even better than they looked.

"Delicious," I said when I could speak again. I dabbed my mouth with a napkin. "Really outstanding. Thank you for the treat, as always."

"My pleasure." He glanced at his order screen and picked up a tall glass to mix a drink.

"I need to go back to the market tonight," I said, with a loud sigh. "That bottle of perfume I ordered is *finally* ready, and I still need food for the week. Since we're off at the same time tonight, I don't suppose you have time to be my escort again and carry my purchases?" I held his gaze. "Or are you too busy?"

To my relief, he took the hint and played along. "I really should stay and work on inventory," he said, sounding reluctant for the benefit of the surveillance.

"Please?" I asked, injecting a plaintive note into my tone. "I know it's a last-minute favor, but I promise it won't take too long. An hour, hour and a half at most. I have to get back too."

"All right," he grumbled. "An hour and a half *maximum*."

"Thank you." I made my voice a little frosty as if he'd irritated me and focused on my drink, pointedly ignoring the berries. Mikas moved his drink-making farther down the bar, his spines prickling visibly.

I hoped we'd sold it well enough to Nubo and my playacting with him earlier about his proposal had been convincing enough that we'd get out of the building and to the market.

Once Mikas and I made it into the perfume shop, I could tell him the truth: Brae and I needed to leave Onat'ras tonight, and I wanted him to come too.

As fast as my set had gone by, the next hour dragged on interminably. It was exhausting to sit and wait to see if Nubo would come up with some excuse to demand one or both of us stay behind and not let the anxiety show. And what if Mikas had changed his mind about leaving? What would I do if I offered to go away with him and he declined? My chest felt tight even thinking about that possibility.

I hated to pretend to be miffed at Mikas and not chat as we usually did. Even *faking* being mad at him made my stomach churn. Or maybe that was just anxiety about our escape. I did eat the jampas, though. Fake argument or not, I wasn't going to waste the most delicious berries on the planet.

An hour later, when our shifts ended, I headed upstairs with Brae while Mikas tidied up behind the bar.

In my apartment, I swapped my lovely teal gown for a much more casual knee-length dress, kept one dagger in my arm sheath, put the rest into my boots, and left my hair loose.

I took what I hoped was one last look around my apartment. I expected to have second thoughts, but I didn't. As much as I'd tried to pretend otherwise, this place hadn't felt like home to me. It was only ever just a place to stay. I hadn't put down roots anywhere except maybe the chair at the bar where Mikas had served me berries and brandy after every shift.

"Are you ready for this?" Brae asked as I slung my cross-body shopping bag over my shoulder.

"As ready as I'm going to get," I said, squaring my shoulders. "Am I crazy for doing this?"

"You know you aren't." He perched on the back of a chair so he could look me in the eye. "You deserve better than living like this. Both you *and* Mikas deserve better."

I took a deep breath and let it out. "Thank you. I just need you to watch for trouble while we figure out what's next."

"I will. Once you talk to Mikas, let me know your plan and what you want me to do."

"Okay." I touched his wing. "Thanks, Brae. I love you."

"I love you too." He nuzzled my hand. "Don't tell anyone I did that."

"Our secret," I promised.

When I opened my door, I found Mikas waiting. "Ready?" he asked, his voice gruff.

"Ready," I said, forcing a smile. "Thanks again for coming." He grunted.

In shadow form, Brae followed us out of the building, and then flew overhead to snack on insects as he accompanied us.

Brae wasn't our only watcher. Slug followed too, as usual without making any effort to disguise herself. Her obvious presence made me wonder whether others might be watching. It was an old trick: keep your quarry focused on an overt shadow to discourage them from looking for others. I wouldn't put it past Nubo to have multiple sets of eyes on us.

Do you see anyone else but Slug following us? I asked Brae, who was circling overhead judging by the telltale warm tingle on the back of my neck.

After a moment's pause, he replied, *No, but I'll keep close watch. She's being too obvious, isn't she?*

Much too obvious, I agreed. *Thank you.*

As impatient as I was to get to the market, I took time to gaze at the waterfall, inhale the sweet scent of the pink water, and feel the mist. Of all the planets, moons, and space stations I'd ever visited, this was the most beautiful and calming place I'd been.

So that was two things I'd miss about Onat'ras: my chair at the bar and this beautiful lake.

Mikas stood at the lake's edge next to me, studying the waterfall with his hands folded behind his back. Would my proposal to leave tonight surprise him, or did he suspect my motives for our trip to the shop? His expression gave nothing away.

With one last look at the waterfall, I turned my steps again in the direction of the market sign. Slug followed about four or five meters behind us.

"It would make the most sense to pick up your perfume first," Mikas said as we walked, making no attempt to not be overheard. He glanced down at me, his eyes twinkling despite how irritated he looked. "Perishable food items should be last."

Some of my unease faded and a warm, bubbly feeling swelled in my heart. If he wanted to go to the perfume shop, maybe he *did* want to talk in private. Maybe he did want to leave.

"I think so too." I bit my lip to keep from smiling. "I'll try not to buy too much for you to have to carry back."

"Next time, you may have to request your purchases be delivered," he said, his voice loud for Slug's benefit. "Or commit to only buying what you can carry yourself."

I knew somewhere beneath that spiky exterior he had a sense of humor. I wanted to see more of it. And I wanted to hear him laugh.

The market was even busier tonight than on our previous visit. I followed in Mikas's wake as he made his way through the crowd, with Slug still trailing us.

Long before we reached the perfume shop, I heard the familiar sound of the Sirrah's breathtaking singing even over the loud chatter and shouts of shoppers, shopkeepers, and other performers. The uneasiness in my stomach and tension in my shoulders lessened immediately—enough that I noticed it.

The last time we'd been here, listeners in the vicinity had seemed eerily enthralled. Simply because her singing was so exquisite? Or did she have some power, or even magic, that made her voice literally captivating and reduced negative emotions? I hadn't thought to ask Mikas at the time. If so, that would add to her value for those who thought of people in those kinds of terms.

We paused outside the perfume shop to join the crowd of listeners and drop coins into the Sirrah's collection box. Once again Mikas made a generous donation. I gave half of what I had in my bag, in case it was my last opportunity to do so. Truly, her voice was like nothing I'd ever heard.

Out of the corner of my eye, I spotted Slug leaning against the wall of the metaphysical shop next door, staring at the Sirrah with a sneer. Who could listen to such a beautiful voice without being moved? The sort of person who could know Mikas and think he'd want to be a raider, I supposed.

Reluctantly, I slipped away from the crown of listeners and into Ycari's shop with Mikas. The doors were closed tonight, so once we were inside I could no longer hear the Sirrah or any market noise. Slug took up a position just past the shop's front windows.

"Isla!" Ycari came flying out of the back hallway, beaming at us, the feathers on the crown of her head ruffling with joy. "And Mikas! My lovelies, how are you this evening?"

"Happy to be here," I said fervently. "Very excited to see what perfume you've made for me."

"Oh, yes, yes! I have made you truly a masterpiece." She shooed us toward the back hallway. "You'll want to experience it fully, I am sure. You must stay at least an hour, my lovelies. The scent will develop as you wear it. I must have your full approval of every note of the scent."

"Did you include the Centenian gregarus?" I asked. "And the Solani violet?"

"Oh, the *violet*," she said, with a knowing smile. "The violet! Of course, of course. That is why you must stay for the full hour. The violet takes time to develop, lovelies." She craned her neck to look at Mikas. "You will not mind waiting with her?"

"I will not mind at all," Mikas rumbled.

My heart leapt.

"Wonderful." Ycari ushered us into the same sampling room as before.

On the counter was a breathtaking pink crystal bottle with a stopper in a strange swirling shape. Next to it was a fabric pouch and a wooden box carved with the same design as the stopper.

With so much of my focus on trying to get away from Nubo and Onat'ras, I'd almost forgotten I was going to get a bottle of real Engareni perfume made by a master perfumer.

I'd never bought something for myself that was so purely indulgent. I'd never had the means. And I hadn't believed I deserved such things until I'd lived free and happy on Fortusia and started to figure out who I was and wanted to be after a lifetime of pain, fear, and danger. This perfume was a symbol of a better life I'd once thought I'd never have.

I didn't regret commissioning the perfume—not one bit. Some things were worth far, far more than their price.

"I hope you love your perfume, Isla," Ycari said, dipping her head to me, her expression sympathetic as if she knew what I was thinking. Perhaps she did. "Three, six, four."

"Three, six, four," I repeated dutifully.

Ycari squawked excitedly and closed the door to the hallway, leaving us alone.

I turned to go to the counter to claim my perfume and found Mikas standing behind me.

His stoic, granite-like façade had evaporated. To my utter astonishment, his expression was now so tender and unguarded that he was nearly unrecognizable.

What in the worlds had come over him? Was this the same stoic, nearly emotionless man who'd watched me sing, listened to me chatter, and served me brandy and berries nearly every night for three months?

Served me *brandy* and *berries*.

Maybe it was the wonder and awe created by the Sirrah's singing combined with the grim reality of her precarious life as having a prized talent, or how gently Mikas had held my hand the last time we were in this shop, or thinking of the brandy and berries in combination with this sudden tenderness that made me consider the possibility it wasn't just a nightly thoughtful gesture between colleagues and friends.

And if it wasn't that…

I sucked in a breath. Great gods above and below, how dense could I be?

He'd quietly offered me food and drink, again and again, as I sat at the bar ever watchful, ever on guard, and yet utterly oblivious to what was quite literally right under my nose all this time:

Mikas.

CHAPTER 14

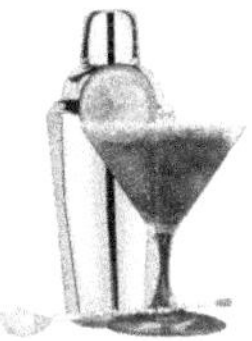

MIKAS

Isla stared up at me, her lovely violet eyes wide and expression suddenly vulnerable for one of the few times since we had met.

"Oh," she said and sat down hard.

If there had not been a couch behind her, she might have ended up sitting on the floor—or nearly so, as I would have caught her. She clasped her hands tightly in her lap as if attempting to hide how they trembled.

I did something I had longed to do for what seemed like an eternity: I knelt in front of her.

"May I touch your hand?" I asked.

She took a shaky breath. "Yes."

Moving cautiously so I did not startle her, I covered her much-smaller hands with my own. Her skin felt like silk against my rougher, scaly flesh. The intimacy of this touch made my hearts flutter.

"The last time we were in this room, my scent told you I feel safe here," Isla said, with a wry smile that faded all too quickly.

Her gaze searched my face. "Between that and all the offerings of berries and brandy and the fact you're kneeling in front of me, I suppose I know what's going on. But why don't you tell me, so there's no misunderstanding?"

I had never seen any sign that she understood the significance of providing her food and drink, but perhaps she had just now realized those gestures were more than mere politeness. And if she knew that on Fortusia a true mate knelt before their beloved, she now suspected the secret I had harbored for so long.

She did not seem angry, dismayed, or repulsed, which was an enormous relief. Her wide eyes, shaking hands, and sweet scent revealed how dumbfounded and flustered she was.

"I believe you are my true mate," I said, my throat so tight that my voice was hoarse. "Or rather, in my hearts and soul I know you to be."

Her little gasp and the shimmer of tears in her eyes made my hands tighten on hers.

"Do you know about Fortusian physiology?" I asked, keeping my tone gentle. "Should I explain?"

She swallowed audibly. "I know about true mates. I'm not an expert," she added quickly. "But I understand what that means. Your body recognized me as biologically compatible."

"It is more than that," I said. "Biological compatibility is only part of the call of a true mate. Our physiology draws us to one whose entire being compliments and resonates with our own in every way, and for whom we offer the same comfort. I think of it less as biological compatibility and more as..." I hesitated.

"Like what?" Isla prompted.

The soldier I had once been, and still was to some degree, protested that I was baring my belly and throat to this woman as I had never done with anyone. Before I met Isla, I could not have imagined doing so, much less going to my knees without a second thought with all my hopes and dreams hanging on her every look and word.

I had not chosen to go to war, or to be injured in battle, or to be shipped home with a medal of valor worth no more than the materials used to make it, but I *had* chosen a quiet life tending bar in Onat'ras, subsisting on tips and living in a small apartment alone with my memories. Had I not done so, I would not have been present when a rainbow-haired human woman came in early one afternoon hoping for an audition. If that did not prove the power of choices, I did not know what would.

And so I chose to speak the truth, and only the truth, to Isla, with my hearts pounding so hard they threatened to escape my ribcage.

"Happiness," I said. "Contentment and safety. And peace."

Gently, she withdrew her hands from mine and leaned forward, her forearms resting on her thighs.

"You're a smart man," she said, with a faint smile. "Observant. Well-trained. And on top of that, your senses tell you a lot about me. So it won't be any surprise to hear I've never had any of those things you're offering."

No, it was not a surprise to hear the depths of her loneliness and pain, but my hearts ached all the same.

"What have you known?" I asked, as if I had not already guessed.

"Mostly fear and danger." She flexed her right wrist. A small but deadly dagger dropped into her palm. She spun it several times without needing to look at it.

In the middle of the third spin, my hand shot out and took the dagger away.

"Nicely done, Mikas." She glanced at my palm, where a thin line of green blood welled. "You caught some of the blade, though."

"Only barely." The little flash of pain was inconsequential to me. "A very fine dagger, and you are very skilled with it."

"I have to be." She retrieved her dagger and returned it to the sheath under her long sleeve. "I've lived in the shadows and by the blade. Much like you when you were a soldier."

The ability to be honest with Isla after so many months of feigning only friendly interest filled me with joy. And truly, her perceptiveness and intelligence caused me to admire her all the more.

Her smile faded. "I'd ask why you've never said a word about me being your true mate, but I think I've worked it out. Nubo made some threats, am I right?"

"Yes." Anger made my chest rumble.

"Damn him." Isla ran her fingertips over mine, sending a shiver of desire down my spine. "He has to steal what he wants because no one will have him otherwise. Pathetic little man."

I had never thought of Nubo in that way, but she was right. I did not pity him and never would, but he *was* a pathetic little man who happened to be the size and weight of a Hardanian mule-ox.

It had not escaped my notice that Isla had steered the conversation away from her past, so she was not yet comfortable enough with me to reveal her history beyond a few vague references. Or perhaps she was not just worried about her own secrets.

She bowed her head. Her beautiful hair tumbled over her shoulders, forming a shimmery, rainbow curtain that hid her face. "It's been so hard," she whispered.

The scent of her tears filled me with the desire to hold and comfort her, but I stayed where I was because I did not know if she wanted my touches.

"All I've wanted since the other night was a few minutes of peace with you away from Nubo's surveillance," she added. "Because you are my friend."

She fell silent for a while.

"I think I knew," Isla said finally, her voice quiet. She raised her head and met my gaze, her face streaked with tears. I yearned to kiss them away. "Subconsciously, I mean. I always looked forward to ending my set and coming to the bar to drink and talk with you. Those were my most peaceful hours, even though I still had to be on my guard. I know humans don't have true mates, but we still have instincts. I guess mine were doing their job. They told me you were safe."

Warmth and joy spread through my body. I took her hand and bowed my head over it. "That is the greatest compliment I have ever received, Isla. If all I could be to you is a place of safety, I would accept it."

"Give me a chance to process it all." She tipped my chin up with her free hand. "I will admit, it doesn't feel as overwhelming as I would have thought."

I could not help myself; I moved closer, nestled my head in her lap, and closed my eyes so I could lose myself in her scent and the sensation of her dress and skin against my face. My chest rumbled in contentment.

"I like that sound you make," she murmured, running her fingers through my hair and along the back and sides of my neck. Nothing had ever felt so good as her caress. "Will you be offended if I say it sounds like you're purring?" she asked.

"No." My voice was barely a whisper. "I am not offended."

For a long, blissful time, her fingertips explored my scalp and the back of my neck, stroking my scaly skin and twirling my hair languidly between her fingers. When she slipped her hand into the opening on the back of my shirt and gently caressed my spines, my knees grew weak. Gods above.

"Can I ask what the source is of your nonhuman DNA?" she asked.

Her tone was curious and affectionate, so I did not feel self-conscious or resistant to replying as I might have been with anyone else.

"I am an amalgamation," I said. "As you may have guessed, I

have primarily reptilian characteristics. These come from the Pallasian bosor. I also have genetic material taken from mammalian species on J'Nora and Muravai."

Isla's hand stilled. "The bosor?"

I raised my head. She appeared startled, but not afraid or dismayed.

Even so, I was quick to add, "I have fangs, but I do not have venom. You do not need to fear me in any way, Isla. I swear it."

"I believe you." She urged me to rise to my knees again and cupped my face with her hands. I leaned into her touch.

Her smile turned mischievous. "You've been honest with me, so I'll be honest with you: I wasn't thinking about you having venom. I probably *should* have been, but I wasn't. I was thinking about a very different characteristic of Pallasian bosors."

Before I could process her words, she slid from the couch to my lap, her knees astride my thighs. I caught her, my hands under her hips. My hearts thundered in my chest.

Her expression solemn, she reached up and tucked my hair behind my ears. "Lift me up a bit," she said. "Let me try something."

I did as she asked, reveling in all the wondrous sensations of holding her in my arms as her inner thighs pressed against my abdomen.

She slipped her hand through my hair to cup the back of my head, drew me close, and kissed me.

Her lips were perfect and soft and she tasted of brandy and jampa berries and *Isla*. Even my most vivid fantasies had not done justice to her kiss.

Everything else in the universe faded away.

I had never kissed a human woman before. In fact, I did not recall kissing any member of any species. Humans were not unique in the galaxy for their desire to touch their lips, but I had never bedded anyone who shared that trait. And I found myself immensely grateful for that.

Isla was the sole proprietor of my lips, along with every other part of my body—including my chest, which rumbled louder with each passing moment until my entire body vibrated against her.

Her mouth yielded under mine, and the tip of her little tongue licked at my lips. I followed her lead and discovered an entire new universe of pleasures and tastes. She even cautiously flicked her tongue along the edges and points of my fangs. I growled. She shivered—but in desire, not in cold or fear. The scent of her need overtook everything else.

For several heartsbeats, I knew nothing else but that siren call and my hunger for her. Blood rushed to my cocks. Luckily, I was holding her well above my lap. I did not wish to startle or frighten her with my arousal.

When she broke the kiss and drew back, I did not resist, but I did not want the moment to end. My chest heaved and my hands trembled with the force of my need.

"I liked that," she said with a wistful smile. Her words were quite unnecessary since her racing heart, rapid breathing, and sweet scent had already told me so.

She rested her head against my shoulder. I held her gently with one arm around her back and the other underneath her, my nose nestled into the crook of her neck and shoulder to drink in her scent.

"If I'd known, I wouldn't have sung 'Warm Waters' tonight," she murmured against my chest. "Or ever joked with you about what people yearn for. Or thought to myself that you weren't the type to yearn. I've never been more wrong."

"Please do not apologize." I caressed her back. "I enjoy that song very much. And you did not know what I held in my hearts. I could not show it."

"Because of Nubo." She looked up, her eyes fiery in a way that stirred heat within me. "He's scum. But we only have this room for an hour at most. I don't want to waste it talking about *him*."

I was more than happy to forget our employer for now. "Speaking of this room, who is Madame Ycari?" I asked. "Is she really a perfumer?"

"She is. Credentialed and certified by the Guild on Engaren. The plaques are on display in the shop." Isla studied me. "She is also more than that."

"Just like you." I took a chance and kissed her again, this time gently. "I would like to know how you came to be on Fortusia, Isla, and who is a danger to you."

"Another time." She surprised me by running her nose and then her lips along my jaw. The brush of her mouth on my sensitive skin made my cocks harden nearly to the point of pain. "You said my scent tells you a lot about me. Do you like it?"

"*Like* is not the correct word." My voice sounded strained, even to my own ears. "For me, your scent is captivating. It transforms me. I am content in my soul when I smell you."

"Just content?" She repeated her slow journey along my jaw, and now my rumble took on a desperate, dangerous edge. "I think you might feel more than that."

I hungered for her so deeply and so intensely that I could think of little else…save the fact I would do nothing unless I knew what precisely she wished me to do. I was no ravening creature like Nubo or the Hardanian I had dumped on the street earlier in the week.

"Isla." I leaned back, though putting any distance between us made my hearts ache. We had only these few stolen minutes to talk, to touch each other. I knew we had to plan what we would do next, but my body sang of her and my need drowned out nearly everything else.

"Tell me the truth." Isla touched my lower lip with her fingertips. "What do you yearn for, Mikas?"

You. Always you.

"What do *you* yearn for?" I countered. "You know what is in my hearts; I have told you."

"I want a home," she said without hesitation, and my hearts broke at the poignant simplicity of her words. "I'm tired of running."

Despite the ache in my chest created by those words, I recalled something I had heard long ago from a friend who had found his true mate and a piece fell into place.

"You asked what it means to be true mates, beyond biological compatibility," I said. "I said peace and contentment."

"And safety." She tilted her head. "And I suppose I could feel those with you. I suppose I already do," she amended. "Because I felt them with you as my friend, before this."

"But there is something else," I said, and now the words tumbled out in a rush. "I have just realized how I feel in your presence. You are my home. And if you can accept me as your own, I will be yours."

She stared at me.

"What is a home but a place of safety, contentment, and peace?" I pressed. "It is a place, yes, but it is more than that. It is a feeling. It is the difference between the place you reside and the place where your heart is full."

"My heart is already full of bad memories and pain." She swallowed hard. "I'm not sure it has room for much else."

"Then I will dedicate my life to replacing the hurts of the past with joys and new memories, if you will let me." I cupped her face with my palm. "I would like a chance to try, but it is your choice."

She smiled. "Somehow, I knew you'd say that." She blessed me with a gentle kiss. "I choose to let you try," she whispered, her lips against mine.

My hearts soared and I found myself speechless.

"We still have some time," Isla added, her eyes twinkling.

"Will you give me a sample of what kind of new memories you'd like us to make?"

I thought of Nubo's threats and Kona, who stood outside the shop's doors waiting for us to emerge and finish our market shopping under her watchful eye. And then she would report everything she had seen to Nubo.

"I do not want to return to our apartments and jobs as if nothing has changed between us," I said, my voice guttural. "I do not want to live like that anymore. I do not want to live without you."

Isla's smile faded. I cursed myself for making her heart heavy, but her disquiet did not last for long.

Her gaze flicked to the blank wall behind me, then returned to my face. She rested her hand on the back of my neck. Her gentle touch drew a rumble from me.

"Do you trust me, Mikas?" she asked.

I did not have to think about my reply. "Yes."

"Okay." She took a deep breath. "Is there anything in your apartment you can't leave behind?"

Leave behind? As in, if we were to depart tonight with only the clothes on our backs? My hearts raced, but not in trepidation or disquiet—only in anticipation.

My belongings were few and I had no particular attachment to any of them. The only thing I possessed that could not be easily replaced was my military medal and that was nothing more than a reminder of years and pain I would rather forget. Why I still had it, I did not know. There was no better reason to rid myself of it than leaving with Isla.

"No," I stated. "There is nothing I will miss."

"Me neither. That used to make me sad, but not anymore." Isla laced the fingers of her free hand through mine. No easy trick, as my hand was so much larger. "We're leaving tonight, Mikas," she said. "You, Brae, and me. Ycari is arranging it. So trust me and forget about Nubo. Only think about you and me."

I thought of that strange exchange about flowers when we arrived at the shop tonight. Isla's tone when she had said *Centenian gregarus* and *Solani violet* and Ycari's response had made me suspect these phrases were code for something. So Isla had already planned a departure? Whatever her plan was, I would follow my beautiful mate.

With her hand on mine, she guided my fingers up her thigh, inching closer to her hip.

Gods, her sweet scent was more intoxicating than any ale or liquor I had ever served and infinitely more precious. My fingertips dug into her skin. I was careful to keep my claws sheathed.

"Yes, hold me like that." She dipped her head to kiss the corner of my jaw where my skin was thinnest and most sensitive. I growled and trembled with need.

But for all my desire, and despite her obvious arousal, I feared Isla's reaction to my nonhuman attributes. She had seen me shirtless many times, but never nude.

"My anatomy is not human," I said before I lost my nerve. "My body may frighten you. Even horrify you."

Her teeth closed gently on the small ridge that ran down the side of my neck. I nearly lost all control at that delicious combination of pleasure and pain. "I doubt it," she said, and licked the spot she had bitten.

Gods above, this woman.

"I don't frighten easily." Now she was smirking, as if my trembling pleased her. "And I think I'll find your anatomy very much to my liking."

She ground herself against me with a moan. Her sweet pussy was so near my cocks, separated only by layers of fabric. A wave of blinding heat rolled through me from the soles of my feet to my scalp.

"Mikas," she pleaded, her lips against my neck. "I see how much you want me. Don't hold back. Touch me, *please*."

I would have crawled across a Solani desert carrying trunks full of stones on my back just for the privilege.

My fingers slid higher beneath her dress and found the dampness between her legs that had soaked into her underwear —and a trace of silken liquid that had escaped the material to run down her inner thigh. This was her response to my touches, my adoration, my own need. No treasure could be greater, except her heart.

The moment my fingertips touched that sweet liquid, every other thought evaporated but one: *my Isla.*

In my soul, my primal, beastly hunger for my true mate raised its head and roared.

CHAPTER 15

ISLA

As Mikas's fingertips grazed the delicate skin of my inner thigh and the edge of my underwear, his vertical pupils suddenly dilated, turning his eyes all black.

In a blink I was on my back beneath him, the back of my head cradled by his enormous hand. As inhumanly fast as he'd moved, he'd made sure I didn't hit the floor, and he braced himself with his other hand so he didn't crush me with his weight.

He ran his nose along my hairline, down the side of my neck, and across my collarbone, growling low, his claws and teeth bared in a way that made me arch up against him.

I felt no fear at all. This, *finally*, was Mikas. Not the reserved, grumpy man he'd pretended to be as long as I'd known him, but the real Fortusian male who'd found his true mate and wanted her with all his hearts and soul. And body too, if the hard heat pressed against my thigh was any indication.

Simply touching me between my legs had done more than

ignite something within him; it had uncaged him. And I would be lying if I said it hadn't uncaged something in me too.

Pallasian bosors were one of the apex predators of the taiga regions of that planet. Their DNA had no doubt helped make Mikas a fearsome soldier. And as a mate, he would be primal. The thought sent a crashing wave of desire through me, and I felt myself dripping for him already.

How he'd restrained himself for so long, I had no idea, unless Nubo had made explicit threats against me if Mikas acted on his desires. The bastard. I hated him so much more now knowing he'd kept us apart.

I ran my fingers through Mikas's thick hair and held him still so I could look into his pitch-black eyes. His body quaked and the claws of his hand that wasn't holding my head scraped on the floor.

"Isla," he grated. "You are my world."

I drew him down for a kiss, then nipped his chin lightly with my teeth. "Show me."

In a flash he moved down my body, pushing my dress up to my waist. I brushed his hands aside and sat up to pull it off over my head. As much as I wanted him, I had enough ability to think rationally to make sure I had intact clothing for when we left the shop.

He knelt between my knees as his gaze caressed me, traveling from my face down to my breasts, over my abdomen, between my thighs, and back up. I found myself caught between self-consciousness while he studied every inch of me as if committing my body to memory and my own desire to look him over in the same way.

When I reached for my arm sheath, he caught my hand and kissed my fingers. "Leave it be," he rasped.

Did my skills with a blade arouse him? If so, I liked that very much. I'd met my share of insecure males who found fierce women intimidating. But if it was true that to be mates we must resonate with each other in every way, then of course he would find my ability to fight appealing. His erection showed clearly through the fabric of his pants. I licked my lips.

I used to curse fate very frequently. But if fate had brought us together, then it had done very well by me in the end.

"You are glorious." His eyes gleamed. "A dream."

"Not a dream." I eyed his shirt. "How do I remove this?"

He unfastened the collar, separated the front of the shirt along the seam, and slid it off over his shoulders and spines with practiced ease.

I'd seen his bare chest many times—more times than any other person's chest in my lifetime, in fact. But never like this, as a lover.

And I'd certainly never been able to explore the contours of his hot flesh. I ran my hands over the hard lines of his pectoral and abdominal muscles, brushed my fingertips across his pierced nipples, and down to the taut skin just above his groin.

Because his claws aroused me so much, I scraped my nails down his chest. They didn't do so much as scratch his skin, but judging by the way he rumbled and the heat and throbbing hardness against my thigh, he enjoyed the sensation very much.

"I want to see all of you," I rasped. "Touch you. Taste you."

"You will." The growly edge in his voice made me shiver hard with need. "But first, I will make you call my name. I have dreamed of hearing it."

Imagining myself writhing under him—or on top of him, or with his face between my legs—elicited a gush of wetness from my pussy.

Despite his obvious arousal, he took his time. His fingertips traveled over my shoulders and along my collarbone, caressing and exploring. Parts of my body I'd never considered sensual came alive at his touch, sending quivers of need sizzling through me.

He cupped my breasts, which had never seemed small until they rested in his hands.

"Your skin is so delicate," he said as he stroked his thumbs lightly over their roundness. "I fear I may hurt you if I lose control."

"I don't fear you," I said, and then gasped when the pads of his thumbs ghosted over my nipples. "I trust you, Mikas. You won't hurt me." I arched my back. "Please, more."

He strummed my nipples with his thumbs. Each touch made me quiver and whimper with need. And then he pinched them —carefully at first, and then harder.

"Use your mouth," I pleaded. "Your tongue."

His lips closed on my left nipple, sucking as he flicked the sensitive nub with his raspy tongue. I groaned and slipped my fingers into his hair to hold him close.

"Please," I gasped, my chest heaving. "Mikas..."

He slid his hand down my stomach and between my legs. I almost screamed as his fingertips caressed me over the thin fabric of my underwear.

"You are so wet," he murmured, laving my nipples with his long tongue.

I mewled when his fingers brushed over my swollen clit. "Yes."

He raised his hand to his mouth and licked his fingers. "Delicious," he rasped. "I want more."

I raised my hips, intending to slide my underwear off. Instead, he unsheathed his claws, slit the fabric down both sides, and ripped them the rest of the way off. No one had ever done something so deliciously decadent with me. My toes curled and I groaned.

"This is a precious gift," he said, running his nose over my tattered underwear. "This is your desire, your need for me."

My arousal made my legs and hands tremble. "Mikas..."

"Already you call my name." He set my underwear aside and

grasped my thighs, pushing them up and open for his hungry stare. A gush of wetness traveled down my slit.

"Beautiful," he rasped. "Delicate and sweet as a flower. And with two perfect holes. I am made for you, Isla."

Oh, gods. The moment he'd mentioned his bosor DNA, I'd suspected what was hidden beneath his pants. Now I knew. The thought of it made me gush again for him. And with my legs wide open, he could witness the effect his words and gaze had on me firsthand.

"Yes," Mikas grated. "You are needful. I will sate you."

He scooped me up, put me on the sofa, and pulled me toward him until I lay on my back and my ass was on the edge of the cushion. Then he pushed my legs open again, lowered his head, and licked me very, very slowly, from my asshole all the way up to my swollen clit.

I screamed.

I writhed in his grip as his mouth delved everywhere along the length of my slit, exploring, sucking, and tonguing me without mercy. Each time I cried out, he focused his attention on that place until he reduced me to nearly incoherent begging.

Finally, he slipped his tongue into my pussy, first swirling its rough tip around the sensitive opening and then spearing me with its length. I rode his tongue and face, crying out his name and pleading for more.

As my release neared, I began to rub my clit, but he brushed my hand away and mimicked my movements. I threw my head back and wailed as his hot fingers circled and rubbed at the swollen, sensitive pearl.

My cries grew louder, and a coil of heat built and built…and then his tongue curled up and rubbed inside me, perfect and rough, and I came with a cry, my back arching off the sofa and legs shaking in his grip. "Mikas. Gods, Mikas."

He withdrew his tongue slowly, holding my legs wide and

licking me inside and out as he did so. "Sweet and perfect," he murmured as my chest heaved and I trembled.

He licked all the most delicate skin along my quivering slit as if he wanted to drink every drop of my release. Each little flick of his tongue made me cry out.

"I thought I could not love your voice more than when you sang 'Warm Waters,'" he added, his breath hot between my thighs, "but I find the sound of my name when you come the most beautiful song of all."

He bit the inside of my thigh. Not hard enough to break the skin, but enough to hurt and leave a mark, and I liked it.

"Mikas," I whimpered.

He smiled—an almost wicked, very toothy smile that was all the more arousing because it was so near my dripping pussy.

"That is what I want," he said, and licked me once more to make me cry out. "My name, and me, as what you plead for."

"Then you should—" I began.

Behind Mikas, a red circle lit up on the wall. It blinked rapidly three times, then faded. My haze of pleasure vanished as if I'd been dunked in icy water.

Moving so fast that he nearly blurred, Mikas leapt to his feet, pulled me up off the sofa, and put himself between me and the door to the sampling room. His spines bristled, and he planted his feet shoulder-width apart as he braced himself to fight.

My legs shook and my slickness dripped down my thigh. If he hadn't been holding me, I might not have been able to stay on my feet.

My wrist chronometer said less than an hour had passed. Had Nubo's people stormed into the shop demanding to know where we were before Ycari had a chance to arrange our escape? Possibly so, if she had activated the warning instead of coming to the room herself.

Brae, I thought. *What's going on?*

I'm not sure, he said, his voice in my head crackling with tension. *Slug is still outside the shop, but a pair of human men just went in and are talking to Madame Ycari. They're two of Nubo's watchers we've seen before. They're very angry. Are you on your way out of the shop?*

We will be in a few minutes. I sighed aloud. *We'll be going out the back way. Together.*

Good. I'll keep watching and let you know if more trouble comes.

The situation called for a clear head, so I tried to slow my breathing and think about what needed to be done.

"Two of Nubo's people are in the shop confronting Ycari." I touched Mikas's clenched fist, which nearly vibrated in fury. "Our time's up. We need to go."

His snarl made my skin prickle. "No one will lay a hand on you. I will not allow it."

Part of me—the part that had taken care of herself for a long time without help from anyone but Brae—resented his words. But he knew I could hold my own, and it was nice to matter to someone so much that they would put themselves in harm's way to keep me safe.

Still, I didn't need him to be a hero right now. "Mikas," I said, very firmly. "Look at me."

He tore his angry gaze away from the door to do as I asked. His expression softened, though the tension in his body didn't abate in the least.

"I understand your instincts are telling you to protect your mate," I told him. "But I need you to listen to me and follow my instructions so we can get out of here."

He snarled at the door. We heard nothing from the shop since this room was soundproof, but trouble would be headed our way soon if it wasn't already.

"You said you trust me," I reminded him. "Now I am asking you to keep trusting me."

He bent his head to kiss my forehead. "I trust you, Isla."

"Good." I bent and picked up my dress. "We're going to let Madame Ycari buy us time and leave out the back way."

"But will she be safe?" he asked, his frown deepening. "If our employer has sent people for us, or decides to come himself, they will not have come alone or unarmed."

"Ycari isn't alone or unarmed either." I couldn't reveal everything about Ycari's shop or allies, but I touched his hand and added, "If Nubo knows anything about her, he might try to demand she turn us over, but he won't want his people to threaten her."

That statement made Mikas's eyebrows go up, but he picked up his shirt. "Then I will follow your lead."

I put my dress on over my head. When I brushed my hair out of my eyes, it was just in time to see him stuff my torn underwear into his pants pocket.

"A souvenir," he said at my look, with another toothy grin. "And we must not leave evidence behind."

"True." I slung my cross-body bag over my head and went to the counter, where my perfume waited, untouched. I put the bottle carefully in the fabric pouch, sealed it inside the wooden box, and put the box in my bag. Then I went to the blank wall perpendicular to the room's only visible door.

I rested my fingertips where the warning light had been. Trailing my fingers along the wall, I took three steps toward the back of the room, slid my hand up six centimeters, and then took four more steps without taking my fingertips off the wall. I pressed my palm to the wall there.

A door slid aside to my right, revealing a narrow, well-lit passageway.

"Three, six, four. Ah, I see now what Ycari meant by that." Mikas joined me at the doorway. He took my hand and squeezed gently. "I very much look forward to learning what your profession was before you became a singer in a bar."

"I've had a lot of different professions." I glanced up at him with a ghost of a smile. His eyes gleamed in the low light. "Not many by my own choice. But this one—" I gestured at the passageway "—and being a singer, I chose. Watch our backs."

He bent and withdrew a blade of his own from his right boot. A Hardanian scythe-knife, in fact, gorgeous and deadly. And all the gods above and below, the sight of it gripped in his hand and the way he showed his fangs made me quiver where his tongue had been only minutes ago.

"I will watch our backs," he said.

CHAPTER 16

MIKAS

I followed Isla into the narrow corridor. The hidden door slid soundlessly closed and sealed behind us.

My shoulders nearly brushed the walls and the top of my head was only a few centimeters shy of the ceiling. Still, wherever Isla went, I would go—whether it be a secret escape from an Engareni perfume shop or a planet far from here.

My sharp ears caught a low hum from the room we had just left. I frowned and tilted my head to listen.

"The room's air and surfaces are purified between guests," Isla explained. "It's a necessary step to ensure each customer gets exactly the scent they want."

"And it is quite handy for removing traces of anyone who has passed through," I observed. "An ideal setup."

Despite the danger of our situation, she smiled. "Yes, it is."

I took advantage of our closeness and ran my nose over her hair. To think I might be able to do so whenever I wanted and no longer had to hide either my feelings or desires…what bliss.

I wanted to know what she planned for us to do, but her most personal scents and tastes remained on my fingers and tongue, a decadent reminder of the intimacy we had just shared —and that our time had been interrupted. I also could not forget that her torn underwear was in my pocket, or that beneath her dress her sweet, bare pussy dripped for me.

"Isla," I ground out, pressing my hand to the wall beside her head. The cold metal helped me focus on our need to get away instead of my need for her. "Where will we go now?"

"We have to choose." Her expression turned grim. "I know I asked if you had anything you can't leave behind, but it's not fair for me to decide for you."

"You are not deciding for me." I cupped her face with my hand. "All my instincts tell me we cannot go back and we must avoid Nubo and his people. To do that, we must leave Onat'ras at least. To be safe, we should leave Fortusia. I do not believe Nubo's reach extends beyond this planet."

She rested her forehead on my chest. "I know," she said, her voice muffled by my shirt. "I knew it couldn't last. I wanted to believe I could live in this beautiful city, on this beautiful world, but in my heart I knew this would be a stop, not a destination."

My hearts ached once again. I had already accepted Isla as my home, but she could not be expected to feel the same. Certainly not until—or *unless*—she truly accepted me as her mate, and perhaps not even then. Human physiology was not the same as Fortusian. We might share much of our DNA, but her body did not respond to mine the way mine did to hers. More than anything, I wanted to find a way to give her the same peace and contentment her presence gave me.

I knelt in front of her again, this time for a very different reason. She let out a little sound of surprise, tinged with dismay.

"I do not wish to cause you pain or regret," I said, and kissed her hand. "I am sorry I have upended the life you built here."

Isla startled me by kneeling too. The corridor was barely

wide enough to accommodate us, so I sat back on my heels and pulled her onto my lap once more, her knees astride my thighs.

"You don't need to apologize." She cupped my face with both of her hands and stared directly into my eyes. "I *chose* to accept you and your feelings for me knowing full well that meant we had to get as far from Nubo as we could. It wasn't something I said in the heat of the moment."

"But if you like your life here—" I began.

She quieted me by resting her index finger on my lips.

"Do you think I'd trade how I feel about you—how I feel *with* you—for a gig as a singer in a bar?" she asked. "Because I wouldn't. I can feel sad about having to leave Fortusia *and* be happy to be your...mate. I'm working on that last part," she added with a wry smile. "Give me time."

"You may have all the time you need." I kissed her forehead. "There is no rush." I glanced at the doorway we had come through, then down the long corridor to where it turned and continued out of sight. "Where shall we go, Isla?"

She kissed my jaw, making my chest rumble. "If we want to leave Onat'ras, we need to go now," she said. "If we can make it to the Delta spaceport, Ycari has a contact there who can get us on an offworld transport using pseudonyms."

"Then we will get to the spaceport." I rose and lifted her to her feet.

"This hallway leads to a hidden exit on the side of a shop much closer to the market's exit." She slipped her hand into mine and tugged. "This way. We'll blend into the crowd and head for the port."

Knife at the ready, I followed, all my senses alert to any hint of danger. The silence and Isla's trust in Madame Ycari and her contact at the port did little to diminish my tension or my rage at the threat Nubo posed to not only our newfound happiness and Isla's safety.

But as we made our way quietly down the corridor, I

recalled Isla's skill with her dagger and the fearless way she looked at the Hardanian. That did not banish my anger or trepidation, but my boots returned to solid ground.

I would do whatever I must to ensure we made it safely away. Fighting was what I did—what I had always done. What better cause could I fight for than Isla and our future together?

Two turns and about twenty-five meters later, we reached the end of the tunnel and another sealed door. But when it came into sight, Isla's steps faltered.

"That orange light above the door is a warning," she said in answer to my unspoken question. "It means our way out of the market isn't clear. Ycari or someone she knows must have gotten word that Nubo's people are searching the whole area, not just the perfume shop and its immediate surroundings."

My spines bristled and tingled anew. "Nubo may be well-connected, but overt violence in the market itself, in front of many witnesses and law enforcement, seems unlikely," I said. "I feel we will be in the most danger once we leave the market area. Many of the streets between here and the Delta Port will be quiet this time of night."

She leaned against the wall and thought. "We could go through the market and head straight for the main boulevard where most of the tourists are. It will be packed with people. We could stick to the crowded areas and head for the Alpha Mega-port instead to book passage offworld on a commercial transport. I doubt even Nubo can prevent us from finding a cabin on a cruiser bound for who-knows-where." She looked up at me, a smile tugging at her lips. "Assuming, of course, you want to share a cabin with me..."

I scooped her up with one arm so I could bury my face against the side of her neck, where her scent was most powerful. "I would share a tent with you on a barren moon, my mate," I murmured, my lips against her skin. "And it would be heaven as long as you were in my arms."

"Well." She drew back to eye me, her smile so gentle that I had to lean against the wall to steady myself. "That is quite the statement of devotion. I'll have to do my best to make sure you don't regret making that pledge."

"I could never regret it." I kissed her temple and put her back on her feet. "To the port, then, Isla. And on to wherever the first ship we find with an available cabin may take us." A thought occurred to me. "Have you told Brae our plan?"

"Yes. He's keeping watch from above."

Quickly, she braided her long hair, perhaps anticipating the need to fight. As she did so, I reluctantly returned my knife to the sheath in my right boot, since I could not carry it openly in the market. I could draw it quickly again, but milliseconds might mean the difference between life and death.

From the market to the Alpha Megaport was a little more than a kilometer if we kept to the crowded streets. The distance had never seemed so close and yet so far.

She settled her bag in place and squared her shoulders. "Ready?"

"Almost." I stole one last kiss. "Now I am ready."

Smiling, she took a deep breath, ran two fingers down along the wall to the right of the door, tapped twice, and waited. I braced myself.

The door unsealed and slid aside, revealing an alcove and a wide alley between this shop and the next. The noise and chaos of the market, which I had not minded earlier, struck me almost like a physical blow after the quiet and stillness of both the sampling room and the corridor.

As the door closed and sealed behind us, I scanned the faces of shoppers passing through the alley, studying their body language with a soldier's practiced eye. No one seemed to pay us any particular notice other than a few casual glances. The alcove was a perfect place for a couple to steal a few moments together out of the stream of foot traffic. With the door now hidden, perhaps onlookers assumed we had stepped into the shadows for romantic reasons.

If only it were so. If only we were not running for our lives.

I affected a casual air and stayed close behind Isla as we joined the stream of shoppers and tourists. Rather than attract attention by running or walking briskly, my mate strolled from shop to shop, looking over the goods on display as we made our way toward the exit closest to the street that would lead to the boulevard.

Meanwhile, even with my spines flat, I had never felt quite so conspicuous. Despite her rainbow-colored hair, Isla blended in with the crowd. At least I was not the tallest person in the market, as I might have been on some other world. Most Fortusians were my height or even taller, and the market was packed. But if Nubo and his people were scanning the crowd looking for us, I would be easier to spot than my diminutive mate. I could do nothing for it though but keep watch for danger.

Just as the arch of the market's exit came into view, Isla paused suddenly. Her hand found mine and squeezed.

"Hello," said a small, very musical voice.

I peered over Isla's shoulder and was startled to see the little Sirrah who had sung so beautifully outside the perfume shop standing in front of us. She had donned a long gossamer coat over her dress and carried a small pack on her back that looked about the size to accommodate her collection box.

"There is a merchant this way with good wines to sell," the Sirrah said to Isla, her hands clasped in front of her. "The shop you like near the exit is no longer open."

The back of my neck prickled in warning. I slid a glance toward the market's exit and caught a glimpse of a hawk-like face in the shadows, waiting just outside the arch.

"Please show us to the wine merchant," Isla said, raising her chin in outward defiance, even as her hand trembled in mine.

I growled low, the sound a rumble in my chest.

To our left, a pair of expressionless human men I recognized as Nubo's employees were making their way through the crowd toward us. From the direction of the perfume shop, Kona approached, her gaze fixed on Isla and hands on her daggers.

I wanted to fight. I wanted to kill them all and get my mate to safety. We could do neither in this market full of witnesses and innocent bystanders. Rather than appearing casual, Kona and the others moved with a purpose, and I did not like the way they seemed to have a coordinated plan. My rage and worry made my stomach churn.

We followed the Sirrah.

She moved with grace through the endless stream of shoppers, weaving her way past a Fortusian dagger artisan's studio and a busy fruit and vegetable shop. My hearts pounded in my ears.

The third shop was indeed a wine merchant, but the sight of its signage and open doors did nothing to diminish my worry. How did we know who or what waited for us inside?

In my peripheral vision, the humans and Kona continued to close in on us. My grip tightened on Isla's hand, and I prepared to bolt with her at the slightest indication of betrayal by our little guide—whose delicate neck I would wring if she had led us into a trap.

All I wanted was to board a cruiser and share a cabin with my Isla, where I could spend our days of travel worshiping her and then every day after that doing the same. My hearts were set on this. My wounded soul had found its home and peace with my true mate. I would let nothing harm her as long as I drew breath.

This shop might be a dead end, quite literally. But Isla showed no sign of trepidation. She trusted the Sirrah—her scent and her body language told me so. And because she trusted, so must I.

As we approached the shop's doors, I caught a scent wafting

through the doorway that nearly made me stop in my tracks in surprise and confusion. I knew that scent and who it belonged to.

What he was doing in the market and why the Sirrah had brought us here I did not know, but we were about to find out.

CHAPTER 17

ISLA

THE AMOUNT OF TENSION IN MIKAS'S BODY MADE IT CLEAR HE didn't trust our guide and he certainly didn't think much of this wine shop as a way to escape the clutches of Nubo's agents. And the closer we got to the shop's doors, the less he seemed to like it.

I squeezed his hand and urged him to follow me, hoping he could tell I had faith we would find help at the wine merchant.

The Sirrah's sudden appearance out of the crowd had startled me, but the moment we'd locked gazes, I recognized a kindred soul. Survivors often recognized each other—or rather, recognized hyper-vigilance and the shadows in our eyes. She might not bear signs of captivity now, as Mikas had noted earlier, but she had faced some of the same horrors I once had. And like me, she had found a way to help those in need of safe passage.

The shop's sign out front was as bright as any other on the promenade. Inside, though, it was quiet and dimly lit, unlike most of the market. It must cater less to raucous tourists and more to locals interested in its offerings of expensive imported wines. And since those were outside my budget and I got my drinks for free at Zaa'ga, I'd never stepped foot inside until now.

With Mikas on my heels and the Sirrah in the lead, we entered the shop. The smell of warm, brackish water hit my nose before my eyes adjusted to the low light.

Rows and rows of bottles, pipes, and other containers in every shape and size imaginable lined the walls, which made sense for a wine shop. More surprising was a terrarium containing a small pool, towering plants, and heated rocks in the middle of the shop's main floor.

As the Sirrah stepped aside, a trio of large, squat, amphibious creatures emerged from the terrarium, waddling on wide, webbed feet. They left trails of water on the floor as they moved. My jaw dropped.

"Singer," the Prylothian in the center of the group croaked. He bobbed his head in greeting.

I'd never seen him outside Zaa'ga. And to my embarrassment, I hadn't really wondered what the bar's amphibious regular might have as a profession. Purveyor of fine wines wouldn't have been near the top of the list even if I had.

Utterly nonplussed, I echoed his head movement, hoping that was the proper response.

The Prylothian's cluster of eyes moved from my face to Mikas's. "Bartender," he croaked.

"Atlath," Mikas said, his tone cautious. "Why are we here?"

"Embassy." Atlath—whose name I hadn't known until this moment—gestured at his companions, who wore plasma guns in holsters and carried rather intimidating swords.

"This shop is on interplanetary ground," the Sirrah said in her musical voice. "Atlath is the Prylothian ambassador to Fortusia. And as this is his official place of residence, the shop and the land on which it sits is an embassy under Galactic Alliance and planetary law."

"Entry granted," Atlath croaked, indicating Mikas and me. Then he pointed out the doorway, where Slug stood, her hands resting on the daggers in sheaths on her thighs. Behind her, two stone-faced human men and a hawklike woman I didn't recognize also waited. "Entry denied," Atlath added, his voice now distinctly menacing. "Penalty… death."

The Prylothian guards raised their swords in unison and hissed, all their eyes fixed on the people standing at the door.

For the first time since our intimate moments in Madame Ycari's back room had been interrupted, I felt Mikas relax just a little.

"Thank you," he rumbled, with another bow of his head. "We are in your debt."

"There is no debt…between friends," Atlath croaked.

I leaned back against Mikas and let him take some of my weight. No sense pretending we weren't a couple now, and I trembled with a combination of adrenaline and nerves. The shop wasn't cold, but I shivered.

Keeping himself between me and the doorway in case our enemies decided to do something rash, Mikas wrapped his arm gently around my upper chest and rested his chin on top of my head. His warmth banished my chills.

"He knows where you are," a rough female voice said from behind us.

Mikas and I turned to see Slug toying with the handle of one of her daggers and smirking.

"You can't hide here forever," she continued, her tone mocking. "Your lives are worth nothing now. You might as well send them outside, Prylothian. You're only delaying the inevitable." Her dark gaze focused on my face. "If you beg, he might spare you, little human. A collar and chain would be better than the death that awaits you."

Mikas's growl vibrated through my body. The Sirrah let out

a hiss that made me wonder if despite her small stature she might be a fierce fighter herself.

"No," I said, my voice cold. "They wouldn't."

"Such defiance." Slug laughed. "I thought at first he wanted you for your beauty alone. Now I see the truth, little human. He'll enjoy breaking you."

The shop's wide doors beeped a warning and began to swing shut.

"The shop is closed," Atlath croaked. "Be...gone."

The door's edge passed within what looked like a centimeter of the Atolani's nose, but she didn't so much as blink, much less move as both doors closed and locked with an impressive *thunk* that reverberated through the floor.

The noise of the market vanished. The doors went from transparent to opaque, cutting us off from the sight of Nubo's henchmen. I sagged against Mikas and rested my forehead on his chest.

The Sirrah smiled up at us. "Such love," she said wistfully. "I still seek my mate. I know in my heart she is out there and our paths will one day cross."

"I hope you find her soon," I said, meaning every word. I didn't yet think of Mikas as my mate, and probably wouldn't for a while, but his presence was a wonderful comfort.

"I am sorry for the disruption to your store," Mikas said over my head, addressing Atlath. "But we are grateful for the refuge."

"No apology necessary." Atlath waddled closer to us, his cluster of eyeballs roving from Mikas to me and back. "You stay upstairs tonight. I will secure transport."

"Thank you," I said. "I'm not sure what we did to earn your help. I know you said no debts, but I feel we owe you, especially since you had to shut your store early."

"No debt," Atlath repeated, now gruff. "You sing beautifully. Mikas pours best wine. We are even."

The little Sirrah chirped. "You sing, Isla?"

My cheeks heated. "Nowhere near as beautifully as you. I sound like howling wingwolves compared to you."

She laughed, but Mikas bristled. "Isla sings just as well," he rumbled. "She is modest."

I did not sing as well as the Sirrah—not even remotely. But I appreciated that Mikas thought so.

"Can I have your name?" I asked the Sirrah.

"I am Pioni." She crouched in a kind of curtsy. "I am friend to Madame Ycari."

"I thought so. Thank you for your help, Pioni." I bit my lip. "Will you be in danger now that you've helped us?"

She trilled in what I realized was laughter. "No, I do not think so," she chortled. "I do not fear Nubo. He is a pest. Ycari and I are not bothered by pests."

"Nubo has dangerous friends," Mikas warned.

Pioni clasped her little hands in front of her chest and tilted her head as if debating how to answer. "I too have dangerous friends," she said, and by all the gods above and below, I believed her.

"Stairs," Atlath said to us, gesturing at the rear of the shop's retail area. "Level Three. Star Bird room. Rest tonight. You are safe here."

"Our deepest thanks," Mikas said, and guided me toward the door Atlath had indicated.

Behind us, Pioni chirped something in her native language. Atlath burbled in response, also not in Alliance Standard, so I had no idea what they said.

Once we were on the other side of the door and on our way upstairs, Mikas chuckled.

"What's funny?" I asked, nearly grumbling as I plodded up the steps. I was more tired than I'd realized and nauseated from so many surges of adrenaline.

"What Pioni said." Without missing a beat, he scooped me up. I squawked in surprise. He kissed my forehead and continued climbing the stairs cradling me in his arms. "She advised Atlath not to disturb us until tomorrow midday because we would be *busy*."

"Nosy Sirrah," I muttered. "I didn't realize it was so obvious how badly I want to get naked with you."

Mikas nearly missed a step, but regained his footing immediately and continued up the stairs at a much faster pace. Apparently, I wasn't the only one excited at the prospect of picking up where we'd left off in Ycari's back room.

On Level Three, we found the doors labeled in a language I didn't know—probably Prylothian. But as we entered the hallway, the nameplates next to the doors blinked out. When they lit up again, the words were Alliance Standard. A scanner must have identified us as not being from Atlath's native world.

The Star Bird room was the third doorway on the right. I waved my hand over the scanner next to the door. It slid open, revealing the dimly lit room beyond.

"Oh," I gasped.

Mikas carried me inside and put me on my feet. The door closed and locked behind us.

To call the room a *room* didn't do it justice. Half the suite was a much-larger version of the terrarium downstairs, complete with a pool, waterfall, and warm rocks heated both by lights and probably radiant heat.

There was also a well-stocked kitchen and a bedroom area near the terrarium with an absolutely enormous bed. The bathroom was as large as the bedroom, with both sonic and water-based cleansing systems. Personal care items catering to a variety of species, including humans, filled the shelves in the bathroom.

"A lovely suite designed for visiting dignitaries," Mikas observed after we'd explored our accommodations. We returned to the bedroom area, standing near the stone steps that led down to the pool and heated rocks. He rested his hands lightly on my shoulders. "But adaptable to shelter a pair of runaway lovers seeking safe harbor for the night."

"Calling us *runaway lovers* makes this seem like a romantic adventure." I craned my neck to look up at him. "Which I suppose it is. It didn't seem very romantic when we were trying to get to the market's exit and all the way to the Alpha Megaport without getting captured or killed, though. At that point, it just seemed scary."

"Yes." Gently, he turned me to face him. "It was scary, but now we are safe for the night." He kissed my forehead and guided me to the bed. "Lie down, Isla. You are exhausted."

I wanted to argue, wanted to follow through on what I'd said about getting naked with him, but now with my rush of adrenaline gone, I was painfully aware that I'd slept poorly for days, I wobbled on my feet from emotional and physical exhaustion, and my hands trembled because I'd had little to eat today besides that bowl of jampa berries.

I sat on the edge of the bed, intending to unfasten and remove my boots and take off my wrist sheath and dagger. Instead, I found myself falling onto my back to stare up at the ceiling. "I am so tired," I mumbled.

Clothing rustled, and then I felt tugs on my boots. I raised my head to see Mikas on his knees next to my feet. "You've really got to stop kneeling in front of me," I said with a sigh.

"No, I do not think I will stop kneeling before my mate." He kissed the inside of my left knee and slid my left boot off. He peered inside my boot and glanced up at me, his eyebrows raised. "How many daggers do you carry, Isla?"

"How many do *you* carry?" I shot back.

"Five." He set my boot aside and reached for the other one. "Approximately."

Chuckling, I dropped my head back onto the bed and closed my eyes.

Once my boots were off, he rose and removed my forearm

sheath. "Do you want me to look for sleepwear that might fit you?" he asked from beyond my closed eyelids. He set the sheath and dagger on what sounded like the small table next to the bed. "I believe the closet contains such items."

I had no energy to change clothes. "No," I murmured. "I'm fine sleeping in my dress."

For the next few minutes, he moved quietly around the room. Then the lights dimmed even further and I heard rustling nearby.

When I opened my eyes just enough to see Mikas, he stood next to the bed in a pair of sleep pants that I would have ripped off his body with my teeth if I'd had enough energy.

"You should be comfortable." He held up a tunic and pants that were a much-smaller version of what he wore. "I found some I think will fit you. I will help you change."

"All right." Sleepily, I sat up and raised my arms.

He slipped my dress off over my head, then put the tunic on in its place and got me into it, his hands gentle. Then he knelt, got my legs into the pants, and drew them up as far as they would go without me raising my hips or standing.

He lifted me with one arm, pulled the pants up to my waist with the other, and set me down. "Better?" he asked, straightening.

I barely heard him. At the moment, his lower abdomen was right in front of my face as I sat on the edge of the bed. The lightweight fabric of his sleep pants clung to the distinct shape of not one but two thick, partially aroused cocks.

Maybe I wasn't *too* tired. One tug on those loose pants, and…

No sooner had the thought crossed my mind than in one fluid movement, he scooped me up, drew back the covers, and settled me into the bed.

Thoughts of removing our sleepwear evaporated. "Oh, gods," I groaned, snuggling deeply into the bedding, which felt as soft as clouds. "The bed is a dream."

"Yes." He climbed into the bed beside me and drew the covers over us both. "Much softer than I prefer, but I believe I am tired enough not to notice." After a hesitation, he asked, "May I hold you while we sleep, Isla?"

"You'd better," I grumbled. "I didn't go through all this just to sleep by myself tonight."

Chuckling, he drew me against his chest so he could tuck me under his chin. I burrowed my face against his hot skin and closed my eyes.

"Whatever comes, we will face it together," he murmured, his chest rumbling in the way that turned my insides to warm honey. "And once we have rested, I will continue in my quest to find all the ways I may touch and taste you that will make you call my name."

I liked the sound of both those promises.

Moments later, warm and secure in his arms, I slept.

CHAPTER 18

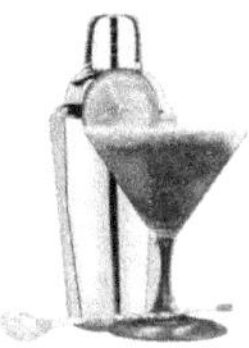

MIKAS

I woke in an instant, launched from a deep, contented sleep to wide awake and alert as if by primitive catapult. My hearts raced like I had been startled by a loud noise, but our room was silent except for the soft sound of the waterfall.

In the next breath, I knew what had roused me: the sharp, almost metallic scent of fear and pain—my *mate's* fear and pain. Isla whimpered in her sleep, her body tense and shaking in my embrace. My hearts ached for her.

My years as a soldier had left me with a reconstructed right leg, intrusive flashbacks, and frequent nightmares. And though I had yet to hear Isla's story of how she came to live on Fortusia, she had told me enough—and I had observed enough—to know she had suffered.

Almost miraculously, from the day Isla had first crossed my path, the frequency of both my nightmares and flashbacks had dwindled significantly. The mere presence of my true mate had granted me a reprieve from torments I had once thought would never cease. Now, as she flinched and trembled in ways I knew all too well, I wished I could do the same for her.

A strange, shuddering feeling I did not recognize rose in my gut and rolled through my chest.

I had a moment to think that I should have felt concern over this strange sensation that could have been a medical emergency, but that thought vanished in a wave of warmth that rose and intensified until it reached my throat. The warmth felt good, and pure, and right. It felt like love itself, as little sense as that might have made if I tried to explain it to another.

I opened my mouth. A low, sweet, vibrant sound emerged I had never made before, and might have said I could not make if I had been asked. Its effect on Isla was instantaneous. She exhaled, her muscles loosened, and the scents of fear and pain faded.

I gazed at her in awe. I had cooed for my mate and eased her distress with the sound.

As a Fortusian, I had known I would have a way of soothing and even relieving any pain experienced by my true mate, but *knowing of* such a wonder and *experiencing* it were very different things indeed.

Experimentally, I cooed again. She sighed contentedly, murmured something unintelligible, and snuggled closer, her palm pressed to my chest over my pounding primary heart. Perhaps even in her sleep, she wanted to feel it beating. Perhaps it comforted her.

I had yearned with all my hearts to bring Isla the same peace in my soul that her presence gave me, and this was one way I could do that. I knew the science of true mates and our unique physiology, but in this moment none of the science seemed important. The way Isla comforted me, and I comforted her, was nothing less than miraculous.

The chronometer on the bedside table indicated I had slept for five hours—more than enough to restore my energy and begin a new day. But as a human, Isla needed more sleep, especially after such a trying and emotional night. I was certainly content to hold her while she slept. In fact, I could not imagine doing anything else.

I lay awake for a long time, cradling Isla and not allowing myself to think about the uncertainty that surrounded us. A few more times she made little worried sounds as if her dreams had taken a dark turn. I cooed softly and she quieted, returning to peaceful sleep.

Once her scent lost all trace of fear or pain, I closed my eyes and nestled my nose against her hair. If another nightmare surfaced, she would not have to suffer it alone or for long. I would instinctually wake just as I would if physical danger threatened us.

I was made to care for Isla, to fight beside her, to make love to her. To ensure she was happy and safe. I had not truly understood how profoundly content that fact would make me until this moment.

Adrift in the wonder of her, I pressed my lips to her hair and dozed.

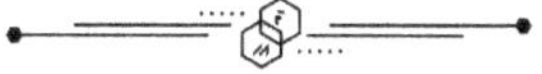

Isla was indeed exhausted and slept soundly for several more hours.

Unfortunately, as much as my hearts and soul wanted to hold her until she woke, my body ached from lying on such a soft bed—especially my right leg.

When the discomfort became pain, I reluctantly gathered the bedding around Isla to form a warm and comforting nest and slipped out of bed, careful not to jostle her. She murmured and snuggled deeper into the blankets. Gods, what a vision she was with her rainbow hair fanning out over her pillow and a hint of a smile on her lips. Perhaps her dream was pleasant. I hoped so, with all my hearts.

And to think only yesterday I had no inkling that when I opened my eyes this morning it would be to the sight of my mate sleeping in my arms.

Silently, I made my way down the stone steps to the glass-enclosed terrarium. While last night Isla's eyes had lit up at the sight of the waterfall and pool, the heated stones had caught my attention. My setup in my apartment was inexpensive. These stones were the same level of luxury as the rest of the suite.

My nonhuman DNA was reptilian rather than amphibious, but everything about the terrarium welcomed me, from its high humidity to the basking stones. I folded my sleepwear in a neat stack—a soldier's habit—and lay nude on the largest stone with a rumbly sigh of contentment.

The radiant warmth soaked into my body from below as the infrared heat from above did the same. It would be heavenly if Isla were here with me rather than still in bed, but I could not imagine she would find this rock anything close to comfortable.

From where I lay, I could just see Isla's still form on the bed. The waterfall masked the comforting sound of her deep breathing, which I missed as much as her touch. Her scent on my skin would carry me through until I returned to her side. In fact, if she accepted me as her mate, I need never be without her scent ever again. I closed my eyes and luxuriated in warmth that radiated from below, above, and within.

I drifted peacefully for as much as a half hour. Time grew hazy, as if often did while I basked.

Thanks to the waterfall and my near trance-like state, I did not hear the bedding rustle. But the moment my ears caught the telltale padding of bare feet descending the stone steps, my thoughts cleared and my body came alive.

At the sound of a splash, I opened my eyes to see my Isla

gliding underwater, crossing the pool from its far side to my basking stone. Her sleepwear lay in a pile near the stone steps.

As graceful and beautiful as a Basilian mermaid, she surfaced beside me, her face upturned and rainbow hair streaming behind her. She treaded water with sinuous movements that enthralled me.

"The water is nice and warm," she said. "How are the rocks?"

"Hot and comfortable, as I had hoped they would be." I reached down to touch her face. She leaned against my hand. "You slept well?"

"Very." A little furrow appeared between her brows. "I had a strange dream that you sang to me. You didn't actually sing me to sleep, did you?"

"No, though I would like to." The thought made me smile. I needed to explain my coo to her, but I did not want to spoil her mood by bringing up her nightmares, so instead I added, "I am sorry I left the bed."

"Don't apologize. I'm sure it's much too soft for you." She made a face. "Don't expect me to sleep on rocks, though. We'll have to work out a compromise."

I chuckled. "I would not expect you to sleep on a rock. I only bask for a few minutes or hours at a time myself. I am still very human-like in many ways, and I sleep in a bed."

"Thank goodness." Her smile returned. "Just not beds that are about as firm as clouds."

She had not commented on my nudity, and while we had talked her gaze had remained on my face. But she had certainly seen all of me now, though not necessarily in the way I had originally planned to reveal my body to her. Then again, perhaps this was better. She could study me with a clear mind rather than in a haze of desire. And maybe subconsciously I had chosen to bask nude knowing she was likely to see me and one of the last walls between us would fall.

To say her body captivated and aroused me infinitely more

than any lover I had ever known would be an understatement, but that was no guarantee she would feel the same about mine. And despite her dismissal of my concerns about her reaction to my body, a knot of tension remained between my shoulder blades and my stomach roiled.

My unease must have shown in my expression, because her joking demeanor gave way to a gentler and more sensuous expression when she said, "Why you thought your body might horrify me, I have no idea."

Now her gaze swept over me unabashedly, taking in every detail much as I had devoured the sight of her with her legs spread wide for me in Madame Ycari's back room. My cocks, already aroused by her nakedness, hardened and beaded with lubrication under her scrutiny. When her tongue darted out to lick her lips, I quaked, and drops of precum welled up and began to drip.

Gods, I would never be able to look at my mate without wanting her with every atom of my being. But far from being a curse, it would be heaven itself, especially after so many months dreaming of a single touch from her.

Isla's voice was husky when she met my gaze again and added, "You're a masterpiece."

Surely there was one masterpiece in this room, and it was not me. "I am hardly that."

"Mikas." She frowned. "Don't argue with your mate."

My breath caught and my cocks leapt at both her tone and how she had referred to herself as my mate.

Rather than continue treading water, she moved to the side of the pool and folded her arms on the edge of my basking stone to hold herself up.

"Ooh, that does feel nice," she said with a little sigh. Perhaps she had expected the rock to be too hot for her to enjoy. "Maybe I could get used to it, at least for a few minutes at a time. Especially if I could lie on top of you instead of the rocks." She eyed my dripping cocks. "Though you seem just as hard."

"I am." And I always would be for my Isla.

I leaned over and kissed her. How it was possible for her to taste better, sweeter, and more perfect with each kiss, I did not know, but it was yet another wonder of my mate I accepted happily and without question.

When the kiss ended, she raised her eyebrows, a playful smile on her lips. "So, are you coming in the pool? Or am I coming up there?"

"I think," I rasped, "you will be coming in both places."

In one smooth movement, I rolled to a crouch and dove into the water to claim my beautiful mate.

CHAPTER 19

ISLA

I had no time to react to Mikas's words, growl, or sudden movement before he sliced through the water's surface in a perfect dive and disappeared into the pool's depths.

This was only the second time I'd seen him move faster than was humanly possible. But unlike how quickly he'd reacted to defend us in Ycari's back room when the warning light flashed, this time he was reacting to me, and it sent a rush of need straight to my core.

As I turned to put my back to the basking stones, he surfaced as quickly as he'd vanished, his hot body sliding up mine until his head and shoulders emerged. He was grinning, his sharp teeth and fangs on full display. I shivered with desire.

Each of his cocks was lovely and thick, with the same iridescent scale pattern that covered him. But unlike the rest of his body, the flesh of his cocks and balls appeared smooth, other than the many textured nubs and bumps along the length of each cock. In particular, imagining how the bumps just behind his cock heads would feel inside me made me squeeze my thighs together.

Gods above, I wanted him. My pussy clenched and gushed at the thought of him taking me with those beautiful, thick cocks.

He nudged me until my back pressed against the smooth stones that formed the side of the pool, and then with his hands on my waist he guided me closer to the waterfall until my ass rested on a little outcropping of rock. It wasn't very big, but it would support me so I didn't have to tread water.

With one hand on a basking stone above us, Mikas cupped the back of my head and kissed me again before trailing his hot lips along my jaw and down the side of my neck. And though his body brushed mine, he seemed to be holding back.

"My Isla," he murmured, his gaze locked on mine. "Do you want my touches?"

Couldn't he tell how much I desired him? I trembled at every movement of his hands and mouth, and doubly so at the sensation of his bare hip against my leg. My scent had to make my level of arousal as clear as this water.

Maybe he wanted to hear me say it, not just because he valued my choices as much as I did, but because he'd waited for so long to hear the words. And I found I wanted to say them too.

I cupped his face in my hands and ran the pad of my thumb over his lower lip. "Yes, I want your touches," I said. "I want your mouth, your hands, your arms and legs, your chest, your cocks, and your incredibly breathtaking ass. I want all of you, just as you are."

Mikas smiled, this time with sweet affection rather than his much more carnal grin. "You think my ass is breathtaking?"

I sighed in mock exasperation. "That's what you heard out of what I said?"

His smile became a look so tender that my heart fluttered. "I heard you say you wanted all of me, just as I am. And that is how you will have me." He rested his forehead against mine. "Eyes on me, Isla. Open your legs."

I obeyed.

His hand traveled languidly from my knee along my inner thigh, brushing my skin lightly to make me quiver and let out little sounds. And he never looked away, as if he wanted to watch every tiny reaction.

His fingertip ghosted along my slit, stroking gently without penetrating. I moaned. "Mikas…"

"Already you whisper my name," he said, his lips brushing my ear. "I dreamed of this last night, hearing you call for me."

His finger slipped between my folds, stroking and exploring as I trembled. "You are very slick," he murmured. "I like this silky liquid you make for me. It is your own perfect perfume. To me, you need no other."

I thought of my treasured bespoke Engareni perfume, still nestled safely in my bag and all but forgotten. Something told me he'd love it if I did, no matter what he thought of my own natural scents—

—But then his thick fingertip slipped inside me, and all other thoughts evaporated.

Gentle and purposeful, he dipped his finger deeper with each little pump. I whimpered for more, so he added a second finger, stretching me and stroking faster.

When I gasped and shuddered, he made a sound low in his throat and focused his attention on that spot, his fingertips curled inside me. My hips moved and my head fell back.

"Eyes open," he reminded me, his mouth against my ear. "Look at me, Isla. I want you to see me when you come."

Gasping and whimpering, I stared into his dark eyes and rode his fingers, grinding against them and crying out, the pitch of my voice rising as my orgasm built. Oh, gods. Oh gods *oh gods…*

"Squeeze my fingers," Mikas rumbled, cupping my chin with

his free hand so I couldn't look away. "Sing for me, my beautiful mate."

I came hard with guttural wails, my fingernails digging into his shoulders as all my muscles clenched.

"Yes," he growled. "Drench me with your sweet nectar, Isla. Give it all to your mate."

I fell against his chest, panting and shaking. He held me close, his lips on my hair, and murmured my name over and over like a song.

"My Isla," he said, stroking my back as I trembled. "You were perfect. So beautiful."

Once I'd caught my breath, he let go of the wall, held me close with one arm, and swam toward the other side of the pool with the other arm and his legs, making sure my head stayed out of the water. The sensation of water streaming over my sensitive, tingling skin was exquisite.

"What are you doing?" I asked.

"Taking you to the bed," he said, his voice rough and chest rumbling.

"You promised to make me come in the pool *and* on the basking stone," I protested weakly.

"And I will." He reached the steps that led out of the water and swung me up in his arms to carry me. "Once I figure out a way to make sure you are comfortable while I do so."

I thought about the problem. "A pillow for my knees would work nicely…and then we can figure it out from there."

He paused, the corners of his lips turning up. "I suppose it would not inconvenience our hosts too much if we relocated some of the bedding."

He carried me up the steps, leaving a trail of wet footprints and dripping water from the stairs to the bed.

When he set me on my feet, though, our height difference made me reconsider my comment about that pillow for my knees. He was too tall for me to kneel in front of him and reach his cocks with my mouth. Hmm.

I recalled from last night how temptingly well-positioned I had been sitting on the edge of the bed. And his sleep pants were not going to interfere this time.

"Isla?" Mikas asked, his head tilted. "What are you thinking about?"

"You." I sat on the side of the bed and beckoned. "Come here."

He obeyed without question.

His body was indeed a masterpiece, from his thick, dark hair to his feet. And wet from the pool, he was even more magnificent.

As often seemed to be the case, the genetic engineers who'd created him had apparently taken all the best and most beautiful —and tantalizing—aspects of various species to forge a man who could have stood on a pedestal in the center of an art gallery and been every bit as much a work of art as the rest of the collection.

But beyond that, he was wonderfully *Mikas*, and nothing of who he was could be credited to any genetic engineers. His kindness and care and everything else I adored about him were his own.

He stood directly in front of me, his dark eyes looking down as I gazed up at him. "Isla," he said, his hand caressing my cheek. The way he said my name was different from anyone who'd ever spoken those two syllables, as if for him the word was both a name and a kind of prayer.

"Do you want my touches?" I asked, my voice shaky with how much I wanted him.

"Yes," he said simply. "Forever, if I may have them."

His beautiful cocks had been erect and dripping for me from the moment I'd surfaced next to his basking stone. They'd also beaded with shimmery liquid.

Near the base of his lower cock, a telltale swelling began under my gaze. And though I'd never encountered one socially before, I recognized it as a knot. My pussy gushed at the sight, and again at the realization that for it to lock inside me for its intended purpose, he would likely be behind me as I bent over for him...and his upper cock would be either stroking along my ass or buried inside it.

Maybe Mikas was imagining the same scene. He closed his eyes and inhaled deeply, his hands shaking. "Gods, Isla."

I took his beautiful cocks in my hands. The shimmery liquid proved to be natural lubricant, and its scent and the sensation of my fingers and palms gliding through it made my pussy and ass clench and ache to be filled.

As gently as I touched him, Mikas's entire body quaked, and his hips moved so his cocks slid in my grip. He made a sound so guttural, so primal, that I moaned.

I stroked him with both hands, exploring the universe of textures, bumps, and slickness, from dripping tips to burgeoning knot and his firm, globe-like balls. And when I trailed one fingertip over the delicate, sensitive skin below his balls, twin releases of precum splattered my arms and face. He groaned and braced himself.

Stroking both cocks evenly and deliberately, I took the head of his upper cock into my mouth. He nearly roared, his hips jerking as he fought to control his thrusts. Oh, gods. I almost came myself from the heat and taste of him and the sounds he made for me. His lubrication was mild and sweet, and his precum's saltiness matched it perfectly.

"Isla," he ground out, his hand resting gently on my head even now and fingers in my hair. "Isla, yes. Gods, yes."

Even with my jaw open wide, I couldn't take more than a fraction of his enormous cock into my mouth, and the prospect of taking its whole girth and length anywhere else made me squirm with arousal. And both...oh, gods above and below.

I released his upper cock from my mouth and gave it a few long licks to make him groan before sliding my lips over the tip of his lower cock. The more I sucked on him, the sweeter he tasted, and the more I wished I had a hand free to rub my clit.

His knot proved to be extra sensitive, so I stroked it very gently. And when I put my mouth on it and sucked, Mikas nearly stumbled.

He drew away, his chest heaving and gaze heavy-lidded. "My mate…"

I reached for him and he came to me, scooping me up with one arm to move me onto the bed so he could cover my body with his. *Finally.*

I gripped his hair tightly, hooked my leg over his hip to pull him to me, and kissed him. "Mikas," I murmured against his lips, "don't make me wait anymore."

"I do not want to wait either." He cupped my face and stroked my cheek with his thumb. "But I worry about hurting you."

"I don't mind a little pain." I leaned against the warmth of his hand and those talented fingers that had wrung so much pleasure out of me in the pool. "I'll tell you if something doesn't feel good, I promise. We can take it slow."

"As difficult as that will be, we will have to." He trailed kisses down my face and neck.

He flicked my right nipple then laved it with his tongue, making me whimper. He returned his mouth to mine to kiss me again and look into my eyes. "If I ever hurt you, even without meaning to, it would break my hearts. I would never forgive myself."

These weren't empty sentiments; the depth of emotion in his gaze and the tension in his body made it clear he meant every word.

After my mother died, other than with Brae, I'd had very little experience with this kind of love—the kind of love that meant my happiness and well-being were essential for someone else's. I was treasured. What a revelation that feeling was.

I cupped his face. He kissed my palm. "Then let me be on top," I said. "I will be careful."

"I will happily let you be on top." He moved down my body again and knelt between my knees, his hands on my thighs. "After you come for me again, that is—this time, on my tongue."

"But..." I took a shaky breath. "I don't think I can, not so soon."

"Oh, I think you *will*." He settled in on his stomach and kissed my inner thighs. "Spread your legs, Isla. Show me how wet you are for me."

My cheeks burning, I did as he asked. He cradled my legs in his arms and pulled me closer to his mouth. I gripped the bedding in my fists.

Carefully, he slipped two fingers along my lips and spread me open. I trembled in anticipation.

"So perfect," he murmured, his tongue delving and sliding along my dripping slit. "My Isla's flower has such sweet, slick petals. And this...little...bud..."

His mouth closed on my clit. I cried out, my hips rising so I could move against his face. He rumbled in appreciation, and that vibration made me shiver.

His fingers slid lower. They pumped into me gently and then not so gently, and I felt him spread them, stretching me a little at a time. Stretching me so I could take his cock. His *cocks*. I quivered, and my pussy and ass clenched.

"I see how much you need me," he said, licking me from my asshole all the way up to my clit to make me wail. "You need me to fill you, my mate. You need my cock in your sweet pussy and my second cock in your ass."

"Yes," I gasped. "That's what I need. I need you to fill me up."

He rewarded me by pumping his fingers faster and returning

his lips to my clit. A delicious coil of heat rose. I moaned and pulled at the bedding.

He didn't stop until I came on his face, and then as I wailed and pulled his hair he lapped at my pussy to drink every drop of my release.

I'd known desire and pleasure before, but I'd never felt this thoroughly wanted and desired and *needed*. And I wanted and needed him too.

CHAPTER 20

ISLA

WHEN I RAISED MY HEAD, HE WAS ON HIS KNEES, HIS EYES smoldering and his cocks dripping in earnest. I licked my lips.

"On your hands and knees, please, Isla," he said. "Before you get on top of me, you will need more preparation."

He helped me move because my legs were shaking so badly. And when I was on my hands and knees in front of him, he groaned and gripped my hips. "Isla…"

He buried his face in my pussy, his tongue delving and sliding sinuously along my dripping slit. I slumped forward onto my elbows, changing my angle, and he rumbled his approval.

He licked me all the way up to my asshole before flicking it with his tongue and then slipping its rough tip into the tiny opening. I wailed and gripped the bedding, hanging on for dear life as pleasure coursed through me.

I heard the sound of him stroking himself, and then a slick fingertip pressed against my ass. When it slid inside, I cried out, my hips moving instinctively to take more of that finger.

Gods, I wanted him. I wanted all of him. I wanted to feel his cocks inside me and have orgasms as he growled into my ear. And I wanted it *now*.

He tongued my asshole as he gathered more lubrication from his cocks and then added a second finger into my ass.

"Yes, take my fingers," he murmured as I moved against his hand, whimpering and shaking with the intensity of the pleasure he was giving me as he gently stretched me. "You are so beautiful and perfect, my Isla. So beautiful and perfect."

With his other hand, he circled my clit to make me shake and cry out. And once he found the right rhythm, he didn't stop. My cries rose in pitch, and my body shook.

Oh, gods, he was going to make me come again like this, on my hands and knees right in front of his face, so he could see every detail of how I came from a different angle.

Just as I thought that, he speared my ass with his rough tongue as he plunged his fingers in and out of my pussy. I screamed and came, yanking on the bedding as if I were trying to claw my way through it or away from him. He held me in place, growling, his tongue thrusting into me until I careened back over the edge in a softer orgasm that made me quake and let out a sound almost like a sob.

In an inhumanly fast movement, he rolled to his back, taking me with him to settle me in place with his hands on my hips and my trembling thighs astride his hard abdomen.

"My Isla," he said, and he licked his lips as if he wanted another taste of me. "Show me how well you can take me, but go slowly. We will stop if you feel pain."

I rose to a crouch and stroked his upper cock, which dripped with both natural lubricant and slick, sweet precum. He groaned and raised his hips to thrust into my hand, then stilled himself as I guided his cock to my pussy. Gods, it was so thick, and so beautiful, with so many textures.

Very carefully, I lowered myself onto the tip. A burst of precum splashed my inner thighs.

Mikas's chest was heaving. He'd fisted his hands in the bedding much like I'd done, but his claws had come out and he'd sliced the fabric. He was fighting to hold back, to keep from thrusting into me because he might hurt me, despite every instinct that demanded he take his mate in the way he'd yearned to do for so long.

The head of his cock was wide but tapered just enough that I was able to slip it inside me. It was so hot and slick.

My cry blended with his groan and he pulled at the covers. *Rrrrrrrip.* The bedding would be in tatters soon and maybe the bed too. This man wanted me so badly he was destroying the bed we lay on.

My gaze on his, I worked my way down one roll of my hips at a time. He snarled and growled and groaned with every movement I made, and I found myself making almost the same guttural sounds as the nubs and textures of his cock rubbed inside me in ways I had never felt before.

The pleasure and pain was so good that my every breath was a gasp.

"Gods, seeing your pussy stretch to take me…" Mikas groaned. "I cannot look away."

I was shaking now and sweating, fighting to take him deeper when I already felt full to bursting.

As if those sensations weren't already overwhelming, his lower cock rubbed against my ass too as I moved, dripping lubricant and precum that made me shiver with anticipation. My asshole clenched, desperate to be filled even as I fought to take one cock.

Mikas sheathed his claws, piled some pillows behind his back so he could raise his torso, and reached for me. "Come here."

My pussy fluttering around him, I lay on his chest, nearly

sobbing with overwhelming emotion and the intense feeling of him inside me. He wrapped me in his arms and buried his face in my hair.

"You can take it," he murmured in my ear. He moved his hips just enough to slip his cock in a little more. I groaned. "Your beautiful pussy can take every inch." Another small thrust. I whimpered. "Take me, my mate."

Another thrust, and then he stopped to let me rest. I panted into his chest. He smelled so good, like warm stones and something else I couldn't quite describe, but that was purely him. Purely *Mikas*.

He caressed my back, soothing me with the heat and tenderness of his touch. I closed my eyes and breathed. He held me gently but firmly, thrust once more, and I finally took all of him.

Hot liquid splashed onto my lower back: a burst of precum from his lower cock. I loved how it felt running down my skin, as if he'd marked me as his own. I was so, so full, and it felt so good. Better than anything I'd ever felt in my life. I would have told him so if I could have said anything.

He cradled my head to his chest and ran his fingers through my hair, his own body shaking as much as mine. "You take me perfectly. I knew you would." His chest rumbled as if he was purring again. "My sweet Isla. You are not in pain?"

"No pain." My voice was ragged. "But it's too much. Gods, Mikas. Sex with you might kill me."

"It will not kill you, I promise." He took my hands in each of his and urged me to sit up. "Show me how you look filled with my cock."

Without him helping, I wasn't sure if I could have moved. The sensations of his cock inside me made my eyes roll back in my head. My vision went a little blurry around the edges.

When I was upright, he let go of my hands to grip my hips as his dark eyes devoured the sight of me.

"Look at your sweet pussy squeeze my cock." With his

thumb, he stroked my clit. I mewled and shuddered hard. "You could come right now, couldn't you?"

"Yes," I whispered. "If I move at all, I'm going to come."

"Good." He laced our fingers together and held his arms out straight so I could brace myself. "Come on my cock, then, my beautiful mate. I want to fill you."

I'd intended to take both his cocks so he could fill me fully. But now, having struggled to take just one despite how well-lubricated he was, I knew I'd need more time and prep to handle both. He must have realized that too.

His lower cock would slide along the cleft of my ass as I moved, but I wanted to give him more than that. I withdrew one of my hands from his grip, reached behind me, and found his slick and dripping second cock.

The moment my fingers wrapped around it, Mikas bucked his hips and roared. That sound—and the intense sensation of his cock moving inside me—nearly sent me careening over the edge.

He had enough control not to thrust hard and come, or hurt me with his claws. His free hand grabbed a fistful of bedding immediately and shredded it. We were going to owe Atlath a new bed.

"Isla," Mikas growled, his fangs bared. "Ride me, my mate."

The sensation of him inside me was already overwhelming. I might not die, but fucking Mikas like this was going to be a level of pleasure that actually frightened me.

I braced myself on Mikas's hand, locked my gaze on his, and rolled my hips. His cock rubbed inside me in a hundred ways I'd never felt before. "*Mikas*," I wailed.

Ever so careful not to hurt me by moving too fast or roughly, he dug his heels into the bed and thrust up gently to meet me as I rode him. I stroked his lower cock in time with our move-ments. His hot precum splattered my back and dripped down my ass. My whimpers became cries, and my cries turned into wails of bliss.

I came on him with screams that were nearly sobs mixed with sounds that were barely human.

Then he was snarling and thrusting harder into my pussy and my hand, bouncing me on his cocks, his head thrown back and hand gripping mine.

When Mikas came, it was glorious.

Roaring, growling, his body wracked with shudders and eyes aglow, he came first from his upper cock in a half-dozen or more massive spurts of beautiful pearlescent cum that filled me and then over-filled me to stream down my thighs and cover his lap.

His orgasm continued to build. With another bellow, he released from his lower cock. Using his grip for leverage, I half-turned and looked over my shoulder to watch. Gods, his cock was magnificent as it leapt and spurted in my grip to splash cum across my face and breast.

I aimed his cock at my open mouth and caught two delicious ropes of sweet cum on my tongue. Did he taste sweet to me because he was my true mate? Or was this his natural taste?

As his cocks released the last of his cum, he quaked and groaned my name. I slid my hand down his slick and dripping lower cock to cradle his tight balls. He roared once more, bucking up into me again and again, his heels braced into the soft bed, until he was spent.

I was full of Mikas's cum, and covered in Mikas's cum, and I loved it. He was *mine*.

Exhausted and content, I slumped against his chest with a sigh.

He wrapped his arms around me, his face buried in my hair. "My mate," he whispered, still trembling. "Gods, you are perfect beyond my wildest dreams."

"Did you dream of me?" I asked, breathless.

"I did." Chest heaving, he held me tightly. "Every day, every night." His voice was rough with exertion and emotion.

How had I never suspected? All those nights talking over brandy and berries, and I'd never had a clue. It was little solace to know our lives had depended on him hiding how he felt.

Maybe I'd been afraid to see it. Maybe I'd let my fears blind me.

"It is embarrassing to admit," he added, "but I fantasized about you as well."

Grumpy, silent Mikas had *fantasized* about me? I moved my head so I could see his face. His eyes twinkled.

"Oh?" I found a streak of cum on my cheek, wiped it up with my finger, and licked it off. Yum. His chest rumbled. "What kind of fantasies?" I asked, my tone playful.

"Moments like this." He scooped up another stray streak of cum from my chin. I licked his fingertips and bit them lightly. "Gods, Isla," he breathed.

"What did you do when you fantasized about us?" I rested my head back on his chest.

"I did what I could to ease my need." He kissed my hair. "It was all I could do, and it was a very poor substitute for the real wonder and pleasure of you."

Imagining Mikas in his apartment fantasizing about me and pleasuring himself was so intensely arousing that I quivered. Maybe I could persuade him to recreate that scene for me later.

I kissed his hot chest. "We've made a mess of this bed."

"*I* have made a mess of this bed." He chuckled. "And of you, though it seems you do not mind."

"I don't mind at all." I glanced at the terrarium. "But I also wouldn't mind a shower or a swim and some rest on the basking stones, if you'd be interested."

"Would I be interested in basking with my mate after the best orgasm of my life?" Mikas tipped my chin up with his fingertips and ran his thumb over my lower lip. "For a brilliant woman, you ask silly questions."

"I don't think I can walk there myself, though," I warned. "You'll have to carry me."

"Oh, no," he said in mock horror. "What a terrible ordeal for me."

I laughed.

He caught my hand in his and drew it to his lips to kiss my palm. "My Isla, to hear you laugh…it is good for my soul."

There was so much about Mikas—the *real* Mikas—that I liked and loved, but this tenderness was the best thing of all. And it was mine too now, along with his beautiful chest, yellow eyes, sexy spines, breathtaking ass, and absolutely exquisite cocks.

CHAPTER 21

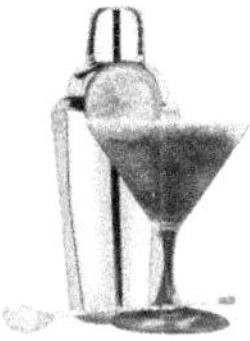

MIKAS

Isla, my mate.

I had thought waiting three months from our meeting to this moment had been difficult. And it had...but not a fraction as difficult as holding myself back from coming before she had a chance to drench my cock in her own release.

No fantasy I had ever entertained had come close to approximating the real sight of Isla's trembling legs astride my hips and her pussy stretched around my cock, or the feeling of her squeezing me in her release as she stroked my second cock. She was a dream, sweating and whimpering, her nipples hard and clit swollen with need.

Even now, simply lying on my chest as we rested, she overwhelmed my senses. We could have been anywhere and it would not have mattered because I saw nothing but her. My hands ran over her soft skin, slick with sweat. The scent of her body and our lovemaking filled my nose and lungs and made my hearts pound. Her tastes danced on my tongue and her cries of ecstasy rang in my ears.

Biting her lip, her body tense as if she feared it might cause her pain to move, she eased herself off my cock. Gods above, her tight, slick heat sliding over my sensitive skin was exquisite torture.

Even lost in my lingering euphoric haze, I rested my hand on her arm and watched closely for any sign of pain or distress.

"You're still hard," she said, her eyes wide. "Don't tell me you could *possibly*…"

"I could," I said, cupping her face. "But I will wait until you are recovered and want more. I would never risk hurting you in any way you do not want."

"Sweet Mikas." She kissed my scaly flesh over my primary heart and freed herself from my cock with a gasp.

"Are you sore?" I asked.

Trembling, she lay on my chest to catch her breath. "Yes," she admitted. "I think I'm going to need some recovery time."

"My cum has healing properties for my mate." I caressed her back to reassure her. "I believe any soreness will fade soon. But there is no rush. We have all the time in the world now."

In truth, we still had to make our way away from Nubo's reach and off Fortusia, but as long as no one came to our room or contacted us, we were safe here thanks to Atlath's diplomatic status and interplanetary law. For all his bluster and desire to possess Isla, even Nubo would not risk ending up in an Alliance prison colony.

I wanted so much to take my mate to the pool for a swim, and then bask with her on the stones, but she did not seem ready to move quite yet. I was more than happy to stay here and hold her.

This was, perhaps, a good opportunity to return to my questions about her past.

"My mate." I cradled the back of her head to soothe her. "I will never demand anything of you, least of all secrets you need to keep to protect others. But please tell me how you came to

Fortusia. I swear, nothing you say to me in confidence will ever pass my lips."

"I know you'll keep my secrets." She took a deep breath. "I'll tell you what's mine to tell."

She took her time gathering her thoughts. I did not rush her.

"My name is Isla Mair," she said finally. "Or at least it is now. And it will be from now on, I hope, because that's the name you know, and I like hearing you say my name. It makes me not want to risk needing to change it. I suppose I might not have a choice if my past finds me."

My hearts ached at the thought of my mate having to take many names, since rarely did that happen by choice or without a threat looming. And my spines prickled because she still lived in fear.

"My mother belonged to a trade baron on Havel Prime," she said. "She was born and raised in a frontier colony raided by mercenaries and sold to the baron when she was twenty standard years old. I was born a few years later. My father was one of the baron's household staff. My mother loved him, and she said he loved her too, but he left the planet after he finished his service contract and never came back for us. I don't remember him at all."

Her matter-of-fact tone sent a sharp pain through my hearts.

"So I grew up in service in the baron's household," she continued. "I was a playmate for his children when I was very young, and then when I turned ten, I helped the cooks in the kitchens. After a couple of years, I didn't get along with the new head chef, so the baron's chief of staff reassigned me to cleaning and preparing the apartments for the baron's guests. It wasn't misery, but it wasn't good. I was lonely most of all, especially after my mother died."

Her hand tightened on mine. "And then when I was twenty-one, one of the baron's guests heard me singing while I cleaned. She'd never heard a human sing before, and she decided I'd be a perfect addition to her palace on Agicord. The next thing I knew, she'd bought me, and I was on her private starship with a travel case at my feet."

"Oh, my love." I nuzzled her hair. "I am sorry."

I had suspected something like this in my Isla's past. Her reaction to the Sirrah in the market during our first outing together had revealed far more about her than anything else I had observed in the three months before that moment.

"She wasn't cruel, but she owned me," Isla said, rubbing her nose on my chest over my primary heart. "She'd bought me from the baron and had the duly registered certificate to prove it. So I came to live at her palace, to sing whenever she wanted me to sing—which was primarily when she had guests. And every time I sang for guests, I lived in fear I'd be sold again, and this time to someone much less kind. Someone who wouldn't just want me to sing."

She raised her head to meet my gaze. "Soon I was less and less of a novelty. It was only a matter of time before she'd find someone or something new she could show off to her guests and want to be rid of me. I knew better than to delude myself into thinking she'd let me stay out of the kindness of her heart. I needed to find a way to escape her palace and get off that planet. A dangerous proposition, but I didn't have a choice. And most of all, I wanted freedom."

My heartache and rage grew to nearly unbearable levels. To think of Isla as *owned*, a possession, a symbol of status, a wonder and curiosity for wealthy visitors to a palace on some distant planet...with my bare hands, I could have killed these people who had bought and sold Isla as if she were a ship or a pretty sculpture.

I could not help but think of my own military conscription. Many nights I had lain awake on my cot in whatever housing I slept in, on whatever planet I served on, thinking of the day I could come home to Fortusia. For all that misery, at least I had a finite term of service and a home planet I could dream of during those long, sleepless nights. Lovely Isla had not had even that solace.

"I had a lover in the palace on Agicord," Isla said, her gaze on mine. "I'll call her Hidel. She was one of the housekeepers. She worked in the palace by choice because it was good wages. Hidel had a wonderful, kind heart. She knew how much I wanted to escape, so she found someone who could help. And one night some people came, took me from the palace, and smuggled me onto a ship bound for somewhere a long, long way from that palace."

I closed my eyes and rested my head against Isla's. *Thank you,* I thought, willing my gratitude to find this nameless woman wherever she was now. Her loving sacrifice had helped make this moment possible.

Isla took a deep, shaky breath. "Because of how suddenly I left, I never got to tell Hidel thank you or say goodbye. It must have broken her heart to give me up. I don't know if I would have had the strength to do it if our situation had been reversed."

"I believe you would have," I said, holding her close. "Your courage and strength astound me. You would have found a way to do what was right even if it caused you pain."

"You are so kind." She kissed my jaw. "After I was free, I decided I wanted to help others as I'd been helped. And that's what I did for three years. When that work came to an end, I came to Fortusia to sing for myself, on my own terms. I wanted to make people happy and earn a living with my voice."

Isla sounded so fierce now. My hearts warmed knowing she had not only devoted her life to freeing others but then chosen to take back her voice and her power. We had both lived under Nubo's thumb, but even so until recently it must have felt enough like bliss and freedom for her to stomach his possessive and vile behavior.

"And how did you meet Brae?" I asked. "Was that after you left Agicord?"

"Yes." She smiled, and I was glad to see it. "I found him on Pallasia, as you probably guessed. He was a baby, orphaned when a transport crashed near his mother's nest. My life wasn't conducive to having an animal companion, but I happened to walk past a shelter and saw his image on the screen out front where they listed companions needing permanent homes. I don't know why, but I found myself going in to ask about him."

She made a face. "They didn't want to let me adopt him. I wasn't a citizen of Pallasia, and I told them I was unemployed since I couldn't very well put my real employer on the application. But then he imprinted on me and wouldn't let go of me, and they had to let me take him."

"Why did he imprint on you?" I asked, smiling.

"Because he was so young at the time, Brae doesn't remember imprinting on me, so he can't very well say why he did it." She chuckled. "Now he says it's because even as a baby shadowbat he could tell if he stayed with me his life would never be boring."

"An exciting life is not necessary." I kissed her hand. "I would happily have a boring life with you, my Isla. A boring and wonderful life."

"I don't think I'd mind a boring life now." She glanced over her shoulder. "Pool?" she asked, raising her eyebrows. "Or shower?"

"Pool." Carefully, I gathered her in my arms and rose from the bed. "I enjoy seeing you swim."

"I like seeing you in the water too." Her smile returned. "But we're going to end up on those stones, right? Like you *promised?*"

"Exactly as I promised," I said very solemnly. "You will come many times on those stones. I will see to it personally."

When we reached the edge of the pool, Isla kicked her feet playfully. "Toss me in."

I blinked at her. "What?"

"Toss me in," she insisted. "For fun."

"How would that be fun?" I asked, puzzled. "You might be hurt." And I would be the cause. The very thought made my stomach roil.

She sighed. "Fine. Put me down, then, please."

I set her on her feet, took her hand, and leaned down, intending to kiss her. But a fraction of a second before my lips met hers, she tipped over and fell backward, taking me with her.

Moving purely on instinct, I caught her in midair, pulled her against my chest, turned us, and hit the water on my back with my arms around my mate. Her laugh ended abruptly in a gurgle as we went under.

My body weight pulled us into the dark depths of the pool before I rotated us and kicked up to bring us back to the surface. I lifted Isla above me so she would reach air as quickly as possible.

When my head and shoulders emerged from the water, I found my mate coughing and laughing.

Scowling and treading water, I grated, "Isla..."

With a chuckle, she swam into my arms, rested her head against my chest, and wrapped her legs around my waist. I suddenly found myself utterly unable to say another word, scolding or otherwise.

"I'm sorry for pulling you into the pool," she said, smiling though she was still coughing. She scratched her nails on my chest to elicit the rumbling sound she enjoyed so much and that I loved making for her. "Don't be afraid to be spontaneous sometimes. You never know what might happen."

"You are right." I kissed her forehead. "I must balance that against my need to keep you safe. All my instincts tell me I must never let you come to harm, most especially by my own actions."

"I'll remember that." She looked around the pool. "This is

such a beautiful room. You'd never know from the shop downstairs that this is an embassy, would you? Or that Atlath's got such luxurious accommodations." She hesitated, then frowned. "Or *did* you know?"

"I did not," I assured her. "I knew his name, but not that he owns the shop *or* is an ambassador. And of course I had no idea he might be in a position to help us."

"He helped us because he knows Ycari and Pioni, and because you're a good bartender and I sang songs he likes." Isla looked up at me, her violet eyes suddenly shimmering. "Do you ever feel like the universe isn't random?"

I rested my forehead on hers. "Are you asking a man who has found his true mate if he thinks the universe is random?"

"Oh, well, that's a good point." She blinked rapidly, fighting back tears. "But my life has been so difficult. The baron sold me to the woman in the palace, Hidel helped me escape, my last mission ended badly, I chose to come to Fortusia to hide, and Brae persuaded me to audition for the job at Zaa'ga, where I met you." Her cough sounded like a little sob. "How do I make sense of it all?"

"My life has also been difficult," I said quietly. "I owe you my own story, but I too have been subject to many winds of fate and others' decisions, as well as my own choices, that brought me to Zaa'ga, where I thought frequently of leaving to work for someone far less objectionable but did not."

"I don't—" She bit her lip. "How can all this feel so much like random chance, but at the same time not like chance at all?"

I brushed her wet hair back from her face. "I cannot explain how our lives unfold, or answer why we suffered, or even why our paths crossed. There are many theories, certainly. Whether one has better claim to the truth than another, I do not know." I cupped her face with both my hands. "What I *do* know is you are perfect, I love you, and if being with me makes you happy, that is all I need or want."

"You have got to stop telling me I'm perfect," she said, with a wry smile that wobbled. "It's starting to go to my head."

"I will never stop kneeling before you, and I will never stop saying you are perfect," I stated. "So you might as well become accustomed to both."

"Stubborn as a Gandarian mule-ox." She sighed. "I suppose if you have to have one flaw, it might as well be that."

I kissed my mate very deeply and for a very long time, treading water. She held on with her arms and legs, trusting me to keep us afloat. Gods, I could spend forever like this, holding her and gently supporting her. For so long I had yearned to swim with Isla in warm waters, and here she was in my arms.

Finally, our lazy circling of the pool brought us to the side with the basking stones. "Are you ready to go up to the stones?" I asked.

"Yes." She looked at her fingertips and then at mine. "I'm all wrinkly from the water, but you aren't. That's not fair."

With a chuckle, I kissed her forehead and guided her to the wall. "Would you like me to give you a boost to help get you out of the pool, or for me to climb out first and lift you?"

She pursed her lips and studied the rocks. "How about you get out first and lift me?"

I left her treading water and clambered up the stone wall to stand beside the pool on the basking stone I had used earlier. When I turned to look down, Isla was smiling up at me, her lovely hair swirling around her shoulders.

"Oh, I like this view," she chuckled, her gaze on my dripping cocks.

"No view could be better than looking at you." I crouched and reached for her hands. "Ready, my love?"

She let me grip her wrists and found a foothold on the wall to push off. "Ready."

I rose, lifting her with ease to set her on her feet beside me. She kissed my chest, then turned in a circle, her arms extended.

"This is wonderful," she said, tilting her head back, eyes closed, to feel the heat from above. "It's warm, but not *hot* hot. I see why you like it."

I sat on one of the stones and held out my arms. "Come to me."

She did so immediately, folding herself into my lap as easily and naturally as though we had done this a hundred times.

I lay back on my elbows as she moved around on top of me to find the most comfortable position, careful not to put her knees or elbows anywhere sensitive.

My mate ended up lying on me as if I were a bed, partly on her side, nestled into my chest with one knee bent over my thigh and her head over my primary heart. The moment she stilled, my body relaxed, as if I had melted into the heated stone beneath me. I exhaled in complete contentment.

"Is this all right?" she asked, biting her lip. "Am I too heavy with a rock under you?"

"Never." I kissed the top of her head. "You will frown at me, but you are perfect."

She did frown, but then she smiled and snuggled closer. "Let me know if you get uncomfortable, or your leg falls asleep."

"I will." I wrapped her in my arms. "Are *you* comfortable?"

"Unbelievably comfortable." She chuckled low in her throat. "I think I could get used to this, actually."

Did she have any idea how much joy she kindled in my hearts and soul with those words?

As we basked, I caressed her back and soaked in her scent. I did not want to spoil the moment, but she had not provided an explanation for something very, very distressing I had noticed last night when we removed her dress.

"Isla," I said gently, "will you tell me about the scars on your back? They appear recent."

She flinched. I stroked her back lovingly until she relaxed again.

"I mentioned my last mission ended badly," she said finally. Her voice was strong and not shaky, but I smelled the pain of her memories. "I can't give you details, but I was shot in the back by a plasma rifle. My body armor took most of it, thankfully."

My chest grew so tight I could not get a breath.

An image of my Isla filled my mind's eye, lying on some distant world, bloody and hurting and shot in the back. My Isla, who could have died in that moment, or afterward if she had not received adequate medical care.

My Isla, who had nearly given her life trying to free someone else from captivity. My body quaked with the force of my rage and sorrow.

"Mikas." She moved her head to look into my eyes. "I'm all right," she said, and squeezed my hand. "I lived. My mission didn't fail, and the person I extracted is living free now."

"I am glad to hear it." I kissed her knuckles. "But is this mission the reason you came to Fortusia? You are in hiding?"

"Yes." She bit her lip. "There's an angry Erotovo on Ngara who believes I *stole* this person from him. He's combing Havel Prime for a woman named Halena Onsulus. That was my false identity for the job."

"How did your mission go wrong?"

"I never found out." She sighed. "I've had no contact with my handler since that day and Ycari doesn't know. My best guess is someone found the holo projector that hid us while we got ready to escape, but I suppose I'll never know for sure." She rubbed her nose on my chest over my hearts. "I received a new identity after it was over. My face, my hair, and even my voice have changed. I don't think the Erotovo will ever find me, no matter how determined he is."

I tried to imagine Isla as she might have looked before she came to Fortusia and could not picture it.

"Mikas." Her voice suddenly had a sharp edge, for reasons I did not understand. "Say something."

"I am sorry your mission did not go as planned." I caressed her cheek, but she raised her head and moved away from my touch.

"Do you not feel the same about me now?" she demanded. Her eyes had become fiery. "Because my appearance changed?"

My stomach churned because I had somehow made her angry. But the more I looked into her eyes, the less I thought my reaction had caused her to be upset.

This was not anger at me, I decided. This was anger at the Erotovo who had held someone captive and now hunted for her, combined with fear that by changing her appearance she might not be herself any longer.

"My feelings have not changed at all," I said, my voice firm. "No matter what color your hair is, or your eyes, or the shape of your face, you are *Isla*."

She studied me for a long time. "So if my hair was brown," she said finally, "or my eyes were blue, or my voice was a little different—"

"—I would love you just the same." I cupped her cheek, and this time she did not move away from my hand. "It is your soul I love, my mate."

She lay back down and let out a breath. "Okay," she said quietly. "I believe you."

We lay like that for a long time, soaking in the warmth and the comfort of being close to each other. Absently, she caressed my arms, my side, my thigh, and my chest, and even played gently with my nipple piercings and spines. Her casual explorations were wonderfully sensual.

I did the same, memorizing every detail of the shape of her ears, the graceful curves of her shoulders and neck, the dip above her collarbone, and the sublime curvature of her hip. I would learn everything about her body, from her toes to her hair.

"How do you feel?" I asked when I judged nearly an hour had gone by.

"I feel loved." She moved her head to look up at me. "Safe and loved. And that's really nice."

I drew her gently up my body so I could kiss her. "It is very nice," I agreed. "What may I do for my mate so she feels even more safe and loved?"

"I'm starving," she said instantly. "Feed me?"

CHAPTER 22

ISLA

RATHER THAN ARRANGE FOR FOOD TO BE DELIVERED, MIKAS declared his intention to cook a meal for us—a very fine and lovingly made gourmet meal that consisted of a half-dozen mouth-watering dishes.

Of course, watching Mikas cook naked might have contributed to how frequently I licked my lips in anticipation. Even with his back to me, he clearly knew I was watching, judging by his smile and the way he flexed his buttocks every so often.

I offered to help with the cooking, but he insisted I relax on the sofa wrapped in a plush robe that was big enough to accommodate both of us, or one generously sized Prylothian.

He brought the feast and a bottle of wine to the sitting area on an enormous tray and set it on a low table in front of the sofa.

"We could sit at the dining table," I protested.

"If we did, I would not be able to do this." He sat next to me, drew me onto his lap, and pulled the tray closer. "I am sorry there are no jampas."

"I guess even as an ambassador Atlath doesn't have your connections," I teased. I looked over the dishes in amazement. "I can't believe you made all this just from what you found in the kitchen. This is enough to feed an army."

"You said you were hungry. So am I." He kissed my temple. "This is my first proper meal I have made and shared with my mate. I could not very well bring you toasted bread, a bowl of fruit, and bits of cheese."

"Thank you for making us this amazing meal." I leaned my head against his chest. "But for the record, I love bread, fruit, and cheese very much and that would have been fine."

"*Fine* is not good enough for my Isla, especially not on this special occasion." He made a sweeping gesture over the tray. "Which would you like to try first?"

I sampled each of the dishes, confirming they tasted even better than they smelled. While many of the ingredients in the kitchen came from Prylothia, there were also staple food items native to Fortusia, and he'd combined them to create absolutely delicious soup, bread topped with layers of meats, sweet sauces, and spicy vegetables, and baked vegetables stuffed with a savory meat and gravy.

Once I'd expressed my approval and appreciation with a long kiss, he began to eat as well. And he ate. And ate. And *ate*.

When I'd said he'd made enough food to feed an army, I supposed I'd meant an army comprised of one hungry Fortusian male.

Long after my belly was full and I'd curled up sitting cross-ways on his lap and nestled into the crook of his arm, Mikas finally pushed the now nearly empty tray away and rested his chin gently on top of my head. "You are content?" he asked.

"Very." With my head on his chest, I listened to his hearts beat in a steady rhythm. "You're going to spoil me, aren't you?"

He kissed my damp hair. "Every chance I get, in every way I can think of."

Smiling, I dozed for a while, warm and full and wrapped in a ridiculous robe I never wanted to take off.

On the one hand, I was so content and comfortable in Mikas's arms that I could have believed we'd been lovers for months or years. But in reality, only a day ago I'd been nervously pacing around my apartment, worrying Mikas might not want to leave Onat'ras with me.

I think he will, Brae had said in response to my concern. At the time I'd wondered why he sounded so wry. Only now did I start to wonder if my shadowbat had some kind of inside knowledge.

"Mikas?" I murmured.

"Yes?" he rumbled.

"Did Brae know about you?"

"Yes." He squeezed me gently. "But I only found out yesterday that he has known for some time."

I found myself caught between surprise, disbelief, and a little bit of hurt that Brae hadn't said a word about how Mikas felt.

"What happened yesterday?" I asked.

"He came to my apartment just before my shift and urged me to get you away from Nubo and Onat'ras." He laced his fingers through mine. "He said 'If she is your mate, you need to do what is right for her.' That is the first time I had ever spoken to him, and the first I knew that he was aware of the situation."

Confused, I asked, "If he knew all along, or even knew for a while, why didn't he say something to me?"

"Perhaps he did not think it was his secret to tell." He stroked my back. Even through the plush robe, the heat of his hand soothed me. "And who but you and I could know the right time for the truth to come out? He loves you very much. I am sure he wants only the best for you. Perhaps he thought you were not ready to hear it until now."

"He might have been right." I sighed. "I don't hold it against him. I had a lot of healing to do after I came to Fortusia. I'm still healing. Maybe it wasn't the right time until it was."

"As difficult as it has been, I think you are right." Mikas squeezed my hand. "I would like it very much if we could heal together."

That was a lovely thought…but the sudden heaviness in his voice compelled me to tug our entwined hands into my lap so I could cradle his much-larger hand between both of mine.

"Tell me how you came back to Fortusia," I said. "And about Slug."

He frowned. "Who is Slug?"

My cheeks heated in embarrassment. "Oh, that's the nickname I gave the Atolani female who thought you of all people would want to be a raider. You didn't tell me her name, so I decided she was a Slug."

He laughed.

Oh, gods, his laugh. It rolled through our suite, rumbly and deep and wonderful. It made me warm inside, but very unexpectedly, my eyes filled with tears.

"My Isla." He lifted me up so he could kiss me, and then he rested his forehead on mine. "Why do you cry?"

"Because this is the first time I've ever heard you laugh," I said, my throat tight.

He cupped my cheek. "My hearts have been heavy for a very long time—since long before you and I met. The moment you came into Zaa'ga they began to heal, but I ached for you. And I was full of rage at Nubo for keeping us apart and afraid he might harm you. I did not have the hearts to laugh until now."

My poor Mikas. I kissed him gently. "Tell me about Slug."

"Her name is Kona Landus." He took a deep breath and let it out. "We served together in the Cludian Corps. I had not seen her for two years when she came into Zaa'ga this past week." He scrubbed his face with his hand. "We were lovers for a time. I can only say that we were soldiers at war and it was a miserable life. In my suffering, I sought some kind of comfort and meaning."

"You don't owe me any justifications or apologies." I held his gaze so he could see I meant it. "I'm not bothered that you shared a bed with Kona. Of course you would want something good in the midst of chaos and misery. Goodness knows I needed the same."

"It was never good." Mikas took my hand and pressed my palm to his jaw. "I do not think I found any comfort or meaning either. At best, it was pleasure."

"Was it more than that for Kona?" I asked.

"Maybe," he allowed. "But mostly it was a matter of pride for her, I think." He rumbled in anger. "I was a commandant. She thought I might advance her career and she was possessive as a result. Regrettably, I tolerated her behavior when I should not have."

"Understandable under the circumstances." I snuggled closer so I could tuck my head under his chin. "Don't be so hard on yourself."

"I will try, for your sake." He kissed my hair. "I was wounded in battle not long before my enlistment ended. Once physicians reconstructed my right leg and the rest of of my injuries healed, I declined to join the raider squad that recruited Kona and instead returned home to Fortusia. The rest, you know."

I wanted to encourage him to tell me more about his early life, his enlistment, and the circumstances of his injuries, but his hand slid up my bare leg under the robe to grip my thigh and I decided all that could wait. We had time to tell each other everything.

"I think it is time for dessert," Mikas said, his thumb stroking my inner thigh languidly. "I find myself yearning for something sweet."

"I'm sure we could arrange to have something delivered to

the shop and brought up to the room," I said innocently. "That bakery near the metaphysical shop has the most delicious cakes."

His lips traveled along my hairline, and his tongue caressed the ridges and sensitive skin of my ear. I shivered.

"No baker could provide what I want." His hand moved farther up my leg until I squeezed my thighs together to pin his hand in place. "My tastes are more refined now. I require a singer to satisfy my needs."

Undaunted by my playful resistance, he slid a single finger between my thighs. Its very tip just barely brushed my slit, but it might as well have been a bolt of lightning straight to my clit. Wetness began to drip from my pussy. I whimpered and squeezed my legs together harder.

Beneath my ridiculous robe, his cocks had hardened to stone. I pictured them slick with his lubrication and dripping precum and licked my lips.

"How merciless you are." He chuckled into my ear. "You would deny a thirsting man a drink?"

"You can't be *that* thirsty," I countered, breathless. "We drank an entire bottle of wine with our meal."

"I beg to differ. I am parched." He caught my earlobe in his sharp teeth, careful not to draw blood. "I need your sweet nectar, my mate. And then I want to see you take my cocks here on this sofa."

I couldn't help it; I moaned.

"I want to see you spread your legs and take me fully," he continued. "I want to give you my knot and pump you full of my cum and hear you scream my name so loudly your voice carries for kilometers. I want you to know what you will have any time you want it for the rest of our days. But first…"

He ran his finger slowly up and down along my dripping slit again, and again, and again, before drawing his hand out from between my legs to show me the wetness on his fingertip.

"First," he said, smiling to show his fangs, "I need to slake my thirst." And then he licked his finger clean.

Gods above and below, this man might kill me with sex before we had a chance to escape the planet.

"Stand up," he said, nudging me with his hips. "Stand on the sofa and put your feet on either side of me."

Trembling and weak-kneed with desire, I rose and did as he'd asked, standing facing him with my feet astride his thighs. The robe was so oversized and so long that it reached the floor behind me.

Slowly, he untied the robe and opened it to bare me to his sight. "Beautiful beyond belief," he said, and gripped my hips to steady me. "Take off the robe."

I slid it off my shoulders, down my arms, and let it fall to the floor.

He drew me to him, slid a little lower on the sofa, and buried his face between my legs. I settled in with a whimper, my knees slightly bent and braced into the cushion.

"I smell my cum in you," he murmured. "This is the smell of mating—of all my dreams come true."

He slid two fingers into my pussy and pumped them slowly, licking his lips at the wet sound they made.

"Do you like being fingered by your mate, Isla?" he asked, looking up at me.

"Yes." It came out as a gasp.

"Do you like sitting on your mate's face?"

My chest heaved. I cupped my breasts and pinched my nipples. "Yes."

He withdrew his fingers and licked them. "Do you like to watch your mate drink your sweet nectar?"

"Yes, I do." I tapped his nose and pulled my hand away when he tried to bite my fingers. "I thought you were thirsty."

With a chuckle, he returned to my pussy, lapping at my slit and teasing my clit. I cried out and rode his face, pinching my nipple with one hand and holding onto his head as he speared me with his tongue.

When he urged me to put one foot on the back of the sofa, I did so, and he rewarded me by turning his attention to my clit. I wailed and held on to him desperately as he took me to the edge of bliss.

I came with a cry, held tight against his mouth by his enormous strength so I couldn't move away until he'd wrung every shudder from me.

When my legs gave out, he guided me down his body slowly, his mouth and tongue traveling over my abdomen to my breasts as my pussy and ass came to rest against his dripping cocks.

As he sucked on my nipples, I slipped the tips of his cocks inside me one at a time. Their heat and size felt so, so good, and I could take him more easily after my orgasm. Bursts of precum splattered my ass and thighs and he groaned.

"Isla," he grated, his hips bucking as he pulled me against his chest. "You will drain me dry."

"I hope so." I stroked him slowly, deliberately, with both hands. "I intend to leave you with nothing left in those beautiful balls."

His cocks leapt in my hands in eagerness. I kissed him deeply.

He held his upper cock steady as I braced myself on his shoulders and worked my way down until the bumps behind his cock head rubbed against my G-spot. I shuddered and whimpered.

"You see, I am made for you," he said, holding me to his chest. "Can you make yourself come, my Isla?"

I could certainly try.

Crying out into his chest, I circled my hips and moved up and down until I found the precise rhythm and angle that sent me careening back toward release.

As the pitch of my cries rose, he gripped my hips and

bounced me gently on his cock until I screamed and came, my back arching and head falling back.

"Gods above, Isla," he ground out. He lifted me free of his cock and rose, positing me on my hands and knees on the sofa. Holding my hips so I didn't fall over onto my side, he pressed the thick head of his lower cock against my pussy as his upper cock rested on my ass.

"My mate," he rasped. "Spread your legs more for me."

Gasping and whimpering, I did, bracing myself with both hands on the back of the sofa.

The head of his upper cock pushed inside me, enormous and hot. My cry blended with his groan.

As if he was savoring every moment or fighting to control himself, or both, he thrust, filling me a centimeter at a time. Every bump and nub made me cry out, even as slowly as he moved.

"Mikas," I wailed. "Mikas, oh gods."

He didn't stop until he'd buried himself all the way to the hilt, including the partially swollen knot at the base of his cock. His upper cock slid over my ass, hot and wet and dripping precum.

"Isla." He caressed my back. "You are so beautiful, and you take me so perfectly."

Slowly, he withdrew from me, the bumps and nubs of his cock stroking me in places I had seldom felt friction. And when that bump just behind his cock head found my G-spot, I wailed again.

"Ah, there it is," he murmured. "This is what you like."

He pumped in and out of me less slowly, stroking that bump over my G-spot so I cried out and clenched around him.

He slipped his lower cock free and plunged his upper cock in. In this position, its distinct shape meant a symphony of new sensations and frictions. My cries turned desperate.

In the midst of that bliss, he slipped his slick fingers into my asshole. I came apart again, this time fluttering and clenching around his fingers and his cock.

"Yes, Isla," he said, his hand on my hip holding me steady as his fingers stretched me gently. "Relax. You are almost ready for me."

He stroked himself to gather more lubrication and added yet another finger for me to grind on. Gods, it felt so good.

His fingers slipped free, he drew back, and then his slick, hot upper cock pressed against my asshole—larger still than three of his fingers. Gods, yes. This was everything I wanted. I clutched the sofa until my knuckles turned white, ready for that delicious combination of pleasure and pain.

But as his hot slickness dripped onto and into me, I felt myself...relax. "Oh," I breathed.

He slipped his upper cock into my ass, and I lost myself in a crashing wave of pleasure and warmth. Heat rolled through me. I sagged in his grip, only marginally aware of how I instinctively arched my back to take him fully.

Oh...gods. This was bliss. I was full—so full—fuller than I had ever been. And not only had there been no pain, the sheer pleasure of feeling his cocks inside me had left me in a haze.

"My mate," Mikas said, his hand cupping my face as he bent over me, one knee on the sofa next to me. His eyes were all black, but his expression was loving and tender. "Is this what you want?"

"Yes." My voice was a wisp. "This is what I want. *This is what I need.*"

Maybe his lubrication had this euphoric effect. And maybe it had relaxed me so I could accommodate his enormous upper cock in my ass without pain or difficulty or fear. Or maybe it had affected me like this because I was his true mate. Those thoughts drifted through my mind, only to drift away just as quickly.

There'd be time to figure it all out later. Right now, I just wanted to be fucked by my beautiful beastly man.

As soon as he began thrusting both cocks slowly, the euphoria was replaced by a pleasure so intense that I couldn't stop screaming and calling his name, sometimes just as single syllables and sometimes as the whole word. He called for me too, every time he thrust, and whenever he paused to hold himself back. And he growled and rumbled each time I tightened around him, my dripping pussy and ass fluttering.

I didn't think I could come again, but when he wrapped his arm around my waist and drew me up on my knees on the edge of the sofa, the sensations were so different and the way his bumps rubbed inside me made me cry out. And when his hand slipped down to circle my clit, I came undone one last time with a sob and a nearly voiceless wail that was some version of his name.

"Will you take my knot, my Isla?" he whispered in my ear, going still with his body hot against mine. "May I give it to you?"

"Give it to me." My voice was hoarse from screaming. "Please."

Gently, he lay us down on our sides and hooked my leg over his arm. "Then watch," he murmured, his lips against my ear as he pumped both cocks into me. "Watch me give it to you."

His cock thrust into me, glistening and slick with my arousal and his own. As his release neared, his knot had swollen almost completely, and even in my haze of pleasure I grew uneasy.

"I can't take that," I said, turning to look at him. "Mikas…"

"You can," he said, very gently, and rested his head against mine. A strange, wonderful sound rose in his chest. And then he cooed. *Oh…*

Once again, my body relaxed, and my head fell back against his chest.

With my leg still raised on his arm, he kissed my neck, and

slipped his knot inside me with the wonderful sensation of coming home. Of completion.

His knot swelled, locking us together, as his lower cock filled my ass to bursting. So perfect. I shivered hard with a soft orgasm.

And then he was coming with growls and groans and my name falling from his lips, his hips jerking as he emptied himself in what felt like a dozen spurts that filled my pussy—and over-filled my ass in hot pulses that streamed down my thigh.

When he finally curled around me, his cocks and knot still buried deep inside me, I let out a little sound that was part sob and part sigh.

Trembling, Mikas rested his head on mine. "Isla."

Strange how my name sounded like a complete sentence when he said it. *Isla, I love you. Isla, you are my world. Isla, let me share this bliss with you for all my days.*

"Mikas," I said, and that was a complete sentence too.

CHAPTER 23

ISLA

MIKAS KISSED MY JAW AND HELD ME TIGHT AGAINST HIS CHEST
with both arms as if even now he worried I might slip from his
grasp.

My gaze drifted to the basking stone, on which I had yet to
come. I was so tired and sated that I didn't mind that we'd
substituted the sofa for the stones. Well, there would be other
basking stones. I certainly hadn't suffered any hardship, and
neither had Mikas. I still fluttered around his cocks, which
throbbed inside me in a way that made my toes curl even now.

Gods, could I have this bliss for the rest of my life? Could a
woman who'd had nothing but a single case of clothing and a
handful of credits to her name only months ago have something
so good and perfect?

Maybe so.

Somewhere nearby, presumably, while Mikas and I were
busy—to use Pioni's phrase—Atlath and our other allies were
working on ways to get us off Fortusia and away from Nubo's

anger. My faith that they would find a way had allowed me to lose myself in Mikas's attentions and the comforts of this temporary safe harbor. And it was worth a lot to have someone at my back, both literally and metaphorically.

I had a home that wasn't a place, but a person—or I would, if we stayed together. The prospect seemed more compelling by the minute.

"You are content," Mikas murmured, his lips against my ear. "At peace."

"Yes." I raised his hand to my lips and kissed it. "You could tell by my scent?"

"Everything about how you feel and smell tells me so." He rested his nose against the back of my neck and inhaled deeply.

"And what about you?" I asked. "Are you content and at peace?"

"Never doubt that I am." He stroked his thumb over my fingers. "You do not mind that I relax and comfort you with my coo?"

"Mind? Hardly." I smiled. "Taking cocks that big, with an even bigger knot, without pain? I like that coo very much."

"My coo does much more for my mate than allow you to take my knot."

"What else does it do?"

He nuzzled the back of my neck. "Last night, you had bad dreams. When I cooed, you were no longer distressed, and I think your dreams became more pleasant."

I'd thought he'd sung to me during the night. Apparently, it was a coo, not a song, that had made me feel so good. And though I had vague impressions of nightmares, I recalled none of them, and woke up feeling more fully rested and happy than I had in a very long time.

"I coo only for my mate," he added. "It is a sound I make only for you, when you are distressed or in pain...and when you want to take my knot."

I closed my eyes and focused on the heat and sensations of his cocks, and thought about the fact he could soothe me simply with his voice. I dimly recalled hearing about that aspect of Fortusian true mate physiology a long time ago, but it hadn't really registered with me as meaningful at the time. I'd certainly had no inkling that someday I might benefit from a seemingly miraculous ability.

He remained fully—and doubly—inside me. The full-to-bursting sensation was a kind of comfort I hadn't known I liked until now.

You don't just like *having your pussy and ass stuffed with Mikas's cocks, Isla Mair*, I thought. *You* love *it.*

"The galaxy is vast." Mikas said, his body so warm and soothing and strong next to mine. "We can go far from here, far from Ngara. Find a beautiful world and make our future there. Where would you like us to go, my mate?"

Us.

Since my mother died, I had never been part of an *us*, even when I was part of the Web.

I thought of the moment last night—had it really only been last night?—that I'd taken Mikas's hand and urged him to follow me into the tunnel that led to our escape route from the perfume shop. In that moment, though I hadn't realized it at the time, I had begun to think of Mikas and me as an *us*. We'd needed to get to safety together. And not just because he'd had my torn underwear in his pocket and my slickness on his fingers and tongue.

In fact, I might have thought of Mikas and me as an *us* long before that, whenever I sat at the bar to talk to him while feeling safe in his presence. And that was probably why I lay here now, so content. Because we'd been an *us* for a very long time.

"I'm sorry it took me so long to figure this out," I said, hoping he understood what I meant.

He kissed my ear. "Isla, no apology is necessary. Our friendship is the best thing in my life. I would not have traded these past few months for anything."

"Me neither." I squeezed his hand. "How long will your knot last?"

"Another ten or twenty minutes. Less if I do not wait until it eases completely." Mikas rumbled. "I do not want to rush. I want to savor this feeling."

"I don't want to rush either." I chuckled. "But if it's up to me, you'll have plenty of opportunities to savor this exact feeling so I can savor it too."

"Of course it is up to you." He pulled me a little closer. "Your autonomy is as important to me as it is to you. In all things, you must always tell me what you wish to do, and what you do not. You have my word I will respect your choices without question."

"But when it comes to our future, we'll make those choices together." I bit my lip. "Do you really want to leave Fortusia?"

"I have many reasons to love my homeworld. If we would be safe here, I would be very content to stay." He rested his head on mine. "But we are *not* safe, so we must go where we will find safety and happiness. What would make you happy, my Isla?"

In answer, I wiggled my bottom. He sucked in a breath at the sensation of his cocks moving inside me. I chuckled.

"Other than that," he said finally, his voice a bit ragged.

"I want to sing," I said. "Besides being here with you, the happiest I've ever been in my life was onstage at Zaa'ga, singing and watching you pour drinks while Brae feasted on insects outside."

"Then that is what we will seek." He hummed. "Do you know of the planet Jakora?"

"I think so." I frowned and thought. "I've never been there. It's a resort planet, isn't it?"

"Yes. By all accounts, it is breathtakingly beautiful, with lavender oceans, beaches with the softest sand, and endless resorts, clubs, and bars where a Fortusian bartender and human singer might find work." He caressed my arm. "It is also far from here, on the edge of Alliance space, but safe—or as safe as any world might be."

He let go of my hand and tapped on his wristcomm. A hologram appeared above his arm of a purple planet swirled with lavender clouds, orbited by a half-dozen moons.

The hologram zoomed in past the moons and showed more details of Jakora while scrolling through images of the ocean, beaches, and resorts.

"It's beautiful." I tore my gaze away from the hologram and looked up at Mikas. "Are there plenty of insects so Brae stays plump and happy?"

"Very rich in insect life," he confirmed after consulting his wristcomm screen. "A shadowbat's paradise, as well as paradise for us. I have enough in savings to keep us comfortable until we find work someplace together."

"I have some savings too—not a fortune, but you won't have to pay for everything." I pulled his head down so his forehead rested on mine and I could gaze into his beautiful yellow eyes. "Should we go to Jakora?"

"That is my vote." He brushed his lips on mine. "What do you say?"

I searched my heart for any hesitation, or reason to suggest something else, or even any fears, and found none. Jakora's beauty had already stolen my heart.

Ours were not the only votes that counted, though. The decision had to be unanimous.

Brae, I thought, reaching out for my best friend. *Mikas and I are thinking about going to Jakora. Would you—*

Book passage, Brae said. His voice in my head was so excited it was nearly a squeak. *I've always wanted to taste Jakoran crickets.*

All right. I smiled, though he couldn't see it. *Anything to report?*

Atlath's shop is closed today, he said, with less cheer in his voice. *I'm perched in a tree next to the shop. I've seen six people we know work for Nubo in the market, and Slug has been outside the shop doors since last night. Either Atolani don't need much sleep or she's highly motivated to find a way to get her talons into you. But everything's quiet. Do you want me to go to Zaa'ga and try to see what Nubo is doing?*

I bit my lip. *Let me discuss that with Mikas.*

I sensed a tingle of warmth through our bond. *I'm very happy for you both*, he said.

Mikas touched my face, drawing my attention. "Isla?"

"Yes." I covered his hand with mine. "I was talking to Brae. That makes three votes for Jakora."

The absolute joy in his smile made me pull him to me for a long kiss.

When his lower cock moved, I gasped against Mikas's mouth. Hot cum that had been held inside me trickled down my thigh. His knot had begun to ease.

A twinge of something like sadness made my chest ache. I'd already become accustomed to the reassuring sensation of his knot—a connection I'd never shared with anyone else.

Mikas wrapped me in his arms and drew me close with my back against his chest once more. "The end of our first knotted mating is bittersweet, but I prefer to think of it as a beginning."

I held his hand in both of mine as his knot eased. His cocks had softened only a little, though. How many times could Mikas come before he couldn't come any more?

Someday I would endeavor to find out, but I suspected today was not that day. We had to book passage to Jakora and find a way to get to the port safely. But I did nothing but be held and comforted until Mikas's knot had gone away.

When Mikas finally eased me free of him, I flinched. "I'm sore," I said before he could ask. "It's not bad."

"You need to soak in a warm bath." He gathered up the discarded robe, wrapped me in it, and carried me to the bathroom, where he sat on the side of the enormous tub with me on his lap. As it filled with fragrant pink water, he kissed my temple. "I will clean up after us and then join you."

"Bathe with me first," I countered, lacing our fingers together. "Then we can clean together after."

"I am persuaded." He chuckled. "I fear I am fated to lose every argument before it begins."

I kissed his knuckles. "I promise to only occasionally take advantage of that fact."

Once we were in the bath, he insisted on washing and combing out my hair. No one had ever done that for me before, and it was marvelous. We were briefly distracted from our mission to get clean while I thanked him with kisses.

As we washed ourselves—and each other—with soap and soft cloths, I told him what Brae had said about the shop and Nubo's agents. He listened, his mouth a tight line.

"Brae could go to Zaa'ga and try to spy on Nubo," I finished. "I'm sure Nubo isn't going to just wait for us to walk out of here. He must be plotting something. I'd like to know what."

"As would I." He drew me close. "Your companion is a very excellent spy. If you think he can do this safely, then I am in favor of it."

I reached out again to Brae. *If you can get into Zaa'ga and find out what Nubo is planning, then go ahead*, I said. *But your safety is more important than anything else. If it's dangerous, just come back.*

I will, he promised.

In the meantime, Mikas and I are going to talk to Atlath about booking travel to Jakora and getting to the port safely. I'll let you know what we decide. Be safe and check in regularly until you get back. I love you.

Love you too, Isla.

I leaned against Mikas's chest and sighed. "He's going to Zaa'ga."

"Good." He kissed my hair. "My Isla, I am ready to be away from Nubo and on our way to Jakora. Are you?"

"Yes." I took a deep breath and let it out. "I'm ready."

CHAPTER 24

MIKAS

Once we finished bathing and cleaning, we opened the door of our suite to find travel cases in the hallway packed with clothing and toiletries for each of us.

Everything in my case smelled of Madame Ycari, while Isla's new clothes carried Pioni's delicate scent. All the clothing was quite practical yet stylish and could be combined to create a number of different outfits. I happily discarded my clothing from the day before in favor of a comfortable shirt and trousers that flattered my build and accommodated my spines.

Rather than discard her own dress, Isla packed it into the case and selected a very plain and practical jumpsuit to wear instead. As she slipped her daggers into their sheaths on her arm and in her boots, I had to suppress the urge to shed my clothing and make love to her again.

Even after bathing, she smelled strongly of me, of *us*. I doubted she was aware of it or of how profoundly her scent affected me. My hearts radiated warmth as they had never done before. And though I was uneasy about the dangers we faced,

Isla had chosen to be with me. I could face anything with Isla at my side.

I carried our cases and followed Isla from the third level to the ground floor. With every step, my mate's contentment evaporated, replaced by the metallic scent of apprehension. This more than my own unease caused my spines to bristle.

We had stolen half a day of sanctuary, but now we must face the grim reality of finding a way safely off Fortusia.

"Any word from Brae?" I asked as we reached the bottom of the staircase, my voice pitched low.

"Yes. He doesn't have anything to report yet." She swallowed audibly. "He's in the bar, waiting for an opportunity to slip into Nubo's office, or for him to come out."

I kissed her temple. I had to bend far less to do so when she wore boots rather than being barefoot. "Have faith," I stated. "He will be all right. Shadowbats are masters of disguise."

"It's not just Brae." She touched my hand. "I feel all prickly, like someone's breathing down my neck. I get that feeling sometimes, and usually it means something is about to go very, very wrong." She bit her lip. "The day my mission on Ngara blew up in my face, I had this same feeling from the moment I woke up."

"I too have sensed rising danger for the past several days." I set my case down and squeezed her hand. "I cannot say which threat is the most immediate—or whether there is something lurking we do not yet know about. We must trust our instincts in all things, now more than ever." I pressed my lips to her ear and murmured, "That includes apparent allies as well as known adversaries."

"I know we can depend on Ycari and Pioni," Isla countered, her voice firm. "And if they trust Atlath, so do I. My gut tells me the danger is outside this building." Her expression turned wry. "Unfortunately, so are all the spaceports."

She waved her hand over the scanner next to the doors to the shop. They slid aside, revealing the dimly lit shop floor and the terrarium in its center. The doors to the market were indeed closed.

As we entered, Atlath emerged from the terrarium and waddled toward us. "Isla," he croaked, and then dipped his head in my direction. "Mikas."

"Good afternoon, Atlath," Isla said, smiling.

Months after our first meeting, it amazed me how her smile made my skin tingle—even in the midst of so much uncertainty.

"Thank you so much for letting us stay in your beautiful Star Bird room," my mate added. "We're so grateful."

"I must reimburse you for damage to your furniture, however," I added, with an apologetic bow. "Please let me know the cost of replacing the bed and bedding."

Atlath's burbly chuckle made Isla's smile grow. "I am not concerned," he said.

"We certainly have to pay someone back for all this." Isla gestured at our travel cases. "Everyone has been so kind to us."

"These are gifts." Atlath burbled again. "A traditional Prylothian blessing on your mating."

Isla's blush melted my hearts and forced me to smother a chuckle.

"Isla and I want to immigrate to Jakora," I informed our host. "We will need passage on transports to at least one or two major transit hubs to make it difficult for anyone who attempts to track us. I have made arrangements for new identities for us, which will be ready soon. With those, we should be able to travel incognito."

Isla blinked up at me. "Just since last night?" she asked, frowning. "I didn't know you did that. When did you have time?"

Unlike my beautiful mate, I could not blush, but my face suddenly became warmer than usual. "I am sorry I forgot to tell you. I began making arrangements a few days ago."

I worried she would be troubled by this news or find my

actions presumptuous, but she slipped her hand into mine and squeezed.

"I can help with travel." Atlath waddled to a counter near the rear of the shop and patted a small case—the kind often used by couriers. "I contacted my homeworld and arranged diplomatic credentials for both of you."

My breath caught. Isla gasped.

Atlath opened a second case and showed us a pair of hexagonal medallions bearing an official seal. "These identify you as my emissaries. You will travel protected by Prylothian and interplanetary law."

"Atlath, this is too much," Isla protested.

"It is not." He grunted and shut the lid of the second case. "You are now my employees. Your task is to deliver this case to the Prylothian embassy on whatever planet you choose as your new home."

"What is in the case?" I asked.

"Nothing dangerous, or even top-secret." Atlath burbled in the way I had learned was the equivalent of a laugh. "It contains sand from a Fortusian beach. A traditional gesture of mutual respect between ambassadors living on different worlds."

"All this because you liked my singing and Mikas's bartending?" Isla asked, her eyes shimmering. "We're so grateful for everything you've done, but—"

"I have been lonely since my mate died," Atlath croaked. "Mikas's hospitality at Zaa'ga gave me solace. And when you sang, I rediscovered happiness."

My mate's tears spilled over. I squeezed her hand and stroked it with my thumb to comfort her with my strength and love.

"I grieve because you are leaving," Atlath continued, "but your love reminds me of my early days with my mate. You should live happily, away from Nubo Wex." He burbled. "I will find another bar."

For three years I had served Atlath and cleaned the pool in which he sat and had no inkling of his heartache or what drew him to Zaa'ga several nights a week. I certainly had not realized fulfilling the duties of my job had provided comfort. He had never tipped me for my service, but leapt at the opportunity to repay us with a gift with value far beyond any amount of money he might have put in my tip jar.

Evil acts caused great pain. Like ripples in a pond, that pain affected more than the victims of those acts. Isla and I knew that harsh truth very well.

But it was also true that acts of selflessness and kindness created ripples too, even when we were not aware of it. Those ripples were at least as strong as those made by evil acts and had just as much to do with the facts Isla's hand was now in mine and we had the means to travel in what I hoped would be relative safety—especially if we had new identities and took sensible precautions.

My wristcomm signaled I had a message from my friend from the Corps.

"Our identification kits are nearly complete," I told Isla after I read the short transmission. "We must choose our pseudonyms from this list or allow my contact to select for us."

"Let me look." She scrolled through the names my friend had offered as options.

With every moment, the sour note of her unhappiness grew. Given our earlier conversation about her past, I suspected the reason for her gloom.

I rested my free hand on her lower back. "You are always Isla," I reminded her. "I am always your Mikas. Whatever our official identification states, we know each other's hearts."

She rested her head against my chest. "Efre Vorda," she said softly, looking up from the screen of my wristcomm. "I like how that sounds."

"Would you like to choose my name?" I kissed her hair. "I have no preference."

My request elicited a smile. She scanned the list, tapping her lower lip with her fingertip and murmuring the names to herself.

"Pelles Vertak," she said finally. "Efre and Pelles. Those sound nice together, don't you think?"

"A perfect choice." I sent those names back to my friend and received confirmation that within the hour the identifications would be ready for use.

Atlath, meanwhile, had selected a pipe of wine from a shelf and brought it to the counter. He reached under the counter and brought out five glasses: two large, two medium-sized, and one very small.

"While we wait for word from your contact, will you join me for a drink?" Atlath asked, opening the pipe with a flourish.

"Of course," I said. "Is someone joining us?"

"Yes." Atlath filled the smaller glasses first and then the large ones. "Pioni and Madame Ycari will be here soon. Ycari wishes to see you off and Pioni plans to accompany you to the port."

"Oh, good." Isla's mood improved instantly. "I really wanted to thank them and say goodbye. I was afraid I wouldn't get a chance."

I recalled her story of how she had left the palace on Agicord without being able to speak to her lover, who had helped her find a way to escape.

I started to tuck her against my side just as her eyes widened. "The perfume," she gasped. "I haven't put it on yet."

She opened her case and searched until she found the wooden box from Ycari's shop. "When Ycari comes, I want to be able to tell her how much I love the scent," she said, looking up at me as she opened the box. "You don't mind, do you?"

"Of course not," I assured her. "Please, go ahead."

Despite my initial resistance to the idea, my lovely mate would smell like Isla to me regardless of any perfumes or scents she used. And I was very curious what scent Madame Ycari had made that would be so perfect without Isla actually selecting any of its ingredients.

The wooden box and pouch that protected the bottle were lovely, but the pink crystal bottle was utterly breathtaking. Its facets shimmered even in the low light inside Atlath's shop. With all my attention on Isla, I had hardly noticed its design in Madame Ycari's sampling room. Now I realized what I had not noticed last night.

"Isla, look at the stopper," I said as she admired how the bottle sparkled. "It is the waterfall. And the bottle is the lake."

"Oh, you're right," she gasped, her eyes widening as she looked from the bottle to me and back again. "Ycari made me a bottle that looks like my favorite place in Onat'ras." She stared at the bottle, turning it slowly at eye level. "I only mentioned it once, in passing," she added, almost to herself. "But she remembered. And now I can take it with me."

Isla carefully unstoppered the bottle and withdrew a crystal wand that dripped with perfume. The scent filled the air, and suddenly everything else faded away as if I had been transported to the moment I had first caught Isla's scent in Zaa'ga the day she came in to audition.

Somehow, through technology and mastery of her craft, Ycari had made a perfume of my own scent and that of my mate, blended with the natural fragrance of the waters of Fortusia. And she had prepared the perfume before I had confessed my love, and before Isla and I had decided to leave the planet together.

I could not help myself; lost in the scent, I went to my knees before my mate.

"Oh, no," she said, smiling down at me. "Not again."

"Again and always." I kissed her palm. "Do you recognize the scent she has made?"

"Maybe?" She ran the wand across her wrists, dabbed it along her neck and cleavage, and stoppered the bottle again before setting it on the counter. She lifted her wrist to her nose and inhaled deeply, frowning.

Her head tilted. "Does it...does it smell like you? And the lake?"

"Yes." I rested my hands on her hips. "And of you."

"Oh." She sank down to sit on her travel case to bring herself eye level with me. "She made a perfume of *us* combined with the water of Fortusia?"

"And floral notes," I said. "Ones I do not recognize by name, but that I like very much."

"So she knew too, somehow." Her smile turned wobbly. "Brae knew, Madame Ycari knew...was I the last to know?"

I kissed her gently. "All that matters is that we know."

"I agree," Atlath croaked. On the other side of the counter, he sipped his wine and kept a tactful distance. "Your employer, I think, was unaware. He may or may not know the whole truth even now. Whether the knowledge would make him more or less angry and vindictive, I am not sure."

I also was not sure what Nubo's reaction might be. Someone less venal might consider the fact Isla was my true mate reason enough to let us leave, but as far as I could tell Nubo had never been troubled by sentiment, much less kindness or mercy.

Isla's expression took on a faraway look that I had learned indicated she was communicating telepathically with Brae. I held her hand in mine, watching for any sign of trouble until she blinked and focused on my face.

"Nubo wants Kona dead," she said, her voice and expression grim. "For letting us get from the perfume shop to here last night. He's sending someone now to get her out of the market and out of sight."

She did not say that Brae had given her the news, likely because she did not want Atlath to know about her shadowbat.

Isla's gaze searched my face. "What do we do?"

I did not want to care what befell Kona. She had threatened me, threatened my mate, taken pleasure in the thought of Nubo breaking Isla and putting her in chains. She had spat in my face and tried to stab me. She had been a mercenary raider and likely killed in cold blood.

And yet…

"We have to warn her," Isla said. Her shoulders slumped. "I know she means us harm, but I can't just sit by and let him kill her. I can't."

"You are too tender-hearted," Atlath croaked before I had a chance to reply. "Too merciful."

His tone was not sharp or unkind, but my spines bristled. I would not hear criticism of my mate.

"Maybe I am." Isla did not appear angry or resentful at Atlath's disapproval, but her mouth compressed into a stubborn line. "But there's too much cruelty in the universe already. I'd rather be too kind than not kind enough."

Part of me—perhaps the more rational part who had undergone military training and served in war—argued Kona's fate was not our responsibility. She had opted to work for Nubo knowing what kind of person he was, and her death would not be our fault.

But all that did not make what Isla said untrue. And had I not just considered how ripples of kindness created effects as much as acts of evil did?

Isla rose. I stood as well and touched her hand. "I will tell her," I said quietly. "Please stay here. She is more likely to listen to me, and it is safer inside."

"All right." She brushed my fingers with her own. "But if anyone so much as looks at you wrong, I'm coming out there with all my daggers."

I caught her hand, kissed her knuckles, and glanced at Atlath. "Do you have anything I can use to write on my skin?"

With a disapproving burble, Atlath waddled to a shelf and found a stylus. He slid it across the bar to me.

If I spoke to Kona, someone was likely to overhear, and Nubo would immediately attempt to find out how his security had been breached. That might put Brae in danger. I needed another way to warn her.

Across my palm, in the coded language of the Cludian Corps, I wrote *Nubo has sent someone to kill you for not preventing us from finding refuge.* It was not impossible for someone to see the message and interpret it, but I could not think of a better solution.

I had no proof of what I said, of course. She might think it was a ploy to get her to leave the market. If she did not believe me, there was little I could do. We could only try.

"Can you open the front door enough for me to step outside?" I asked.

Atlath accessed a control panel behind the counter and tapped on it. One of the front doors swung open about a meter. The noise of the market spilled into the shop along with a slant of mid-afternoon daylight.

I strode to the door and stepped outside.

At a glance, I noted five watchers I recognized as Nubo's agents—and Kona, who stood to the right of the doors, hands on her daggers, her dark gaze fixed on me and fury blazing in her eyes.

Moving slowly so she did not interpret it as an attack, I held out my palm. Her gaze dropped from my face to my hand, then flicked back up. I dropped my hand to my side.

For a beat, she studied me, her eyes narrowed almost into slits. I could well imagine she was reading my body language and expression and weighing the odds of whether I was telling the truth or simply trying to trick her. Would I believe me if I were in her place? I did not know.

My gaze on hers, I stepped backward through the doorway. The moment I crossed the threshold, the door swung closed again.

Isla was waiting just inside. She wrapped her arms around my waist and rested her head on my chest. "That was the longest fifteen seconds of my life," she said, her voice muffled by my shirt. "Did she believe you?"

"I do not know." I kissed the top of her head and glanced at Atlath. "Is she still there?"

"She is leaving," the Prylothian croaked, all his eyes fixed on his control panel. "I do not understand why you warned her or why she would take your word, but it is done."

The rear doors to the shop slid aside. Madame Ycari entered, followed by Pioni. Both smiled at the sight of Isla in my arms.

"Ycari!" Isla slipped from my embrace and hurried to greet them. I followed in her wake.

She grasped Ycari's outstretched feathered hands. "Thank you so much for the perfume. It's more wonderful and perfect than I could have imagined."

"You are most welcome," Ycari said. Her gaze moved to my face. "You approve as well?"

"More than words can say." I gave her a deep bow. "It is the finest scent I have ever encountered except Isla's own."

Her feathers ruffled in obvious pleasure. "I am so glad you approve."

Pioni folded her little hands in front of her chest. "You are both beautifully in love today," she said to us in her musical voice. "Atlath says you have chosen your destination and will soon leave for the port. He mentioned I would like to go with you?"

"Yes." Isla took my hand. "Thank you so much for everything. How can I repay your kindness?"

"When next you may help another, you can do so in my name. I need nothing more than that, except one thing." Pioni dipped her head. "Will you sing for us before you go? I would be very grateful."

"Oh." My beautiful mate blushed again. "Pioni, I can't—your voice is so beautiful that it made me cry. I can't come close to that. And I haven't warmed up at all."

"I have heard from many sources that your voice is marvelous," Pioni countered. "We are not in competition. You have admired my voice. I want very much to do the same for yours."

I stroked Isla's palm with my thumb in silent encouragement.

"All right," she said finally with a smile. "I'll do my best, then."

Humming to herself, she selected a song on her wristcomm. As the music began to play, I let go of her hand, surreptitiously tapped my wristcomm, and joined Ycari, Pioni, and Atlath at the counter.

Wineglasses in hand, we listened to Isla sing the Fylorian ballad she had performed for her audition at Zaa'ga. Despite her nervousness about singing for Pioni, the questionable acoustics of the wine shop, and her lack of warm-up, her voice soared, filling the space.

Gods above, I loved her.

When Isla reached the third and final verse, Pioni began to sing, turning the song into a duet. Isla's eyes widened, but she did not stop singing or sing more softly in deference to the Sirrah.

Their voices blended, sweeping through the shop and leaving us all mesmerized. Ycari's feathers ruffled with every high note, and for all his love of wine, Atlath's glass went untouched, as did mine.

When the last notes of the song faded, I tapped my wristcomm again to end the recording. Isla would surely treasure this recording of them singing together, as would I.

"Thank you," Isla said to Pioni. "Thank you so much. What an honor to sing with you."

"Truly, the honor was mine." Pioni handed Isla her glass of wine, then raised her own. "A toast to Isla and Mikas, friends. To love."

"To love," we echoed, and clinked glasses.

Isla tucked herself under my arm and nestled against my side. "Brae says Nubo is angry because Kona got away," she murmured. "He can't figure out how you knew, or why you warned her. Apparently he's arranged for someone to come in and scan his office for listening devices. I told Brae to come back here and keep watch outside while we get ready to leave."

"Good." I kissed her temple. "We want him to be safe."

"I have arranged transportation to the Alpha Megaport," Atlath interjected. "My embassy guards will escort you to the market gate, where you will board the vehicle. Ordinarily I would have you board on the landing pad on the roof, but I think it will be to your advantage for your diplomatic credentials and escort to be clearly seen. Once your observers see those medallions, I expect your way to the port and off-planet to be clear."

"I hope so." Isla toyed with her wineglass. While the rest of us had finished our own drinks, hers was almost untouched.

For all Atlath's planning and preparation, he could not guarantee our safety. Neither could I, and that gnawed at my insides. Isla must be safe. Nothing else mattered as much as that. My beastly hearts pounded, even as I rubbed her back and projected calm I did not feel.

My wristcomm beeped. *Identification sets complete*, the message read. *Best of luck*. I replied with my thanks and transferred Isla's new identification to her wristcomm.

In our own names, we could travel from Fortusia to another world with a major transportation hub, and then use our new identities to make our way eventually to Jakora.

Efre and Pelles, I thought. *Efre and Pelles*.

I liked how the names sounded together. Isla had chosen well. But we would always be Isla and Mikas to each other.

CHAPTER 25

ISLA

Hand-in-hand and wearing our diplomatic medallions in plain sight, Mikas and I stepped out of Atlath's shop, flanked by two armed embassy guards and Pioni.

One of the guards carried our travel cases while the other brandished a shield emitting an energy field large enough to enclose and protect all of us from weapons fire and even incendiary devices. Not that we expected Nubo to attempt overt violence in full view of a market full of witnesses, but angry people were unpredictable.

The moment our entourage crossed the shop's threshold, everyone in the vicinity turned to look at us. I recognized four of Nubo's agents in the crowd. Mikas's hand tightened on mine. He saw them too. As did our guards, who hissed.

Letting Nubo's agents see our guards and medallions would hopefully keep us safe, but Mikas vibrated with unease. If only we could retreat to the beautiful Star Bird room and find comfort in each other's arms.

Think about the cabin aboard the cruiser, I told myself. *Think about making love to Mikas as stars and planets pass by the windows. We won't have to leave the cabin for the whole trip if we don't want to. It'll just be him and me—and Brae, when Mikas and I aren't busy. I can lie on top of Mikas all day long if I want to.*

I fixed that image in my mind and hung onto it.

Mikas, Pioni, and I followed the guard with the shield toward the closest market exit—the one we had attempted to use last night before Pioni ushered us to Atlath's shop. The crowd cleared a path for us, murmuring in a dozen languages and clearly wondering who we were.

I never minded an audience when I was onstage, but I despised this kind of attention. Mikas clearly felt the same. I wanted so badly to be done with this part of our journey and get safely out of sight in our cabin.

I sensed Brae's presence overhead. *I see four of Nubo's people,* I told him. *But it's the ones I don't see that worry me. Do you see anyone else we know lurking around? Do you see Scar? Or Kona?*

No, he replied, his voice tense. *Neither of them. Is that good or bad?*

I don't know, I said. *Do you want to ride with us to the port, or fly?*

I'll fly. Don't worry—I'll stay close.

Just ahead, on the other side of the market gate, a small armored ground transport waited. Atlath had done so much for us. My throat grew tight.

Mikas squeezed my hand again. He was so wonderfully attuned to my emotions and ready to provide comfort and strength almost before I knew I needed it.

We stepped through the market gate. The guard with the shield cleared us a path across the busy walkway to the transport's door, which slid open as we approached.

We all spotted Nubo at the same time.

With a thunderous expression, he stepped out of the crowd of pedestrians and in front of the transport, blocking its path forward with his bulk. An unfamiliar Hardanian male—not one of the brothers who'd expressed interest in me a week ago—stood behind him, clearly acting as a bodyguard.

Our guards hissed, Mikas snarled, and I flexed my wrist to drop my dagger out of its sheath into my hand.

I didn't care anymore if Nubo knew I wasn't who I'd claimed to be. I was done pretending to be a scared little human needing protection. I'd played that role long enough. It had served its purpose and now I just wanted to be myself.

I met his stare and raised my chin.

Let him see my blade and think about it. Let him wonder whether it would be worth it to pursue us, given our list of allies and the diplomatic credentials we wore. A smart man would weigh the risks and rewards—the latter of which were pretty damn slim—and decide to cut his losses.

But judging by the way he bared his teeth and flexed his hands, Nubo wasn't going to be a smart man.

Then his gaze moved to Pioni and his expression turned calculating. My fingers twitched on the handle of my dagger.

No matter what she or anyone else said, Pioni's voice made mine sound like a braying Solani desert ox. And now Nubo was in the market for a new singer.

"Please board the transport," the Prylothian guard holding the shield croaked. "Anyone who blocks our way will find themselves under the vehicle." He definitely intended Nubo to hear that warning.

With his gaze on Nubo and the Hardanian, Mikas ushered me into the transport. Pioni followed, and the embassy guards got in last, using the shield to block the opening until the door slid closed.

In the passenger area of the transport, I found myself sitting between Mikas and the guard who'd carried our travel cases and across from Pioni and the shield guard. As small as I felt between Mikas and a male Prylothian, Pioni looked positively tiny next to the guard.

"I don't like how he looked at you," I said to Pioni as the transport's engines powered up. "I know you said you're not worried about him, but—"

"I am leaving Fortusia as well," Pioni said. She smiled at my obvious confusion. "I sent my luggage ahead to the port earlier today. So you've no need to fear for me."

The transport glided smoothly into motion and accelerated. Nubo must have moved out of the way. Pity.

"But why are you leaving?" I asked. "Because of Nubo?"

"No, not because of him." Pioni crossed her ankles. "My kind are wanderers. I have been restless for some time, but stayed because Fortusia is so lovely and Ycari has been a wonderful friend and confidant. The instinct to roam has become too strong for me to ignore now." Her hands and arms flushed. "I feel someone is calling to me. Perhaps my mate has reached maturity."

"Oh, that's wonderful," I said as Mikas clasped my hand in both of his. "Where do you plan to go?"

"I do not know," she confessed. "I will go to the port and wander until I am drawn to a particular voyage. I will know which ship to board by listening to my heart. And wherever I go, I will continue to help those who need it."

"I hope to do that too again someday." I bit my lip. "When you say you'll be *drawn* to a destination, what does that feel like?"

"It is difficult to describe." Pioni hummed as she thought. "I have heard it described as the feeling of solving the last piece of a puzzle, or finding the right key after trying many that did not fit. I do not have the words to describe it more clearly than that, especially as I have not experienced it myself."

I rested my head on Mikas's bicep.

Two years ago, despite being arguably a terrible candidate to adopt an animal companion, I'd been walking down a street on Pallasia and felt drawn to go into a shelter and inquire about an orphaned shadowbat who'd then instinctively imprinted on me. Brae and I often teased each other about how we'd met, but we both felt certain in some way it had been meant to happen.

The night I'd shared a bunk and a bottle of moonshine with Novee, I'd chosen Fortusia as my destination. All I'd known of the planet was images I'd seen of its beauty and some general knowledge about Fortusians' use of genetic engineering.

Brae and I had discussed several potential destinations, but from the moment I found out the Web had put me on indefinite leave, this beautiful world had been top-most in my mind. Had I felt *drawn* to Fortusia? It would be easy enough to say so now, knowing Mikas and I would meet here, but thinking back to that night aboard the cargo carrier, I didn't remember the kind of feeling Pioni described. But even so, I had come to Fortusia, to Onat'ras, to Zaa'ga, and found Mikas waiting for me.

I hoped with all my heart Pioni would find her way to her mate and they'd be happy together for the rest of their lives.

The Alpha Megaport was a little over a kilometer from the market. The trip took only a few minutes once the transport reached the transit path that ran alongside the main boulevard. As much as I wanted to get aboard a ship, I wished this leg of the journey could have been longer. Jakora would be beautiful too, but I would miss this city.

At the port, the embassy guards escorted Mikas, Pioni, and me not to one of the many kiosks or a gate but the office of a private booking agent. I had never arranged travel with an agent before.

Atlath had already purchased our berth on a cruiser bound for the enormous Section VII transit hub on the ice planet Aloris. Once there, we would book our own travel under our new identities, changing ships in several places until we reached

Jakora. All we needed to do in the office was have our travel documentation loaded onto our wristcomms.

Pioni and the guards accompanied us to the entrance to the docking ring for passenger ferries. Smaller ships could dock at the port, but the larger cruisers stayed in orbit, accessible only via these ferries. I saw no sign of anyone I recognized as one of Nubo's agents, and neither did Brae, but the back of my neck wouldn't stop itching.

My farewell with Madame Ycari had been tearful enough, but saying goodbye to Pioni made my heart ache. She was a kindred spirit. We were both singers who'd once been prized and possessed for our talent and decided to take that power back and sing for ourselves.

"Come visit us someday if you can," I told her, fighting back tears. "You and your mate."

"We will," she promised. "I know in my heart I will see you again, my friends. This is not goodbye—it is *ula'nagora.*"

"Fortusian, for *until we meet again*," Mikas translated for me, his thumb stroking my fingers. "Be safe in your travels, Pioni."

With a smile, she left with one of the guards, while the other accompanied us to the ferry. Our cases had gone ahead in a cargo transport and would be waiting for us on the ship.

"Please keep Ambassador Atlath apprised of your well-being until you reach your destination," the guard croaked at the gate. "Safe travels to you both."

We thanked our guard and boarded the ferry. Our seats were near the front, allowing us a good view of the rest of the passengers. Neither of us saw anyone we recognized or anyone watching us with more than a passing interest. In shadow form, Brae nestled himself into a corner above my head.

When the hatch closed, Mikas tucked me under his arm and kissed my temple.

"We are only minutes away from our cabin," he murmured

into my ear. "You will need to ask Brae to explore the ship for a few hours once we are settled in."

Brae's shadow discreetly slipped away toward the back of the passenger compartment. I bit the inside of my cheek to stifle a chuckle.

"Oh, I know. I'm sleepy too," I said, with an exaggerated yawn. "I love to sleep on a starship. The engines are so soothing."

"You will get no sleep for a while," he warned, his eyes gleaming. "I want to make love to my mate as we look down on Fortusia from orbit."

My sweet, insatiable Mikas. "Your mate might agree to that," I said. "Under certain conditions."

His eyebrows rose. "What conditions?"

"You'll find out," I said with a smile. Chuckling, he kissed me.

The ferry's engines powered up, sending a strong vibration through the small ship. I activated the screen in front of my seat to watch the exterior view during our flight up to the cruiser.

The ferry launch was so smooth and the stabilizers so advanced that I might not have known we were in flight other than the way my stomach lurched when the ship rose from the docking bay and the exterior view.

"Goodbye, Fortusia," I murmured as Onat'ras grew smaller and smaller on the viewscreen. "Or maybe *ula'nagora*."

Mikas rested his chin on top of my head and cooed softly. With a sigh, I snuggled against him and listened to his hearts.

CHAPTER 26

ISLA

Midway through Fortusia's pink atmosphere, the ferry's viewscreens switched to a forward view.

Several enormous cruisers orbited the planet. Other than its name, I had no idea which was our destination until the ferry's flight path turned and headed straight for a magnificent luxury cruiser.

"Oh, gods." I gaped at the screen. "I've never been on one of these."

"Me either." Mikas cradled my head against his chest. "It is certainly a far cry from military transports and cargo carriers."

I watched in awe as our ship entered the open docking bay on the side of the cruiser, rotated, and landed precisely on the pad. The viewscreen switched to the cruiser's logo as the ferry's engines shut off.

Once we disembarked via a walkway, hosts escorted us into the cruiser and divided passengers by assigned decks and sections. Only then did we discover our cabin was located on a secure level.

Mikas, Brae, and I followed our escort into a private lift accessed by biometric scanners. It rose smoothly sixteen levels before opening to reveal an enormous multi-level artificial conservatory filled with colorful rain forest flora from a dozen worlds, walkways, small waterfalls, and several pools.

Wide galleries ringed the atrium, providing three hundred and sixty-degree views of the rain forest on the inside. The cabin doors lined the outside of the galleries.

I would have liked to spend a few minutes admiring the atrium, but our host guided us directly to our designated cabin, Epsilon 42. We scanned our wristcomms to open its doors. My mouth fell open.

"There must be a mistake," I murmured to Mikas. "This is some kind of royal suite."

"With your pardon, Emissary, it is no mistake," our young Engareni host warbled. "Your booking agent was quite clear about which suite would be most appropriate for you. This level is reserved for diplomats and others needing secure accommodations."

"Thank you for escorting us," Mikas said. "And for the explanation."

The host dipped his feathered head. "Please contact me via the comm panel in your suite with any and all requests."

"We will." With his hand on my lower back, Mikas urged me into our suite.

I'm going to explore the ship while you two get settled, Brae said in my head. *Let me know when it's safe for me to come back.*

My face heated. *Thank you. Be careful.*

Always. His shadow flitted away in the direction of the atrium.

Without warning, Mikas swept me up in his arms in full view of our host and a dozen other passengers and carried me through the doorway into our cabin. The moment the doors slid closed, he kissed me with enough heat and hunger to make my toes curl in my boots.

"What is this?" I asked breathlessly when he drew back.

"You blushed so prettily at whatever Brae said to you that I lost all control," he said, eyes twinkling. "And you encouraged me to be spontaneous, as I recall. I believe your exact words were, 'You never know what might happen.' I await the consequences of my spontaneity."

"The consequences could be dire," I warned.

He kissed my forehead. "I very much hope so."

We stood in a spectacular sitting area with floor-to-ceiling windows offering a breathtaking view of space. Through an open doorway, I saw a bedroom no smaller than this room and beyond that a bathroom. The bed was enormous—larger even than the one in Atlath's embassy.

Exploring our palatial cabin could wait. After all, we had several days here before we reached Aloris.

"Take me to the window," I said.

Obediently, he carried me across the sitting area to the windows and their breathtaking view of Fortusia.

"Computer, dim lights," Mikas said. The suite plunged into near-darkness. He pressed his lips to my temple. "It is a beautiful planet, but it pales in comparison to you."

I reached up to run my fingers through his hair. He rumbled at my touch. "What did I say about that kind of flattery?"

"I do not recall." He turned his head to kiss my palm. "I was too captivated by my beautiful mate to make note of it."

I pulled his head down to mine and kissed him. "You remember offhand comments I made months ago, but you don't remember me telling you earlier today not to flatter me so much?"

"Selective memory is a regrettable condition," he said with feigned sorrow. "I hope you do not find it too difficult to live with."

"Luckily, *my* memory is sharp." I raised my eyebrows. "Remember how I said you might get your wish to make love overlooking Fortusia under certain conditions?"

He pretended to think. "I do recall that, yes. What are these mysterious conditions I must meet in order to give my mate many orgasms at this window?"

My toes curled again at his promise. "Put me down and I'll tell you."

With obvious reluctance, he set me on my feet. I found the seam of his shirt and pulled it apart slowly. I slid the palms of my hands over his hot, scaly skin, reveling in how he rumbled and trembled at my touch.

I dragged my nails down his chest and pressed myself against the hard lengths of his cocks, already straining the fabric of his pants. His gaze had gone dark with desire. Slowly, I licked his right nipple before catching the piercing in my teeth. His gasp was ragged.

I let go of the piercing and flicked his nipple with the tip of my tongue. "Show me what you do when you fantasize about me," I said, my voice husky. "I want to see."

Mikas cupped my face and ran his thumb over my lower lip. "What do you want to see, my mate?"

"I want to see how you pleasure yourself." I tugged at the fastening of his waistband until it released, leaving his pants barely clinging to his hips. "I want to see what your face looks like when you think about me with your hand on your cocks."

He growled, his pupils dilating to turn his eyes fully black.

On my tiptoes, I wrapped my arms around his neck and lifted myself a few inches until he picked me up so we were face to face.

"And I want to see your primal self again," I murmured against his lips. "The Mikas I saw at the perfume shop when you touched me for the first time. But this time, I don't want you to hold back. I told you I want all of you just as you are, and I meant it."

"You do not know what you are asking," he grated. "I must be as human as possible when I am with you. There is a beast inside me."

"I know, and I want it inside *me*." I slipped my hand into his pants and discovered he wore nothing under them. He growled again, this time from deeper in his chest, but still he held back.

I caressed the area of his lower abdomen where his rougher scaly skin turned soft just above his groin, nudging his pants down his hips as I did so. His beautiful cocks sprang free, already hard as stone, beaded with lubrication, and dripping. His entire body vibrated and his chest heaved as I stroked them gently one at a time, from base to tip.

I'd pushed him to the edge until he was clinging to the shreds of his control. He wanted me with every fiber of his being, and yet he didn't give in. There could only be one reason for that: he worried he would frighten or hurt me.

"I'm not afraid of you," I said. "The only thing I fear is you feel you can't be yourself with me. If you can't be yourself with your mate, when *can* you be yourself?"

His arms tightened around me. "I do not deserve you," he rasped.

"Don't you ever think that." I took his face in my hands. "Don't you dare, Mikas Auren. You were meant for me and I was meant for you. Now let me see *all* of you, the way you've seen all of me."

With a snarl that made me shiver with desire, he kissed me hard. "My mate," he said, his voice guttural. "Choose a word you can say to let me know you are afraid, to tell me I must stop whatever I am doing because I may go too far. I have to know you are safe with me."

"All right." I kissed his jaw. "The word will be *trava*."

He rumbled. "Fortusian for *stop*. Yes, that is perfect."

"So," I said, my hands on his chest. "What did you do first when you fantasized about me? Did you take off all your clothes?"

"Yes." He set me on my feet next to an oversized chaise lounge with two backrests clearly designed for passengers to relax on as they enjoyed the view out the window.

As I watched, he dropped his shirt to the floor. Moments later, it was joined by his boots and pants and then he was beautiful and naked, his dripping cocks curving enticingly toward his abdomen.

I licked my lips. "And then what did you do?"

"I would lie on my basking stone in my apartment," he said, his gaze locked on mine. "But for now, this lounge will do."

He reclined against the pillows on one end of the chaise lounge and gestured at the opposite side. "Please, my mate."

I took off my boots but left my jumpsuit on and mirrored his pose. I was dripping already. Could he smell my arousal?

"I imagined you onstage, singing," he continued without being prompted. His hand traveled languidly over his chest, flicking his nipple piercings and gliding over his abdominal muscles. "I heard your voice and imagined your smile."

He took his cocks in his other hand, slipped a finger between them, and stroked once.

Gods. I let out a shaky breath edged with a moan.

"I thought about how beautiful you were beside the lake." Another slow, gentle stroke, and twin streams of gleaming precum spilled out to trickle down his fingers. "The waterfall's mist on your face, glistening in the lights. I imagined how your lips would taste." His tongue slid over his own lips, and his strokes became less gentle and more purposeful. "I wanted to kiss you. To feel your lips on mine. I wanted to fill your mouth with my cocks."

His hand slid up and down his cocks. My own fingers

twitched, aching with my desire to take over. And my mouth watered thinking about taking his cocks in my mouth.

In desperation, I opened the front of my jumpsuit along its seam and cupped my breasts, pinching my nipples. Oh, delicious pain. "And then what did you imagine?"

His breathing turned ragged. "I imagined my cocks in your pussy and your ass. You were calling my name."

I couldn't help it—I slid my hand into my jumpsuit and between my legs, where I was sopping wet. "Mikas," I whispered.

"Yes." His eyes blazed with need as he stroked his cocks. "Touch yourself, my mate."

With a whimper, I slipped my fingertips into my dripping slit.

"Show me," Mikas growled. "I want to see how wet you are for me."

Trembling, I withdrew my hand to show him my glistening fingertips.

"Beautiful," he said, his chest heaving. "Shall we continue?"

I couldn't imagine saying no to that. "Yes."

I wriggled out of my jumpsuit and tossed it on the floor next to my boots. I wanted so badly to climb on top of him, but there was something so decadent and satisfying about watching him pleasure himself to me.

So I settled back into the pillows on my end of the lounge, spread my legs, caressed my slit, then dipped my fingertips inside myself. I moaned and cupped my breast with my free hand.

"Gods, Isla," Mikas groaned, his chest and stomach muscles tightening as he stroked himself harder. "I want to come."

"No," I said sharply. "I'm not ready. You have to wait."

He shuddered hard, almost doubling over, but he slowed his movements. "Gods," he repeated, and that time it sounded like a prayer.

My fingers slick and dripping and my gaze on Mikas's face, I circled my swollen clit. "Mikas, what else did you imagine when you thought about me?"

"I cannot say," he rasped. "You are too beautiful. I am trying…not to come."

I imagined it for myself: Mikas, on his basking stone just like this, head thrown back and cocks splattering precum over his hand and stomach and legs as he envisioned what I would look like under him or on my hands and knees in front of him.

But I didn't have to imagine what that felt like because I'd already come with his cocks filling me up and making me scream. My pussy and ass clenched, desperate to feel those overwhelming sensations again.

That sent me over the edge with a wail, eyes closed, one hand on my clit and the other pinching my nipple hard.

A moment later, hot hands pushed my own hand aside and Mikas's face was between my legs, his tongue spearing me and lapping at my slit.

I cried out, my legs closing instinctively on his head until he pushed them open again and held me against his mouth so he could drink my release.

I ran my fingers through his hair. "Mikas," I gasped.

With a snarl, he turned his head and bit my inner thigh.

A millisecond of pain—and then the universe exploded.

CHAPTER 27

MIKAS

When my mate came on her own fingers, her head thrown back and mouth open in a desperate scream, my beastly hearts roared, demanding to be freed to feast—to mate not just in the human way but in the way of the bosor, the predator.

I am not afraid of you, Isla had said, and demanded I show her all of myself. My mate would not lie to me, and her scent confirmed she did not fear me. I was her *safe place*.

With wild abandon, I threw open the door of the cage that had kept my beastly self contained since I had left the battlefield behind and let all the darkness and hunger rise. The joy of freedom, of trust and being trusted, coursed through my body and ignited every cell.

Lost in a haze of need and pleasure, my face buried between her thighs, I feasted on the taste and scent of her orgasm as I had never done before. I was hungry. Hungry for *her*. Hungry for her ecstasy. Hungry for our future, so long denied.

I licked Isla's sweet flower, my tongue seeking every drop of her release. She gripped my hair and pulled, the pain delicious and demanding. I could never get enough of being needed by my mate.

A shiver ran through my body, bringing with it a wave of heat that tightened my balls and nearly made me come though my hands were on Isla and no longer on my cocks. A sweet liquid dripped from my fangs and landed on my tongue. The taste was like nothing I had ever experienced. It set my soul alight and sparked a new kind of need.

Mate, my beastly hearts roared.

I tightened my embrace of her hips and sank my fangs into her inner thigh. Her flinch was brief, and then she moaned.

The sweet liquid pumped through my fangs into her flesh. I tasted a hint of blood, but she did not bleed from the wounds.

Instead, she came.

My Isla screamed and screamed, her heels pushing against my shoulders and body thrashing in my arms. Her sweet juices splattered my face and the scent of her release filled the air, tinged with notes of the liquid from my fangs.

As she wailed, gasping and glistening with sweat, I caught fragments of my name in the midst of her cries. I withdrew my fangs and licked the tiny punctures, which leaked droplets of that sweet liquid I had made for my mate. Isla trembled and moaned every time my tongue rasped against her skin.

Her chest heaving, she reached for me. I crawled up her body and gently thrust my upper cock into her sweet pussy as it fluttered and clenched around me. She wrapped her legs around my hips and pulled me closer in an unspoken demand.

"Isla," I rasped, and buried my upper cock to the hilt in her tight, slick heat.

Somehow all the sensations of making love to my mate were more vivid now—more visceral, more electric, impossibly more satisfying. The sounds I made with each thrust were far from human. And Isla responded in kind, crying out each time the nubs and ridges on my cock entered her.

"Use both," she demanded, her eyes wild with need. "I want to feel them both."

I withdrew completely from her and plunged my lower cock in. My slick upper cock rubbed over her clit, again and again, and she came with a cry, tightening and fluttering around me so powerfully that I had to slow my movements to hold back my own orgasm.

When her screams quieted, I gathered her in my arms, moved to the side of the lounge, and turned her to face the window. "Bend over," I rasped. "Spread your legs and put your hands on the glass."

With a whimper, she obeyed.

With beautiful Fortusia before us, I spread her ass with my hands and speared her with my tongue. She cried out and nearly fell, but steadied herself against the window.

Slowly I stretched her open, first with my tongue and then with my fingers, until she was sobbing and pleading, her fingers scrabbling on the glass.

When I drew her to me with my hands on her hips, she backed up, eager and ready to take me. I held my upper cock steady for her. "Slowly," I said.

Without hesitation, her fingernails digging into my thighs, she took my cock head into her lovely ass, pushing it in a little farther each time, moaning and shaking. My precum splattered her ass and lower back. A beautiful sight, but not half as beautiful as the sight of my cock disappearing into her.

An inch at a time, she took me, and despite my roaring desire I held still and let her set the pace. I would not hurt my mate—not for anything.

Once she nearly reached the base of my upper cock, she withdrew almost to the point of freeing herself, reached for my lower cock, and positioned it at the entrance to her pussy.

The moment she slid it inside her slick heat, I nearly roared.

"Yes," she said, arching her back. "My beautiful beast."

I wrapped my arms around her, picked her up, and pulled her to me, burying my cocks into her past the halfway point. She screamed and screamed, her sounds pure pleasure and delight.

She rode me like that, bouncing on my cocks slowly at first and then faster, her cries rising in volume as she took more and more. I guided her with my hands on her hips, watching and feeling her stretch to take my slick cocks.

I had wanted so much to make love to my mate as Fortusia turned outside the window, but I found myself unable to see or care about anything but Isla: the way the dim light shimmered on her sweat, her reflection in the glass, her breasts bouncing as she rode me, the way she called my name.

My orgasm built to a nearly frightening crescendo. But I would not come until my knot locked us together, and I did not want to knot until my mate clenched around my cocks one last time.

I reached around and circled her swollen clit. Her gasps rose in pitch in a way I had come to know so well already. And moments later my mate's head fell back as she wailed, tightening around both of my cocks in a way I should be so lucky to feel in my dreams.

My knot swelled inside my mate as if my body had learned it must wait until she came to lock us together. Isla cried out and her hands tightened on my thighs.

"Fill me," she begged, turning to look into my eyes. "Please. I want to feel you fill me."

With growls and rumbles, with arms around my mate and claws extended, with full hearts and wild soul, I came in great spurts that wracked my body and hers. My beautiful mate took all I had to give.

When I laid us down on our sides on the lounge, still locked together by my knot, she trembled violently. I held her tightly in my arms and licked the perspiration on the back of her neck, so sweet and salty and tasting of me, of *us*. I had never done so before—never felt a desire to until now. My beastly needs were basic. I wanted to devour all of her. Everything about her sustained me.

"M-Mikas," she said, her arms wrapped around mine as if she was holding on for dear life. "I've never c-come so hard in my life."

"Neither have I." My voice was gravelly. "I have never let myself be so free. You asked me to give you all of myself, and that is what I did."

"You bit me." She ran her trembling hands over my forearms. "I loved it. *I loved it.* It felt so good."

Her scent and reaction had already told me so, but I was glad to hear confirmation that she had enjoyed that moment as much as I. To savor the memory, I licked my fangs to catch any remaining traces of that sweet liquid.

"My fangs produced something new just now," I said, my lips against her hair. "I was drawn to bite you and share it."

"I felt it," she said, to my surprise. "It was so warm and loving. Pure comfort. And it made me come from everywhere, like my entire body had an orgasm. Did you know you could do that to me?"

"No, I did not." I pressed a kiss into her hair. "Sometimes genetic engineering leads to unexpected abilities. The substance and orgasmic bite must be something I can do only for my mate, like my coo."

"You didn't need to coo for me this time." She wiggled against me and I quaked at the sensation of my cocks moving inside her. "But I miss it, so please coo for me now."

Happily, I cooed. She seemed to melt in my arms, her scent so thoroughly contented that my racing hearts slowed simply from smelling her tranquility.

"Did making love to me with the planet outside the window live up to expectations?" she asked.

Careful not to break her skin, I trailed the edge of one of my fangs very lightly along the nape of her neck and enjoyed her shiver. "Is there a planet outside?" I asked.

She laughed softly. "Yeah, I didn't notice it either." Her hand found mine and squeezed. "I see it now, though. It's beautiful."

We lay like that for a long time, savoring the sensations of our joined bodies and watching Fortusia turn.

Finally, I raised myself up onto my elbow and pressed my lips to her ear. "Show me my bite," I said.

She moved her leg and revealed two pink, almost invisible puncture marks on her luscious inner thigh.

The sight of the marks next to where my cock was still buried inside her, held there by my knot, made my balls tighten.

I stroked her clit gently with my fingertips. She moaned. "Mikas…"

"If you want me to stop, you can say the word," I said, my mouth still on her ear, as I circled her swollen bud. "In all things, I obey my mate without question."

She whimpered. "I don't think I could come again."

"Oh, I think you *can*." I closed my teeth gently on her earlobe. "Would you like to place a wager?"

"No." It came out breathless. "No, I know better than to underestimate you."

I moved my slick fingers to the little bite and caressed her delicate skin. She shivered hard. "Oh, that spot is so sensitive now," she gasped.

I stilled immediately. "Pain?"

"No." She took my hand and guided it back to her clit. "But this is where I want you to touch me. I want to watch us in the glass while you make me come one more time."

As did I. "Computer," I called. "Lights off."

The cabin plunged into darkness other than faint glow from the comm panel near the door and the starlight outside the window. Now our reflections were easy to see.

Her gaze on mine in the glass, she hooked her leg behind my knee so I had total access to her sweet clit, and we had a perfect view of my cocks buried inside her.

"Heaven has nothing on this moment," I said, my head resting against her as her chest heaved. I curled my arm underneath her and cupped her breast in my free hand. "Do you see us, my beautiful mate?"

"Yes." She gasped, her fingernails digging into my thighs in what had rapidly become one of my most favorite sensations. I wished my skin was not so thick and scaly so her nails would hurt more and she could leave marks on me as I had left on her. "Gods, Mikas, I've never watched myself come before," she breathed.

"I do not mean to spoil the surprise," I said, trailing my lips along her neck. "But you are beautiful and perfect when you come."

Her laugh dissolved into ragged gasps.

When I took her over the edge, her orgasm was soft rather than hard, and her breathless moan and the way she clenched around both of my cocks made my hips jerk.

I could have made love to her again, perhaps twice more, but she was tired now and sated.

"My mate," I said, and licked her sweet juices off my fingertips. "This will be how we spend our journey to Aloris. Do you object?"

"No." She drew me down for a kiss. "Not in the least," she murmured against my lips. "Not in the least."

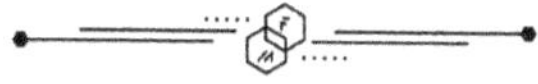

OTHER THAN OUR FIRST NIGHT TOGETHER IN ONAT'RAS, THE three-day journey to Aloris were the best hours of my life.

As pleasurable and satisfying as it was to make love to my mate without worrying about our safety or interruptions, it was pure bliss to simply hold her and talk—about ourselves, our pasts, our hopes for the future. We talked about inconsequential things too, from the gourmet food delivered to our suite to the planets we passed as we lay on the lounge in the main room, in the bed, or on the luxurious, almost throne-like basking stone in the bedroom.

"We're officially spoiled." Isla sat sideways on my lap facing the floor-to-ceiling bedroom window with her head on my chest. The radiant heat from the stone and the warmth from the overhead lamps could not compare to the summery contentment of my hearts.

"I'm sure whatever accommodations we have for the rest of the trip won't be anything close to this," she added wistfully. "And Brae won't have nearly as big of a ship to explore either, or a beautiful rain forest conservatory that reminds him of home."

"It has been far from a tent on a barren moon," I agreed with a chuckle, my chin on top of her head. She smelled strongly of me, and I of her, and I could not get enough of those scents. "To me, the real luxury is having you close every moment of these past few days. A smaller cabin simply means I will be *more* spoiled."

She kissed my chest. "You're not the only one of us spoiled by all this closeness. But if our next cabin doesn't have a basking stone, you may be cold and singing a different tune."

"I do not anticipate being cold," I murmured into her hair. "I will simply put you on top of me and we will generate our own heat."

"I like that plan." Isla laced her fingers through mine. "We could probably book our travel now if we wanted to, rather than waiting until we get to the port on Aloris."

"We could," I allowed. "I have never been to Aloris, or any ice planet, and thought we might do some sightseeing before continuing on our journey."

"Oh, that sounds like fun." She wiggled happily. "We can be tourists. I've never been a tourist."

I grimaced. She laughed and kissed the soft skin at the corner of my jaw. "We'll be *good* tourists," she amended. "Not the ones who came into Zaa'ga and made us miserable by being loud and demanding and not tipping."

"We will be *travelers*," I countered. "Lovers seeing the wonders of the galaxy on our way to our new home."

"I like that." She snuggled into my chest. "Once we've seen Aloris, we can choose where to go next. Maybe a desert world like Solan? Or Tivor's oceans? Or maybe our diplomatic credentials could get us permission to visit Hyderia—"

"My love." I kissed her knuckles. "Happiness and freedom to choose your destination has made you even more beautiful than before, and I did not think that could be possible."

She scoffed. "You're just saying that so I'll let you do more naughty things to me on this basking stone before we disembark."

"I would not mind doing so," I said, cupping the side of her face. She was so warm on the basking stone, and that made me deeply content. "But I mean every word. I have longed to see you so happy."

"I wanted you to be happy too." She leaned into my hand and closed her eyes. "If I'd paid more attention to the fact your unhappiness made *me* so unhappy, I might have figured out what you really meant to me earlier."

Her sorrow and regret had a distinct scent—one that made my spines bristle. Despite my assurances, she still carried guilt she did not deserve to carry.

"We have discussed this," I said softly. "Think of all the nights you sat at the bar and we talked while you ate your jampas. You were happy?"

She took a shaky breath. "Yes, I was."

"So was I." I stroked her cheek with my thumb. "We have a

lot to be grateful for and no need for regrets." A distressing thought made me pause. "Isla, you do not feel guilty for being happy, do you?"

"No." Her voice was soft. "Well, maybe."

I feared as much. I wrapped my arms around her. "You deserve happiness. You deserve joy and pleasure and to be treasured. These are not privileges you have to earn. This may be difficult for you to believe, and I am sure you cannot simply accept what I say. But it is the truth."

She went quiet for a while. Finally, she said, "Why is it I feel that way about you, but it's so difficult to believe it for myself?"

"Because we have led difficult lives, and too often we extend grace and kindness to others that we do not believe we deserve for ourselves. It is a strange state of being." I nuzzled her hair and forced myself to add, "At first, I questioned what I had done to deserve for you to come to Zaa'ga."

She raised her head. Her violet eyes had never looked so beautiful as they did now, reflecting the starlight that passed by outside the window as the ship traveled at hyperspeed—other than when I looked into her eyes as we made love.

"Oh, that's very close to how I feel." Isla bit her lip. "How did you convince yourself otherwise?"

"I am still working on that," I admitted. "But I have the benefit of feeling the comfort and joy of finding my true mate. I now accept that I am meant to care for you and love you. I hope in time you will share that feeling. I have heard that is often the case with humans who have Fortusian mates."

"That's a lovely thought." She smiled, which lightened my hearts immediately. "I think I'll get there. I've been contented in your presence almost since the moment we met. That bodes well, doesn't it?"

"Yes, it does." I glanced at my wristcomm. "We have a few hours before we must get ready to disembark. How would you like to spend that time?"

"Right here," she said immediately, then seemed to reconsider. "Oh, you can't just sit on the stone for two more hours. We've already been here a while."

"I do not mind." I caressed her arm. "But we have done little exploring of the ship since we boarded—"

She huffed. "Wasn't that the plan?"

"I did not say it was not," I said with a smile. "But I do not want you to feel you have missed out on seeing the wonders of a luxury cruiser because I kept you prisoner in this cabin."

"I've been a very willing prisoner, and my guard has been extremely generous." She studied me. "You'd like to look around before we arrive at the port, though?"

"I would like to walk with you on the promenade," I said. "And visit the observation deck."

"Brae did say the observation deck was beautiful." She made a face. "Ugh, *clothes*."

I laughed at her expression. "Such an inconvenience."

"It's not the inconvenience so much as I've enjoyed spending the last few days looking at you," she shot back. "I suppose you intend to put on a shirt as well as pants?"

"I do." I caught her hand. "Unless you demand I do not. I told you I obey my mate in all things."

Her expression turned thoughtful. "In all things, you say?"

"In all things." I eyed her. "What is my mate plotting?"

"You'll find out later." She rose and tugged on my hand to draw me to my feet. "Let's find Brae and do some exploring before it's time to disembark and play tourist—I mean, *traveler*."

To be teased by my mate was one of my greatest joys of all.

CHAPTER 28

ISLA

Ice pellets and howling wind scoured the windows and hull of the crawler taking our small group of intrepid travelers across the blue ice for an up-close look at an enormous glacier two hours' ground travel from the port.

From orbit, Aloris's stark, frozen beauty had enthralled me. As the crawler trundled along its path, the harsh reality of surviving on this planet's surface made our journey equal parts wondrous, thrilling, and unsettling. My stomach roiled from the moment we boarded the crawler, despite our guides' assurances about our safety during the excursion.

I'd traveled to more than a dozen worlds in my lifetime, but the scale of natural wonders here, combined with the bluish-white landscape, made judging both size and distance nearly impossible.

From the port, the glacier we planned to visit was easily visible on the horizon, and I'd questioned why the journey would take two full hours. By the time the trip reached the halfway point, I realized the size of the glacier's face and the mountains around it were deceiving. What appeared from the port to be a cliff of ice the width and height of a city block in Onat'ras was in fact more than five hundred kilometers wide, more than a kilometer tall at its terminal face, and an astounding two thousand kilometers in length, stretching deep into the mountains. And it was only the fifth-largest glacier on the planet. The mountains around it soared more than seven thousand meters into the gray, almost sunless sky.

Inside the crawler, Mikas's natural body heat kept him comfortable in regular clothing. I, on the other hand, had to don a thermal suit, hood, and gloves designed specifically for humans. My emergency helmet was attached to my seat, within a moment's reach.

Other species in our group who were even more sensitive to cold wore full-body suits with helmets even in the crawler. Our gear was a stark reminder of the omnipresent dangers of the planet's climate. Poor Brae had to stay behind in the port terminal, since our guides had no way to guarantee his safety if the crawler lost power. Exposure to cold would be fatal for him.

Like other hot-blooded passengers, Mikas could put on an emergency suit if needed, but the rest of us wouldn't survive long enough in the brutal cold to do that.

Despite the necessity of our gear, Mikas grumbled under his breath for the entire journey to the glacier because he wanted to touch my skin but had to settle for cradling my gloved hand.

"Well, you wanted to see Aloris," I teased from my seat beside his as the crawler made its way along the ice. "This is the price of bringing a human mate to an ice planet."

"It is a steep price." He squeezed my hand and rested his head against my thick hat. "But one I suppose I must pay to see a glacier nearly the size of my home province."

For all my teasing, I was thrilled to go sightseeing. It was a joy to explore a new place and learn about life here and the environment, even if we only stayed for one day.

I hadn't been joking when I told Mikas I'd never gotten to be a tourist. We were far from carefree, thanks to Aloris's brutal environment and lingering worry about Nubo's wrath, but gazing out the window at the mountains and the jagged columns of windswept ice that lined our path, I could lose myself in awe.

The crawler's destination wasn't the glacier itself, but a scientific research post ten kilometers from the glacier's face. At long last, our transport trundled into a large bay at ground level. Once the door sealed and the bay was deemed safe, we all exited the crawler and took a lift to the circular observation level at the top of the research station.

Mikas took my hand and led me to the glass wall. We stood in awed silence, utterly transfixed by the glacier, which from this vantage point spanned the entire horizon.

This was a harsh world, as far removed from the lush beauty of Fortusia as I could imagine. And yet it was beautiful beyond imagination, just in a different way. The view from the observation deck and the sensation of feeling so small and in complete awe inspired quiet soul-searching.

Sharing this moment with Mikas made me deeply contented, though I wished Brae was here too. Surreptitiously, since it was against our guides' policies, I took off my glove and slipped my hand into Mikas's. He was so wonderfully warm. The uneasiness that had plagued me since we boarded the crawler dissipated—at least, mostly.

"To see such a wonder in person is like finding my true mate," Mikas said, smiling down at me. "To know of such a wondrous thing, to read about it or study it, you may think you understand it. But when you see it and feel it for yourself, you realize you knew nothing." He kissed my fingertips. "My awe of you is beyond words."

He clearly loved complimenting me at every opportunity. As awkward as it made me feel because I didn't deserve a tenth of his admiration, I tried to resist the urge to be self-deprecating or ask him to do it less because it made him so happy. And unlike most people I'd met, who used flattery primarily for manipulation, he meant every word.

To be able to trust him completely was pure joy and comfort. For the first time in my life, I felt like my feet were on solid ground. And if Mikas was right about how our feelings would develop over time, this happiness would only get better.

Mikas squeezed my hand. I'd gotten lost in thought and forgotten to answer out loud.

I blinked back sudden tears and quipped, "So, the glacier reminds you of me? Are you saying I'm distant and cold?"

"Anything but." Eyes twinkling, he bent to kiss me, utterly unbothered by the presence of the travelers around us. They were probably too focused on the glacier to notice us anyway. "I am saying you are beautiful and leave me speechless."

Our guides offered an opportunity for those interested to go outside the research station and walk on the snow. While about half of the group declined due to the extreme conditions, Mikas and I both jumped at the chance—though he was obviously uneasy at how vulnerable I'd be if anything went wrong.

Bundled up in special gear and having heard a grim lecture about safety, our group of a dozen adventurous travelers descended to ground level via a lift and exited the station through an airlock. Our gear kept us warm despite the frigid temperature, but beyond the shelter of the station's thick support piers, the wind made me stagger and nearly fall. I was the smallest member of the group. No others my size had opted to venture outside.

Mikas tucked me against his side and positioned himself to take the brunt of the wind. "Very inhospitable to off-worlders," he said via our helmets, which allowed us to communicate privately. "The people of this planet love their homeworld and thrive here, but you and I are ill-equipped."

"It's beautiful." I turned in a circle to take in the vast beauty around us. "Even if I adapted to living inside a dome, I think I'd miss the feeling of real wind on my skin too much to live here." I took his gloved hand again and squeezed it. "I'm so happy we decided to leave the port and see what it's like on Aloris. Thank you for insisting we do this."

I couldn't see his expression under his helmet, but I heard the smile in his voice when he said, "I want us to experience all the joys we can find to share, from the simple to the exotic."

"From luxury cruisers to standard-class single-room cabins," I teased. "And from pink waterfalls to enormous glaciers."

"And eventually to a little home overlooking a white sand beach and lavender ocean." He drew me tight to his chest and turned us to put his back to the wind when a gust roared across the ice. "If we can find work together and live in such a place, I will have all I need to be happy for the rest of my life."

"Me too." I couldn't kiss him, so I settled for bumping his helmet lightly with my own. He chuckled and bumped mine in return.

We spent the rest of our time outside exploring the designated safe area around the station and soaking up the stark beauty of Aloris's ice fields and blue-gray sky. After living in busy Onat'ras, packed with pedestrians and ground and air transports, the emptiness and silence were simultaneously refreshing and unnerving.

Despite the wonders around us, my uneasiness returned with a vengeance. The back of my neck prickled and my stomach churned, even with Mikas at my side and no apparent danger near other than the slim chance of disaster striking somehow during our excursion or the trip back to the port. Knowing all the equipment was triple-checked for safety before every outing meant the odds of trouble were slim, but something was making me acutely uneasy. I wished I could figure out what and why.

Mikas was unsettled too, judging by the way he scanned our surroundings and gripped my hand as if he worried I might drop through the ice or blow away in the wind at any moment.

Our guides corralled us back to the airlock just as I began to feel a chill even through my double layer of protective gear. Once we removed our outerwear, it was time to board the crawler for the return journey to the port. Mikas and I took a last lingering look at the glacier and joined the rest of the group in the crawler loading bay.

My apprehension didn't abate much even after we were seated and underway. Mikas's spines bristled, but he studiously kept them flat after an Engareni female in a full-body thermal suit sitting behind us squawked in alarm.

"I am too accustomed to having you on my lap with nothing between us," Mikas murmured in my ear as the crawler trundled over the ice at what felt like a truly glacial pace. "I am anxious to book the next leg of our journey and get to our cabin."

"That makes two of us," I said, happy to have something to talk about to distract from my unease. "What do you think? Solan? Tivor?" I thought about it. "Or do what Pioni did and wander the port until we feel drawn to a particular ship or destination? Maybe we should let or hearts or fate decide."

"I am not sure what is best." He rested his forehead on mine. "I am uneasy. I do not know why. I thought it was the danger of the ice, or our lack of a definite plan, but now I wonder if there is some other cause."

"I know what you mean." I leaned against his bicep and did my best to lace my gloved fingers through his bare ones.

I would have given a lot to be able to curl up on his lap, but we had to stay secured into our seats in case of trouble. My argument that I'd feel safer in Mikas's arms than in the harness, or that we were in more danger while traveling through space than in this vehicle, was unlikely to persuade the guides to let me flout their rules. And I'd promised Mikas to be a good tourist, so I stayed in my seat.

Some of our group slept during the journey while others watched the scenery via the windows and viewscreens. I tried to relax and enjoy the trip, occasionally scanning the faces of the other passengers—those I could see, that was. Nearly a third wore protective gear that hid even their heads and faces from sight. When Mikas and I weren't discussing our next potential destination, I entertained myself by trying to guess what species those in full-body gear were based on body size, number and locations of appendages, and mannerisms.

As much as I wanted to continue with our journey and get back to sharing a clothing-optional cabin with Mikas, I hoped we'd have time to have some drinks and food in the port and watch the seemingly endless parade of travelers from across the galaxy. In the hour between our arrival from the cruiser and boarding the crawler I'd seen dozens of unfamiliar species, some of which even Mikas couldn't identify. We both enjoyed people-watching, as did Brae, so I suspected neither would object too strenuously to relaxing in a lounge prior to boarding our next ship.

When we were within minutes of the port, I reached out to Brae. *We're almost back,* I said. *The glacier was beautiful. What have you been doing?*

There are four hot biospheres in the port, he replied immediately, his voice high-pitched with excitement. *I've been basking and snacking.*

I gasped softly. Mikas glanced at me and raised his eyebrows. I patted his hand in reassurance and mouthed *Brae.* He chuckled and kissed the top of my head through my hood. I missed the heat of his lips.

Please don't tell me you've been eating anything you shouldn't have in those biospheres, I said to Brae. *You know those are carefully balanced environments.*

I'm not uncivilized, my shadowbat huffed. *They stock special feeding areas.*

Oh, good, I said, relieved. *We'll be arriving at the same gate we departed from in a few minutes. If you'll meet us there, we'll go book our next ship and then decide what to do before it leaves.*

I'll meet you there.

I relayed what Brae had said to Mikas. He chuckled. "Trust Brae to find a feast of insects on an ice planet."

"A shadowbat's instincts are strong when it comes to danger and food." I nestled my head against his arm. "Gods above, I'll be glad to get out of this thermal suit. I've had an itch on my back for the last hour and I can't scratch it."

"Where?" He slipped his hand behind my back and scratched between my shoulder blades with just the tips of his claws, carefully not to shred the suit. "Here?"

I had to bite my lip to stifle an inappropriate moan. "Lower," I murmured. "To the right."

Obediently, he moved his hand and scratched. *Ahhh.* I might have slumped over if it hadn't been for the harness. "Oh, that's the spot," I groaned. "Thank you."

He gave the rest of my back a thorough scratch for good measure and took my hand as the crawler reached the ramp that led to the dock inside the port. Our guides had told us at the beginning of the excursion that all forms of transports on Aloris were designed to withstand the climate but were stored in protected and temperature-controlled areas to lessen the chance of damage or deterioration due to weather.

Once the crawler safely docked and connected to the port's climate system, we released our harnesses, stood, and stretched. My stiff muscles protested the long hours of sitting. Now my fantasy of what Mikas and I would do once we boarded our ship began with a hot bath or shower and a long massage. Something told me Mikas wouldn't object to this new plan.

While some of the passengers opted to wear their gear all the way into the port, several guides and other passengers opened their thermal suits. I took my suit off to the waist and tied the sleeves around my hips with a sigh of relief. My jumpsuit was quite warm enough inside the port.

With Mikas in front of me, we made our way up a series of ramps from the crawler to the gate on the lower ring that led to ground transportation. At this massive five-level port, one of four terminals on Aloris, passenger ferries belonging to large cruisers loaded in the second-level ring. Small and medium-sized ships loaded from the third and fourth rings. The fifth ring at the top was a hotel and resort.

Hand-in-hand, Mikas and I emerged through the gate and into a crowd waiting to board crawlers and other ground trans-portation. I scanned the area, looking for Brae and the place we were supposed to leave the rest of our protective gear to be cleaned and reused, but it was hard to see anything through the crush of travelers.

A three-legged creature I didn't recognize stepped on my foot, and a massive, lumbering Biltrobian bumped into me hard enough that I nearly fell. He rumbled something that might have been disgust. His equally enormous companion made a gesture indicating my relative height and chortled.

I scowled at their disdain. Just because I wasn't two and a half meters tall and built as solidly as a meteorite didn't mean they could just—

Icy cold sliced through my back and deep into my chest.

I blinked a few times, puzzled by the sensation. A draft of outside air coming from the gate we'd just passed through? The cold spread through my insides. Suddenly, I couldn't get a full breath.

"Isla." Mikas's voice seemed to be coming from a long way

away. He was holding me by my upper arms, his expression part stricken and part pure rage. "*Isla...*" The word was a distant roar.

Somewhere nearby, Brae screeched, which he almost never did in public—especially when he traveled in shadow form.

"Mikas," I said, or tried to say. The word turned into a gurgle. My legs went out from under me.

Mikas caught me, cradling me to his chest. He was bellowing something but I couldn't tell what he was saying. I also thought there was a lot of screaming and frantic movement around us, but that was vague too. Everyone but Mikas were just shadows.

Brae? Even my thought was wispy. *Help...*

No reply, or at least not one that I heard. That was strange. Where was Brae?

When the pain arrived, it was distant too and not at all like when I'd been shot on Ngara. Whatever had happened, I must not have been hurt that badly, but thinking had become difficult.

Stranger still, something hot and sweet ran over my lips and into my mouth. Was someone giving me a drink?

"Isla, *swallow,*" Mikas said through the ringing in my ears. His voice sounded like his mouth was pressed to my ear. "Drink, my love."

My back hurts. I'd meant to say that out loud but the words got no further than my brain. One of us was trembling violently. I wasn't sure if it was him, or me, or both.

I coughed. Warm liquid bubbled up and spilled down my chin.

"Please do not leave me," Mikas rasped. "I will not make it a day without you."

The sweet, hot liquid in my mouth tasted like Mikas—like sun-warmed stone and love, like what had come from his fangs when he bit my leg. That made no sense, but very little made sense at the moment.

"Drink," he begged. "Isla, *please*."

With the last of my waning strength, and with darkness closing in, I struggled to do as he asked. He was hurting and I didn't want him to hurt. I didn't want to leave him all alone.

Oh, my beautiful Mikas. My heart. My mate.

He clasped me to his chest and roared.

CHAPTER 29

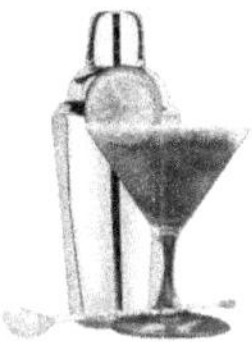

MIKAS

PANDEMONIUM REIGNED AROUND US, BUT IT MEANT NOTHING to me.

The smell of Isla's blood overpowered everything else. I raged and bellowed, my spines flaring, fangs bared, claws extended. My beastly fury swallowed my humanity and reduced me to a vicious monster cradling my dying mate as she gurgled her last breaths.

Rage fragmented my thoughts.

A flash of metal. A dagger, driven hilt-deep into my Isla's back. A gloved hand that withdrew the blade and disappeared into the crowd. Brae screeching in fury as he flew off in pursuit of the assassin.

I had failed to protect my Isla. My life had only one purpose and I had failed catastrophically.

Her blood was everywhere. It spilled from her mouth and poured from her back and covered her clothes, my clothes, and the floor. There was too much blood. *She has lost too much blood.*

My roars filled the port and sent everyone running out of reach of my claws, fangs, and spines.

I held my torn wrist to Isla's mouth as I pleaded with her to drink. My other hand pressed the sleeve of her thermal suit, soaked with my blood, against the wound in her back. I had no memory of ripping into my own flesh for the blood needed to try to save my mate's life, but I had sliced myself on both arms nearly to the bone.

Even on the battlefield I had never become this creature, this beast. My humanity had never so fully given way to my darkest, most monstrous rage.

I must save my Isla. My Isla must live. My own life was worth *nothing* if she did not live.

A male voice cut through the chaos. "Sir—" he said in Fortusian.

I snarled and spun, ready to shred whoever had dared come near us.

The speaker was an enormous Alorisian soldier flanked by medics. One led an antigrav medical stretcher and the other a trolley of emergency triage equipment.

"We are here to help," the soldier said, still in Fortusian. He spoke calmly and kept a respectful and cautious distance. "You have done what you can by sharing your blood."

I must not let anyone's hands touch her but mine. No one could be trusted. Only my blood and other bodily fluids could heal my mate. I growled low in warning.

The medics took a step back, but the soldier held his ground. "We can provide the care she needs to survive, but you must let us reach her. Please, sir."

Isla let out a garbled, broken sound that cut through my haze of rage like a sword and doused me with ice-cold dread.

Oh, gods—had I frightened her? Please, no. I could not bear to see fear in her eyes.

Her eyelashes fluttered. "*Trava*," she whispered thickly, the word barely audible. Then her head rolled to the side and rested against my chest.

"Isla?" I rasped.

She did not respond. My mate had lost consciousness.

Rage threatened to sweep over me again, but Isla's last word to me rang in my ears like bells:

Trava. Stop.

I had sworn that if she said that word, I would cease whatever I was doing immediately and without question. *I must know you are safe with me*, I had said, and I had meant it with all my hearts and soul.

My love and devotion to Isla was perhaps the only force more powerful than my rage.

For the first time, I saw the soldier and medics with human eyes and a clear mind.

What if my blood and the force of my will were not enough to save my mate? If that were so, then Isla's death would be not at the hands of her assassin, but mine. There would not be a hell deep enough for me then.

I got to my feet with Isla in my arms. She had swallowed enough of my blood and enough of my blood had gone into the wound in her back for her to lapse into what I hoped was a healing sleep. Her breaths were shallow and gurgling, but as long as she continued to breathe, I could as well.

"She must live," I told the soldier and the medics. "She is everything to me."

"She will live, Commandant," the soldier said, drawing himself up. "I swear it."

Only then did I recognize him. Morolo. Lieutenant Morolo.

The last time I had seen him was on Ryoxv. He had been covered in blood and missing his lower right leg below the knee. I had seen him fall. While others in our cadre ran past him, I had slung him over my shoulder and carried him to a medical transport. My uniform had remained stained with his blood for days until I had a chance to clean it. A month later, I was promoted and left Ryoxv for another battle on another world.

He was older now and more scarred than I recalled, but clearly physicians had reconstructed his leg much like they had done for me after my own injury. Our kinship resonated so profoundly that I felt it in my bones.

"Send someone to find me and bring me to her," I told Morolo as I settled Isla on the stretcher. It activated immediately, scanning her and sending data to the screens on its side and the medics' wristcomms. Nearly all the indicators immediately turned red.

"Yes, sir." Morolo did not salute, but he dipped his head to me. "Where will you be?"

I caressed Isla's face. She was terribly cold. The stretcher had already sensed her condition and begun to radiate heat. "I have another duty I must see to," I grated. "I must find the one who did this."

"We will be in the medical wing. Third ring, port side." And they were off at a run.

My guts wrenched to watch Isla taken away, but it had to be done. I tilted my head back and bellowed, *"BRAE!"*

In the distance, in the opposite direction of where Morolo was taking my Isla, a familiar screech split the air. I ran. Everything and everyone around me blurred as travelers cleared a path.

Brae's screeches led me past a dozen gates, up a ramp, and down a short corridor to its end, where a half-dozen uniformed and armed soldiers had gathered just short of an airlock.

I smelled blood long before I reached the group: unfamiliar blood I thought might belong to Brae, which made my stomach churn, and another scent I recognized on a visceral level before my brain registered whose it was. My snarl felt and sounded as if it had risen from the darkest part of my soul.

I might have plowed straight through the soldiers to get to their prisoner if three of them—two larger than myself, and one just as large—had not turned to face me, using their long staff-like energy weapons to bar my way. Even my white-hot rage did not blind me to the fact those weapons would bring me down and leave me if not unconscious, at least incapacitated. And I could not be incapacitated when Isla counted on me.

I stopped a meter from the soldiers, my chest heaving and blood dripping from my fingers.

"Does this shadowbat belong to you?" one of the soldiers demanded. The insignia on his collar indicated he held the highest rank of the group.

"He belongs to my mate," I grated. "Whom the female behind you just tried to murder in cold blood. Lieutenant Morolo has taken my mate into protective custody."

I had not intended to use Morolo's Corps rank, but in my distracted state, old habits had kicked in. The soldier straightened. "You know Protectorate Morolo?"

I nodded once. "We served together."

My words had a seismic effect on the soldiers' expressions and body language. The three with weapons stood down but did not step aside, and almost as one they came to attention. Perhaps they too had served in the Corps.

"I want to see her," I said, jerking my head in the direction of the female they had cornered. When they did not move, I added, "You have my word of honor I will not touch your prisoner."

A rough, garbled chuckle came from behind the soldiers. My spines, already stiff, flared with the force of my rage.

The soldiers stepped aside.

Kona had slumped to her knees against the wall, bleeding profusely from a dozen deep gashes and talon marks—including a severe set of lacerations on her neck that had cut down to the bone.

Brae was a predator as much as I, and nothing made that

more evident than the shredded mess he had made of Kona's flesh. He had obviously not been satisfied with those wounds, because he had also buried his fangs into the back of her neck. Shadowbats produced a paralytic venom that could prove fatal to some species, especially if a large quantity was pumped into the wound. And it appeared Brae was determined to do just that, regardless of what the soldiers wanted him to do. His wings trembling and eyes glowing with rage, he had wedged his body between Kona and the wall, making himself almost impossible for them to reach even with their weapons without going through Kona.

My gut contracted. Kona wore the same full-body thermal gear we had donned for our excursion. She had been with us on the trip to the glacier, hidden under a helmet and coverall, only feet away from Isla and me.

"Why?" I asked, my voice like gravel. "We saved your life."

Kona's laugh gurgled. Black blood dripped from her mouth. "Do you think Nubo is so stupid that he didn't know about your spy?" she scoffed and coughed thickly. "It was a sham. You're pathetic."

A wave of cold washed through me, turning my rage from volcanic to ice. Nubo had never intended to kill Kona. The entire incident had been orchestrated to manipulate us—to manipulate *Isla*, whose kind heart had influenced mine and persuaded me to venture out of the wine shop to warn Kona of a nonexistent threat.

"So he sent you to hunt us down?" I asked. My voice was deceptively calm. All the soldiers watched me uneasily. I gestured at my medallion. "In violation of interplanetary laws prohibiting violence against diplomatic envoys? Is he that desperate to end up in the prison colony on Ymar II? Are you?"

"It's not as if I planned to be caught." She spat out blood and glared up at me. "And he didn't send me. This was *my* mission."

Was that the truth, or a lie to cover up Nubo's involvement? Both seemed equally likely.

"I know you despise me, but you have no reason to hate Isla," I said. "Our former employer, however—"

"I do have every reason to hate you," she hissed. "You betrayed me."

"I never betrayed you." There was little point in arguing, but I could not understand why her hate ran so deep. "You left to become a mercenary. I wanted no part of that life. More than two years have passed. Why seek me out now?"

Her eyes narrowed into slits. "Atolani do not forgive. I lost honor when you refused to join my raider squad. I would never be made a squad leader among our people with tarnished honor. The only way to regain it was to avenge your betrayal."

It was a logical explanation as far as it went, but her actions today still made no sense. "Then why not kill me if it was my supposed betrayal you came to avenge?" I demanded. "Why target Isla?"

"What satisfaction would there be in killing you?" she snarled. "You always cared less about your own life than the soldiers you served with or who were under your command. You certainly care more about that screeching human you stole from Nubo than yourself. So why would I kill *you* if I wanted *you* to suffer? I regain my honor either way, and this gave me far more pleasure."

Gods, she was heartless. The thought I had once shared a bed with her made me want to be violently ill.

In my mind, I envisioned ripping her away from Brae and the soldiers and tearing her apart a piece at a time so she could feel the pain and fear I had experienced seeing my mate's blood spurt through the air, and my terror that neither I nor anyone else would be able to save her life.

I would have done it in a heartsbeat given a chance, but it would be murder in full view of a half dozen soldiers. Even pleading provocation, I would be taken away from my Isla. Even my beastly hearts told me revenge would be sweet but not as sweet as my life with my mate.

Kona could go to the deepest hell. It would be a hell of her own making.

"You are a coward," I said, my voice cold. "You have no honor at all. You stabbed a human woman in the back. I hope whatever prison you end up in, everyone knows the cowardice of your crime. I will do everything in my power to see they do." I glanced at Brae. "Give her to them, please. We have no use for her anymore. Isla needs us."

"She must be dead by now," Kona said, making Brae hiss and sink his fangs in deeper. "That was a very special blade. By the time they got her to the medical bay, she bled out. Poor, sad Commandant." She slid a glance at Brae. "Poor worthless little bat. Left all alone."

Brae gnawed on Kona's neck. She twitched and groaned in pain.

"Brae," I said quietly. "She is trying to get you to kill her so she does not go to prison. Isla is not dead."

"Liar," Kona spat.

"I am many things, but I am not a liar." I crouched to bring myself eye level with her and raised my bloody arms to show her the wounds I had made with my own teeth and claws. "Isla is my true mate, Kona. That means my blood heals her."

Her head jerked as if I had punched her. A half-dozen emotions flashed in her dark gaze: shock, fury, dismay, and most of all jealousy.

It was very possible she *had* followed us here to kill Isla entirely of her own accord and not on Nubo's orders. If she did not admit the truth, we might never know whether he was behind this brutal act. That was a bitter pill to swallow.

"My mate will not die," I said. "But even so, you are going to prison for a very long time."

Kona's breathing turned ragged. *"Tor'gar efet,"* she hissed.

An Atolani insult—a very vicious and vile one. One last attempt to get me to attack. But nothing she might say could reach me now. I was done with her. Only Isla and Brae mattered.

I rose. "Come with me to see Isla, Brae."

With one last rip at her flesh with his claws, he released Kona's neck and took to the air. The soldiers did not try to stop him as he passed overhead and flew away in the direction of the promenade. I turned my back on Kona and followed.

Scuffling sounds and cursing indicated she was trying to fight the soldiers despite blood loss and paralyzed limbs. Just as I turned the corner, a sizzle told me the soldiers had thrown a stun net over her. Her truncated shriek was a very satisfying sound.

Halfway down the ramp, as Brae followed above in shadow form, I encountered a soldier coming from the opposite direction. "Auren," he said, with a nod. "Protectorate Morolo has asked me to escort you to your mate's bedside."

"Thank you," I grated.

I had feigned certainty about Isla's condition when speaking to Kona, but my guts churned and my spines bristled with fear.

Brae landed carefully on my shoulder and hooked his talons into the fabric of my tunic. "She lives," he said, his voice pitched so only I could hear him. "But she isn't awake."

"No," I murmured. "She lapsed into a healing sleep after consuming my blood."

Brae made a rough sound. "I didn't see the danger. I only saw someone hidden in protective gear. It wasn't until Kona left the scene and removed her helmet that I realized who she was."

"You did what I could not and captured her." My throat was tight with rising dread at what we might find when we reached the medical bay. "If you had not, she would have escaped justice. I am forever in your debt."

"You saved Isla." He whined softly. "The debt is on my side."

Like on most ports this size, the medical bay was enormous, as it could be called upon to deal with a wide variety of potential emergencies. The moment we entered its main doors, however, I knew precisely where my mate was: to my right and down a short corridor. The scent of her blood and pain was unmistakable. I rushed past my escort and down the hall with Brae still on my shoulder.

I froze on the threshold of a private room.

My beautiful Isla was so pale that her normally rosy skin had a bluish tinge. Eyes closed and chest barely moving, she lay naked on her side in a blood-soaked medbay pod, draped to the waist with a thermal sheet.

A grim physician and two nurses tended to the wound in her back. Their demeanor as much as Isla's pallor and wheezing breaths stole my ability to move.

"You are the mate?" one of the nurses, a blue-skinned Ymarian, asked.

"Yes." My voice did not sound like my own. *Isla.*

With a raspy sound, Brae rose from my shoulder and settled above Isla on the ceiling. The scent of his grief added to my heartache.

"Why has she lost so much blood?" I asked.

"The knife the assassin used was poisoned and doused in anticoagulants," the physician said without looking up. "Officers recovered the blade from a refuse chute and we were able to identify the poison. Your quick reaction to share your blood gave us a chance to fight, but she is in very grave condition."

My hearts thundered in my ears. I held out my bloody arms. "Then take more. Take it all."

"This is not something your blood will heal," the Ymarian nurse said with surprising gentleness. Most Ymarians I had met were very matter-of-fact. "What is needed is the antidote, transfusions of human blood, and the replacement of flesh lost to the poison's cytotoxic properties."

Replacement of flesh? My Isla's flesh was *decaying?*

My legs grew unsteady, forcing me to lean against the wall. "You have the antidote? You can counter the anticoagulants?"

"Yes," the physician said, finally sparing me a glance. "You need to clean yourself up and change clothes. When you've done that, you can come back and stay with her. I don't want a mess in this room while she's vulnerable to infection, even with air and surface sanitization at maximum." She returned her attention to Isla's back. "And if she opens her eyes, I don't want my patient to see you looking like this and worry about you. She'll need all her strength to fight for her life."

"The facilities for washing are at the end of this hall," the Ymarian nurse added. "You will find clean clothing. It is best to dispose of everything you are wearing. When you come back, we will have someone treat your wounds."

I spotted something in a bin on top of the pile of Isla's discarded, blood-soaked clothing: her forearm sheath with the dagger still in place. My steps robotic, I went to the bin and picked it up.

"Everything in that container is hazardous and designated for disposal," the other nurse said, her voice sharp.

"This belongs to my mate," I said. "You will have to take it from me by force."

Scowling, the nurse opened her mouth to reply, but the physician raised her gloved hand. My gut wrenched at the sight of Isla's dark, discolored blood.

"He can take the knife and sheath with him and have them sanitized," the physician stated in a tone that brooked no argument. "We're busy with more important things."

Holding the sheath tightly to my chest, I turned my steps to the hall, leaving Brae to hold vigil until I returned.

When I was out of sight, I leaned against the wall, raised the sheath to my nose, and inhaled to drink in my mate's sweet scent. My vision tunneled.

Gods, Isla. I could not bear to imagine what my life would be like without her. My chest hurt as though massive talons were shredding my flesh and organs. I had to force myself to start walking again. My steps were uneven and I bumped into the wall several times.

In the cleansing suite, I threw all my clothing into a refuse chute and put the sheath and dagger into a sterilizer as I used the sonic cleanser. The full cycle took less than two minutes, but it felt like an hour before the unit shut off and the doors opened.

I found a set of medical coveralls and boots that fit comfortably and reclaimed Isla's dagger and arm sheath. They bore no trace of her scent after medical-grade sanitization, but that heartache was only a fraction of the pain I would have suffered if I had not been able to save her treasured weapon.

When I returned to Isla's room, the soldier who had escorted me to the medical bay was on guard in the hallway. We exchanged nods.

"Better," the physician said without looking up when I entered. "Sit."

I sat in the chair beside the medbay pod. Was Isla's breathing even more shallow and labored now? Had she been this pale before?

"What do I do?" I asked.

"Hold her hands and talk to her," the doctor said. "When the nurse comes to treat your arm wounds, let him do what needs to be done without arguing. Those are your only jobs until I tell you otherwise."

I would have given anything to lie down beside Isla and hold her in my arms, but that was not possible as long as she was in the medbay pod.

So instead I put the sheath and dagger on the chair next to me, focused all my will on Isla's survival, and clasped her cold hands in both of mine.

And there I stayed.

CHAPTER 30

ISLA

My mate sang to me while I slept.

He cooed too, and sometimes he talked as if he knew I was listening. Other voices came and went but his was always nearby, deep and loving and strong. I drew on that strength. His rumble kept me from wandering away so deeply into darkness that I couldn't find my way back.

Most of all I wanted him to hold me. I didn't understand why he didn't. Pain lurked on the edges of my awareness, and sickness, and a strange numbness. My mate reassured me that I was safe and cared for and I could rest. And I did rest, but I was so cold I'd almost forgotten what it felt like to be warm.

When he finally wrapped me in his arms and nestled my bare skin against his, it was the most wonderful comfort. The chill in my bones abated and my dreams were much more peaceful.

After a particularly lovely dream of lying on a beach in the sun, warm in Mikas's arms, I opened my eyes to find myself held tightly against hot skin. Our position was so like my dream that it took me a little while to understand that I was awake.

The unfamiliar room in which we lay was dark except for the faint glow from machines behind me that hummed. Even so, I immediately recognized Mikas. His beautiful scaly skin. The scar below his left pectoral muscle. The piercing through his dark green nipple. The beating of his three strong hearts. His chest moving with deep, even breaths. The scent of warm stones that told me I was safe and home.

"Mate," I whispered.

He went completely still. "Isla?" His voice was ragged.

I pressed my lips to his sternum. "Do you have another one?"

He let out a strangled sound and leaned back so he could see my face. His eyes were shadowed, his cheekbones more prominent, his jaw muscles pronounced, his skin almost sallow.

My stomach lurched. With a shaking hand, I touched his face. "You look terrible."

He leaned against my palm and closed his eyes. "I did not know if I would ever hear your voice again, and you wake teasing me." When he opened his eyes, he looked at me as if he wasn't sure I was real. "Am I dreaming?"

In answer, I pinched his earlobe. He flinched and chuckled, burying his face in my hair. "I am not dreaming, then," he murmured. "Gods, Isla. You must tell Brae."

I didn't sense my shadowbat nearby, so I nestled my head against Mikas's chest and reached out with my mind. *Brae?*

A wordless reply seared me with its forcefulness: *!!!*

I winced.

Isla! Brae's voice in my head was nearly a screech. *You're awake?*

Yes, I'm awake. Mikas is here.

Warmth spilled into me from my shadowbat. *I'm out hunting,* he said excitedly. *I'll see you as soon as your mate is ready to share your attention.*

That made me smile. *Thank you. I'll let you know.*

Mikas's lips traveled to my forehead. "He is happy?"

"Very happy." I kissed his chest again. "He says he'll come back when you're ready to share me."

His smile turned my insides to warm honey. "He is thoughtful. I will need some time alone with my beautiful mate." His smile faded. "You have been asleep a long time."

His nearness soothed me, but my stomach churned. "Where are we? What happened?"

"It is a terrible story." He rested his forehead on mine. "I do not know how much to tell you now."

"Whatever it is, I can take it," I promised, lacing our fingers together. "I'd rather know everything at once so I don't have to wonder. Not knowing is worse."

"I will stop if you become too distressed." When I started to protest, he kissed my forehead. "Supervising Physician Nvornik will have my hide if I upset you too much. That is a direct quote, by the way. We owe her and her nurses your life, so I will not cross her."

That made me smile despite the ball of dread in my stomach. "I like your hide where it is, and I try to never get on the bad side of someone who saved my life, so we're agreed."

He held me close and told me about Kona's attack and the aftermath. Then he caressed my back and cooed as I huddled, trembling and nauseous, against his chest, trying to make sense of what he'd said.

I struggled to accept that we'd been here for two entire Alorisian weeks—the equivalent of nearly twenty-four Fortusian days. For damn near the entirety of that time, I'd remained unconscious in a healing sleep caused by sharing Mikas's blood, and then a medically induced twilight state, fighting to survive a terrible stab wound and massive dose of poison.

After the first week, my physician had moved me from my original room to a secure suite in the port's medical bay, guarded by soldiers trusted by Protectorate Morolo. Only then had Mikas been able to share my bed, and he hadn't left my side for more than a few minutes at a time since.

"Nvornik warned us your memory might be affected," Mikas murmured, one hand cupping the back of my head and the other rubbing my back. "Not just the attack itself, but you might have lost an entire day or more." The prospect clearly upset him immensely.

"I remember everything," I said softly. "Docking here at the port, the trip to see the glacier, coming back…and being stabbed. The blade was icy cold."

His chest rumbled. "Protectorate Morolo said they tested the blade. In addition to revealing the type of poison Kona used, it showed clear evidence of having been exposed to outside air and ice."

The implication left me stunned. "Kona chilled her dagger on purpose, then. To make a point? That her revenge was cold?"

"I think so." The words were a growl. "She probably exposed the dagger during the excursion. Maybe even just meters away from us while we were admiring the glacier. But we did not know who she was because of her protective gear."

"We both felt uneasy," I reminded him. "Maybe there was something familiar about her that we saw subconsciously but didn't recognize at the time."

"Maybe. Or maybe we both suspected our escape from Fortusia had gone too easily." He inhaled my scent from the crown of my head. "We may never know Nubo's true level of involvement, unless during her trial Kona decides to speak plainly."

"I'm not going to hold my breath for that." I sighed. "I think we should stick to our plan to get far away from Fortusia under our new identities."

"I agree." He growled quietly. "We chose to help Kona when we thought she was in danger, and this was her repayment."

"I don't regret that we warned her about the threat, even if it was all a sham." I rubbed my nose on his chest. "I would rather have a kind heart and risk suffering for it than force myself to be hard. The universe needs more kindness, not less."

"My Isla." He kissed my hair. "I am sorry you remember the attack. I did not want you to have lost memories of that day, but I confess I hoped you would not recall the act itself."

"Don't be sorry." I cupped his face with my much-colder hands. "I'd rather remember so I don't have to wonder how it felt or what I went through." I stroked his cheeks with my thumbs. "What I remember most, though, is what you said to me, and what you did to save me from a truly horrific death. I wouldn't want to have forgotten that. I'll never forget it…my mate."

"I have never heard sweeter words." His voice was rough again, but now it was happiness and not grief that made it gruff.

Mikas kissed me then, finally. My body came alive as if I hadn't yet fully woken up until his lips were on mine. His kiss was gentle at first, and then much more hungry when I ran my fingers through his hair and pulled. His growl made me shiver and not with cold.

When he lifted his head, he cupped my face with his hot hand. "I have one more thing I must tell you. The cytotoxins in the poison caused significant damage to the skin and muscles on your back. You are still healing and those regenerated muscles will be weak until you strengthen them." His gaze searched my face. "But what you must know is because the skin is new, all your scars from…before…are gone."

I wasn't sure how to react to that. Not relief, exactly, and not regret. Maybe it would take me more time to process this news.

"I wasn't ashamed of my scars," I said softly, because Mikas was waiting with obvious unease for a reply. "I only kept them covered to avoid having to explain how I got them." I squeezed his hand. "Scars mean I survived—that someone tried to hurt me, or kill me, and failed. The agent who took me away from the palace on Agicord told me that when she saw me looking at hers. I'd never heard anything that made as much sense as that."

I'd shared that sentiment with Novee after our escape from Ngara. She'd wept at the news her back would be scarred after the plasma rifle shot. She had every right to be upset, and I would never have said otherwise, but she had asked why I wasn't more distressed. My explanation had helped her then, and I hoped it still did, wherever she was.

Mikas touched his right leg. It bore no visible scars but had been reconstructed after he'd lost the original limb in battle. "Survival is no small thing," he agreed. "It is a triumph."

"It feels like a triumph to me," I said. "I'm alive, Kona is in custody, Nubo is light-years behind us, and as soon as I can get out of bed, we'll be on our way to Jakora, by way of a few more beautiful planets."

"There is nothing I want more." He kissed my forehead. How I loved forehead kisses now.

The thought of continuing our journey made me think about clothing-optional cabins, which in turn made me think of something else. "Mikas, since they moved us into this suite, when the physician and nurses come to check on me, are you naked in bed with me?"

"Where else would I be?" He tilted his head. "They know I am your mate. I believe they would have found it strange if I were *not* naked in your bed holding you as you recovered. This is how mates care for one another. In fact, Nvorkin believed skin contact between us would be essential for both your physical and emotional recovery. That is why she moved you from a medbay pod to a standard patient bed I could share as soon as she could. She is Tocanian, and they also experience strong mate bonds."

I blinked at him. "She prescribed being naked in bed with my mate for healing?"

"Yes, she did," he said, very seriously. "Obviously, I was reluctant, but she insisted."

Oh, my heart. He was *teasing me*.

To play along, I feigned sadness. "I hate to be a burden, you know. I'm sure there are other accommodations in the port. You don't have to share this little bed with me."

Very, very carefully and slowly, he wrapped his arms around me and rolled to his back so I lay on him as I'd done on the basking stones. I braced myself for pain, but felt none—only some stiffness in my muscles and the weakness in my back and shoulders he had warned about.

Oh, gods. He was so warm. I melted against him until I lost track of where I ended and he began.

"I take it back," I murmured, my head on his chest above his hearts. "You are not allowed to leave."

He kissed the top of my head and stroked my back, his chest rumbling in that way that felt and sounded like a purr. "My mate, I simply must stay. Doctor's orders."

CHAPTER 31

ISLA

Four days later, Mikas, Brae, and I secretly boarded a mid-sized cruiser bound for the desert world of Solan.

As Efre Vorda and Pelles Vertak, we booked a midship cabin with a basking stone in the bedroom and windows in both the common area and bedroom. The entire cabin would have fit in the sitting area of our luxury suite with room to spare, but I didn't mind. As Mikas had pointed out, a smaller cabin simply meant we were closer to each other. And after what we'd survived on Aloris, I minded closeness even less than before.

There were no botanical gardens or insectivoriums aboard the ship, so we had to pack food for Brae and he had far less room to roam than aboard the luxury cruiser. Still, he said he was so happy I'd survived and we were on our way to Jakora again he would travel in the cargo bay and subsist on protein pellets if need be without complaining.

As the ship left the port and climbed toward Aloris's atmosphere, I stood at the window to watch our departure as Mikas unpacked our scant belongings.

With the luxury of time these past few days between physician visits and painful exercises designed to develop my repaired and regenerated muscles, I'd researched Fortusian true mate physiology and behavior so I better understood what Mikas had been experiencing since the day I walked into Zaa'ga.

What I'd learned so far had been eye-opening. I found information designed for non-scientists most helpful, and even located a trove of first-hand accounts about mating between Fortusians and humans. But since no two Fortusians were exactly alike and the species varied so widely in biology as well as life experience, each individual pairing was unique.

Nowhere did I find an example of a Fortusian male with Mikas's exact genetic composition, much less one whose true mate was a human female. Mikas and I were making our own way, in our own way. I didn't need any research or geneticist's theory to tell me who or what we were together. Our hearts knew those answers. We just had to listen.

I caught sight of Mikas out of the corner of my eye putting my beautiful perfume bottle, arm sheath, and dagger on the table next to the bed. He adjusted them until they were just so, and slid my travel case into a storage area next to the doorway that led to the bathroom.

Mikas, according to my research, was *nesting*. There was a more scientific term for the profound urge he was experiencing to make and keep a home for his mate, but I liked the idea of a nest very much. On Pallasia, bosors made beautiful and strong nests capable of withstanding powerful storms and harsh conditions, as did several of the mammalian species whose DNA contributed to his genetic makeup.

All that science aside, he loved me. He wanted me to be happy and comfortable, and to make me a home as well as be my home, and that was *Mikas*.

When he wrapped his arms around me from behind and

rested his head against mine, I smiled and leaned back against him. Mmm, so warm.

I caught chills more easily now. Whether that was a permanent effect of the poison or only temporary, time would tell. Luckily, Mikas had heat enough for both of us—and most cruisers, even smaller ones, featured cabins with basking stones or similar technology. Many species from many worlds liked or required intense radiant heat.

"My mate," he said. "You have been smiling all day today. I am glad to see it."

"Well, I'm no longer in protective custody in the Aloris port medical bay, stuck in bed with you all day," I said with an exaggerated sigh.

His chest shook with silent laughter. "My poor Isla. How ever did you survive the hardship?"

"I don't know. Sheer determination, I suppose." I drew his hand up to my lips so I could kiss it and inhale his scent. "And now we're trapped in this little cabin for days. How terrible."

"Indeed." He turned me to face him and cupped my face, his expression surprisingly serious. "I ache for you, Isla, but I will do nothing that might cause you harm."

"I know you won't. I trust you." I covered his hand with mine. "And I ache for you too. It seems like forever since we last made love on the cruiser before it arrived at Aloris. Sharing a bed with you in the medbay was wonderful and so comforting, but I need another kind of comfort. So do you." I separated his shirt along the front seam to reveal his chest and rested my hand on his hot skin above his primary heart. "Please, Mikas."

"If you say you are well enough, then I accept your word." He tucked my hair behind my ear. "We will be gentle and take it slowly."

Until I'd met Brae, I'd always had to hide my feelings and fears from everyone. Even after he and I had bonded, I still had to hide my true self and play roles, even with lovers. I'd always had to be on guard. Judging from what Mikas had told me about his life, he'd been forced to do the same.

To be able to be honest with each other, and vulnerable, and feel completely safe doing so, was maybe the greatest gift of all.

"Gentle and slow is what I want right now," I said, swallowing hard around the lump in my throat. "That's what I *need*. We almost lost everything. My heart hurts, Mikas."

"Mine too." He bent his head and kissed me softly, his hand cupping the back of my head. "We will heal together," he promised, his lips against mine.

And then he knelt at my feet, his arms around my legs and face buried against my middle. I wrapped my arms around him and kissed the top of his head—which was not something I got to do very often. I decided I liked it very much.

His hands slid up my legs and gripped the back of my thighs. He looked up at me, eyes dark with desire. "Dress off," he said.

With trembling fingers, I unfastened my collar and separated the dress down the front along its seam. He brushed my hands aside and drew the sides of the dress apart, revealing my chest and underwear. My nipples hardened as the fabric slid over them.

"Beautiful," Mikas said, his gaze traveling up my body to meet my eyes. "I will never tire of this sight, my mate."

"And I think I might be coming around to seeing you on your knees," I said, my voice husky. "That's a nice view too."

Smiling, he eased my dress off my shoulders and let it fall to the floor. Then he unfastened my boots and helped me step out of them, leaving me in just my underwear.

But when I reached for his shirt, he caught my hands. "I must worship you first," he said, nibbling at my fingertips. Each little bite made me shiver and caused more wetness to drip along my slit. "I can think of nothing else."

He unsheathed his claws and cut my underwear from my

body, careful not to so much as scratch me as he did so. And then I was naked with my beautiful mate kneeling at my feet.

"Another souvenir?" I teased.

"A new tradition," he said, pressing the torn fabric to his nose, his glowing gaze on mine. "If you do not object."

"I might if you leave me without any to wear." I ran my fingers through his hair and tugged to make him smile and show his fangs. "Or maybe I'll just stop wearing any when I'm with you."

"I like this plan." He licked his lips and nudged my legs apart. "Let me taste you, my mate."

He kissed his way up my thighs before he reached my quivering, dripping slit. His hands cradled my ass and held me still as he drew his tongue slowly along my most sensitive skin. And though he'd licked me like that so many times, the sensation felt as good and electrifying as if he'd never done it before.

I cried out and gripped his hair. "Mikas…"

His tongue delved along my slit, drinking me in. Taking his time. Savoring me. *Worshiping* me.

When my legs began to tremble, he rose, picked me up so I could wrap my legs around his waist, and carried me to the bedroom. His cocks strained the fabric of his pants. I longed to touch them, stroke them, taste them, but he was a man on a mission.

With a satisfied rumble, Mikas lay me gently on the bed and settled in with his head between my thighs. He raised my hips to bring me to his mouth, watching for any sign of pain or discomfort. When his tongue slipped into my slit, my fists twisted in the bedding.

He raised his head. Gods, the sight of those gleaming eyes with fully dilated black pupils made slickness drip from my pussy.

"Grab my hair," he grated. "I want to feel your need."

I ran my fingers through his thick hair and tugged his mouth back to where I wanted it most. He growled low and closed his lips on my clit. I cried out.

With his raspy, long tongue, he circled my clit, wrenching gasps and cries with every stroke. Gently, he slid a finger inside my pussy and pumped it in and out slowly, then added another, curling his fingertips to stroke lightly over my G-spot.

"Mikas," I gasped. "Yes. More."

His fingers moved more purposefully now, and he raised his head to meet my gaze. "My mate. My beautiful mate. Come for me, my love."

His mouth returned to my swollen clit as his fingers stroked inside me. A coil of delicious heat and tension built and built, and finally broke.

With a cry, my fingers gripping his hair, I went over the edge. Mikas didn't stop stroking inside me or tonguing my clit until he'd wrung gasps and pleas for mercy from me.

Fabric ripped, and then he was above me, gloriously naked, his cocks dripping onto my abdomen.

"Beautiful and perfect," he growled, burying his face against the side of my neck, his fingers stroking inside me as I quaked. "You are mine and I am yours."

"I know," I said, holding him close. I kissed his hair. "I need both of your cocks. I need to feel you fill me. *I need you.*"

Rumbling, supporting himself on his arms so he didn't put too much weight on me, he slipped the head of his lower cock into my pussy. I whimpered and wrapped my legs around his waist, urging him to thrust a little more each time. Gods, it felt so good to be stretched again, to feel his heat and every little bump and ridge, to have his upper cock rub over my clit, a promise of pleasures still to come. Better than anything I'd ever known.

When he was finally inside me to the hilt, he stilled above me. "No pain?" he asked, his voice rough.

"Only the best kind. Don't move." My gaze on his, I reached for his slick upper cock.

He groaned, and a shudder ran through his entire body. Even his spines bristled. And I hadn't done anything more than wrap my hand around him—as much as I could, anyway.

I squeezed him gently and held tight. "Now you can move."

"Isla." It was a moan. He shuddered again, his back bowing. "You may kill me."

"Sex with me won't kill you, I promise," I teased, my voice husky. "Or at least that's what *you* told *me* the first time."

Trembling, his chest heaving, he withdrew slowly. We both quaked every time the nubs and ridges on his cocks passed through my fingers and the entrance to my pussy. The sensations were all the more powerful because we were sharing them.

"Isla," he groaned. "Isla…"

I drew him toward me with my leg, wordlessly encouraging him to thrust. And he did, slowly, savoring every sensation as much as I did. His groans matched my whimpers.

"You feel so good," he gasped. "So perfect."

"So do you." I took a shaky breath. "Mikas, make your mate scream."

He thrust into my pussy and my hand, slowly at first and then more quickly, every muscle in his body rigid with the strain of holding himself back. Oh, it all felt so good, so intense. So wonderful. I cried out, pleading for him to go faster.

"Call me your mate," he rasped, lowering his head to kiss my jaw. "I need to hear you say it again."

"Mikas, my mate." I caressed his face. "My beautiful beast of a mate."

He groaned and thrust harder. I slipped my thumb into his mouth. He sucked on it as he pumped into me, and that was a new sensation that somehow made all the rest even more delicious.

I didn't want him to hold back. I wanted him to lose himself for me, to fill me and fill me again. I wanted everything he had to give.

As he thrust, I tightened my grip, stroked him harder, and ghosted my thumb over his cock head. He shuddered hard and made a sound somewhere between a groan and a snarl. "Isla—" he grated.

"Come for me, my mate," I said, my hand cupping my breast and pinching my nipple. "Cover me with your cum."

With a guttural bellow, he came first from his upper cock in great spurts that splashed over my body, across my face, and into my mouth. I held out my tongue to catch what I could.

And then he came from his lower cock in a rush of heat that spilled out freely because there was so much, and because no knot had kept it inside. The movement of his lower cock sent me over the edge with him.

As I gasped for air and licked his cum from my lips, he withdrew from me, formed the pillows into a mound, and rolled me to my front, careful even now not to put strain on my back or shoulders. He bent me over the pillows, spread my legs with his hands, and plunged his tongue into my ass. I screamed and held on to the pillows for dear life.

He tongued me and stretched me, rumbling as I wailed and ground against his face and hands. And then he was thrusting his cocks into my pussy from behind, alternating between them until the different angles and sensations made me come hard. I was nearly sobbing with the pleasure he gave me.

When he stroked his upper cock so it dripped over and into my ass, that wonderful warmth of total relaxation and acceptance really did make me sob.

"Isla?" he asked, his hand resting on my hip. "Talk to me."

"Please," I gasped, reaching behind me to find his thigh. "Please give me your cocks, Mikas. My mate. *Please.*"

With a guttural sound, he did as I asked. Oh, all the gods

above and below—the feeling of both his cocks pushing into me was pure heaven.

When my ass was against his hips and he was fully and doubly buried inside me, he stopped again to kiss my back and lave it with his tongue. My skin was so sensitive that every raspy lick made me shiver and clench around his cocks.

I would have liked to ride him like this, for him to sit back and let me bounce on his lap, but my healing back wasn't strong enough to do that yet.

"My mate," he said, his hands cupping my breasts as his thumbs stroked my hard nipples. "This is what you want?"

"Yes." I wanted him to thrust, to send me crashing into bliss, but I understood what made him pause. "I want this forever. I *need* this forever. As long as I have you, I have everything."

He moved ever so slightly, withdrawing an inch and then pushing back in. His knot was swelling quickly. I shivered hard at the sensation of it bumping against me. I'd come so quickly like this, and then I would take his knot.

I am made for you, Isla, he'd said in Ycari's back room. I hadn't believed it then, not really, but I did now. How could I not? We fit together so perfectly, in every way.

"I am made for you, Mikas," I said, and ground against him so he would shudder and growl. "Fill your mate."

"I will." He kissed my back one last time and bent to whisper in my ear, "I obey you in all things."

Moments later, on his third hard thrust, I came with a scream, squeezing around him and wrenching a rough sound from his chest.

He cooed, then slipped his knot inside my pussy. I groaned. Feeling him swell inside me was so satisfying. He was *mine*.

The ship's engines thrummed, the vibration traveling through the floor, the bed, and the pillows on which I lay. Outside the window, the stars streaked past at hyperspeed. We were on our way to Solan.

And when Mikas came with a roar and filled me completely, I was home.

CHAPTER 32

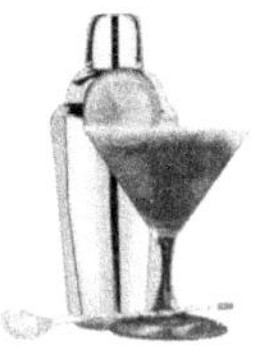

MIKAS

One Year Later

When my Isla took the stage, all the world stood still—or at least it did for me.

"I do not need to go to any heavens above," she sang in Tivoran, her rainbow hair and teal dress shimmering in the multicolored lanterns hovering around the stage. Her sparkling violet eyes met mine. *"Or see starlight shine or moonlight glow to be happy. I only need to be with you."*

Smiling, I filled a tankard with Bacorian mead and a glass with Terran sake and slid them across the bar to the green-skinned server. She added them to her fully laden tray to deliver.

The weight of the tray was no challenge for a Hardanian female. The servers casually competed nightly to see who could carry the most drinks at once, with the winner pocketing a modest purse. As long as no drinks were spilled, I pretended I did not know about their wagers.

Unlike most bars along Jakora's Angel Coast, Silver Sails Tavern did not use service 'bots or drink kiosks. Nor did it have holos or vidscreen entertainment. Instead, our tavern offered live bar service, live entertainment, and a spectacular lavender ocean view as a backdrop. And it had proven an effective business plan, much to the delight of its humble and hard-working owners.

"So, you're living the dream," Brae rasped in my ear. In shadow form, he was perched carefully on my bare shoulder, his claws gripping my spines to hold himself steady as I moved around behind the bar. "How does it feel to own the most popular bar on the Angel Coast?"

I chuckled quietly. "All I need is to see Isla happy. If she is happy, then I am happy." I scanned the packed bar and allowed myself a moment to feel pride in how few empty seats I saw. "But it does feel good," I admitted. "Damned good."

My order screen displayed a long list of drink requests awaiting my attention. Our newest bartender, a human woman named Abril, was as busy as I was at the other end of the bar. She seemed to be keeping up without any trouble. Not surprising, given she had been bartending for years.

Abril had jumped at the chance to work at Silver Sails when we posted a job notice. She moved here almost overnight from the central port area. Her explanation for her willingness to relocate more than a thousand kilometers from her previous home to take the job was the very business plan our financing agent had met with extreme skepticism.

It was, that same agent had grudgingly admitted at our last meeting to go over the bar's finances, a business plan that seemed to be catching on in the area. More bars and resorts advertised live service and entertainment and fewer 'bots and kiosks. Customers were happier, profits rose, and the area had drawn more interplanetary visitors who before had stayed closer to the planet's primary port. Isla and I had changed the Angel Coast with our vision.

And it did feel damned good, but what filled me most with warmth and contentment was my Isla's unending joy.

In the months following our departure from Fortusia, Madame Ycari's sources reported the Erotovo on Ngara had given up his search for Halena Onsulus. Nubo had run afoul of rivals and fled Fortusia for parts unknown. Soon after, Atlath had purchased Zaa'ga and promptly replaced all the drink kiosks and service 'bots with live bartenders and servers. He had also hired local singers and musicians to perform nightly. Ycari reported the bar rarely had any empty seats. We had promised to visit as soon as we could.

Kona had received a thirty-year sentence in the Ymar II penal colony for attempted murder, with no chance at early parole because she had targeted a diplomat. If Nubo had sent Kona after Isla, she had never mentioned his involvement. Either way, I hoped justice in some form would find him wherever he was hiding.

Isla no longer wished to work as an undercover operative for the Web, but she, Brae, and I had discussed becoming local agents on Jakora in the way Madame Ycari helped those in need on Fortusia. Though the risk was far less than what my mate and her companion used to do, we had many considerations to weigh and would not rush making a decision.

My beautiful mate was happy day and night. She smiled at work and at home, in my arms and swimming in the lavender ocean, and even when she slept. Her heart was at peace here, and so was mine.

Gods above, ours was a good life.

I made four Bacorian fullwells for a pair of six-armed, two-headed Boltanians. Fullwells were not as popular on Jakora as they were on Fortusia, but every so often someone would order one and I was reminded of my time at Zaa'ga, which now seemed a lifetime ago.

"I'm off to forage," Brae said, rubbing his round belly. "I'll see you and Isla back at the house later—unless you're going to be down on the beach when I get back."

"We might be," I said with a smile. "You know Isla likes to sit under the stars with a brandy after our shift."

"Yes, I'm sure it's the *brandy* she likes to have on the beach after her shift." Brae chortled. "See you later, Mikas." He launched himself off my shoulder and disappeared into the night in search of the area's tastiest insects.

Unlike the bars and clubs on Fortusia and those on Jakora close to the port, establishments on the Angel Coast closed generally around 0100 or 0200 hours. The area was less tourist-oriented and at least half to two-thirds of our guests were local residents. It was, in my opinion, an ideal situation, because it meant Isla and I returned to our little home by 0200 or 0300 at the latest nearly every night—sometimes earlier.

Tonight, Isla and I took a blanket, our dinner, and a bottle of Bacorian brandy to our usual little secluded cove on the beach. As much as we loved Silver Sails, the quiet of an empty beach and the gentle sounds of waves were a welcome respite from the pressures and noise of our workplace.

The only ache in my hearts was that even on a mild night Isla had to bring a second blanket to keep herself warm. She always reminded me we should be grateful the poison's only lingering aftereffect was sensitivity to temperature, and I *was* grateful, but it was a never-ending reminder of what I had almost lost.

We made love under the stars and moons, and then I settled her on top of me with a blanket draped over us and my arms holding her close. She nestled her head against my chest and made little contented sounds as we caught our breath.

Another benefit of this stretch of beach was its view of the night sky without interference from light pollution. In deference to local residents and late-night beachgoers, ordinances required non-essential lights to be dimmed or shut off after the bars and restaurants closed.

"Tell me which moons we're seeing tonight," Isla murmured.

"The small moon just there is Kyri," I said, running my fingers through her soft hair. "The gray moon without an atmosphere is Lirai. And the large purple moon is called Iosa."

"I'd like to visit some of the moons." She snuggled deeper under the blanket. I tucked it more tightly around her. "I've heard Iosa is lovely when it's not hurricane season. Can we go?"

"Someday," I promised, raising my head to kiss her hair. "There are no resorts there and only a small population, but the oceans are lavender like here and the wilderness is unspoiled. It would be beautiful and quiet, I think."

"Sounds like it." She let out a contented sigh. "I miss Fortusia, but we live in paradise, don't we?"

Isla was my paradise, but Jakora was certainly one too. "Yes, it is wonderful." I reached into the bottom of the bag that had contained our meal. "I have a gift for you."

She chuckled. "Another one? You already gave me…" She counted on her fingers. "Three?"

I nipped her fingertips with my teeth. "*Only* three. Not my best effort."

"I'm always more interested in quality over quantity." She rubbed her nose against my chest. "And every one of those was of the highest quality—especially your bite."

"I very much enjoyed my bite as well." I caressed her wonderfully soft thigh, which was draped over my hip. My cocks leapt at the thought of the little marks my fangs left in her skin. "I am sorry you have to stay quiet when we make love on the beach. I would much rather hear you scream."

"Greedy man, I scream enough for you at home. And we don't want everyone in the area knowing what we're doing down here." She rested her chin on my sternum and looked up at me, her eyes twinkling. "What was that you said about a gift?"

I sat up, leaned against a stone, and settled her in my lap wrapped in the blanket.

She took the package and studied it. "No sign of where it's from or what it is," she said, frowning at me. "Give me a hint."

I shook my head. "No hints. Open it."

Scowling, she found the latches and raised the lid. She gasped.

The first item in the case was a wooden box. Wide-eyed, she opened it and withdrew a cloth pouch. "Mikas! Is this what I think it is?"

"Yes." I kissed her temple. "Go on."

From the pouch she took a delicate hand-carved crystal perfume bottle in the shape of a miniorinae, a purple flower native to Jakora. The flower's stamen was the stopper. When she freed the stopper and lifted the glass rod, a wonderful fragrance filled the air.

"Oh," she breathed, closing her eyes to inhale. "It's the scent of *us* again…but with Jakoran florals. Oh, Mikas." She applied the perfume to her wrists and stoppered the bottle carefully before setting it in her lap and kissing me deeply. "Thank you. This is the most wonderful gift. All the way from Madame Ycari on Fortusia!"

"To celebrate our first year on Jakora." I nestled her head under my chin. "Now the rest of what is in the package."

"What?" She blinked at me. "There can't be more. This is already too much."

"My love, nothing is ever too much." I nudged her arm. "Lift the divider and look at what is underneath."

She found the release and popped open the lower section of the case. And shrieked.

"Jampas!" She bounced on my lap in glee, holding up the case so I could see the bright red berries, preserved for the long journey from Fortusia to Jakora. "Mikas, *jampas!*"

"Yes, I know," I chuckled. "Jampa berries…and seeds."

She gasped. "Seeds? To grow our own jampa bushes?"

"Yes." Gods, her joy warmed me like a sun. "We will need specially blended soil since they are not native to this planet, and they will have to grow indoors, but—"

She silenced me with a kiss.

I fed my mate two berries and watched her savor both, and then I kissed her again. She was so perfect: so sweet, so fiery, so full of passion and joy. So wonderfully *Isla*.

Her hand slid down between us to stroke my cocks. I rumbled.

"I would like to thank you properly," she murmured against my lips. "That is, if you have the energy, and you'd like to see me take your knot tonight after all."

"There is nothing in the universe that would keep me from saying yes to that proposal." I cupped her face. "I love you."

"I love you." Isla's smile made my hearts sing. She rolled off my lap to her hands and knees and frowned at me over her shoulder. "Don't keep your mate waiting."

"Of course not." I rose to my knees and kissed her shoulder. "As you know, I obey my mate in all things."

She laughed, and then she gasped, her back arching. "Mikas…"

"Yes, my love," I growled, my fangs grazing her delicate skin. "The best is yet to come."

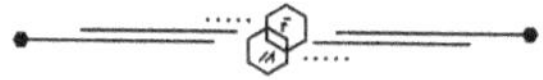

THANK YOU FOR READING

Thank you for reading *Needed in the Night*, the second book in the Fortusian Mates series! I hope you enjoyed the story.

More novels featuring Fortusian males and the fierce human women they love are coming soon.

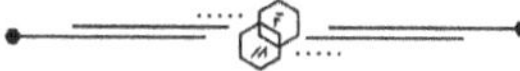

Reviews are very much appreciated by all indie authors, if you have the time to share your thoughts.

ACKNOWLEDGMENTS

I am so grateful to so many people who helped bring this story to the page:

My editor, Friel of Grey Moth Editing, who is a wonderful hype woman in addition to providing absolutely invaluable advice and encouragement;

Artist Lindsey Staton, aka @honeyy.fae, for yet another gorgeous cover;

Flavia and Bojana of FlavulousArt for the lovely art of Isla and Mikas in the bar included at the front of this book;

Carly of Carly's Bookish Beasts for the spectacular chapter art inside the book; and

Megan Van Dyke, who created the cover typography for this book and the others in this series.

Thank you to my Discordant Owl Squad for your awesomeness, love, and support. I owe you all more than I can ever repay.

As always, all my love to to my close family and friends, all of whom do not need to read this book. This includes my sister Michelle and brother-in-law Josh, my cousins Antoinette and Felicia and their partners John and Mike, my dear friends Marie, Adrienne, and Stacey, and my father Mike and stepmother Teri. Your support has meant the world to me.

And last but far from least, to my husband Bill, who is my heart: I love you. Thanks for putting up with my nonsense.

ABOUT THE AUTHOR

LISA EDMONDS

URBAN FANTASY & ROMANCE AUTHOR

Lisa Edmonds was born and raised in Kansas. She studied English and forensic criminology at Wichita State University. After acquiring her Bachelor's degree in English, she considered a career in law enforcement as a behavioral analyst before earning a Master's in English from Wichita State and then a Ph.D. in English from Texas A&M University.

For ten years, she was an associate professor of English at a college in Texas, where she taught a variety of writing and literature courses. Now a full-time author, she shares a cute Victorian-style home called The Storybook House with her husband and their pets, and enjoys writing, reading, traveling, spoiling her niece and nephew, and singing karaoke.

Don't miss new releases, commissioned art, and sneak peeks at works in progress! Join my reader community at LisaEdmonds.com.